AMERICA

AMERICA

Stephen Coonts

ORION

First published in Great Britain in 2001 by Orion Books
an imprint of The Orion Publishing Group
Orion House, 5 Upper St Martin's Lane, London WC2H 9EA

A CIP catalogue record for this book
is available from the British Library

ISBN (hardback) 0 75284 633 7
ISBN (trade paperback) 0 75284 634 5

Printed in Great Britain by Clays Ltd, St Ives plc

ACKNOWLEDGMENTS

The SuperAegis space-based missile defense system and the submarine USS *America* that are featured in this tale are products of the author's imagination. Many of *America*'s capabilities and features were suggested by the *Virginia*-class of attack submarines currently under development, but the design is entirely the author's. Patent applications are pending. It was not the author's intent to write a treatise on submarines, which are among the most complex devices ever invented by man, so, as usual, the author has taken creative liberties where necessary in the interest of readability and pacing.

Engineer and physicist Gilbert Pascal was kind enough to illuminate numerous technical points as the author slashed his way through the arcane jungles of Star Wars and underseas warfare. Submarine experts Malcolm MacKinnon III and Chris Carlson read and commented upon the underwater portions of the manuscript. The author is deeply grateful to all three.

Culpability for this literary crime is shared by the author's wife, Deborah Coonts, to whom all complaints should be addressed.

The author's editor at St. Martin's Press, Charles Spicer, deserves a special tip of the baseball cap. His enthusiasm for adventure fiction, wise counsel, and patience throughout the creative process make him a pleasure to work with.

AMERICA

PROLOGUE

"Thirty minutes and counting," the loudspeaker blared.

Jake Grafton held his hat on his head against the breeze as he tilted his head to look up at the massive three-stage rocket towering into the blue sky. He squinted against the glare of the sunlight reflecting off the frost that covered the rocket's white skin. The cold fuel had lowered the skin temperature, causing moisture from the warm sea air to condense, then freeze.

"It's three hundred fifty-two feet, three and a half inches tall," Commander Toad Tarkington said expansively. He was full of facts and figures, enormous, meaningless numbers that managed to convey only the impression of stupendous size.

"You're sure of that?"

"Give or take a half inch. Shooting that thing is going to be a hell of a way to celebrate the Fourth of July."

"It is the holy Fourth, isn't it?"

Tarkington had spent the last month aboard the Goddard launch platform, a converted deep-sea drilling platform, and liked to play tour guide whenever his boss, Rear Admiral Jake Grafton, showed up with the international entourage in tow. Jake had been visiting the platform, which was sitting on the edge of the continental shelf fifty miles east of Cape Canaveral, for a couple of days every two weeks or so. This had been going on for months while the rocket was being assembled and tested.

Now it was ready. So the experts said, and there were a great many of them, from NASA, the air force, Europe, and Russia. Atop the third stage was the first of the SuperAegis space-based antiballistic-missile defense system satellites. The satellite contained a nuclear reactor and a laser, which would be used to shoot down ICBMs as they rose from the atmosphere. When fully operational the system would consist of eight killer satellites in mid-Earth orbit. It would take another three years to get the other seven launched. Assuming the first one successfully passed its operational tests. But all that was for other days in the hazy future.

SuperAegis was being launched from here as a sop to the Florida politicians, who were worried about contaminating Cape Canaveral and the Florida east coast if the rocket blew up on launch. The sea launch also ruled out use of the space shuttle as a launch vehicle.

Today the assembly crane had been moved back and only the gantry carrying the electrical umbilical cords stood next to the rocket.

"I confess I never thought we'd get this far," Toad murmured.

The other tourists were crowding onto the small work area below the rocket, so Jake and Toad moved to the very edge of the platform, against the safety rail. The sea was a hundred feet below. Dark blue water, a few whitecaps. Jake took a deep breath, reveling in the smell of the salty sea air.

"Smells good," Toad said, reading his mood.

Three helicopters were orbiting the platform. Two of them were military birds, and the third belonged to a television pool, which was sharing the video feed. The buzzing of their engines came and went, depending on whether they were upwind or downwind.

A mile from the platform lay the aircraft carrier USS *United States*, barely making steerageway. Even from this distance Jake could see the hundreds of people lining the deck. By launch time most of the carrier's crew and the thousand or so members of the press and dignitaries who couldn't be accommodated on the launch platform would be standing on the four-acre flight deck. Several destroyers were also visible, though farther away, steaming back and forth between the launch platform and several dozen civilian boats—yachts—crammed to the gunwales with protesters.

The antinuclear, peace, and environmental activists were out in full force, having a wonderful holiday and making as much of a nuisance of themselves as possible.

With their onboard nuclear reactors, the SuperAegis killer satellites certainly had something for everyone to worry about. The threat of nuclear contamination if a rocket failed to reach orbit had been minimized but could not be eliminated. Then there were those who felt that an effective ICBM shield made nuclear war more likely, not less so. Finally there were those who felt that it was obscene to spend so much money on a system that would in all likelihood never be used. All these cares and concerns had worked their way through the political process . . . and here sat the first component of the SuperAegis system, ready to launch.

One of the civilians standing nearby surrounded by aides and colleagues was the secretary of state, whose idea it had been to include Europe and Russia under the SuperAegis missile shield. That master stroke had cleared the way politically. The rockets lifting the satellites were made in Russia, and the launch was funded by the Europeans.

The antiballistic-missile defense system itself, the SuperAegis satellites, were purely American. The general details of how the system worked were of course common knowledge, had been publicized around the globe and argued at great length in legislative halls from Washington to Moscow, but the technology at the heart of the system was highly classified. It would have to remain that way to ensure it could not be defeated by rogue, pirate, or outlaw states that might in the future get an itch to launch a ballistic missile at the Western allies.

The secretary of state had plenty of company today. With him were the secretary of defense and the national security adviser. No doubt the president and the rest of the cabinet would also have been here if one of the protesters had not pointed out that if the rocket exploded on the platform—an unlikely event—conceivably the entire government delegation might be immolated. This, the protester said wryly, would not be a complete disaster. So the president stayed home.

One of the civilians, in a tailored gray suit standing at the secretary's elbow, was General Eric "Fireball" Williams, a former chairman of the Joint Chiefs. These days he was the president of Consolidated Aerospace, the prime contractor for SuperAegis. After the protester's immolation crack Williams had publicly announced that he was going to be in the control room during the launch.

SuperAegis had saved Consolidated, according to the press. Fifty billion dollars spent so far, with more to come.

Most of the other big-ticket American weapons procurement programs had been canceled to fund the ICBM shield. Many people in and out of uniform had argued bitterly about the wisdom of that, but the public wanted protection, and a hundred billion dollars was a lot of gravy to be spread far and wide, so Congress had gone along. After all, the argument went, America was the only superpower, with planes, ships, and tanks enough to defeat anyone on Earth, so the real threat was from third-world regimes developing weapons of mass destruction. SuperAegis, the argument went, would be a big first step in protecting Western civilization. And with a hundred billion to spread around, there was something for everybody, as one commentator pointed out. What's not to like?

"If it works," Jake Grafton muttered.

"Oh ye of little faith, it *will* work, Admiral!" said the man beside him after glancing at his uniform and name tag. His name was Peter Kerr, and he was the engineer in charge of SuperAegis. Jake recognized him from several meetings that he had attended chaired by Kerr. To the best of Jake's recollection, Kerr had never spoken to him before. In fact, he would have been amazed if the man even remembered him.

"In fact, SuperAegis is the only antimissile defense system that would work," Kerr said as he looked at the dignitaries peering into the rocket's first-stage exhaust nozzles and gazing up, up, up. "All the academics said it couldn't be done, but there it is. The sensors in the satellite detect the exhaust of an ICBM booster lifting out of the atmosphere, the reactor powers up, generating the energy to track the warhead with radar and destroy it with a pulse laser. Solves the detection and interception problems neatly, cheaply, and automatically."

"A better mousetrap," Jake agreed. Peter Kerr looked at him sharply, glanced again at his name tag, then turned away.

"There went your naval career," said a cheerful British voice at Jake's elbow. The owner, Wing Commander Alfred Barrington-Lee, was the British military liaison officer to the SuperAegis team. Toad Tarkington liked to refer to him as "Hyphen," although Toad called him "sir" to his face. He was in his late forties and sported a nice potbelly that appeared larger than it really was due to his stooped, narrow shoulders and nonexistent hips. Jake hadn't managed to spend much time these last few months with Barrington-Lee. Toad had, and respected him, which was a positive recommendation.

Beside the RAF officer was Maurice Jadot, the French civilian on the liaison staff. He was a medium-sized, nondescript man who smoked Gauloises cigarettes—outside of course—and often loitered, flirting outrageously, around the female secretaries' desks. This open sexual tension in the workplace awed the Americans, who had been so browbeaten by the sexual Gestapo that they hadn't seen it done at the office in decades. Jadot spoke English with a pleasant accent. According to Tarkington, who was a connoisseur in these matters, the accent added to his sex appeal.

The German was Helmut Mayer. An urbane, witty, intelligent man of the world, Mayer was the most extroverted of the four, the one most often at the center of conversation. Just now he was shaking hands and muttering pleasantries to the dignitaries, many of whom he apparently knew well enough to greet by name. His humor was self-deprecating and he had a delightful laugh. The women in the office found him fascinating. Unlike Jadot, Mayer treated all the women the same, friendly on a social, not sexual, level.

The fourth member of the team, who was looking around at the lively crowd as if he were attending his first hockey game, was Sergi Kuznetsov, the Russian. He was the only one of the four who was an acknowledged intelligence professional, yet he probably knew as much about ICBMs and the problems involved with shooting them down as any of the others. He was taciturn to a fault, spoke only when spoken to, and never made small talk. Tarkington referred to him as a stranger in a strange land, which Jake thought an apt description. Apparently America had overwhelmed him. When asked, he once admitted that this was his first foreign assignment.

Jake was the deputy to the team leader, Air Force Lieutenant General Art Blevins, who was somewhere below with the launch team. Tarkington filled an administrative assistant's billet, although in addition to his admin duties he functioned as Jake's assistant. He and the admiral had been together on various assignments for years.

Looking around, Jake decided he was probably the junior flag officer on the platform today. A good many three- and four-star flag officers were on the flight deck of the USS *United States* or one of her escorts. And truth be told, from that vantage point they would have a better view than the bunch on the Goddard platform, who were going to watch the launch on the control room monitors.

More people were filing up onto the tiny platform under the rocket, so Jake eased his way down the steps to the catwalk. From here he could see the giant flame deflectors that would vent the rocket's exhaust away from the platform's massive legs. He took a last look at the carrier, destroyers, frigates, and protesters' yachts as he made his way along the catwalk. He entered the personnel module and began climbing the ladders, working his way up six stories while uniformed NASA launch personnel filed down to make their final checks. The ladderways reminded Grafton of those in aircraft carriers.

The control/launch module was designed to contain everyone on the Goddard platform during the launch. The module was a bomb-proof, fireproof vault with small, three-inch-thick windows that looked as if they could withstand anything up to a nuclear blast. Huge monitors were spotted strategically throughout the room, and it was at these that the spectators looked. Cameras all over the platform were focused on the rocket, which gleamed on the monitors like . . . "the administration's phallic symbol."

Congresswoman Samantha Strader made this observation in a clear voice. She had the ability, honed through the years, to make herself heard in crowds. The babble died abruptly. A few people tittered nervously.

Strader had buttonholed the secretary of state, who had reached the command module just moments before Jake arrived. He was huddled with the secretary of defense and the chairman of the Joint Chiefs. Strader was the senior minority member of the House SuperAegis subcommittee, which was why she was here. She was the administration's most vociferous critic of SuperAegis and had used that issue to catapult herself to national prominence. In fact, in some quarters she was seen as presidential timber. If she made a splash in the primaries, she certainly had a shot at the vice-presidential nomination.

"Man, she ought to love SuperAegis," Tarkington whispered. He had followed Jake up the ladder with the international liaison team in tow. "Got her on the cover of *Time* magazine last week."

Jake didn't hear the secretary's retort, but he heard Strader's riposte. ". . . should be issuing hara-kiri knives to you gentlemen, in the event this bottle rocket goes in the water. After squandering fifty billion on it, hara-kiri is the least you could do for your country."

The secretary had had enough of Sam Strader. "I'd be delighted to do the dirty deed on those terms, Ms. Strader," he said loudly, "if you'll promise to use the knife if SuperAegis works as advertised."

The public address system buzzed to life, ending the bantering with an order for all personnel on the Goddard platform to enter the command module. "Ten minutes and counting," the announcement ended.

The launch technicians sat at computer consoles butted against each other, all in a row, against the forward bulkhead. A second row of consoles sat behind the first, also oriented toward the windows. This arrangement allowed the controllers to peek through the bombproof portholes at the waiting rocket if they could somehow tear their eyes from their computer screens. Few, if any, did. The technicians wore headsets and concentrated fiercely on the screens before them.

Walking behind the technicians and looking over their shoulders were the scientists and engineers who designed and supervised the construction of SuperAegis. This launch was the culmination of years of effort, a lifetime of study and theorizing for most of these men and women.

They reminded Jake Grafton of expectant parents, chewing fingernails, strolling aimlessly, lost in their own thoughts. Here and there one of them would pause to study a computer monitor, then move on, apparently reassured.

At five minutes to go, all conversation behind the consoles stopped. The audience stood silently, watching.

Jake glanced at Strader, who was watching the proceedings with rapt attention.

The launch director's name was Stephen Gattsuo. He reminded Jake of an orchestra conductor, and in many ways he was. Grafton and the liaison team had attended many practice countdowns, so many that the admiral felt he could have written the launch order and got it pretty close. If anything, the real countdown was going much smoother than the practice sessions, which were full of emergencies and every malfunction the fertile brains of the engineers could conjure up.

A minor electrical problem delayed the countdown for several seconds, perhaps twenty, but the technicians rerouted data around the malfunctioning distribution bus so smoothly most of the observers didn't know there had been a problem.

Tick by tick, the clock worked down. All conversation ceased among the spectators.

Ignition!

With a roar that was awe-inspiring, the first-stage rocket engines ignited. For only a moment was the beast still chained, then it began to rise. Through the bombproof windows only white-hot fire could be seen, so everyone not staring at a computer screen looked at a monitor.

Slowly, majestically, the rocket rose on a pillar of fire, perceptibly accelerating.

As the intensity of the noise began to diminish, the view on the monitors became an upward look at the dazzling exhaust plume of the rising rocket.

Jake Grafton realized he had been holding his breath. His skin tingled. He exhaled, then forced himself to breathe regularly as the rocket slowly shrank to a dot of brilliant flame on the monitors.

Now he was aware of the controllers' voices, talking to chase pilots, talking to each other, talking to tracking stations downrange. He clearly heard the first hint of trouble. "Bahamas tracking has gone off the air, apparently power failure."

He was watching the monitor when he saw the flash that meant the first stage had expended its fuel and dropped away as the second stage ignited.

The exhaust was a white-hot star in the monitors, low on the horizon, high in the atmosphere, accelerating. . . .

"Azores tracking is down. We are the only station with contact, and we're going to lose it in twenty-five seconds."

"Missile is changing course! Two, three, four degrees left . . . six, eight . . ."

Jake glanced at Gattsuo, the launch director, who stood like a statue staring at the monitor, listening to the reports. The missile should *not* be changing course. With a nuclear reactor aboard the satellite, the United States could not afford, ethically or politically, for the missile to wander off course and crash wherever, contaminating the crash site for thousands of years. On the other hand, if the missile managed to place the SuperAegis satellite in orbit, perhaps the orbit could be successfully altered later, saving the mission and the billions of dollars involved. Gattsuo was the man on the spot; the decision to destroy the missile his to make.

"Second-stage burnout in five seconds . . . four . . . three . . . two . . ."

The star in the center of the monitors that was the second-stage exhaust winked out. Leaving . . . nothing!

"Third stage has failed to ignite," the male voice on the PA system intoned flatly. "Missile seventeen degrees off course. We'll lose contact in nine seconds . . . eight . . ."

As the seconds passed, Gattsuo's face reflected his agony.

"Self-destruct," he ordered. "Destroy it."

Nothing on the monitor. No flash, nothing.

"Three . . . two . . . one . . . radar contact lost!"

In the crowded launch module dead silence reigned. It was broken finally when Stephen Gattsuo said disgustedly, "Shit!"

In the seconds that followed that comment, Jake Grafton distinctly heard a strident feminine voice ask, "Where's the knife?"

In the hours that followed, a parade of helicopters ferried the VIPs off the Goddard platform. They were a subdued lot, even Congresswoman Sam Strader, who knew better than to gloat. As they filed up onto the helo platform and stared at the empty place where the rocket had been, they even ignored each other. It was as if they had witnessed something obscene and were ashamed they had been there.

Jake Grafton and the liaison team remained behind. As the hours passed, the tracking stations came back on the air one by one, but no one could explain why the stations had all experienced power failures at the most inopportune time. "The odds are a billion to one that all the stations would lose power at the same time, and by God it happened!" exclaimed Gattsuo and smashed the flat of his hand against a bulkhead.

"Or someone made it happen," Toad Tarkington muttered.

"Why did the rocket go off course?" Jake Grafton asked the launch director.

"We don't know that it did."

"It sounded to me like it was wandering around."

Gattsuo had other things on his mind. "Maybe it drifted a little off course," he said distractedly. "We'll study the data."

"Why didn't the third-stage engines ignite?"

"We don't know."

"Did it self-destruct or didn't it?"

"We don't know."

"If it didn't self-destruct, where did the third stage—and the satellite—come down?"

"Goddamn it, Admiral, *we don't know*!"

Three days later when Jake and the liaison team finally went ashore, none of those questions had been answered. The SuperAegis killer satellite was lost.

CHAPTER ONE

A small band played lively Sousa marches as USS *America,* America's newest nuclear-powered attack submarine, prepared to get under way on its first operational cruise. The raucous crowd on the pier was in a holiday mood that balmy September Saturday morning. As seagulls skimmed over the heads of the happy onlookers, the band swung into a heartfelt rendition of "Anchors Aweigh." The line handlers on *America's* deck threw the last of the lines to the sailors on the pier, severing the connection between the sub and the land.

The sailors in white uniforms standing on the small, flat, nonskid surface atop the curved hull were going to sea for three months. As the gulls cried and the music floated away on the sea breeze, they took their last fond look at America—wives and kids and girlfriends and scores of navy officers high and low, miles of gold braid, and despite the early hour, barely eight A.M., dozens of civilian dignitaries up to and including an undersecretary of defense and the secretary of the navy. The congressional delegation from Connecticut was there—the boat had been constructed at Electric Boat—and of course various other senators and congresspeople high and low, those who were on defense committees in their respective houses and those who merely wanted to be seen on the evening news back home. Most of the political people even had a pithy sound bite ready if they were lucky enough to have a microphone thrust at them.

As the distance between the sub and pier widened, sailors blew their families kisses and everyone waved. When the last notes of "Anchors Aweigh" drifted off on the breeze, the band began playing "The Navy Hymn." Many of those on the pier and the sub's deck swabbed moisture from their eyes.

"Oh, hear us when we cry to thee, for those in peril on the sea," the skipper of the sub sang under his breath as he watched the pier slide aft.

"What a day!" the officer of the deck said, glancing at the wispy cirrus high above in the cerulean sky. This morning the sea breeze was light, just enough to roughen the surface of the water and make the sun's reflection on the swells twinkle wildly, as if the sunlight were reflecting off diamonds. Gulls hovered almost within arm's reach of the sail, begging for a handout.

America's commanding officer, Commander Leonard Sterrett, was shoulder-to-shoulder with the officer of the deck and two lookouts in the tiny, cramped bridge atop the sail. A temporary safety railing had been rigged around the bridge, but it would be removed and stowed before the boat dived. A hatch would then be lifted hydraulically into place to seal the opening.

The tug pulling the sub away from the pier seemed to be pulling effortlessly, with little white water from her screw.

With the band still playing, Captain Sterrett ordered everyone except the watch team on the bridge to go below. Time to say goodbye to earth and sky and families and get about the serious business of taking a brand-new, state-of-the-art attack submarine on patrol for the very first time.

Leonard Sterrett had been eagerly anticipating this day from the moment he had been told, three years ago, that he was to be *America*'s first commanding officer. He had been working to earn a submarine command since that summer day twenty-three years ago when he walked through the gate at the Naval Academy in Annapolis to begin his plebe summer. Now he had it. The responsibility for a capital ship worth two billion dollars manned by 134 men was all his.

He turned in the cramped open bridge and waved one last time at the people on the dock, especially his wife and parents, who had shared his dream all these years. He could see them and his teenage daughter waving back.

Then he turned to face the sea.

The officer of the deck, Lieutenant Ellis Johnson, seemed to read the CO's mood. "Congratulations, sir," he murmured, just loud enough to be heard.

"Thank you," the skipper said and smiled at the sea and sky.

A mile or so away, barely making steerageway, USS *John Paul Jones*, a guided-missile destroyer, kept a watchful eye on the covey of boats that had gathered to watch *America* get under way from the New London submarine base. For the last hour a small Coast Guard cutter had done most of the work of keeping the spectator boats corralled, mainly through use of a bullhorn. Overhead a helicopter belonging to a television station circled slowly, shooting footage for the evening news. One of the boats contained a delegation of antinuclear activists who had tried their best to raise a rumpus and be noticed by the camera folks in the news chopper. The Coast Guard skipper had threatened them with arrest and confiscation of their borrowed boat, so they were behaving themselves just now.

Aboard *Jones,* Captain Harvey Warfield focused his binoculars on *America*. The sail on the sub was located far forward on the hull, almost as if the attack boat were a boomer full of ballistic missiles. Well behind the sail was the squarish shape of a miniature submarine, a fifty-five-ton delivery vehicle for special-warfare commandos, SEALs. Although it was hard to judge from the portion of the submarine visible above water, to Warfield's practiced eye *America* looked slightly longer and sleeker than the navy's *Seawolf* boats. Perhaps the fact that he knew its dimensions exactly, 377 feet long and 34 feet in diameter, colored his perception.

Certainly not the fastest or the deepest-diving U.S. submarine, *America* was the quietest, without a doubt the ultimate stealth ship. Designed for shallow-water combat, the most difficult environment submarines could fight in, *America* packed more computer power inside her hull than all the other submarines of the United States Navy combined. Originally the submarine had been laid down as USS *Virginia;* the name had been changed to get a few more votes in Congress, which was the way things worked in Washington in this age of Pax Americana. These things Warfield knew from press releases and briefings—he wasn't cleared for the really juicy classified stuff, the secrets the submariners put in the I-could-tell-you-but-then-I'd-have-to-kill-you category.

Which was just as well, Warfield thought. Submarines had never interested him much—months submerged, the crew packed into the tiny ship like sardines in a can, the ever-present threat of drowning or being crushed when the hull imploded. . . . Just thinking about it was enough to make Warfield's skin tingle. Submarining was tough duty, obviously, and somebody had to do it. Those who did certainly earned their extra dough every month, Warfield thought, and were welcome to it.

Warfield checked his watch. *America* had cast loose her lines right on time, just what he expected from Lenny Sterrett.

Today the Coast Guard seemed on top of the small-boat situation, the navigator and senior quartermaster were on the bridge, and Warfield's officer of the deck was the best he had, so the captain reached for a pile of paperwork on the small table beside his raised bridge chair. After one last glance around, he picked up the first document in the pile and began reading.

Standing in the wheelhouse of the tugboat pulling *America* away from the pier, Vladimir Kolnikov lifted his binoculars and aimed them yet again at *John Paul Jones*. The destroyer was making only a couple knots, yet it was there, ready.

Ready for what?

That was the question, wasn't it? Ready for what?

How good was the skipper of the destroyer? How fast could he handle the unexpected? How quickly could the crew obey unanticipated directives?

"What do you think?" Georgi Turchak asked in Russian. He was at the helm of the tugboat. The captain of the tug lay in a corner of the small bridge, quite dead.

"You knew there would be destroyers," Kolnikov replied without lowering his binoculars. "We are lucky there is only one."

"What if there is another submarine out there?"

"Then we will soon be dead. Do you wish to back out now?"

"No, damn it. I wish you would tell me comforting things to make me think that we are going to pull this off, get filthy rich, and live to a ripe old age enjoying our money."

Kolnikov turned the binoculars, focused them on the captain of the submarine. He could see the features of his face plainly, see him talking to the officer of the deck, the OOD, and the lookouts, who were looking all over the horizon with their binoculars and paying no attention to the tugboat.

"He's going to want to release the line any moment now," Kolnikov said, more to himself than anyone else. He walked to the head of the ladder leading down.

"Are you ready, Heydrich?"

The man below looked about him at other men hidden from Kolnikov's view. "Eck? Boldt? Steeckt?" There were fourteen men belowdecks, one on the fantail, and of course here on the bridge Kolnikov and Turchak, for a total of seventeen.

Now the man below looked up the ladderway at Kolnikov. His face was one of large cheekbones and tiny eyes. "We are ready, Russki. Give the word."

"Very soon, I think."

The band was playing "America, the Beautiful" when the OOD used a bullhorn to call the tugboat. He could still hear the music plainly even though the sub and tug were about seven hundred yards from the pier. "We are ready to release the tow," he called.

Releasing the tow was a relatively simple maneuver. When the tugboat reduced power, the towline would go slack so the submarine's deck crew could release it from the towing cleat. Then the tug would accelerate away and the sub would proceed under its own power.

Kolnikov signaled to the man on the fantail of the tug, who began winding the towline tighter around a power winch as Turchak at the helm gently reduced power on the tug's engines.

The distance between tug and submarine began to decrease, while the men on the sub's deck waited in vain for slack to develop in the line.

It took several seconds for Captain Lenny Sterrett and the OOD, Ellis Johnson, to comprehend what was happening. Sterrett spoke sharply to Johnson, who barked into the bullhorn, "Get off the winch and give me some slack."

The white foam coming from the tug's fantail ceased as the distance between the two vessels closed. Kolnikov shouted at the man on the winch, waved his arms excitedly, and the distance continued to close until only a few feet of water remained between the two hulls.

Then smoke erupted from the fantail of the tug. Three seconds later, a minor explosion along the tug's waterline blew water into the air. The man on the fantail went over the side. Kolnikov rushed down the ladder from the tug's bridge and raced for the afterdeck.

Two more crewmen appeared on the tug's deck and ran aft.

"Man overboard, civilian from the tug!" The OOD shouted this message into the intercom, and in seconds it blared on the boat's loudspeakers.

In the control room the chief of the boat pronounced a curse word. "Oh, man!" he said. "First *Greenville,* then this!" Everyone in the control room knew what he meant—if the civilian in the water drowned before the sub crew could pull him out, the media would savage the navy and Captain Lenny Sterrett, which would probably sink his naval career.

Meanwhile the two vessels drifted without power. No slack developed in the towline, which continued to pull the vessels together until the tug's stern gently contacted the anechoic skin of the submarine below the waterline.

In the sub's tiny cockpit, Lenny Sterrett was trying to sort it all out. The men on the line-handling party on the submarine's deck threw the man in the water a line. He came clambering up it hand over hand with surprising agility.

"Cut that tow line," Lenny Sterrett roared at the senior petty officer on the sub's deck, who turned to grab an ax that had been thoughtfully carried on deck, just in case.

Too late. The man coming up the line pulled a weapon from beneath his loose-fitting wet shirt and shot the six unarmed men in the line-handling party as fast as he could pull the trigger. Then he scrambled for the open deck hatch.

All Lenny Sterrett heard were pops from the silenced reports, but the sight of falling men galvanized him, cleared away the cobwebs. He keyed the intercom and roared, "General quarters. Close all watertight doors. Prepare to repel unauthorized boarders."

Those were his last words, because even as he said them, a man with a sniper rifle standing on the wing of the tug's bridge shot him.

When the skipper went down, bleeding profusely, the OOD stood for a second, too stunned to move. The sight of two men crossing the line that held the sub to the tug hand over hand galvanized him. He jumped down the hatch into the sail. "You two, clear the bridge!" he shouted back up at the lookouts.

Neither man made it down the hatch. The sharpshooter on the tug didn't miss.

When he realized what had happened, the OOD closed the hatch and feverishly worked to dog it down. This evolution could not be done quickly. Unlike World War II submarines that patrolled on the surface and crash-dived to evade enemies, *America* was designed to submerge when leaving port and stay submerged for months.

Meanwhile, in the control room, the radioman punched a button to allow him to transmit on the ship-to-ship plain-voice frequency, Navy Blue. He was wearing a headset. "Mayday, *America,*" he said. "Unauthorized armed personnel attempting to board *America*. Request assistance ASAP. Mayday."

The chief of the boat, who had been standing behind the helmsman, for in this new class of submarine there was only one, reached above his head for the safety cover that shielded the SCRAM button, which would drop the rods into the reactor, stopping the nuclear reaction. He broke the safety wire on the cover and lifted it.

Valuable seconds were wasted as the OOD wrestled with the hatch dogs. Finally he got them secured to his satisfaction, then he dropped down the ladder to the first deck, where he rushed below to the control room.

"Boarders," he roared. "SCRAM the reactor. Close all the hatches. Don't let them—"

At that moment two men carrying silenced submachine guns rushed in and shot Ellis Johnson. They each fired one aimed shot; the bullets struck the lieutenant square in the back. The chief of the boat already had his hands up, reaching for the SCRAM button, so they ignored him. He jabbed in the red button.

And nothing happened! Warning lights should have lit up like a Christmas tree, the power in the boat should have switched to battery backup. . . .

"Hands up," the intruders roared, and one man stood with his weapon on the sailors as his companion dashed aft toward the engine and reactor spaces. The radioman was listening to excited voices from *John Paul Jones*.

He keyed the mike with his foot control. "Intruders in *America*—" he began, then they shot him.

The American sailors stood stunned, shocked, speechless. Unsure of what they should do to resist, most of them simply raised their hands and remained frozen. Those who had other ideas were mercilessly shot by the gun-toting men who came pouring through the main deck hatch in front of the sail and ran through the submarine.

Kolnikov was the last of the intruders to board. He paused on the deck, watched one of the Germans chop the towline through with an ax. The fantail of the tug was already awash. The demolition charges had produced noise and smoke and blown a nice hole in the side of the tug below the waterline, all of which was calculated to cause confusion on the American sub, where the sailors' innate caution would be overridden by the obvious peril of the man in the water and those aboard the tug. And it worked.

The downwash of the helicopter buzzing overhead made it difficult to stand on the open deck. Kolnikov lifted his submachine gun and squeezed off a burst. He was so close to the chopper that he saw holes popping in the Plexiglas. The machine veered away rapidly.

The destroyer was still a mile or so away, barely moving.

Good.

Kolnikov lowered himself into the open hatch.

"Captain, we have received a radio message from *America*. Armed intruders are boarding."

Aboard *John Paul Jones,* Captain Harvey Warfield took about two seconds to process that information.

"Verify," he barked at the OOD, a short, heavily built female lieutenant who used a telephone to call the radio room.

After listening a moment, the OOD said, "Put it on the loudspeaker on the bridge."

At the bottom of the ladder, Kolnikov found himself in a tight compartment above the control room. One of Kolnikov's men held a submachine gun on four Americans, who had their hands raised.

"Out," Kolnikov said to the American sailors, gesturing toward the ladder. "Up, into the water."

When the last of them was out, Kolnikov and the gunman went forward, opening the hatch to the space in the forwardmost part of the boat, which housed the sonar computers. One man was there. He was unceremoniously rushed aft at the point of a gun and pushed toward the ladder leading to the open air.

Kolnikov went aft, through the crew spaces and mast housings that protruded down from the sail. "Get them out," he told the two men there holding weapons on the Americans.

Then Kolnikov went into the control room. He knew what to expect—indeed, he had studied wall-sized photographs of the displays. Still, the massive screens and control consoles were so different from those on the submarines that he had served aboard in the Russian Navy, and before that the Soviet Navy, that he stopped involuntarily and took a deep breath.

The bodies of two men lay on the deck between the consoles, two wearing khaki. One was the body of the OOD, the other the control room chief. The radioman was slumped in his cubicle beside the control room.

"Get them out," Kolnikov told Heydrich, meaning the American officers and sailors who stood there with their hands raised. "The bodies too. Put them in the water."

"The men in the engineering spaces have secured the hatches," Heydrich said, "and jammed the dogs."

"You know what to do," Kolnikov replied.

Heydrich turned to the nearest man wearing khaki. He grabbed him by the arm, then turned to a sailor wearing a sound-powered telephone headset. "Tell them they have ten seconds to open that hatch, and if they don't, I shoot this man. Ten seconds later I shall shoot a second man. You will be last. Tell them to take all the time they want."

Heydrich put the muzzle of the pistol against the forehead of the sound-powered telephone operator. "If they SCRAM the reactor, we will kill each and every man on this boat. All of them. Every single one. The ten seconds start now. Tell them."

The operator was about twenty, with fair hair and acne. He began talking. He looked as if he were about to faint. Heydrich lowered his gaze to his watch, studied it. The talker was still delivering his message when Heydrich pointed the pistol at the man whose arm he held and killed him with one shot in the side of the head. The talker almost lost it on the spot.

He began babbling to Heydrich and Kolnikov, "No, no, they are opening the hatch. They are opening it!"

On the bridge of *John Paul Jones,* the captain and watch team listened without breathing to the garbled sounds of Heydrich and the sound-powered telephone operator. The dead radioman's foot rested on the push-to-talk pedal, so everything picked up by his lip microphone went out over the air.

"Are they recording this in the radio room?" Harvey Warfield snapped to the OOD.

The OOD spoke into the telephone she was holding against her ear. "Yes, sir."

The report of the silenced pistol was barely audible on the destroyer's bridge, but the fear in the voice of the talker and Heydrich's accented English came across plainly.

Harvey Warfield had heard enough. "General quarters," he roared. "All ahead one-third, Ms. OOD. Steer for the sub. Have the radio room send a flash immediate message to Washington telling them what's going on." The general quarters alarm began bonging away. The captain merely raised his voice to be heard above the hubbub. "Get some helicopters out here right now to sit on this sub and get the admiral at New London on the radio. Right now, people! Make it happen!"

The sullen men from the torpedo room and berthing spaces came slowly up the ladders and filed forward. The men from the engine room came through the reactor tunnel one by one. They looked at the dead men lying on the floor, at the Russians and Germans holding weapons, and filed on by.

The last American out of the engineering spaces was a second-class petty officer named Callahan—Heydrich was behind him with a pistol in his back. "This is the reactor man," he told Kolnikov in English. "He was at the panel."

"Half of them out now," Kolnikov told Turchak, "the other half later." He held up a hand to Callahan. "Not you. You stay here."

At that moment one of the SEALs stuck a knife into a German and grabbed his weapon. Heydrich killed the American sailor before he could get his finger on the trigger.

"Get them out of the control room," Kolnikov roared. "Get some into the water and the others down to the mess hall. Make the men going into the water carry the bodies. When they are in the water, shut the forward hatch. Turchak, let's get the boat moving."

He sat down at the control console and smoothly pushed the power lever forward a half inch. The motion of the boat steadied out. "Steeckt, up into the cockpit. Quickly now. We have no time to lose. Turchak, put the radar display on that screen right there," and he pointed.

"*America* is making way, Captain," the OOD reported to Harvey Warfield. "The lookouts report that men seem to be jumping into the water from the deck forward of the sail."

Warfield focused his binoculars. The radio transmission from *America* had ceased. The dead radioman's foot was no longer holding down the transmit switch; Warfield didn't know that, and it really didn't matter. The silence, however, was ominous. "Give me her course and speed," he snapped to the watch team.

"Little over a knot, sir. Coming starboard, heading passing one zero zero."

"Distance?"

"Thirteen hundred yards."

He could see people going over the side into the water. Jumping. Three or four jumped as he watched. Two men shoved someone— a body, perhaps—into the water.

"How many people in the water? OOD, ask the lookouts."

That was futile. He could see only the starboard side of the sub... the tug was just now coming into view as the sub turned. The tug was down seriously at the stern.

"More than a dozen, Captain."

"Get that Coast Guard cutter to pick them up."

"She's steady at two knots, Captain, probably just enough to keep the rudder effective, heading one two zero."

Aboard *America,* Kolnikov and Turchak studied the computer displays and controls on the consoles, the analog instruments, all the labels in English. . . .

The whole thing—the control room, the computers, the displays, everything—was overwhelming. They had studied all the available information, had run through simulation after simulation, but neither of them was prepared for the reality of *America*'s control room. Workstation after station, the sonar control group, the combat systems group, the engineering group—the enormity of the task before them hit them with hammer force. For the first time, Kolnikov was truly frightened.

Two of the men with them, both Germans, were computer experts. They were seated now at the consoles, taking it all in. Unfortunately, there was little time. A few minutes at most.

Rothberg, the American, was there, thank God. He was dashing from console to console, setting up displays, checking computerized data, selecting automated operating modes wherever possible.

"How does it look, Rothberg?" Kolnikov asked.

"No sweat," the American said without looking up from the console he was working on.

America was unique, in Kolnikov's experience, because the control room did not sit under the sail, but behind it, in a section of the hull that was clear of the machinery necessary to raise and lower the radar, communications, and photonics masts. This positioning was possible because *America* didn't have a conventional periscope, which formed the center of every other submarine's control room. The telescoping masts were housed in the sail, and none penetrated the pressure hull. Aboard *America* the periscope function was performed by the photonics mast, so-called because it contained sensors and cameras for capturing photons of light and heat, which were converted to digital form, run through the computers, and presented as images on one of these large screens in the control room. The information from these sensors could also be integrated with the data from all the other sensors, such as sonar and radar, to form a complete tactical picture for the control room team and its leader, the commanding officer.

"How is the reactor functioning?" Kolnikov asked Callahan, the American sailor who was standing with Heydrich near the main tactical display in the center of the control room. This display was horizontal, a high-tech chart on which the boat's position and the position of all contacts, friendly and hostile, were automatically plotted by the computer in real time. And of course, the display could be advanced to predict positions at any future point in time, which allowed one to instantly see the closest point of approach, study possible attack headings, visualize possible defensive maneuvers, etc.

"Reactor's perfect," Callahan said. "Someone should be on the board, though, every minute."

"We don't have that luxury," Kolnikov muttered, more to himself than anyone else.

All the boat's systems were controlled from this room—the reactor, turbines, sonar, weapons, life-support systems, everything except the stove in the galley and the commode in the head. Of course, the reactor control panel in the engine room had more complete instrumentation—doctrine in the American and Russian navies demanded that the panel be monitored constantly, twenty-four hours a day, even if the reactor were shut down. Unfortunately, Kolnikov didn't have enough men. And the ones he did have didn't know enough to make sound decisions. He was going to have to monitor the readouts himself from the control room and trust to luck.

Kolnikov bent over and looked at the German the SEAL had stabbed. The knife had gone into his heart. He was still alive, but he would die soon. He motioned to two of his men. "Carry him below."

They blanched.

"He's dying. We can't help him. Do it."

Callahan took a step closer to Kolnikov, glanced around the control room to ensure none of his shipmates were there, then said, "Hey, listen. I've done my part. The only SCRAM button that is still wired up is in the engine room. How about letting me get off now? You guys sail over the horizon and bon voyage."

Kolnikov glanced at Callahan, then nodded at Heydrich.

A wave of relief crossed Callahan's face. He started forward with Heydrich following.

Twenty seconds later Heydrich walked back into the compartment, his pistol in his hand.

"He knew too much," Heydrich said to Kolnikov as he slid the weapon into his belt. "We'll get rid of the body later."

Kolnikov nodded. He had other things on his mind. He had read and studied every scrap of information he could get about this submarine from every conceivable source. "Are you certain you can handle this boat?" the man in Paris had asked last week at their final meeting.

"No one could be absolutely certain unless he had read all the manuals and spent many hours in the simulator," he had replied, a reasonable response, he believed.

"So you are willing to try it?"

"Assuming the boat is not damaged in the hijacking, we will be able to take the boat to sea, submerge it, and proceed slowly away from the North American continent. Then we will spend three or four days figuring out what we have, how it works, what we can do with it."

"What are the dangers of this approach?"

Kolnikov had maintained control of his face, though his shoulders twitched. "Submarining is not chess," he said coolly. "Mistakes can be fatal. We must pray the boat functions as it should. We have had a limited time to prepare, we haven't seen the real ship. We will be unable to properly deal with malfunctions or emergencies until we discover exactly how the boat is laid out, how the control systems work."

"And the reactor?"

"The operation of the reactor is mostly automatic. All the critical parameters are automatically monitored by a computer, which will shut down the reactor if anything goes wrong. People monitor the parameters to back up the computer—we will have to forgo that luxury. If the computer shuts down the reactor, we will abandon ship. That is our only option."

"And if the Americans come hunting for you?"

"I have no doubt that they will," Kolnikov had replied. "We must ensure that they are unable to find us until we are ready for them."

The man in Paris had looked at him as if he had lost his sanity. Perhaps he had.

Yet Turchak had believed, for the man was here. A former

boomer skipper himself, Turchak had been the hardest sell. When he agreed to come, the others did too.

Now, as Kolnikov stared at the horizontal and vertical large-screen displays and the keyboards on the consoles surrounding him, the cold truth hit him like a hammer. They had been damn fools to attempt to sail this thing. It would take hours to work through the options of the weapons program; their only option just now was to run and pray that no one shoots.

Still, this was Vladimir Kolnikov's big chance, as it was for Turchak and the other Russians. On the beach, with no money or prospect for earning any, stranded in the midst of an absolutely corrupt third-world country—yes, Turchak and the others welcomed a chance to steal a submarine. Whether they would ever see any money for their efforts remained to be seen, but the Russians had nothing to lose.

Nothing to lose but their lives, and after all, what were they worth?

And if Kolnikov and Turchak and the others died trying for the gold . . . well, submariners risked their lives every time they went to sea.

The Germans were also here for the money. None of them had experience in nuclear submarines, but they were computer and sonar experts. Heydrich was neither. He was here because the man in Paris demanded that he be included.

How willing we are to volunteer for unknown risks when we are broke and hungry, standing on dry land.

Kolnikov turned to his most pressing problem, the American destroyer. Everything depended on what the skipper of the destroyer decided to do. "What is the destroyer doing now?" Kolnikov asked.

Eck, one of the German computer men, had a tactical display on the large-screen vertical display in the forward port corner of the compartment. Boldt, the other, worked on the ship's main system computer. Rothberg ran from one to the other, coaching them, reaching over their shoulders and pushing buttons when required. Eck's display showed tactical information from the main combat system computer, information derived from radar and photonic data. In fact, the image from the light sensor in the photonics mast, the tip of which was raised several feet above its housing, was presented on a large-screen vertical display that formed the centerpiece of the control room. The destroyer was about a thousand yards away, clos-ing. Five more vertical displays hung on the port bulkhead, four on the starboard, and one each in the forward corners of the compart-ment. At the forward end of the space were two ship-control con-soles, with vertical displays above them. Seven consoles to manage the integrated sonar suite lined the port side of the room. Four com-bat control station consoles were on the starboard side; the navigation engineering stations were behind the ship-control consoles and in front of the horizontal tactical display. A momentary twinge of panic gripped Kolnikov. Operating these systems with just five men—only one of whom, Rothberg, knew the systems cold—was idiocy, he thought.

"Close the main hatch and report when it is accomplished," Kol-nikov ordered. "Have Steeckt ready the sail cockpit for diving."

At the starboard ship-control console, Turchak examined the in-formation displays. He pushed buttons, tentatively at first, then with more confidence as he recalled the long conversations he had had pre-paring for this day. The joystick that controlled the boat was there before him, waiting for his hand. He caressed it, then ran his fingers along the power lever. The rudder, he knew, was tied in with the joystick, so the boat would always slide through the water with min-imum resistance. However, in the unlikely event there was a control computer failure, they would shift to manual controls to move the hydraulic valves that controlled the rudders and planes.

Digital images of the undersea world constructed from sonar data could be displayed on any of the vertical screens in the room. These images presented a three-dimensional picture of the undersea space around the submarine. The images could be rotated to display the situation in any direction from the submarine, or indeed, put the sub in the middle of a three-dimensional world, but for now the displays showed only the sea ahead, below and on each flank.

The displays were divided into two halves, both of which were transparent, by a wriggling line. The line was the water's surface. Above the line, the images were derived from data from the pho-tonics mast, below the line from the sonar.

The sonar was the top-secret black magic of which Kolnikov, Turchak, and the others had heard rumors but had little specific information. Revelation, the Americans called the gear—or multistatic passive sonar, MSPS—because it made the sea transparent, revealing all. Using only the noise present in the sea from every natural and man-made source, listening from acoustic arrays in the bow, chin, sail, flanks, and stern of the submarine, the computers processed the data into a three-dimensional presentation that was awe-inspiring. The acoustic sensors themselves produced data at the rate of about thirty million bytes per second, which was processed by a system capable of handling twenty-five gigabytes per second. The sonar-processing system had more capacity than the computer systems of all the other U.S. submarines combined.

Magic!

Kolnikov stood looking, dumbstruck. The sea appeared clear as glass. He could see hulls of other boats, buoys, the bottom of the sound, the shards of a sunken ship. . . . The ocean was a tough, nonlinear medium. Temperature and salinity variations led to speed of sound changes that refracted and reflected sound waves, causing ducting, "mirrors," and other effects that required real-time modeling on board to predict what in- and outbound sound was going to do as a function of depth, direction, and distance. Submarines changed depth periodically to measure actual conditions, to provide input to the computer models.

The pictures that Revelation generated, Kolnikov realized, were going to be only as good as the computer model. If the model were wrong, the pictures would be dangerous fiction. He would have to keep that fact firmly in mind.

"Nine hundred yards, Captain, bearing zero nine zero relative, speed five knots," reported Heinrich Eck, referring of course to the destroyer. "We are steady on course one two zero degrees, making two knots. The destroyer is flashing us with an Aldis lamp." Of course none of them knew what the Aldis lamp message was about, but Kolnikov thought it was probably an order to heave to.

"When the hatches are closed, we will accelerate," he said.

Kolnikov found a chair and settled in. Behind him four Russian and German technicians stood watching the horizontal tactical display and fidgeting nervously. Leon Rothberg sat at a terminal checking automated defaults. Heydrich stood together behind the tactical display.

With studied casualness, Kolnikov removed a pack of unfiltered

Pall Mall cigarettes from a trouser pocket. He extracted one from the pack, tapped it gently on a thumbnail to seat the tobacco, then lit it. He inhaled deeply, then blew out the smoke with a sigh.

"Smoke will foul the air filters and trigger the smoke alarms," Rothberg said irritably.

"Turn off the smoke alarms," Kolnikov said and took another drag.

"What will the destroyer do?" asked Gordin, one of the Russians.

"I don't know," Kolnikov replied curtly. Gordin was another former submariner, a veteran of the Arctic icepack—he should know to keep his mouth shut.

"Hatches shut, Captain," Boldt reported. He was working feverishly on the computer displays and now had one up that showed every orifice in the hull. All were now sealed.

"Obtain verbal confirmation, please," said Kolnikov, refusing to hurry.

Another minute passed. Gordin looked as if he were going to pee his pants when Steeckt finally came into the control room, out of breath. "All hatches secure, Captain."

"It's all yours," Kolnikov said to Turchak. "All ahead one-third." He took another drag on his smoke.

With his eyes on the reactor display and the steam pressures, Turchak slowly advanced the power lever, careful not to cavitate the prop or stir up the mud on the bottom of the sound. The power lever was merely a computer input device: The computer pulled rods from the reactor and opened valves in the engine room to route steam to the turbines. Here in the control room, Turchak could feel the submarine respond to his power command. The sonar picture began changing as the sub surged forward. The effect was mesmerizing.

Kolnikov leaned over and studied the touch-screen reactor information. The temperatures and cooling flow rates seemed smack in the middle of the normal ranges.

"Magic," Eck whispered as he stared at the sonar display, unintentionally voicing the thought all of them were thinking. "Pure magic."

Kolnikov shook his head, trying to clear his thoughts. There was so much to be done. "Gordin, you and Müller check the emergency gear. Extinguishers, hoses, nozzles, flashlights, tools, emergency breathing apparatus—all of it. Ensure that every man knows where everything is stowed."

"Aye aye, Captain."

"Admiral, it looks like somebody just hijacked your new submarine," Harvey Warfield boomed into the telephone. The people in the *Jones*'s radio room had the commander of the Submarine Group on the other end of the hookup. Apparently the admiral had been on the pier watching *America* get under way and had only now arrived in his communications center.

"Are you sure?" the admiral demanded.

Try as he might, Warfield couldn't remember the flag officer's name. "We received a radio transmission that I interpreted that way, sir. A lot of people from the tugboat boarded the sub, and the sub sent a Mayday, which wasn't repeated. The mike seemed to get stuck open, and it sounded as if the intruders were hijacking the boat. There are people in the water right now, and we're closing on them."

"Who is in the water?"

"Sir, I don't know."

"Well, goddamn it, Captain, I think we had better find out just who is in the water and what the hell is going on aboard that submarine before we go off half-cocked."

"Admiral, in my considered judgment, a bunch of pirates are stealing that submarine."

"What do you want to do about it?"

"Sir, the decision to disable or sink an American submarine needs to be made way above my pay grade."

"Jesus fucking Christ! You expect me to authorize that based on some unverified crap you heard over the radio?"

"No, sir. I'm just advising you. People are falling in the ocean off that sub, the tug is sinking, we've been signaling the sub, ordering it to stop. Whoever is running that show is ignoring our signals. They refuse to answer our radio calls. Something is terribly wrong! It looks to me like the goddamn sub has been hijacked."

The admiral mulled that comment for about two seconds. "Well, before we stick our dicks in the meat grinder, Captain, we need verification of this tale. I assume you've notified national command authority in Washington. Have you sent a flash message?"

"Yes, sir. I think we're drafting our third now. You should have received copies."

On that note, the admiral terminated the conversation.

"Asshole," roared Harvey Warfield as he slammed the telephone receiver down onto its cradle. He jabbed the squawk box. "Radio, get me the goddamn Pentagon. If I'm gonna sit here like a wart on a dog's ass watching that pigboat sail off over the horizon, I want a four-star on the hook with me."

He released the button and shouted to the OOD, "That sub is accelerating. Stay with it. Close to parallel at its four-thirty position at a range of a hundred yards. And give me some reports. I want to know when the gun and torpedo tubes are manned and ready. Tell me about the people in the water."

"The Coast Guard cutter will pick up the men overboard, Captain."

Hijacked!

Yes, he was sure of it, though Harvey Warfield had to admit to himself that the evidence was sketchy. Although it sounded compelling, the radio show they had listened to could have been produced anywhere. The exploits of Orson Welles came immediately to mind.

Do this right, Warfield! There won't be any second chances.

He trained his binoculars on the white Coast Guard boat, which was now dead in the water. He could see the sailors rigging nets over the side and lowering a small boat.

Of course the admiral didn't want to take responsibility for sinking a brand-spanking-new two-billion-dollar submarine and killing a bunch of American sailors. Who would?

But if he, Harvey Warfield, didn't ring the fire alarm, the sub was as good as gone.

Hijacked!

The thought occurred to Harvey Warfield that there might be other submarines about, submarines that did not belong to the United States. He jabbed a squawk box button: "Combat, bridge, are there any subs on our plot?"

"No, sir. None."

"Unidentified aircraft?" Even as he said it, he knew the answer.

"A couple dozen, Captain. Five non-transponder-equipped targets; the rest, I believe, are light civilian planes not under positive radar control. But I have no way to verify that."

A feminine voice in his ear: "Captain, one of the lookouts reports that a television news chopper is hovering over our fantail. It appears to have bullet holes in the Plexiglas. We think the pilot wants to land on the fantail, sir."

"Let him land. See if he has any videotape of that sub. If he does, get it and put it on the ship's system. I want to see it here on the bridge. And transmit it to Washington. And I want a report on those people in the water. Get that Coast Guard skipper on the horn and get a report."

"Aye aye, sir."

"The Pentagon war room is on the line, Captain," said another voice.

Harvey Warfield picked up the telephone and identified himself. He tried to succinctly sum up the situation by citing only hard, verifiable facts.

The war room duty officer was a two-star. "Are any Americans still aboard *America*?"

"I don't know," Warfield replied bitterly. He could almost hear the other man thinking in the silence that followed.

"What is his course and speed?" the admiral in Washington asked.

"Up to ten knots now, sir, still heading one two zero for the open sea."

"Depth of water?"

"Two hundred feet at the most."

"Captain, you are the officer on the spot. I am not going to grant you permission to do anything. Anything you choose to do is your responsibility."

"Yeah," said Harvey Warfield, who didn't join this man's navy yesterday. He hung up the headset.

"Is the gun manned?" he called to the OOD.

"Yes, sir. Manned and ready."

"Have the gunnery officer fire a warning shot. Have him telephone me before he shoots."

"Yes, sir."

In seconds the telephone rang. "Captain, gunnery officer."

"A warning shot across their bow, Mr. Turner. Do not hit the submarine or any of those goddamn little boats running around out there."

"Yes, sir."

"Whenever you are ready, Mr. Turner."

"Aye aye, Captain."

Twenty seconds later the gun banged. The shell hit the water a hundred yards ahead of the sub, made a nice splash.

And the sub kept right on going. It was up to thirteen knots now.

Warfield jabbed the button on the squawk box labeled Radio.

"Tell everyone in the world, flash immediate: We have fired a warning shot across *America*'s bow and it was ignored."

When Warfield looked up, his XO was standing there, the finest naval officer he had ever been privileged to serve with, Lorna Dunnigan. He felt better just having her there. As usual, she got right to it.

"What do you intend to do, Captain?"

"I don't want the responsibility for killing a bunch of Americans either," Warfield admitted. "I want more facts before I pull any triggers."

Vladimir Kolnikov was on his second cigarette when the splash of the warning shot showed on the integrated tactical display and on the sonar. He glanced at the photonics image—yep, there too.

"How deep is the water here?" he asked Eisenberg, his navigator.

"One hundred eighty feet below the keel, Captain."

"How long to the hundred-fathom curve?"

"Three hours at this speed."

"Fifty fathoms?"

"An hour."

Kolnikov leaned back in his chair and put his feet on the console in front of him. "I need an ashtray," he remarked to no one in particular.

"Aren't you going to sink this destroyer?" Heydrich asked. He was seated in an empty sonar operator's chair, watching.

"With what? It will take all night for us to figure out how to aim and fire a torpedo."

"So he can kill us at his leisure?"

"That's about the size of it. But he won't. The captain of that destroyer does not know what happened aboard this boat. He certainly suspects, but he doesn't know. None of the Americans know, and we are not going to help them find out. I wouldn't shoot at that destroyer even if I could."

"They will fish some of the Americans from the sea and question them. Those men will talk."

That process would take time. And no two of the Americans would tell the story the same way, Kolnikov reflected. Half-drowned men would tell disjointed tales, disagree on critical facts. "They'll talk," he told the German. "And they will say that there are still Americans aboard this boat."

"So?"

"That fact means nothing to you, Heydrich, but it will mean a great deal to the Americans. Trust me."

A half hour later Harvey Warfield had two pieces of critical information. He knew that about fifty Americans remained aboard *America,* and he was convinced that the submarine had been hijacked. In addition to the testimony of the *America* sailors pulled from the sea, he had a videotape from the camera of the television news helicopter, which was sitting in the helo spot on the destroyer's fantail. Two navy helicopters were circling over the sub and destroyer, neither of which was equipped with a dipping sonar or any of the other high-tech paraphernalia of antisubmarine warfare. Warfield talked to the Pentagon duty officer on a scrambled radio voice circuit as he watched the video on a monitor mounted high in a corner of the bridge.

"At least a dozen men," Warfield said. "They spoke accented English. One of the crewmen thought they were Russians, two thought they were Germans, one guy thought they were Bosnian Serbs, two swore they were Iranians, no one knows for sure. I'm watching them on videotape, though, shoot a submachine gun at the helicopter taking pictures. The guy just turns and shoots, like he was swatting at a fly."

"How many Americans were killed?"

"At least eight that we know of. The Coast Guard has already recovered that many bodies."

"Captain Sterrett?"

"Dead. Shot once at the base of the throat with a bullet that went all the way through."

"I'll pass this along to the national command authority."

"Better pass along this fact too, Admiral. This sub is going to dive in the very near future. If it is as quiet as everyone has been saying it is, I'll lose it unless I'm shot with luck. Whatever the brains in Washington want to do about this had better be done before this thing slides under."

"Try to stay on it."

"Aye aye," Warfield said without enthusiasm and hung up the headset.

"What if this guy squirts a torpedo at us, Captain?" the OOD asked.

"He won't," Warfield said with conviction. "I doubt that he has any torpedoes in the tubes ready to go, but even if he does, he won't shoot. This guy kept fifty hostages to ensure that we wouldn't shoot at him."

"If he didn't have any hostages," the XO asked, "would you sink him?"

"Right now. This very minute."

"So the choice is to sink him with the gun or let him go."

"Or try to ram him, disable the screws."

Even as he said the words, Harvey Warfield was considering. If he could bend or break off just one blade, the sub would lose a great deal of speed and become a real noisemaker. He picked up the handset, asked for the Pentagon war room again.

The admiral there was unenthusiastic. "The evidence for a hijacking hasn't changed in the last five minutes, has it?"

"No, sir."

"Still thin."

Harvey Warfield had had enough lawyering. "We fry people in the electric chair with less evidence than we have right now," he told the admiral. "The Coast Guard has eight dead American sailors stretched out on their deck." Warfield lost his temper. "Are you going to wait for autopsies, Admiral?"

"If you ram the sub you will damage both ships, perhaps severely."

"Yes, sir."

"Perhaps crack the sub's reactor, have a nuclear accident right there in Long Island Sound. With thirty million people strewn around the shore."

"There is that possibility," Harvey Warfield admitted. He felt so helpless, listening to this cover-my-ass paper pusher while he watched a brand-new, genuine U.S. attack submarine armed to the teeth sail for the open sea with a bunch of criminals at the helm. Killers. Murderers.

"This decision needs to be made by the national command authority," the Pentagon admiral said. By that he meant the president of the United States. "We'll get back to you."

"Yes, sir."

That was the situation twenty-seven minutes later when Kolnikov decided the water was deep enough. Two freighters were nearby, on their way out of Long Island Sound into the Atlantic, and several fishing boats. The Block Island ferry was about to cross the sub and destroyer's wake when Kolnikov reduced power. As two Coast Guard helicopters buzzed angrily overhead, the sub decelerated, gradually flooded its tanks, and settled slowly into the sea. The destroyer was abeam the submarine on the starboard side when the top of the sub's masts disappeared from sight. Crying raucously and soaring on the salty breeze blowing in from the sea, a cloud of seagulls searched the roiling water for tidbits brought up from the depths.

Aboard *John Paul Jones,* Harvey Warfield knew that he didn't have a chance of tracking the submarine unless he used active sonar, so he gave the order. *Jones* was a guided-missile destroyer, its systems optimized to protect a carrier battle group from air attack. The ship had an antisubmarine capability, but it certainly was not state of the art.

The sonar operator tracked the sub as it turned into the swirling water disturbed by the destroyer's passing, then lost it.

"This guy is no neophyte," Harvey Warfield muttered darkly when the tactical action officer in combat gave him the news, but there was little he could do. He turned the destroyer, slowed to two knots, and waited for the wake turbulence to dissipate. All the while the sonar pinged on, probing for the submarine that was actually going back up the destroyer's wake at five knots, steadily opening the distance between the hunter and the hunted.

The TAO called the captain again. "The water is very shallow, sir. The sound is echoing off the bottom and other ships and thermal layers. It's like we're pinging inside a kettledrum. The scope is a sea of return. *America* might be one of those blips, but we would only be guessing. We could go passive, see if the operator can pick him out."

"He'll never hear him. I'll bet a silver dollar that he's under that ferry this very minute."

"That would be a good bet, Captain, but we can't pick him out of the return at this range. If you want to close, we can keep trying."

"This guy won't wait for us to search the haystack," Harvey Warfield said with conviction. He knew that pinning a submarine in shallow water under less than ideal conditions was an impossible task for a guided-missile destroyer like the *Jones,* equipped with fifteen-year-old sonar technology. He needed a helicopter or two, or a second destroyer. Even if he had those assets at his disposal, stealthy as the *America* was, he would need a pot full of luck. "Do whatever you think best," Warfield told the TAO.

"Just like that," Captain Warfield stormed at his XO. "Just like that! I will make a prediction. I predict that before very long those bastards in the Pentagon are going to wish to God they had given the order to destroy that boat before it submerged."

Kolnikov did use the ferry, not by running along under it, but by keeping it between the submarine and the destroyer when he left the destroyer's wake. As he stole slowly away he was careful not to put the destroyer directly astern, in his baffles, so he could still see it on the sonar presentation. The active pinging from the destroyer's sonar resembled flashes of light on the screen.

When the destroyer was miles behind, Kolnikov threw the sub into a series of hard, tight turns designed to allow him to check his baffles to see if an American submarine was trailing him.

The sea was empty. *America* was alone.

"It feels strange going to sea without an American boat following along with his nose up our ass," Turchak remarked.

Kolnikov thought this remark amusing. American attack subs usually picked up Russian boomers as they left port and followed them for months, quite sure the Russians didn't know they were there.

"I think this time we are really alone," Kolnikov replied jovially and slapped Turchak on the back.

With the sonar presentation showing open sea ahead and to all sides, *America* swam deeper into the gray wastes of the Atlantic.

CHAPTER TWO

Rear Admiral Jake Grafton and his wife, Callie, awoke Saturday at their beach house in Delaware. They had guests this weekend, both of whom were apparently still asleep. The Graftons pulled on pants and shirts, and tiptoed down the stairs and out the front door. They sat on the porch steps to put on their shoes, walked the block along the crushed seashell street to the public parking area, then crossed the dune on the boardwalk. Standing on the beach in deep sand, they took off their shoes again, tied the laces together, and draped them around their necks.

The wind this morning was off the sea. The Graftons walked along arm in arm as seabirds ran along the sand probing for mollusks and the September breeze played with their hair. They tried to get to the beach several times per month, but with two hectic schedules they were lucky to get there once every other month. This weekend trip had been eagerly anticipated for three weeks. Jake normally spent twelve hours a day at the office, seven days a week.

When the couple bought the beach house years ago they anticipated living here when Jake retired. As Callie walked the beach this morning, she suddenly realized that she and Jake hadn't discussed retirement in quite a while. He hadn't mentioned the future in months.

She glanced at him. He had thinning hair, which he combed

straight back, and a lean face with a nose that was a trifle too large. His tan, she noticed, was pretty much gone. She reminded herself to make sure he put on sunblock when they returned home.

Now he smiled at her and squeezed her hand. "We've got to get over here more often," he murmured. "It isn't fair for me to keep you cooped up in that flat in Washington."

"If I wanted to come by myself, I could. I just don't like coming here without you."

"I know how you feel." He smiled again.

"Last night was a lot of fun," she said. "I really like the Russian, Ilin." Last night Toad Tarkington, Jake's executive assistant, arrived at the beach house with Janos Ilin, a Russian.

Jake absentmindedly released her hand and jammed both fists into his trouser pockets. "He's really smart," Jake said tentatively. "Supposed to be a bureaucrat in the Russian defense department, an accountant, he says. He's certainly a people person, smooth as old scotch. Almost too much so. This guy could sell magazine subscriptions at a home for the blind or charm his way out of jail. At times I wonder what the man who lives in there is really like."

"Supposed to be a bureaucrat?"

"I think he's a very senior officer in the foreign intelligence service, the SVR, which is the successor to the KGB. Same paranoid bunch running it, doing all the nasty stuff they always did, but they aren't Communists now, they say. As if that makes a difference in an authoritarian society."

"Do you really think having him here is a good idea?"

"Maybe not, but Ilin didn't want to spend the weekend at the Russian embassy and Toad didn't want to just turn him loose to see what trouble he could get into. Hell, the guy's first taste of freedom—he might run off to Vegas with a topless dancer sporting a new boob job and never be heard from again. You can imagine the repercussions!"

She made a rude noise.

"Toad had to do something with the guy," Jake said with a shrug. "His wife's on a cruise and the kid is at his grandmother's. Toad knew you and I were coming to the beach, so he brought him here."

"Ilin makes a nice houseguest. I enjoyed visiting last night."

Jake smiled. Callie, the linguist, had been studying Russian for the last year. Last night she refused to speak to Ilin in English, which he spoke well. The two of them had laughed merrily as she chattered away in fractured, broken, semi-intelligible Russian.

"Even if he is a spook, he's very charming," she said as they strolled along, Jake with his hands in his pockets, Callie with her arms crossed in front of her.

Jake took his time choosing his words, then said slowly, "He replaced the last Russian six weeks ago, two weeks after the Super-Aegis satellite was lost. The other guy was called home for a family emergency, according to Ilin. The other guy went back to the embassy one evening and Ilin showed up the next day with credentials and an explanation."

"So have they figured out what went wrong?" Callie asked now. She touched Jake on the arm and he automatically reached for her hand.

"NASA is investigating. And the Russian rocket experts and the European experts. Someone said that every time three people meet in an office, it's like a session of the UN Security Council. I hear they even have the FBI turning over rocks and going through waste-baskets. In any event, no one is telling us diddley-squat."

A thorough, comprehensive search had failed to find the satellite or the reactor it contained. Nor could any trace of excess radiation be found, which one would expect if the reactor had been damaged in the crash. Even worse, no one knew why the launch had failed or the entire tracking system had shut down.

"Surely there must be some theories," Callie murmured.

"Theories are four for a dollar," her husband admitted ruefully. "NASA insists the prelaunch and launch procedures are not the problem, the Russians insist there is nothing wrong with Russian rockets, the Europeans deny that the expedited testing procedures they demanded for cost-containment purposes are to blame . . . but the fact is the satellite didn't reach orbit. It was presumably lost at sea."

"I don't understand why it hasn't been found. It must be somewhere under the launch path. Shouldn't it?"

"Well, there's a debate about that. The trajectory was curving to the north when the third stage failed to ignite. Apparently. Then the tracking stations lost it. At that speed and altitude, it could be anywhere from Africa to the Bahamas."

"You don't really think that something just 'happened,' do you?"

"No. I think it was sophisticated sabotage. Someone changed a few lines of software here and there. After the missile was lost, he or she went back in and changed it back. Someone else could have killed the tracking stations for several minutes. The FBI is investigating and apparently coming up dry."

"And the Russian response to the SuperAegis disaster was to send a spy to be a member of the liaison team?"

"It's that kind of world, I guess," Jake said lightly. "Drop a satellite and here they come. But who knows, there's a chance—a small one, of course—that Ilin is indeed what he is says he is, a career paper pusher, a bean counter."

"So why didn't he get a room at the Washington Hilton?"

Jake chuckled. "The times, they are indeed a-changin'," he said. "But they don't change overnight. Used to be a senior spook like Ilin couldn't leave the Russian embassy without an escort. They're afraid their people might defect or turn traitor or something. Presumably Ilin's chock-full of state secrets that Russia's enemies would pay huge money for. He says his boss thinks he's growing up. They would like him to sleep at the embassy, but now he can play outdoors without adult supervision."

"How senior is he?"

"Equivalent of a major general, I think. Maybe a lieutenant general. The CIA says they think he's the number-two or -three man in one of the SVR's chief directorates."

"Are you and Toad corrupting him?"

"I'm just trying to be a decent host. Toad is probably trying to rot Ilin's Cyrillic heart. I don't know. Or care. Ilin may be trying to show us that he isn't SVR because he can sleep outside the Russian embassy. Whatever. At some point you stop peeling the onion and let it be."

"Is he going to defect?"

"God, I hope not! It would be a disaster if he did."

"Do you like Ilin?"

Jake shrugged. "I haven't thought much about it. He is charming, but he's way too smart. Being around him makes me nervous."

Callie laughed. "Phooey. You're in his league, Jake Grafton." She shook her head. "Just for the record, though, I wish you and I had a little more time alone to practice this husband-wife thing."

"Me too," Jake agreed warmly and reached for Callie's arm. "I'm sorry the guys showed up. I could tell Toad to take him down to Ocean City this afternoon, get a hotel room with a good television and watch some football."

"No, no. They can stay. I didn't mean that."

"Honest. I can run 'em off."

"I know. But it would be impolite."

They walked on hand in hand.

"Last night was fun," Callie said, remembering. Ilin had asked the origin of the name of the project—SuperAegis. Jake replied that the space-based missile defense system was first christened Galahad, after the good knight with the enchanted shield. "Galahad's shield," Jake explained, "had a marvelous property; it would protect only those pure in heart. The president thought that this close to the Clinton era, people would think the name was some kind of political joke."

That remark got Ilin started on political jokes. He regaled the Americans with an hour's worth, all of which Callie forced him to repeat in Russian. Then somehow the conversation turned to grandmothers. Jake Grafton grinned as he walked the beach this morning, remembering.

"My father's mother liked to invite her friends over for cards in the afternoon," Callie had told her audience. "They smoked and drank gin until they were so snockered they could barely walk and thought they were so wicked. Grandmother would call me over to her and announce, 'Callie is going to help me cheat. Look at the other ladies' cards, honey, and tell me if you see any jacks.' My other grandmother was also a pistol. She's the one who taught me to pee without taking off my swimsuit." That comment brought a gale of laughter. "She also liked to skinny-dip and would wake me up at midnight to go skinny-dipping with her in her pool. She loved splashing around naked in the darkness, listening to the crickets and frogs, speculating about what the neighbors would say if they ever found out."

That got Toad talking about his grandmothers. He then mimicked the way they talked. Jake and Callie had never heard him mimic other voices before, so they encouraged him. He did an excellent John Wayne, good Jimmy Stewart, Jack Benny, Bill Clinton, and a passable handful of others. Although Ilin didn't know many of the voices, the Graftons did; Toad had them in stitches.

"What are you grinning about?" she asked her husband this morning as they walked the sand.

"Being alive," he shot back. "Like your grandmother, I enjoy it immensely. Come on, let's get our feet wet." Jake led Callie into the surf runout area. The water was cold on their ankles. In seconds a wave forced them to retreat. Back and forth they went, like children, as the surf chased them.

Eventually he misjudged a wave, which soaked his trousers from the knees down. He grinned ruefully at his wife, who was wearing a wide smile as the cold salt water swirled around her ankles.

They were crossing the beach, heading for the boardwalk across the dune, when Jake's cell phone rang. He removed it from his pocket and flipped open the mouthpiece.

"Grafton," he muttered and inserted a finger into his left ear to block out the sighing of the wind and surf.

Callie sat down on the boardwalk to put on her shoes as Jake concentrated on the telephone conversation. He didn't say much. Callie felt her spirits sink. The cell phone was nonsecure, Callie knew, so official business could not be discussed on it. More than likely this was a summons to return to Washington. When Jake glanced at his wristwatch, she knew.

"Okay," he said and closed the phone mouthpiece. As he put the phone into his pocket he looked at her and shrugged. He looked tired, she thought.

"Someone hijacked a submarine—if you can believe that. Big meeting in Washington. They're sending a helicopter. It'll be here in about an hour."

"Oh, Jake. I'm sorry."

"Damn!" he said. "You'll have to drive the car back to Washington."

"A submarine?"

"New London, he said. This morning."

"Is there any chance you could get back here tonight?"

"I don't know. Perhaps."

"Why don't you call me from Washington, let me know? I could thaw steaks and Toad can cook them tonight on the grill. I'll thaw one out for you."

"Okay."

She touched his cheek. "You seem happier than I've seen you in years, Jake. You're fully engaged."

"They keep me jumping, that's for sure."

"And you love it."

He grinned. "It's the niftiest job I've had in years. Maybe ever. The truth is that it's fun working with really smart people, like Ilin. Man, I didn't know there were this many geniuses in the world. At times I feel like I'm the dumbest kid in the class, but what the hey. I'm giving it my best shot. And yeah, that's fun."

They found Toad and Ilin sitting on the screened-in porch drinking coffee. In his mid-forties, Janos Ilin was a tall, lean man with craggy features and lively, expressive features. He greeted Callie now with a phrase in Russian, and she fired a few words back at him.

"Good morning, Jake," Ilin said to the admiral with a smile. Ilin liked to use first names. Apparently someone had told him that was the American custom and he took it to heart.

"So did you sleep okay?"

"Fine, Jake. Just fine."

"I'm going back to Washington in a few minutes," Jake said, more to Toad than Ilin. "You guys make yourselves at home. Callie is going to thaw steaks for tonight."

"Will you be returning this evening, sir?" Toad asked.

"I don't know."

Jake took his coffee with him when he went upstairs to pack. As he climbed the stairs he heard Callie speaking to Ilin in Russian, probably asking him what he wanted for breakfast. When Jake came back downstairs carrying his overnight bag, he found Ilin inspecting the bookshelf.

"Help yourself," he told the Russian. "Toad, how about driving me down to the hospital helo pad."

He kissed his wife, then went out to the car with Tarkington. As Toad piloted the car along the highway, Jake told him of the submarine hijacking. "USS *America,* according to the Pentagon duty officer. It's on television, he says; all the channels are running news specials. Turn it on when you get back, watch Ilin's reaction."

"Why?" Toad asked, referring to the theft of the sub.

"I dunno. Someone wanted a sub."

Toad whistled. "Holy . . . !"

After a bit Jake asked, "What do you think of Ilin?"

"He's sharp as a razor, Admiral. It's hard to figure what he's thinking, but I suspect that he has a low opinion of you and me. It's just a feeling I have, nothing specific."

"We are sorta small-caliber guys," Jake muttered.

"He speaks great English," Toad continued. "Has an excellent vocabulary. Seems to know a lot about a lot of stuff. He has something to say about every subject I could think to raise. This morning you saw him checking out your taste in literature."

As Jake mentally cataloged the thrillers, mysteries, and action-adventure novels that filled his shelves, Toad added, "He thinks we're nincompoops."

"There's nothing on my shelves that will disabuse him of that notion," Jake replied. "Let's let him hang on to it as long as possible."

Kolnikov had *America* running at three knots, five hundred feet below the surface of the sea, when he engaged the autopilot. He had seen submarine autopilots before, of course, but not an autopilot that was designed to run the ship all the time, except in the most dire emergency. He had never seen a submarine with completely computerized, fly-by-wire controls operated with a joystick, either. No fool, Vladimir Kolnikov knew the reason that naval engineers didn't trust submarine autopilots—if a stray electron galloped sideways through the system, the boat could be endangered within seconds. An out-of-control submarine could easily dive too deep, past its crush depth. The faster the sub was going when control was lost, the sooner crush depth would be reached. This one, Kolnikov knew, was operated by three computers that constantly checked on each other and compared data. Any two of them could outvote and override the third.

Still, engaging the autopilot was an act of faith, Kolnikov told himself as he pushed the final button and took his hands off the boat's joystick controls. If Rothberg and the Germans didn't have the computer system functioning properly, this was going to get very exciting very quickly.

Now Kolnikov watched the attitude indicator and the depth gauge, waiting.

All steady.

The machine kept the sub on course, without varying the depth a detectable amount. But for how long? And if something went wrong, how long would he have?

He looked around. Turchak, Eck, Boldt, and the other two Germans were frozen, staring at the gauges. Leon Rothberg was working on the master combat control station on the starboard side of the control room.

"Don't go to sleep," Kolnikov muttered to Turchak, who nodded in full agreement.

For the first time since he submerged the sub, Kolnikov left the captain's post. He was relieved to find the radio gear and encryption computer in the communications space, or radio room, in the area on the starboard side of the control room. No codebooks in sight, which meant they must be in the safe. He examined the safe, which, alas, was locked. He had been worried that the communications officer or his subordinates might have destroyed the crypto computer and the codebooks when they realized the sub was being hijacked. Apparently not.

As nifty as the sonar was, the codebooks and cryptographic computer were solid gold. Or would have been if the Americans hadn't known the submarine was stolen. No doubt they would change the codes within hours, if they hadn't already.

Yet any new system would be based on the encrypting algorithms contained in the computer, which meant that it was a prize without price for many of the world's intelligence agencies.

Kolnikov patted the machine once, then left the compartment and went forward through the control room into the crew's living area. He looked into the captain's cabin—very nice, bigger than he expected—and looked into each of the officers' staterooms, the wardroom, and the head. Finally he went down the ladder to the third deck. The galley and mess hall were under the control room. Right now the mess hall was jammed with Americans, packed like sardines. Two Germans were guarding them. Kolnikov didn't say a word, merely looked.

Under the mess hall were the cold rooms and auxiliary machinery space. After inspecting both compartments, Kolnikov climbed back up to the mess hall and went aft, into the torpedo room.

America had only four torpedo tubes, two on the starboard side and two port. All were empty just now. Eight Mk-48 torpedoes rested on cradles, ready for loading. Two contained dummy warheads, but six were war shots. In the center of the compartment was a compact berthing module, which had bunks for the six SEALs who would use the minisub. This module could be disassembled and removed from the boat in port, and the space used for more torpedoes.

His inspection complete, Kolnikov went through the galley—avoiding the mess hall where all the Americans were being held just now—into crew berthing. The berths were tiny, about the size of coffins, stacked three deep. Personal privacy could not be had here. There were, Kolnikov knew, not enough bunks for all the American sailors the boat normally carried—the junior men took turns sleeping. None of this surprised Kolnikov, who had spent almost twenty years serving in submarines.

Forward of the berthing area was the pressure bulkhead and, beyond that, the vertical launch tubes. The missiles were inside their tubes, which were sealed units. There was no provision for reloading tubes at sea—the thirty-four-foot diameter of the pressure hull meant that there just wasn't enough room, which was why the tubes were outside the pressure hull. Forward of the tubes was the bow sonar dome with its huge array. Beneath that array was another, a conformal array.

When he had seen all there was to see, Kolnikov closed the hatch and went back through the tunnel. Part of the ballast tank space, he knew, was utilized by the winch and cable for the towed array, but access to that compartment was on the first deck. On the second deck he went through the control room—Turchak was poring over a computer—to the hatch opening into the tunnel that led through the reactor compartment. The shielded tunnel was designed to prevent crewmen from absorbing any unnecessary radiation.

He exited the tunnel into the reactor compartment. There was really little to see. Everything was spotlessly clean. The control panel was in the engine room.

Kolnikov reentered the tunnel and went on aft to the engine room.

Gordin and two others were there. A normal engine room watch team was three men aboard this class of sub, one fewer than the *Seawolf-* or *Los Angeles*-class.

On a Russian sub, one man would be enough, but American boats were not as highly automated. The Russian Navy could never get or keep enough qualified men, so they had to automate. For safety reasons, the Americans had never taken automation as far. *America* was more automated than any past boat, but still, a normal engine room team was three men, who spent their watch checking gauges and turning valves. Kolnikov had Gordin, Steeckt, and Brovkin, none of whom knew much about the reactor but had been taught to rush from station to station, checking this, adjusting that to keep everything within normal limits.

They were impressed. "This is a beautiful ship, Captain," they gushed and expounded loudly as they touched and pointed.

The ship was beautiful, Kolnikov admitted ruefully. Everything reeked of quality. Everything the eye beheld was a wonder of design and manufacture. Nothing shoddy, quickly made, quickly finished.

It feels as if we are inside a giant watch, Kolnikov thought. He recognized the major assemblies, but that was all. He studied the control panel that Callahan had manned. According to him, the only SCRAM button still wired up was the one on this panel. SCRAM— there was an acronym! It stood for safety control reactor ax man, a title given to the man responsible for cutting the rope holding the control rods in the first nuclear core under the stadium at the University of Chicago should anything go wrong.

He would not attempt to rewire the SCRAM controls, he decided. One stray volt during the rewiring would drop the rods into the pile, killing the fission reaction. The reactor could be restarted, of course, if they knew what they were doing and had plenty of time and electrical power, but why take that risk?

"The electrical complexity is beyond my experience, Captain," Brovkin said as he explained the intricacies of one of the major circuit-breaker panels. He led Kolnikov from panel to panel, showed him the fiber-optic wire bundles that carried information to the computers and actuators located throughout the ship. "I have never seen anything like this. Without diagrams one would be hopelessly lost." The electrical diagrams, several thousand of them, were in the computer, of course. Finding the right diagram was the biggest problem.

If anything went wrong, anything...

Brovkin grinned at him. The fool!

Kolnikov knew that he was on a tightrope without a net. If the reactor had a problem, he couldn't kill it from the control room. If he accidentally SCRAMed it, he probably couldn't restart it. Either way they were all dead men.

He wondered if the others had carefully considered the risks. Or were they here because they thought he had? Maybe they just didn't care. "At some point in life you gotta just grab for it, man." That was the American, Leon Rothberg's, explanation, and it was probably as good as any.

Kolnikov spent another hour exploring the boat, examining everything, trying to absorb all of it. The boat was two technological generations beyond anything he had seen in the Russian Navy or on the drawing tables. The torpedoes, fired by computers that displayed the tactical problem on large screens; the cruise missiles, with their breathtaking capabilities; and the remote periscope—all these things were marvels, yet the main technological jewel was the multistatic passive sonar. Truly it was a Revelation, revealing all things.

As he walked through the boat he paused often to listen and marvel at the quiet. He put his head against bulkheads, for any vibration or noise would be magnified by its transmission through a solid. Essentially nothing. As he listened he could hear his own heart beating. Years ago the Americans pioneered techniques to acoustically isolate mechanical noisemakers so the sound would not be transmitted throughout the hull of the boat. Now the Americans had taken that technology to a whole new level.

He would have to do something about the Americans crammed into the mess hall. Kolnikov conferred with Heydrich. "I intend to find a ship and surface near it before dusk, put these men into the water, get rid of them."

"Do you want to keep anyone?"

"No. We would have to watch anyone we kept, keeping our people up around the clock. Put them over the side."

"Several of them probably have the combination of the crypto safe. No doubt I can persuade them to open it. The codebooks would make us extremely wealthy men."

"They will be worth pennies when we find the time to peddle them; they aren't worth the effort. Put all the Americans over the side."

Heydrich grimaced. "These people will tell tales. Why not just shoot them, then jettison their bodies through a torpedo tube in the middle of the ocean?"

"You'd like that, wouldn't you?"

"I don't take unnecessary risks."

"Risks are my department, Heydrich. We do it my way."

CHAPTER THREE

As he rode the helicopter across the Delmarva peninsula and the Chesapeake Bay on his way back to Washington, Jake Grafton speculated about the urgent summons. He knew nothing about submarines—had spent his entire career in naval aviation.

He smiled to himself as he recalled Callie's enthusiasm this morning. When he was handed the assignment to the military liaison staff of the anti-ICBM project—SuperAegis—he had been depressed. He knew enough about the navy to understand that the job was a dead end, on the career path to nowhere. The liaison team would get no credit for a job well done. Problems that led to complaints from foreign governments, however, would earn everyone involved sufficient notoriety to force his or her retirement.

Callie hadn't seen it that way. This job was a fine opportunity, she said, a challenge. "Someone chose you for this job because he knows you can do it well."

Jake just nodded. He didn't tell her that Admiral Stuffy Stalnaker put Jake in this job because he didn't want to give him a job with a shot at promotion.

Ah, well. Bureaucracies were the same the world over. And regardless of how it went, Jake was ready to retire. Sharing the days with Callie would certainly be fun. And yet, as Callie had predicted, he was enjoying the challenge of the liaison team.

The space-based missile-defense system was a technological marvel, a marriage of computers, reactors, lasers, and infrared sensors that many said could never be made to work. That many didn't want to work. The system had certainly been expensive, more than fifty billion dollars so far, yet the politicians had approved the expenditures every step of the way. If SuperAegis worked—there was that caveat again—the industrial superpowers would be protected from the missiles of the great unwashed who hadn't been invited to share the prosperity of the booming world economy masterminded by the superpowers. That was the cynical view, of course, argued loudly and vehemently in Congress and the world press, but it lost out when the votes were counted. Politicians liked big-bucks defense projects and the public wanted protection. SuperAegis was a military-industrial PR dream come true, a hundred billion bucks for Congress to spend on something for everybody.

As the helicopter carrying Jake to Washington droned along, he reflected on the political battles and diplomatic maneuvering that had won approval for SuperAegis. Sharing the antimissile umbrella with Europe and Russia had been the masterstroke—an insight of pure genius from the secretary of state, Wallace Cornfeld—that had made SuperAegis diplomatically possible. And created a host of problems for the liaison team.

Inherent in the entire concept was the premise that the technology must be protected from states not under the SuperAegis umbrella, the so-called aggressor states. If an aggressor state learned enough about SuperAegis to defeat it, all the treasure and effort would have been expended in vain. Of course, the nations under the shield wanted to ensure that once SuperAegis was in the sky and operational, the United States could not turn it off if the winds of fortune shifted into another quadrant. In addition, the Americans did not want the Russians or Europeans to learn too much about the system for fear they would figure out ways to defeat it in some future crisis, nullifying its capabilities. SuperAegis presented a monstrously complex technical and political problem; military liaison was the place where many of these cares and concerns came together, generating heat and smoke and—who knows?—maybe fire.

Jake's boss was an air force three-star, Lieutenant General Art Blevins. Jake had tried to explain to General Blevins that the liaison team faced an impossible challenge. "There is no way," he argued, "that we can absolutely prevent leaks or prove that leaks have not occurred. And to the extent that any potential enemy penetrates the security walls and learns about the technology, the SuperAegis shield is less effective. For the countries under the umbrella to have absolute protection, security would have to be absolutely perfect. The only way to get close to that standard would be to execute everyone who knows anything about SuperAegis as soon as the system is operational. Even then, we might get 'em too late."

"I would appreciate it if you would put that recommendation in writing," Art Blevins said. Although he never smiled, he did have a sense of humor. A small one.

"Security is never perfect," Jake acknowledged, marching bravely where no one else cared to go. "Still, a hundred billion bucks isn't peanuts, and it's being expended for a system that an aggressor may know how to defeat when crunch time rolls around. And the protected nations will not know about the holes in the shield until the missiles fall on their heads."

Blevins didn't seem disturbed by Jake's theorizing. "All military systems have that flaw," he remarked.

"Sir, it strikes me that SuperAegis is our Maginot Line. And you know what happened to the French."

"Indeed. A great many politically connected French contractors made a lot of money selling concrete to the government. Presumably the people in Congress and the White House also remember their history."

"For Christ's sake, Art—"

"The SuperAegis decision has been made at the highest level, Jake. It's far too late for us to bitch. Let's see if we can make it work. Who knows, the politicians might actually be right, for a change."

SuperAegis certainly was a knotty, challenging problem, Jake reflected this morning. And for that reason fun to work on.

He leaned his head back on his seat and closed his eyes. The drone of the engines made him sleepy.

After another round of looking, touching, seeking to understand, Vladimir Kolnikov returned to the control room, the heart of the ship. Rothberg had the sonar picture on the right main screen, which was huge. Kolnikov got close, studied the visual presentation of what was out there. This, he reminded himself, was not a television picture but a computer presentation. More magic!

He told Rothberg he wanted a ship large enough to take all of the Americans, and Rothberg played with the range controls on the sonar. Fifteen minutes later Kolnikov saw it, a fuzzy, indistinct irregularity almost hidden in the shimmering, inverted plane that was the surface.

Turchak listened without comment as Kolnikov told him what he wanted, then he disconnected the autopilot with a sigh of relief. That infernal machine would take some getting used to. Turchak turned *America* toward the small freighter, which was still eight or nine miles away, and began rising slowly from the depths.

Kolnikov sat on the captain's raised leather-covered stool in the center of the compartment. That Heydrich . . . what facts could the American sailors tell that the FBI would not learn within days? The identities of the men who stole the sub? How many of them there were? These things were impossible to keep secret, so having the sailors confirm them to investigators cost nothing. Sparing the sailors' lives also sent a message to the Americans that the thieves were reasonable, rational men.

Kolnikov grinned at the thought.

"We've just returned from the White House," General Flap Le Beau, commandant of the Marine Corps, told Jake Grafton, who had just been shown into the commandant's office by an aide. Flap shook Jake's hand, pointed toward a chair. Admiral Stuffy Stalnaker, the chief of naval operations, merely nodded at Jake when he came in, didn't say anything or offer to shake. Stuffy looked unusually dour this morning. For that matter, Flap didn't look happy either.

"Someone hijacked *America* this morning as she got under way for her first operational cruise," Flap said as he dropped into the padded swivel chair behind his desk.

Flap summarized what he had learned at the White House briefing. He related how the hijackers had used the tug, sank it alongside as they boarded, forced half of *America*'s crew into the water, and sailed away. He also told Jake about Harvey Warfield and *John Paul Jones*.

Jake Grafton glanced at Stuffy, who looked as if he had sucked on a lemon.

"The FBI is investigating, of course. We'll know more soon. Apparently sixteen or seventeen men stole the boat. The FBI director thinks the men who did it were a CIA team trained to operate a sub with a minimum manning level."

"Say what?"

"Yep. The CIA trained some Russians and Germans whom they wanted to insert into Russia to steal a submarine. The CIA guys think the big thoughts. Whatever, the project didn't work out, apparently. Maybe the risk was too high, maybe the president had second thoughts. In any event, the CIA director said the project was canceled last month, and these guys were just loafing around waiting for the agency to come up with a better idea or pay their way home. Then this."

Jake found his tongue. "Why?"

"That's the sixty-four-dollar question. The thinking at the White House is that the hijacking has something to do with SuperAegis. Maybe they're going to torpedo the launch platform or something."

"A CIA team?" Jake exclaimed, still trying to digest the news. "These guys didn't just rip off a boat because they had nothing better to do on a Saturday morning. Who is behind this?"

Flap Le Beau squared his shoulders. He was a muscular, fit black man, several inches over six feet, whose thinning hair was turning frosty. He and Jake had flown together when they both were junior officers, years ago during a carrier cruise to the western Pacific as a member of a marine A-6 squadron. Born in a ghetto, Flap Le Beau had found a home in the corps, which was the perfect place for a natural leader who knew how and when to fight and loved to do it. He was an expert with rifle and mortar and the best man alive with a knife.

"We are going to find out," Flap said now. "The president handed me the job of investigating the hijacking. He thought the navy shouldn't investigate itself, so he asked me to do it." He glanced at Stuffy Stalnaker, who was lost in his own thoughts.

He's probably trying to figure out how many people are going to get court-martialed when the dust settles, Jake thought. Hell, he's probably wondering if he is going to be one of them.

"Admiral Stalnaker mentioned your name," Flap continued, "since you were working liaison with the foreign military reps on the SuperAegis project. When I heard your name I decided I wanted your help. You know the navy, you know bullshit when you hear it."

Flap picked up a television remote and clicked it on. He channel-surfed a moment and, sure enough, found the video shot from the helicopter by the Boston television station. The officers in the room watched in silence. They said nothing as Kolnikov squirted a burst of submachine-gun fire at the chopper, and remained silent as the last of the footage showed *America* under way in Long Island Sound.

As the talking heads speculated, Flap said, "A disaster of the first order of magnitude." He used the remote to kill the television audio.

"This ranks right up there with California falling off into the Pacific," Stalnaker said.

"Why?" Flap asked. "Why did they steal it?"

"More to the point," Stuffy Stalnaker said heavily, "what in the name of God are they going to do with it?"

"Why did the White House staff think the hijackers are off to do the Goddard launch platform?" Jake asked.

"Because Russians headed the CIA hijack team," Stalnaker replied. "The Russian government never wanted SuperAegis. They went along because they had no choice. Maybe . . ." He threw a pencil across the room. "Hell, I don't know. Nobody does. Those bastards killed six Americans and stole our goddamn submarine and sailed off over the fucking horizon, bold as brass. One of the news types says the tugboat crew is missing, presumed dead. We've got a goddamn Russian Blackbeard on our hands, sailing off in a U.S. Navy warship to do God knows what. Double-crossed the spooks and stole the newest, sneakiest sub on Planet Earth right out from under our noses."

Jake was not thinking about embarrassment just now. He was thinking about a sub in the North Atlantic, that great gray ocean, deep and wide.

"Twelve cruise missiles, six live torpedoes and two practice rounds, and a SEAL minisub on the back of the boat." Stalnaker sighed. "Obviously we're doing all we can to find our lost pigboat. Our SOSUS nets are going to get a hell of a workout." SOSUS was an acronym for sound surveillance system, a network of underwater acoustic sensors on the seafloor in the open ocean and strategic straits and waterways, sensors designed to listen for submarines. "We're putting every antisubmarine asset we have east of the Mississippi and west of Suez into the North Atlantic. We're sending a battle group to guard the Goddard platform for the next few weeks. Maybe we'll get lucky—somebody will find this guy."

"How probable is that, sir?" Jake asked.

"Truthfully, the chances are damned slim," CNO shot back. "I've followed the development of the *America*-class for years. Losing her is an absolute disaster. She's more stealthy than we've told the press. And more capable."

"How come," Jake asked, "the *Jones* didn't sink *America* this morning when they saw what was going down?"

"The skipper wanted to. The White House said no. Apparently the thinking was that Americans might kill Americans, which would go over like a three-hundred-pound canary with Congress and the electorate. Can't go killing our own, they said, not without solid-gold verification of what's going down."

"The crypto gear, the codebooks, Revelation, the software, the weapons..." Jake ran through the list so softly that Flap Le Beau had to strain to hear. "Oh, boy."

Stalnaker merely nodded. "The president was really pissed at us. But he was outraged at the spooks. 'You people let this happen,' he raved. 'You picked these men, you trained them, now this!'"

"Anybody claiming responsibility?"

"Not that I know of," Stalnaker said gloomily. Flap shook his head.

"Stealing a submarine to knock off the Goddard launch platform strikes me as ridiculous," Jake Grafton said. "They went to a lot of trouble and took a huge risk. We're not going to launch any more satellites until we find out why we lost the first one. Even if we were going to, damn near anyone with a wild hair and some guts could screw up our launch with a speedboat and a scoped rifle."

"If I wanted to sabotage the launch, I'd pay a guy or gal to change a line of software code," Le Beau said thoughtfully. "One keystroke would put the rocket in the water. Hell, one keystroke probably did. That's my theory about why all the king's horses and all the king's men can't find the satellite or figure out why it didn't get into orbit."

Jake Grafton nodded. "Unless someone gets religion and confesses everything, we'll never know for sure whether the loss of that satellite was an accident or sabotage. And until the engineers can pinpoint the cause of the accident, there will be no more launches. I don't care what the politicians say, it won't happen. Someday the Goddard platform is going to be a cruise ship port of call. So why a sub?"

"Maybe they stole it to see what we've been up to in the shipyard," Stalnaker said. "We wanted theirs for the crypto and the weapons. Tit for tat. But who the hell knows? I suspect the who and why will become painfully obvious all at once."

Flap Le Beau studied his fingernails, then glanced at the CNO. "They stuck you with me when you said you weren't sure the navy could find that boat. In fact, you implied to the president and secretary of state that finding the thing would take a miracle."

"I didn't use the *m* word," Stalnaker protested.

"You might as well have."

Stalnaker studied his toes.

"So what do you want me to do, sir?" Jake asked Flap Le Beau.

"I want you to go to New London, see what the FBI is finding out, ask the questions they won't think to ask. I don't believe for a minute that a little band of ex–submarine jockeys on the CIA payroll thought this stunt up all by themselves. Our first job is to find out who is behind this."

"If we find out what they want, the who will take care of itself," Stuffy Stalnaker opined.

"Maybe," Flap said. "And maybe not."

"I've got a Russian houseguest this weekend," Jake said, remembering Ilin. "He's supposed to be a Russian rocket expert, but I think he's SVR. Former KGB."

Flap's eyes narrowed. His fingers beat a barely audible tattoo on his desk.

"Makes you wonder, doesn't it?"

"Yes, sir."

"Why don't you take him to New London with you? Try to figure out if he knows anything about this little deal."

"The minute he learns something that isn't on television, he'll tell Moscow."

"As if they don't know all about *America*," the commandant said scathingly. He waggled a finger at Grafton. "I want to know if the Russian spook on the SuperAegis project knew about the hijacking in advance. You get the slightest hint, let me know immediately."

"Aye aye, sir."

"Throw your weight around, Jake," said Flap Le Beau. "Get answers."

Tommy Carmellini went to bed that night with a beautiful woman. She was one Sarah Houston, an American expatriate who resided in London. For the past six months she had returned to the United States on business for half of every month. The bed was in Carmellini's apartment on the Upper West Side of Manhattan. At least, Houston thought it was Carmellini's apartment. Actually it was a CIA safe house, one that Carmellini was using to woo Ms. Houston. In the line of duty, of course. She didn't know that either.

As Carmellini kissed Sarah Houston and reveled in her ripe sensuousness, he thought about the three-month campaign that had led up to this moment. When he was told the part he was to play and shown Houston's photo, he had readily agreed. In her early thirties, with high cheekbones, startling green eyes, and shoulder-length brown hair, Sarah Houston was a striking presence.

"It's nice work if you can get it," his boss commented, a little wistfully, Carmellini thought.

They had met "accidentally" several times as they left the building, a condominium townhouse, for early morning runs, so they ended up running together. As the weeks passed those runs led to Sunday sandwiches, a televised ball game at a sports bar, then several movies with ice cream after, and finally a formal dinner date at a terrific Italian restaurant on the East Side in the Fifties.

Getting to know her had been a pleasure, yet a bittersweet one. She was a delightful human being, and he had known the relationship was going nowhere! She had a wicked sense of humor, a quick wit, and a nice laugh. Tonight, when he finally unlocked the door to his apartment and led her inside, she had looked at him so wonderfully that for a moment there Tommy Carmellini felt like a real jerk.

In truth, he was a jerk. He let the CIA trap him into this . . . well, okay, he got himself into this fix by being who he was. So being Tommy Carmellini made him a jerk.

Knowing that, he smiled at her anyway.

When they showered together he remembered his boss's comment about nice work.

If she was surprised that Carmellini was solid as a brick she didn't show it, though she repeatedly ran her hands over his arms and shoulders. He told her he was a rock climber, which was true. She had seen the free weights in the apartment, knew he ran . . . she just didn't know how much he worked out or how far his runs took him.

At dinner she told him her life's story, the parts of it he hadn't heard before. It had the little family triumphs and tragedies, a couple of failed love affairs, college, wise and foolish friends, stupid vacations, an interesting job, and she told it well, paused in all the right places, made him laugh along with her.

His turn came after dinner, as they walked the sidewalks of New York. They had talked about the stolen submarine earlier in the evening and had moved on to other subjects. Most of his story was historical truth, as far as it went, right up until he was about eleven years old. Then he told her the story he told anyone who questioned him closely. He omitted the sneaking around, picking locks, peeping, the fun of getting into and out of places without anyone else knowing. Nor did he mention the safecracking and burglary that came later. Of getting caught he said not a word. He failed to mention the fact that he worked for the CIA.

For the first time in a long time Tommy Carmellini felt a twinge of conscience about the lies—he never ever told the truth about himself to anyone, male or female, business or pleasure.

When he finished his tale, she was silent for a moment, walking with her head down, one arm wrapped around his. Then she said, "One of the girls in the apartment above mine said that you work for the CIA."

Carmellini snorted, trying to hold in the laughter. That comment was so hilariously funny! He snorted again, trying not to burst out laughing.

"That's a good one," he said, his eyes twinkling, shaking his head. "Wait until the folks at the firm hear that one."

"I promised my mother that I would never date a lawyer," she told him solemnly.

They talked about lawyers, about what egotists most of them were, the rest of the way back to the building.

Inside his apartment he poured her some wine. When it was obvious that she was going to drink only about half the glass, he led her into the bedroom, undressed her, and took her to the shower. After that they fell into bed in each other's arms.

She was a great kisser. He let himself go, let the fire of her warm him to the core.

Then she went to sleep. One second she was there, then she was limp, breathing deeply, sound asleep. Carmellini put his fingers on her wrist, took her pulse.

Strong, steady and slow. Okay.

Tommy Carmellini waited a moment, then got out of bed. He donned a robe and made a telephone call.

Five minutes later the doorbell rang. Carmellini checked the peephole, then unlocked the door and admitted the two men who were standing there.

"How much did she have?"

"Half a glass."

The man's name was Joe May. He opened a valise, removed a hypodermic needle, drew twenty cc's from a bottle, then went into the bedroom. In half a minute he was back. He checked his watch. "Five minutes," he said. "Then she'll be deeply under. She won't remember a thing."

The other man was named Fernando. No other name that Carmellini had ever heard. Just Fernando. "When we're done, you can have her, big guy," he said with a sneer. "She'll sleep for hours and won't remember a thing. This is your chance."

"Did your mother ever tell you that you are a foul little asshole?"

Fernando chuckled and began unpacking the two cases made out of aircraft-grade aluminum that he had carried in.

As Fernando and Joe May set up the equipment in the bedroom, Fernando peeled back the sheet to look over the merchandise.

Carmellini's hand shot out. He wrapped his fist around Fernando's wrist and squeezed.

"Jesus, you son of a bitch, you're going to break my wrist." Fernando went to his knees as Carmellini forced his elbow down.

"Come on, Tommy," Joe May said as he worked with the electrical cords. "He's an asshole. Let it go at that."

Carmellini covered up Houston as Fernando massaged his wrist. "You almost broke my wrist," he said in amazement.

"Shut up and help," May told him.

Working carefully and as quickly as he dared, May took impressions of all ten of Sarah Houston's fingers in a soft clay. Two of the fingers he did twice. Only after he examined every impression with a magnifying glass did he let Fernando pack them away.

They rigged a tripod with an arm that extended out at a right angle. On the arm Joe May attached a sophisticated camera and two bright lights.

Carmellini watched as Joe May meticulously measured the distance from the camera's lens to Houston's right eye, which Fernando was holding open. After a series of photographs of both eyes had been taken, the first camera was removed from the arm and another camera, one with a much different lens, was attached. This camera was lowered to within a half inch of Houston's right eye. May took another series of photographs, then rearranged the camera over Houston's left eye and shot another series.

Finally May snapped the lights off and took down the camera and tripod and repacked them in their cases. "We've got it," he told Carmellini, who had been in the kitchen going through the contents of Houston's purse. "Let her sleep. She'll come out of it in about five hours, won't remember a thing."

"You're sure?"

"Positive."

"This is your chance," Fernando muttered at Tommy, who ignored him.

Five minutes later the two men were gone. Carmellini turned on the lights, checked the apartment to ensure that all traces of the two had been eliminated, then went back to the kitchen table and studied the contents of Houston's purse one more time.

In her wallet she had British and American currency, a couple of hundred-dollar traveler's checks, credit cards, a California driver's license, and eleven business cards from people all over Europe, ten of whom were men. A checkbook: she had a balance of 1,744 pounds . . . maybe, since it didn't appear that she ever bothered to reconcile the account. Let's see, nope, no checks for outrageous amounts. The usual feminine hygiene and cosmetic items. Seven photos, mostly of women, two of Houston with men. Carmellini didn't recognize either of them. Two ATM cards, both in paper envelopes with her secret PIN numbers written on the envelopes in ink. Bits of paper torn from an appointment book bearing telephone numbers and addresses. A small address book filled with women's names—first names only, most of them—addresses, telephone numbers, some E-mail addresses. A few stray keys, a button, an unwrapped piece of hard candy that was partially stuck to the bottom of the purse, and two paper clips. He sighed and carefully repacked all this stuff in her purse.

Finally he turned off the lights in the apartment and crawled into bed beside Houston. She was breathing deeply, totally relaxed.

"Sorry, kid," he told her. "With you it would have been good."

He fluffed her pillow and made her as comfortable as he could. He kissed her once, then stretched out and tried to go to sleep himself.

It was after midnight on Sunday morning when the Pentagon helicopter dropped Jake at the hospital helo pad in Delaware where it had picked him up. Callie was waiting in the car.

Jake kissed her, thanked her for coming.

"We spent the day watching television," Callie said. "If Ilin knew about the hijacking before it happened, I didn't get a hint of it. He looked as stunned as Toad. And probably me."

Jake grunted. He had expected no less.

"Have they found the sub yet?" Callie asked.

"No."

"Why did they want you in Washington?"

"I'm supposed to help look for the thing."

"People are frightened, Jake. I've never seen professional news-people panic like they have today. That congresswoman, Samantha Strader, has been all over the news, demanding that all American submarines be recalled to port and kept there until the American people are satisfied with the navy's security measures. Other people want to permanently retire all the submarines."

"We deserve it, I guess," Jake said. He couldn't ever remember being so ashamed of his service.

Reading his mood, Callie said, "You missed a good steak."

"Yeah."

A talk show was on the radio. People were venting about the submarine hijacking. Jake turned the radio off. The streetlights illuminated cars, people out for ice cream, dog owners with their pets on leashes. Lovers walked hand in hand in the shadows, unwilling to give up the September evening.

"It all looks so normal," Callie said.

"Yes," Jake said, watching the people. "For how long?"

When they got out of the car in front of the house he could hear the surf hitting the beach. He took her hand and led her along the street to the boardwalk across the dune. The wind was off the dark sea. As the surf broke, the foam of the breakers was just visible. A few stars enlivened the dark sky. Holding Callie's hand, Jake breathed deeply of the cool salt wind.

The sub was out there somewhere, in that vast sea.

Well, the men who stole it wouldn't remain hidden long. Stalnaker said the White House thought the sub would go to some third-world country, perhaps be used to threaten a neighbor. All of which was ridiculous, of course. The politicians didn't want to face up to the reality of the disaster. They should have ordered the *Jones* to sink the sub when the destroyer had the sub under its guns.

Jake half turned, glanced toward the beach house. The Russian, Ilin, was there. Were the Russians behind the theft? Ilin was a spook—did he know about this?

Callie held him tightly as the wind played with her hair.

He wrapped his arms around her.

CHAPTER FOUR

Kolnikov and Turchak were poring over the cruise-missile universal target databases in the computer when Rothberg finally yawned and asked permission to find a bunk to sleep in. Kolnikov nodded his assent. Boldt went with him. For the first time since they seized *America,* the two Russians were alone.

"While they sleep, we must collect all the weapons," Kolnikov whispered.

"But the boat! Who will watch it?"

"We will leave it on autopilot."

Turchak's eyes widened. With no one to monitor the performance of the computers that formed the autopilot, there was no safety margin whatsoever. "Oh, man. Why don't we just shoot ourselves now and get it over with? This really is Russian roulette."

"We must get the guns."

"We may have to kill Heydrich."

Kolnikov grunted.

"You and I could run the boat," Turchak admitted. "The automation is quite extraordinary. We could not respond quickly to anything, and there would be no safety margin—none—which makes my flesh crawl. The first casualty, the first equipment failure, and we will be dead men. With people on watch in the reactor and engine room, we have a little breathing room. Someone on the sonar will help enormously. We will need all the people we have if we need to reload a torpedo tube. Still, we know so little. A tiny fire, an electrical problem . . . we'll be dead."

"That is the risk we agreed to take," Kolnikov insisted.

"Talking about risks on dry land is not the same as living them."

They stood looking at the displays. Finally Kolnikov shook his head. "There is no way to undo what we have done. We must go forward."

"I know. I know! All of this frightens me—that is the honest truth. I wish—"

Turchak left the thought hanging. After a bit he asked, "What are we going to do with the guns?"

"Jettisoning them through an empty torpedo tube would be best. I don't want them aboard."

Kolnikov checked the navigation display. The boat was five hundred feet deep, running southeast at four knots. Except for the grunting of some distant whales, the sea was silent, empty in all directions, surface and subsurface. A few minutes ago there had been the telltale signature of noise from an airplane passing overhead, a jet running high. It was gone now.

Kolnikov pulled the pistol from his belt, checked that the safety was on, and went forward.

Pistols and rifles were strewn carelessly near the sleeping men. The two Russian officers picked up every firearm they saw. One man was sleeping with his pistol belt and holster still wrapped around his waist, so Kolnikov put his pistol against the man's forehead and waited for him to awaken. In seconds his eyes came open. Kolnikov undid the buckle and pulled the belt from under the man.

They had an armful of guns by the time they reached the torpedo room. All four of the tubes were empty. They put the guns in number one, then proceeded to the engine room in the aft end of the boat. Three men were awake there, checking lubrication levels and monitoring the turbines. Kolnikov held a pistol on them while Turchak took their weapons and carried them forward. Kolnikov followed.

When they had the tube closed for the second time, Turchak asked, "Where's Heydrich?"

"I don't know. He must have been in one of the heads when we went by." Or in the aux machinery room, cold storage . . .

"And Steinhoff?"

"I don't know."

"Someone may have told them we are confiscating the weapons."

Kolnikov and Turchak gripped their pistols tightly as they approached the door of the control room.

The two Germans were there, examining the control panels.

Steinhoff turned, saw that the Russians had pistols out, and immediately decided to jerk his automatic from its holster.

Kolnikov shot him once. Steinhoff sagged to the deck and lay there moaning.

Heydrich stood frozen with his back to Kolnikov, his hands half raised.

"May I turn around?"

"Not yet."

Turchak inched forward, pulled the pistol from Heydrich's holster, and patted him down for more weapons. He also had a pistol in his pocket, which Turchak transferred to his own pocket.

Turchak put the guns in the torpedo tube while Kolnikov sat in the control room with his pistol pointed at Heydrich and Steinhoff moaned softly and writhed on the deck. Heydrich made no move to examine the man, see how badly he was hurt.

When the guns had been flushed from the tube into the sea, Kolnikov remarked, "Take your friend to berthing and put a bandage on him." He pocketed the pistol.

Heydrich jerked Steinhoff off the deck and slung him over his shoulder, oblivious of his wound.

"The game isn't over, Kolnikov."

"Get your head out of your ass," the Russian shot back. "This is no game. You can't run this boat without me, but I can certainly run it without you. As far as I'm concerned, you're expendable ballast. At the first sign of disobedience I'll shoot you as quick as I shot Steinhoff."

"You know, I believe you would."

When they were alone, Turchak said, "You should have killed him, gotten it over with."

Vladimir Kolnikov rubbed his face. "We must take split watches, you and I. One man will run the boat while the other sleeps."

When Jake Grafton descended the stairs in the beach house Sunday morning, Toad Tarkington and Janos Ilin were drinking coffee at the window nook while Callie cooked eggs. She had the television in the corner tuned to CNN. Jake kissed her, dropped into a chair at the table.

"You two look chipper this morning," Jake remarked to the men, both of whom looked slightly rumpled. "Sun and sand seem to agree with you."

Toad eyed the admiral suspiciously as he sipped his coffee.

"We spent yesterday in front of the television," Janos Ilin said, "until we couldn't stand it anymore." He felt his pockets, probably feeling for his cigarettes. He had picked up the fact that Americans didn't smoke indoors.

The Sunday paper lay on the table. The headline screamed, "Sub Stolen." Under it was a photo of the hijackers entering the submarine taken from the television video. To the right was a smaller shot of Kolnikov shooting at the helicopter.

The admiral helped himself to the coffee and cream. He was sipping it when the telephone rang. He picked it up.

"I'm a reporter with—" the voice began. Jake put the telephone back on the cradle.

"So who did it?" Toad demanded.

"Some Russian and German ex-submariners." Jake didn't mention the CIA.

"Wow!"

"Quite amazing," Ilin said. "How in the world could they have learned enough about the submarine—*America?*—to take it to sea? Aren't submarines extremely complicated?"

"Like a space shuttle."

"Surprising," Ilin said and helped himself to more coffee.

Callie served him an omelet as the group discussed what the thieves might do with a stolen sub. The telephone rang two more times. Each time Callie answered it, said a few words, and hung up. "Reporters," she said.

"I have been asked to assist in the investigation of this matter," Jake said, addressing Ilin. "Since several of the men involved were Russian nationals, I was wondering if you would assist me? On an informal basis, of course."

"Do you know their names?"

"Not yet."

"I assume," Ilin said slowly as he buttered a piece of toast, "that you have discussed this matter with General Blevins?"

"Yes."

"And other people?"

"Of course."

"May I ask who they are?"

"I think I'll reserve that."

Ilin ate the toast before he spoke again.

"The theft of the submarine is certainly a tragedy, but I fail to see how I can be of assistance in investigating that theft."

"Maybe you will have a glimmer as we go along."

"I tell you frankly that I know nothing of submarines. I have never even been aboard one. In fact, to the best of my memory, I have never actually seen one. They are an uncommon sight in Moscow."

"Perhaps," Jake said, also choosing his words carefully, "the news has been so unexpected that you have failed to grasp the implications. If Russian nationals were involved, persons in some quarters might suspect that they are acting on behalf of—or at least on the orders of—the Russian government. The event might have serious implications for U.S.-Russian relations."

"I appreciate that. Yet I fail to see how I can assist you. I know absolutely nothing about submarines or ships or any of that."

"Are you refusing?"

"No. Merely trying to force your expectations down to rational levels and make you air them. Just now I fail to see how I can be of any assistance whatsoever."

"Ah, we'll have to await the event to see if you can aid me. But perhaps you can aid your government. If these . . . pirates . . . use the submarine against Russian shipping or naval vessels, the Russian government might be very interested in your observations."

"Perhaps. And it might not. In any event, I tell you flatly that regardless of what I say, the people in Moscow will draw their own conclusions."

"Would you care to call the embassy? Discuss this with someone there?"

Both men knew the Graftons' telephone was nonsecure, and both knew that the American government would record the conversation since it was made to the Russian embassy.

"Perhaps later," Ilin said, refusing to close the door or pass through it. "How do you propose to begin your investigation?"

"The navy will have a plane pick us up at noon at Dover Air Force Base. Callie can drop us there on her way back to Washington. The plane will fly us to Connecticut. The FBI will have an agent there to brief us. They might have learned something about the thieves. No doubt we can also learn something about the stolen submarine."

Janos Ilin helped himself to more coffee. "Admiral, I am sure my government will not object to my tagging along. You understand, I am under no obligation to withhold anything from my government, nor will I." He grinned disarmingly at Jake. "I will of course also report this conversation."

Jake Grafton grinned right back, his best I'm-holding-four-aces look. "Of course."

He was upstairs packing when Callie came up. "Well?"

"I don't know," she said. "He's a master at handling his face."

Jake made a noise.

"So what are you going to let him see?"

"Everything. The technology is compromised anyway." That was an oversimplification, which might or might not prove true. If the submarine could be found and destroyed and the thieves killed, they wouldn't compromise anything. If they hadn't already passed on the secrets. On the other hand, Jake didn't believe that Ilin was a technical expert...in anything. He was an intelligence professional. Showing him a sonar presentation did not mean he could tell Russian engineers anything they would find of value.

"They put Flap Le Beau in charge of the investigation so it won't look like the navy is investigating itself," Jake explained. "He picked me to assist him, and I discussed bringing Ilin along. Having an SVR man involved is unconventional as hell, but . . . we've never had anyone steal a submarine before."

"So heads will roll?"

"Oh, you bet. Finger-pointing, JAG Manual investigations, courts of inquiry, careers ruined, sackings, courts-martial, at some point a congressional investigation. We're going to get the whole military entertainment experience."

"Do you think the thieves will torpedo the Goddard platform? Maybe shoot a missile at it?"

"At this point I don't know what to think. They might even fire off a missile at Moscow. If they do, at least the Russians will know that we didn't put these guys up to it."

"If they believe that the submarine was really stolen."

"Yeah. If." He got his shirts the way he wanted them, then went to the window and looked out. Ilin was standing in the street smoking a cigarette, drinking another cup of coffee.

"It was a theft, wasn't it?" his wife asked.

Jake glanced at her, a startled expression on his face. Sometimes her insights stunned him. It was almost as if she could read his thoughts. He wondered if Ilin thought him equally transparent.

"I can't imagine that it wasn't, but I want to see the bodies," he said.

He glanced again out the window at Ilin and froze. "The binoculars. Where are the binoculars?" he hissed at Callie. "Quick, get them for me, will you?"

She turned and flew from the room without a word. He heard her run down the steps, then back up. When she dashed into the room carrying the binoculars he was standing on the bed, well back from the window.

He focused the glasses on Ilin. Yep, his lips were moving. He was talking.

Certainly not to himself.

Either he was wired or someone was pointing a directional mike at him.

Jake did his best to scan across the street from his perch on the bed, where he should be essentially invisible from the street. Houses lined the other side of the street, many of them rentals, and vehicles filled every available parking space, the usual state of affairs this close to the beach. One of the parked vehicles was a van, a custom job without back windows. It was unfamiliar to him, but then most of the vehicles were. Who the heck ever noticed cars? From here he couldn't see the license plate.

He lowered the glasses, sat down on the edge of the bed.

He had underestimated Ilin. Underestimated the Russians.

This whole house could be wired. Probably was. The Russians had listened to every word that was said all weekend.

Callie was looking at him with an amused expression. "I wish I had a picture of your face wearing that look," she said.

He took her into the bathroom, turned on the shower and the exhaust fan. Then he put his mouth near her ear. "Ilin is standing alone in the street smoking, drinking coffee, and chattering away. The whole house is probably wired. Someone is listening."

She accepted his assessment without question. "What do you want me to do?"

"Take us to Dover and put us on the plane. Then drive back to Washington. On the way find a pay phone and make a telephone call. Don't use your cell phone. Call from an inside phone, like at McDonald's, so no one can aim a directional mike at you." He gave her a number, told her whom to talk to, what to ask for.

"Oh, God! I am so sorry," Sarah Houston wailed. "What a lover you must think I am! It must be jet lag. I must have fallen asleep in midkiss."

"You were exhausted," Tommy Carmellini said.

"That's never happened to me before. Is it old age? Already? Oh, my God! What you must think! Well, I'm wide awake now. I hope. Give me some hugs and kisses, big guy."

Tommy Carmellini knew he wasn't enough of an actor to pull it off. He felt like a real jerk. He had wined and dined her and taken unfair advantage, and alas, sex hadn't been involved. He glanced at the clock on the bedside table. "I've got to be at JFK in two hours," he said. "I'm catching a flight to London. The next time you're in New York, could I have another date?"

"London?" She brightened. "Perhaps we could have dinner this coming week in London. I'm going over on Wednesday."

"Friday?" Tommy asked hopefully, wanting to end it on that note.

"Do you have any aspirin? Or Tylenol?"

There was a small bottle of aspirin in the bathroom cabinet. He remembered seeing it there. He got her two tablets and a glass of water, which she drained.

"Friday, lover," she whispered as she handed him the empty glass.

Sarah was still naked under the sheets—hung over from the drugs—when he threw his toothbrush and shaving gear into his bag and zipped it closed. There was nothing compromising in the apartment, so he didn't need to worry about that.

Tommy kissed her, wished that they . . . kissed her again, then rushed for the door. "Friday evening. London. I'll call you. Lock the door on your way out."

She blew him a kiss.

Down on the street he legged it toward Columbus Avenue. He would catch a southbound cab there, although he wasn't going to the airport. He was going to Penn Station to catch a train to Washington, and he had all day to get there. The trains ran practically every hour. On Columbus he slowed to a walk, ambled along thinking about things.

He had plenty of time. What the heck, why not stroll over to Fifth Avenue and look in jewelry store windows?

Two FBI agents met the plane in Connecticut. "Two cars," Jake Grafton told them. He rode with the agent in charge, Tom Krautkramer, while Toad Tarkington and Janos Ilin piled in the second car. Krautkramer was a large man of about forty, with a frank, open face and huge, meaty hands.

"Ilin may be wired for sound," Jake said after a look at Krautkramer's credentials. He told him about the incident this morning in the street outside Jake's house. "I doubt it, but I want you guys to check him out without letting him know he's being swept. Can you do that?"

"You bet," Krautkramer said. "However, the better way is a thorough, quick search."

"Okay, doctor. Do it." Jake thought about all the things that had been discussed within Ilin's hearing since he reported to the SuperAegis project. There was nothing there that couldn't be shared—indeed, by disclosing it to the foreign liaison officers the American government was indeed sharing the information—but Ilin didn't seem to want to wait to get back to the embassy. He was passing along everything he heard as quickly as he heard it. One assumed that he was passing along only the information that Jake and Toad provided. If he had other sources . . .

"If he's wired," Jake said, "there is a van somewhere with an antenna that picks up his transmissions. Maybe he isn't wired and they use a directional mike that picks up what he says when he goes outside for smoke breaks. He's probably been doing that since he got to the States. Left to himself Ilin is a three-pack-a-day man. He spends more time outside than a beach lifeguard. Find the van, if there is one."

"Do you want us to stop it? Arrest the occupants?"

"Not yet. What I would really like is for Ilin to chatter away through this sub base visit, then after we leave for Washington, you bust the van and listen to what he had to say."

"That's feasible. We're going to need more people, a lot more. We're already bringing in people to dig into the submarine hijacking; sounds like we may be facing a major counterespionage investigation."

"I don't know what is going on," Jake replied. "Let's get some idea of what Ilin is up to before we go to general quarters."

"It'll take a little time to bring in the right people and equipment."

"Check with Washington. They'll have to assign the priority."

"They already did. General Le Beau has been on the telephone this morning with the director, who called me." Krautkramer glanced at Jake, who was wearing civilian slacks and a sports coat. "That was the first time I ever talked to the director. Who are you, anyway?"

"Just a naval officer."

"Yeah, right!"

"A stolen warship attracts a lot of attention. The next time your telephone rings, the president may be on the other end."

"I hear you. Let me tell you where we are. There were fifteen men in that CIA team; they stayed in one wing of the BOQ while they were here for training, kept pretty much to themselves. Both the CIA and the navy had people with them every minute, and we are talking to those escorts.

"Yet when the CIA dropped the Russian project, they left the team in the BOQ for almost a week while they made up their mind what they wanted to do with them. During that week, indications are that no one paid much attention to them. The stewards say many of the crewmen played pool in the rec room, they watched television, whatever. It is entirely possible they sneaked out. One of them was supposedly seen at the base exchange buying junk food.

"Then the team left the BOQ. The CIA supposedly knows where

they went, but we don't. We're talking to the CIA, but apparently they don't want to tell us much. Yet Saturday they were in the harbor on a tugboat, so they had to be nearby on Friday night. We're trying to find where they spent that night, who they talked to, how they got to the tug pier Saturday morning, find witnesses who saw these people, saw the vehicles that delivered them. The surviving sailors from the sub said there were seventeen people in the hijack crew, so we have an apparent discrepancy. They could also be wrong about that number."

"Okay," Jake said. He glanced in the mirror to see that the other car was still following faithfully.

The day looked like another normal fall Sunday afternoon in New England, families out in cars, people jogging, kids on skateboards and bicycles.

"I assume that the National Security Agency is looking at all communications."

"That's a safe assumption," Jake replied.

"The CIA supplied dossiers on the team that trained here." He patted an attaché case that lay on the seat between them. "I thought you might like to look at it."

Jake opened the case, took out the top file. Vladimir Kolnikov.

"We've got a crime artist working with the surviving crew members. He's trying to put together facial sketches of the two men who aren't in the dossiers as a first step to identifying them."

Vladimir Kolnikov. Ex–Russian naval officer, captain first rank. Twenty-five years' service, almost all of it in submarines based on the Kola peninsula. Was driving an illegal taxi in Paris when recruited by the CIA.

Jake looked at Kolnikov's photo. About two hundred pounds, if the rest of him matched the head-and-shoulders shot. Partially balding, with a short haircut, unsmiling, wearing civilian clothes.

He flipped through the other files, scanned them: Turchak, Steeckt, Eck, Gordin, Eisenberg, Boldt . . .

"There's gotta be more paper than this," Jake said, tossing the files back into the attaché case. "There should be security evaluations, background investigations of some sort, reports, all that stuff. Someone decided these men could be trusted, that they weren't SVR agents. Who made that decision? What was it based on?"

"You'll have to talk to the CIA, Admiral. They aren't in the business of sharing information like that with FBI field types."

"I suppose not."

"What questions should we be asking?"

Jake took his time replying. "Who are these people? How did they steal a submarine? If you can figure out what they did, we can analyze our security plans and figure out what we need to do to prevent another theft."

"And kick ass."

"I guarantee you, if people haven't obeyed orders or have used bad judgment, they are going to be in deep trouble. An armed, state-of-the-art capital ship worth two billion dollars just slipped out of Uncle Sam's grasp."

"I understand, sir," Krautkramer said contritely.

"There are specific questions that must also be investigated carefully," Jake continued. "When they realized that *America* was being boarded, surely one of the officers or chiefs or petty officers—someone—would give the order to kill the reactor, SCRAM it, which means stop the fission reaction by slamming in the control rods. With the reactor subcritical, the sub would be impossible to move very far. Oh, it might go a mile or two on residual steam pressure, but that would be it until the reactor could be restarted, a process that would take hours. Even if the SCRAM order wasn't given, I am amazed that one of the crew didn't hit the button anyway. It was so obviously the right thing to do. Why did this submarine nuke off over the horizon unSCRAMed? And when it did, why wasn't the destroyer authorized to sink it?"

At the naval base, Jake, Toad, and Ilin were met by a captain in uniform, Piechowski, and a chief petty officer, Hyer. They led the visitors into the simulator building.

After the introductions, the captain spoke directly to Jake. "You wanted to see an *America*-class submarine, but of course there aren't any. *America* was the first of her class. The next one is a floating shell, two years away from being commissioned. The next best thing is the simulator."

"Okay."

Captain Piechowski and the chief led them into a dark, cavernous room in the rear of the building. The walls were painted black, there were no windows, and the interior seemed to soak up the small spotlights that illuminated a desk and two chairs, the only furniture, which stood in one corner between two large steel cabinets.

"This is it," Piechowski said. The chief unlocked the cabinet and removed five helmets with faceplates. "It's a virtual reality simulator." He gestured around him. "This used to be the base gymnasium."

Toad Tarkington looked at Jake, looked at the helmets, pursed his lips to speak, then changed his mind. Ilin took one of the helmets, examined it skeptically.

"Let's put on helmets," Piechowski suggested, "and we'll give you the two-dollar tour. We have a set of gloves we'd like you to wear, Admiral." Chief Hyer helped each man don a helmet and connect it to an electrical cable that led to a large bus on the wall.

When the system came on, the effect was extraordinary. With the helmets on they were standing outside the submarine, which was semitransparent. Captain Piechowski took Jake's arm and led him through the steel hull and ballast tanks and bulkheads to the control room. As Jake stood in the control room looking around, Piechowski went back to escort Ilin. When all of the guests were in the control room, the chief began talking. His voice sounded in their helmet headsets.

"Welcome aboard USS *America*, the most capable submarine in the world. We will do a complete tour of the ship in a few moments, but first I want to acquaint you with the main features of the control room, including the crown jewel of *America*, the Revelation sonar system."

The large computer screens on the bulkheads came alive. Forward, on both sides, and in the rear of the room, the screens became windows that allowed the helmeted visitors to look directly into the sea. "We are sixty feet below the surface," their guide told them, "under way at seven knots. If you will look at the starboard screen, you can see the hull of a ship protruding down into the water." He used a pointer to enlarge the ship's hull, which grew in size as the computer zoomed in, until it became recognizable as a warship hull, one with a sonar bulb on its bow. The photonics mast was up, so the camera image was laid over the top half of the sonar picture, and now the superstructure of the warship leapt into view. The chief explained the mast and sonar, demonstrated some of their capabilities, then moved on.

Jake found himself staring at the joystick that controlled the sub.

He reached for it and found that the image moved in his hand, although he could of course feel nothing. He moved the image with his hand, and the submarine reacted.

"Ooh boy!"

"Sensors in the room tell the computer where the helmets are, where you are looking. Sensors also track the position of the gloves."

"So I can touch and manipulate the controls?"

"All the controls, levers, valves, knobs, switches, the works. We train the crew here in the virtual sim, teach normal and emergency procedures."

The captain led them aft to see the reactor and engineering spaces, then forward through the boat, looking at pipes and valves and tanks and torpedoes and cruise missiles. They didn't go through the hatchways, although they could have; they walked through bulkheads and sealed hatches. The visitors examined the sonar hydrophones, looked at the intricacies of the computers and the ship's electrical systems, played with the photonics mast controls, inspected the radio room and torpedo room, walked through the solid mass of cruise missiles standing erect in their launchers, visited the galley and captain's cabin.

Finally their guide suggested they take off their helmets. The submarine disappeared, and the five of them were again standing in the large, dark room. Jake Grafton fought back the urge to reach out to feel for the submarine that had surrounded him just seconds ago.

Janos Ilin had his feet braced wide apart. His hands did move, probably involuntarily, trying to find something to restore his sense of balance.

"Hot damn," muttered Toad Tarkington.

"And that, gentlemen," said Captain Piechowski, "is the submarine the hijackers stole."

"Did you see all those computer consoles in the control room?" Toad Tarkington whispered to his boss.

"Yeah," Jake whispered back. One thing was crystal clear: Someone who knew a lot more than an ad hoc group of German and Russian submariners could learn in a couple of weeks had gone to sea with them in *America*. The systems would require highly trained experts to operate, and the Russian, Kolnikov, must have known that.

So who was that person?

———

When the cabdriver dropped Zelda Hudson in front of an old brick warehouse in Newark, he was dubious. "You sure about this address, lady?"

"It's the new economy," she replied, "rising from the ashes of the old."

"Ashes still look pretty cold to me," he said, and got out of the car to help get her bag from the trunk and pull out the airport handle.

After she paid him she said, "Wait for a minute until I get in."

The door was the tip-off that this building was not a crumbling wreck like the others that stood nearby. It was solid steel, inset so that it could not be jimmied, with an inletted cylinder lock. Of course there were no windows on the ground floor; the ones on the second, third, and fourth were covered with wire mesh and steel bars. Small video cameras were mounted unobtrusively high on the corners of the building.

The number of the building was above the door, in peeling paint. Beside the door, bolted to the brick of the building, was a sign that said, in inch-high black letters, "Hudson Security Services." Under the sign was a telephone. She picked it up, pushed the button, waited until it buzzed. "Hi, it's me."

The door unlatched with an audible click.

Zelda Hudson pulled the door open, waved to the cabdriver, and pulled her bag in. She made sure the door locked behind her. To her right was a wire-cage elevator. She used the lever to close the door, then pushed the Up button.

The first three stories of the old warehouse were open, with a magnificent high ceiling supported by a latticework of massive oak beams and trusses, barely visible amid the dusty gloom and cobwebs. The only light was from the dirty, painted-over windows. The thought struck Zelda Hudson, not for the first time, that this building could be renovated into a marvelous place, with lights and modern furniture and walls of glass bricks. She could almost hear the sound system playing jazz and the party laughter.

The top floor, "world headquarters" of Hudson Security Services, looked lived in. Lights hanging from the wooden beams illuminated rows of wooden tables sitting on sawhorses. Covering the tables were computers, monitors, and printers. Servers, storage units, and back-up power supplies sat on the floor wherever they would fit. Shelves held boxes of software, developers' kits, and manuals. Over, under, around, and through the clutter ran a veritable jungle of wires bundled with network and power cables. Piles of pizza boxes and mountains of computer paper overflowed from gray plastic garbage cams. Mounted high in the corners of the room were television monitors, which just now were tuned to CNN, MSNBC, and two other twenty-four-hour news networks.

In one corner sat a large caged system with racks of tapes and storage disks housing samples of almost every computer bug extant, as well as Hudson Security's own proprietary designs—Zelda's "unfair competitive advantage," as she liked to say. Ideas and codes came from every source, acquired legitimately from libraries used by the international security industry, from hacking into government activities, and from stealing from some of the most creative elements of the hacker community.

Another system quietly hummed away in another corner, logging every network, computer, and software event seen by the SuperAegis contractor's own security systems. Algorithms would analyze those events without human involvement, searching for irregular activity, and setting off alarms when something was detected. Hundreds of thousands of these recorded events would eventually comprise the "audit trail" for postevent analysis of security breaches and routine security assessments.

Electronically projected on a recently painted section of wall in front of the workstations were duplicates of the very displays watched by the targeted contractor's security managers, complete with the highlighted yellow and red alarms that drew instant attention to suspicious activity.

That was almost the only vertical area within six feet of the floor not covered with politically incorrect posters and cartoons attacking anything and everything, but especially management, inelegant programming, and advertisements hyping "secure systems" that had been broken into and exploited.

Amid this clutter three people sat on folding chairs staring at the television monitors, two women and a man. They wore jeans or shorts, T-shirts, one of the women was smoking, all were young. Zelda's crew. On a normal workday there were a dozen.

No one paid any attention to her as she walked to her desk. She looked at the television to see what had them captivated. For the fifty-second time, CNN was running the video from the Boston television station helicopter. She was just in time to see Kolnikov squirt a burst at the camera.

"Someone hijacked a submarine yesterday morning," the young man told Zelda. He was a tall, pale, intense youth with a scraggly beard. His name was Zip Vance. He had a Ph.D. from Stanford and an IQ close to two hundred. "It's still on every channel," he added. "Been on since yesterday morning."

The four of them watched the coverage for another hour. Little was said. Finally the women said good-bye and took the elevator, leaving Vance alone with Zelda.

"The White House asked for a news hold in the name of national security. The station in Boston told them hell no and put it on the air."

"And the navy?"

"They're moving heaven and earth to get assets out there to find it. So far no luck."

"What do you think?"

Zip Vance grinned. "I think we pulled it off," he said and laughed aloud.

Zelda Hudson joined him in laughter. After a bit, Zip went to the refrigerator in the far corner and returned with a cold bottle of champagne. "I bought this to celebrate," he said, and made a production of popping the cork, which shot away. He didn't bother retrieving it. As they sipped champagne from Styrofoam coffee cups, Zelda kicked off her shoes, put her feet up on her overnight bag, and tousled her long hair.

God, she felt sooo good!

"We did it!" she said, and laughed again.

CHAPTER FIVE

"How does this system work?" Jake Grafton asked Captain Pie-chowski. Jake, Toad, and Janos Ilin were standing with the two simulator experts near the desk in the corner of the dark, old gymnasium.

"The ship is in the computer, if you will, Admiral. The helmets contain sensors that locate them for the computer and provide the direction of orientation. Same with the gloves. The computer presents a three-dimensional holographic image on the faceplate of the helmet as you move in cyberspace."

"Remarkable."

"Much cheaper than a simulator made of hardware, which by the way also requires a computer to give it life."

"Has the virtual sim replaced hardware completely?"

"No, sir. Not yet. We still have an actual control room sim to teach crew coordination and procedures. The rest of it is done here. With the exception of *America*'s reactor and engineering personnel, who do their training in the base reactor and engineering simulators. Those devices are also used for *Seawolf-* and *Los Angeles*–class boats; the plants are sufficiently similar."

"How big is the computer that runs this thing?" Toad Tarkington asked.

"It's a mainframe. The system is capable of simultaneously handling ten people and ten sets of gloves, so the computing capacity must be generous. We have a smaller portable system that we take to other bases for refresher training and retraining on procedural revisions. It will handle just four people at a time."

"How portable?"

"An enhanced laptop runs it."

The admiral glanced at the Russian. "Any questions, Mr. Ilin?"

"It all seems quite amazing," Janos Ilin said, and carefully scrutinized the helmet he held in his hand. "Too bad you still use cords." He was referring to the electrical wires that connected the helmets and gloves to the computer. The use of the wires required the wearer of the helmet and gloves to be careful not to get tangled or wrapped around a fellow trainee.

"We could go wireless," the chief commented innocently, "but wires make the system more secure. I am told there are people in this world who have the capability of intercepting wireless transmissions. Over time they could duplicate the contents of the mainframe, thereby discerning hardware and software design characteristics of *America*."

Jake Grafton was tempted to smile, but the urge died before it reached his lips. Someone had stolen the whole submarine, not just the design.

"Thank you for your time, Captain. You too, Chief. You've been most helpful."

"Captain Killbuck, I asked for the best submariner in the United States Navy, and they tell me you're him." General Flap Le Beau, commandant of the Marine Corps, made this remark when he was introduced to Captain Leroy "Sonny" Killbuck in the Pentagon war room. Killbuck was on the briefing platform and Le Beau was seated in his usual chair, one of the large ones reserved for the Joint Chiefs arranged in a semicircle in the front of the room. In the chairman's seat was General Howard Alt.

"That's very flattering, General," Killbuck said. "I heard you were the toughest marine in uniform."

"They've lied to both of us, then," Le Beau shot back. Killbuck was a year or two over forty, just screened for flag, with a lot of American Indian in him apparently. He had high cheekbones, dark brown skin, jet-black straight hair, and a rugged, craggy face. Some-one said he was Shawnee. A star on the staff of Vice-Admiral Na-varre, the assistant CNO for underseas warfare, he was being groomed for high command.

An African American, Le Beau was just a shade darker than Killbuck. He was a veteran of Vietnam and several brushfire wars since, a fearless knifefighter with the knack of inspiring people to give the very best that was in them. He liked to tell people that his name, Le Beau, was from his white ancestors, a family of Louisiana planters, but in truth he had no idea where it came from. His mother, who had called herself Twila Le Beau, died of a drug overdose when he was in his early teens; he never knew who his father was, and if he had grandparents who outlived his mother, he never knew them. He was, he told his closest friends, a Brooklyn sewer rat. Those who knew him would tell you that he had given himself to the marines body and soul, that he embodied the heritage and values of the corps; the troops said that even his blood was green.

"So where's that submarine?"

Sonny Killbuck gestured toward the map that formed the wall behind the podium. "We drew the black circle an hour ago, sir. The submarine was hijacked thirty-six hours ago, so this is a circle with a seven-hundred-and-twenty-nautical-mile radius, centered on New London. The submarine is somewhere within that circle."

"I thought *America* had a maximum sustained speed of nearly thirty knots." Le Beau shot a glance at Stuffy Stalnaker, the CNO, who was sitting in his usual seat, looking sour. Vice-Admiral Navarre was sitting beside him. His face was stony.

"It does, sir, but at anything over twenty knots the boat will begin to make some noise—and we haven't yet detected it on SOSUS." Beginning in the 1950s, the United States placed hydrophones on the ocean floor all over the world and gradually built a complete system. Today the raw data from hydrophone arrays was processed through a regional evaluation center, and the processed results were then passed to the main evaluation center in Washington, where they were correlated with information from other sources, such as satellites, human intelligence, patrol planes, etc.

"The senior hijacker was apparently a former Russian submariner named Kolnikov," Sonny Killbuck continued. "Presumably he knows a great deal about SOSUS, knows to keep his speed down."

"The yellow circle?"

"That is the ten-knot circle, sir, with a three-hundred-and-sixty-nautical-mile radius. Obviously both circles continue to expand; eventually the submarine could be under any of Earth's oceans."

"Okay."

Killbuck used a pointer. "This is the Goddard SuperAegis launch platform, east of Cape Canaveral. We have a battle group proceeding into that area at twenty knots. Two of our attack boats that were in port in Georgia are now at sea, and two are being readied for sea. We have four boats on patrol in the North Atlantic; those are being diverted back to the seaboard of the eastern United States. Our antisubmarine patrol assets are flying patrols searching for the boat. In addition, Space Command is retasking their reconnaissance satellites to concentrate on the North Atlantic."

"What is the range of the Tomahawk missiles aboard *America*?"

"About one thousand nautical miles, sir."

"So the Goddard launch platform is already within range of *America*'s weapons?"

"Yes, sir. That is correct."

"I understand that *America* surfaced south of Long Island to put the rest of the crew in the water. Did any of these P-3s or satellites see her?"

"Not to my knowledge."

"What else should we be doing, Val?" General Alt asked Vice-Admiral Navarre.

"We are doing everything within our power to find that ship, sir," Navarre shot back. "We'll not find it, though, until the hijackers start doing something with the boat, torpedo something, shoot a missile, or surface. We must be ready to close in if and when they break cover."

"You think they'll use the ship's weapons?"

Navarre took his time before he answered. "Taking the sub to sea is a hell of a feat for an untrained crew, or an undertrained one. Operating the ship's weapons systems is a whole different ball game. The submarine combat system is a fully integrated package, constructed like a telephone network. There is no one single monstrous software package, but a series of packages, all of which work together. Parisian taxicab drivers who once went to sea in old boats back when the world was young aren't going to have a clue."

"This whole scenario is improbable," said General Alt. "But the fact is the damn submarine is gone and our crew is on dry land." Alt was a politician-bureaucrat to his fingertips, and he looked it. Smart, well educated, from a prominent family, Alt was the possessor of a large inherited fortune, which made him an anomaly in the armed forces. The American military had drawn its officers from the middle and lower middle class almost exclusively since the end of the Korean War. Perhaps Alt had seen the military as a bureaucracy to be conquered; in any event, he attended the Military Academy and made the army his career while his brothers went to Ivy League schools, then burrowed into the merchant-banking business.

"When we get some idea of why they stole the ship," Stuffy Stalnaker said, "then we'll get a glimmer of where to look for it."

"Do you have anything to contribute to this conversation?" Flap asked Killbuck.

"They broke cover once already, surfacing," the captain said. "We heard the boat surface. We didn't know it until two hours later, when the sound could be matched to an event. We haven't yet listened to *America* enough to collect a decent database."

"This boat has been to sea numerous times for workups and testing," Flap objected.

"Yes, sir. We haven't yet run it through the acoustic range off Andros Island. We are going over the sea trials and SOSUS records now, doing statistical studies. In forty-eight hours or so we hope to have a database we can work with."

"Anything else?" Alt asked with the slightest edge in his voice. He, not the other chiefs of staff, ran the war room.

"Yes, sir. During the night the SOSUS sensors picked up a sound that we could not identify. I'll play it for you."

Killbuck signaled to one of the enlisted men who worked in the war room. Flap took a deep breath, exerted control over his own emotions. Parading useless information before the brass was an old, old briefing technique designed to deflect criticism when one had nothing tangible to report.

Flap half closed his eyes, listened to a faint, faint sound. Definitely metallic. Killbuck played it four times.

"And?"

"The SOSUS people refuse to identify it," Killbuck said. He paused for a heartbeat, then added, "It's a low-frequency sound, perhaps a torpedo tube being flushed with compressed air. And that's just a guess."

"Where?"

Killbuck used his pointer. "What you heard is sound picked up by four sensors and mixed together by computer. We think it originated here."

"Did you get a P-3 over there?" Flap Le Beau asked.

"Yes, sir. He came up dry."

"We must do better," General Alt said. "We must have planes out there to investigate anything suspicious. Let's get out there and get after that sub. Find him."

"Yes, sir."

"We find it, we're going to sink the son of a bitch," Stuffy Stalnaker said. "Shoot on positive identification. We aren't going to run over to the White House and watch the politicians wring their hands while those assholes sail off into the sunset. We're going to send those sons of bitches to Davy Jones."

"Getting positive identification is critical," Val Navarre remarked. "We're putting our attack boats out there to look for *America*. The best way to find a sub is with another sub. We should have six boats at sea by tomorrow night. Other nations will do the same. There are going to be a lot of submarines in the North Atlantic very soon."

After dinner in the sub-base officers' club, Janos Ilin excused himself and walked across the street to the bachelor officers' quarters, the BOQ, leaving Toad alone with Jake Grafton.

"The FBI has the place surrounded," Toad said in a low voice, trying not to be heard by diners at other tables. "If he leaves the BOQ he'll be followed."

"Ilin knows that. Or suspects it. He won't leave."

"I saw you talking to that FBI agent just before dinner," Toad continued. "A report?"

"They've found where the hijackers stayed for the past two weeks. The place is a cheap motel near Providence. Thirty-dollar rooms. And the FBI went into our beach house after we left this afternoon. The place is bugged, and the bugs are wired to a low-power transmitter."

"Russian?"

"Apparently."

"But you didn't invite me and Ilin for the weekend until Friday."

"The house has stood empty all summer, Toad. When Ilin joined the security team he learned the identities of everyone on the team. The FBI is checking, but it wouldn't surprise me to learn that our apartment in Rosslyn is bugged, and Blevins's townhouse, and your house. . . . The FBI will check all of them."

Commander Toad Tarkington leaned back in his chair. He was a few inches shorter than his boss, with a perfect set of white teeth and deep laugh lines that grooved his tan face. An F-14 radar intercept officer, or RIO, early in his career, he had spent the last few years as Jake's aide or executive assistant.

Jake told Toad of seeing Ilin talking in the street during a smoke break that morning. "I don't think the Russians can get a surveillance team onto the base, but they might. If he does it again, we'll be listening too. And we'll burn the surveillance team."

Toad looked speculatively at Jake. The admiral thought he knew what the younger man was thinking. "Yes, I know having Ilin around is a risk. But the Russians are our prime suspects for the theft of *America*. We need to determine if they are involved, and the sooner the better."

"Are you going to tell Ilin that the hijackers were a CIA team being trained to steal a Russian sub?"

"Yes. If he doesn't already know."

"What if the Russians weren't behind it?"

Jake turned over a hand.

"The Russians are going to get a good laugh over that one."

"As long as a laugh is all they get!" Jake muttered.

Toad tapped the table with a finger three or four times. "Were you thinking what I was thinking when the simulator guys told us about that portable sim?" he asked, glancing up at Jake's face.

"Yeah. The FBI is going to follow up on that. If the portable computer went off base to train the hijackers, someone took it off."

When Toad went back to his room in the BOQ, Jake called for a car and rode to the base communications center. There he used a secure telephone to put in a call to General Flap Le Beau.

"Jake Grafton, General. Thought I would give you a progress report." He did so. When he had finished talking, the marine told him that the rest of the *America* crewmen had been pulled out of the ocean by a freighter several hundred miles off the New Jersey coast.

"So there are no more American sailors aboard that sub, sir?"

"Not to our knowledge. Two are unaccounted for and may have been killed. Or they may have drowned at sea, although we don't think so. The *America* sailors think the missing men were killed by the hijackers. Fourteen are known dead and four are wounded."

"Do the sailors have any ideas about what the hijackers are up to?"

"They are full of ideas," Flap said heavily. "Nothing to back up their ideas, but they have them."

A moment later in the conversation, Jake said, "I'm troubled about possible Russian penetration of the SuperAegis liaison team. We've done routine sweeps in the office and taken all the usual precautions, but we haven't been suspicious enough. The FBI says they've bugged my house at the beach. Ilin's dancing around chattering to himself. They're playing games, General."

"I'll pass that to General Blevins."

"I recommend a complete, thorough security review for the project, top to bottom, reexamine the credentials of everyone. I get this feeling that Ilin's onstage, that he expects us to catch him sooner or later."

"And?"

"Maybe Ilin's a diversion. He wants us to catch him. I would bet some serious change that he's just the first layer of the onion."

Jake told the driver to park the car two blocks from the BOQ. He walked toward the building with his hands in his pockets. He saw smoke rolling out of an open window in the upper story of the building just seconds before he heard the fire alarm ring. People came running from the building, some half dressed. In less than a minute two fire trucks rolled up. Firefighters charged into the building while another group attached a hose to a hydrant with a minimum of lost motion.

Jake was leaning against a tree a block away when Krautkramer found him ten minutes later. "We waited until he was in the shower," the FBI agent said, "then popped the smoke bomb and pulled the fire alarm. We unlocked the door, hustled him out with a towel around his waist within twenty seconds. He didn't flush the commode."

"And?"

"His black leather belt contains a microphone and battery-operated transmitter. There is an on-off switch so he can get through electronic scans."

"A black leather belt? I've only seen him in that a couple of times."

"He has three belts. Another black and a brown. Both are clean. Everything else in his luggage seemed innocent enough. We didn't have time to inspect everything closely, but we ran everything he had through a portable X-ray machine."

"No cyanide pill in the heel of a shoe?" Jake asked savagely. "A bottle of invisible ink, maybe a cipher pad? A code ring from a cereal box?"

"Ahhh . . . no."

"Okay. Thanks for your help."

"Sure, Admiral."

"Someone or several someones who know that submarine inside out went to sea with it. Either they boarded the boat with the hijackers or they were already aboard. Who were they?"

"We don't know yet, Admiral."

"That boat is a giant, seagoing computer. No sane man would go to sea in it without an expert or two at hand. If the hijackers didn't force the U.S. sailors to stay at their posts and operate the boat for them, and apparently they didn't, it is only because they already had an expert. This is an inside job. Find the people on the inside."

"We'll do our best," Krautkramer said. "We are going through the base files right now. There are people on leave, civilians on vacation, people out sick—all those people have to be accounted for. Then we have to figure out who knows what. It's just going to take time."

"Send Toad Tarkington out to talk to me."

Toad came walking down the sidewalk three minutes later.

"I'm going back to Washington now," Jake told him. "You and Ilin stay with the FBI. Keep me advised. I told Krautkramer that someone who knows that submarine inside out went to sea with it. When they figure out who that person is, call me."

"Aye aye, sir."

"And keep an eye on Ilin. So far he's played us for suckers. Don't let him out of your sight."

When the others had gone for the night, Zip Vance was alone with Zelda Hudson. She was, he knew, not going anywhere. The bathroom in the far corner of the upper story of the old warehouse had a shower in it. A couch piled with several blankets and a pillow was shoved against the wall near the door, beside the refrigerator and sink. She lived here, worked the computers at night until she finally wound down and slept. He had never seen her sleeping but knew that she must.

"This is a dangerous game you're playing," he said tentatively.

The remark irritated her. "We've been all through that."

Indeed, they had argued many a night. Smart as he was, Zip Vance didn't understand Zelda Hudson. He chewed a fingernail and thought about what he wanted to say.

"They'll never convict us of anything," she said flatly. "We'll know if they get a sniff. And if they surprise us, we've got the money to hire an army of smart lawyers."

"It had better never come to that."

"It won't. I know what I'm doing. You know what you're doing. These others"—she waved a hand dismissively—"what are they going to say? Zelda did this? Zip did that? Naw. They don't *know* anything. They think we're doing just what we always did, hack into other people's networks, see what the vulnerabilities are, then get a contract to plug the holes."

Irritated, he brushed her argument away with a flick of his fingers. "They may not know about this operation, but when the heat arrives, they'll turn state's evidence to save themselves from jail. Half of them have already been there, and they don't want to go back."

"A few hacking charges! We'll pay a fine and get probation, and business will boom. The publicity will be wonderful. Pfffft!"

"What they'll say will make the FBI dig deeper. I'm not talking about hacking, Zelda, and you damn well know it."

"We'll be long gone by then, Zipper. Absolutely gorgeously, filthy rich, rich beyond your wildest dreams. Maybe not as rich as Warren Buffett, but we'll be younger and will have had a lot more fun, and we won't be stuck in Omaha."

"Actually, I think you're doing this for fun, for the challenge of it."

She eyed him carefully. "You know me pretty well," she conceded.

Zip Vance stood. "I want to leave you with one thought. The United States government may never get enough evidence to prosecute, and granted, they may even offer immunity if we'll cooperate and tell them what we know." He shrugged eloquently. "But remember this—Antoine Jouany and Willi Schlegel don't play by civilized rules. They've paid us huge heaping piles of money and are going to pay mountains more. And you aren't playing straight with them. They aren't the type to call their lawyers."

"We've been all through this, Zip," she said, her voice rising, "time and time again. I know what I'm doing. If you don't want to play the game, maybe you'd better go now."

Their serious conversations on this subject always ended like this. Zelda was . . . well, shit, she was Zelda.

"Maybe the game is worth the risks," he said lightly and headed for the elevator. "I just don't want you to forget what the risks are."

Vladimir Kolnikov stretched out in the captain's bunk aboard *America*. He glanced at his watch, made sure the cabin door was locked, then turned out the light. Lying in the darkness, he closed his eyes, tried to force his body to relax.

He had a hell of a headache, so he snapped the light back on, wet a washrag at the sink tap, and lay down again. After turning off the light a second time, he arranged the cool, wet cloth over his forehead and eyes.

He had first gone to sea thirty-five years ago, a diesel-electric sub that rattled underwater. The Soviets had not known then how good American sonar was. Or would become. If there had been a war with the United States, that old boat would have been quickly sunk.

Didn't happen, of course. After all the propaganda, all those lies about the superiority of the Soviet system and the moral and financial bankruptcy of the free nations of the West, the whole Soviet edifice shattered and collapsed. All the lies the Communists had told, the crimes they committed, the lives they shattered, the people they murdered—that was the foundation of the Soviet state, and the whole colossal sand castle fell of its own weight.

If that wasn't bad enough, then came the aftermath! The now

anti-Communist *nomenklatura* soldiered on as before, spouting propaganda about freedom and democracy. Same people, different song.
They stole the foreign aid donated by the West, looted the national
treasury, sold military equipment, literally robbed their fellow citizens of everything they owned to line their own pockets. They
wanted to continue to live the privileged life they had enjoyed in the
workers' paradise of Stalin, Khrushchev, Andropov, Kosygin, Brezh-
nev, and all the others.

Civilization collapsed in Russia. That was the optimist's take on
it. Cynics said it never existed there. Certainly the liberal civilization
of the West never existed in Soviet Russia, which had gone directly
from a totalitarian society ruled by czars to one ruled by absolute
dictators. Now, with the dictators gone, no one ruled. That would
change of course, Kolnikov knew. Another dictatorship would inevitably follow, he thought. The Russians liked dictatorship, were
comfortable only in an authoritarian, autocratic society where everyone behaved and did as he was supposed to do. And the people at
the top set the standard. The Russians did not know how to live any
other way.

Except Kolnikov. He had refused to wait for the inevitable. So
had Turchak. The two of them gave up on Mother Russia and
sneaked out of the country. Now they were criminals. Traitors.

Captain First Rank Vladimir Kolnikov, criminal. Thief. Terrorist.
Pirate!

He lay now in the silent darkness listening in vain for sounds of
the ship.

God, she was quiet!

He turned to the computer screen mounted beside his pillow and
touched it with a finger. A menu appeared. He studied the options,
then selected one. The boat's depth, course, and speed appeared instantly. Another touch showed him a variety of reactor temperatures
and pressures. All normal. He turned his head, closed his eyes, tried
to relax.

Before this adventure was over he was probably going to wish
he had stayed in that Paris hire car. It was a living. An honest
one, even.

The hell with it. He had made his choice, cast the dice. However
it came out . . . well, it didn't really matter how it all came out. He
knew that. And in truth, didn't really care.

The National Security Agency is a collection of buildings behind a chain-link fence on the edge of the army's Fort Meade complex between Baltimore and Washington. It is bordered on two sides by major arterial highways. South of the complex across one of the highways sits a regional military jail surrounded by concertina wire. The ugly, gray NSA buildings are festooned with an odd assortment of antennas, although no more so than many other high-tech headquarters in the Washington area. What is not readily apparent from the highway, however, is the size of the complex, which employs sixteen thousand people and houses the largest collection of computers in the world. Most of the complex is underground.

It was three in the morning when Jake Grafton arrived by helicopter at the National Security Agency. A gentle rain was falling as he walked across the helo pad.

The woman who met him shook hands, led him through a security checkpoint, and took him into a nondescript government office where three other people waited, two men and another woman.

"As you know, we've lost a submarine," Jake said to get them started. "We need all the help we can get to find it. I was hoping you folks could do a study of telephone traffic for the last two or three weeks around Providence and New London."

"It doesn't work quite that way, Admiral," the senior NSA briefer said. She was in her fifties, looked like she had just gotten out of bed an hour ago, which she probably had. "As you are probably aware, we use the Echelon system to monitor foreign telecommunications traffic—hardwired, wireless, satellite, all of it—but legally we can't monitor U.S. domestic communications: That is the FBI's job. And we don't have the storage capacity to record even a statistically significant part of the traffic we do study. We sample conversations and automatically record those that use certain keywords; for example, *terrorists, bomb, assignation,* etc. But we have to choose our keywords in advance." She explained how they did it, discussed interception techniques, hardware and software.

"I guess the horse is gone," Jake said finally, when she appeared to be through.

"Apparently."

Jake Grafton slapped his knees. He too was running on empty. "Let's do this: Can you monitor all the traffic in the New England area, and the Washington area, and do a study on all conversations that talk about the stolen submarine? *America*."

"Not legally. But we can ask the British to do it and give us their results."

"That is legal?"

"Oh, yes. We do the British, they do us. Keeps the politicians happy."

"When you get the study, what will you be able to tell us about those conversations?"

"Everything. We'll have the conversation, where it originated, where it went, voices that can be identified. . . ."

"What if they use some sort of code?"

"Breaking codes is what we do. We examine all suspect conversations to see if they contain a code. It's almost impossible to talk in code without revealing the fact that a code is involved. If it's there, we'll find it. Given enough time and some idea what the coded conversation might be about, we can break it."

On that note, Jake rose to go. He took a step, then turned and returned to his seat.

"You got my security clearance?" he said questioningly, looking at the senior woman, who nodded. "Let's do this. Give me a summary of what's going on in the world that isn't in the newspapers. What are you people working on here?"

They looked at each other. Intelligence projects were discussed on a need-to-know basis, not in wholesale form.

"Pretend that you are writing a morning briefing for the president, who has been on vacation for a week. What would you tell him?"

They began. SuperAegis headed the list. Korea, Middle Eastern terrorists, Iraq, oil, an assassination attempt in Ireland . . . the list was extensive. Almost by the way, one of the men mentioned Antoine Jouany, the financier. "He's making huge bets on the euro, shorting the dollar. We also think he's betting billions on the index futures market. How much, we don't know."

"What does that mean?" Jake asked.

"He thinks the American stock market and the dollar are going to get hammered in the near future."

"Don't people buy and sell futures every day?"

"Of course. But Jouany has a massive position, we believe. Just how big we don't know."

"How big is massive?"

"Ten billion dollars. Maybe twice that. We hope to know more next week. We're working with the CIA, trying to discover just how big the position is, what Jouany thinks is going to happen. His main office is in London, but he operates worldwide."

"I know he's one of the world's richest men," Jake said slowly. "Is this unusual behavior for him?"

"He's never bet more than two billion on a market move before, and even then, he hedged in the derivative markets. We think this is a ten-billion-dollar position, but we don't know. It could be smaller."

"Or a lot more," one of the men said. "Maybe he's been reading tea leaves or studying technical charts. Maybe he knows something we don't. Whatever, we hope to find out what induced him to make such a massive commitment."

"Have you asked him?"

"The Brits did. He told them American interest rates were going to move."

"Are you monitoring the calls to and from his company?"

"Oh, yes."

On that note Jake thanked them and headed back toward the helicopter. He wanted desperately to go home to snatch a few hours' sleep. General Le Beau would want a briefing first thing in the morning.

"These are the targets," Vladimir Kolnikov said to Leon Rothberg and handed him a slip of paper containing three sets of coordinates.

Rothberg looked at the paper in amazement. "What are they?"

"Targets."

"You want to shoot a Tomahawk?"

"Three of them."

Rothberg studied the paper. He was sitting on one of the two chairs in the captain's cabin, Kolnikov was sitting on the bunk. "We're almost five hundred miles off the coast."

"We'll close to about four hundred by dark," Kolnikov said. "I want you to rise to periscope depth—"

"We don't have a periscope."

"Whatever. Stick the damn communications mast out of the water, update the inertial with the GPS. Then shoot. I want the missiles to hit their targets before midnight."

"You know that the missiles must be programmed. I doubt that the United States database is in the mission-planning computer."

"Of course it's there."

"Don't tell me my business, Ivan. You are wasting air. Even if the U.S. is in the database, it will take hours to set up each missile." He glanced at his watch. "We don't have anywhere near enough time."

"We have enough. I know what is involved. Let's go to the control room and do it, shall we?"

"Shooting missiles wasn't in the plan. Heydrich won't like this. The plan was approved—"

"I don't care what Heydrich likes or doesn't like. He has no choice. The plan has changed. And you will do it right, won't you? The missiles will hit these targets."

Leon Rothberg wanted to argue. He was a small man, thirty pounds overweight, a twisted genius who owed money to half the bookies in Boston. "Heydrich paid me. And he still owes me a ton of money, a shit-pot full."

"Heydrich keeps his promises. He can be relied on to pay his debts. I assure you of that."

"But he won't like this. This wasn't in the plan! We weren't going to shoot weapons, except as absolutely necessary in self-defense. If we shoot Tomahawks at anybody, every navy in the world will hunt us like we're rabid dogs."

"It seems I must repeat myself. The plan has changed." Kolnikov reached for Rothberg's face, latched onto his chin, held it as he looked into his eyes. "I want to be sure that you understand the situation. You will program the Tomahawks to fly the routes and profiles I chose and hit the targets I have designated. We will launch the missiles, they will strike their programmed targets, and we will hear that fact verified by news broadcasts on commercial radio. If the missiles don't hit their targets, I will kill you, Rothberg. No excuses, no reprieve, no second chance. Have I made myself clear?"

"I hear you," Leon Rothberg said contemptuously. He brushed away Kolnikov's hand. "Now you listen to me! If anything happens to me you won't have anyone who knows how to operate the boat's systems. You think this boat is something you order from Dell and figure out by reading the fucking manual? There isn't another submarine in the world with a system like this. Without me you people will die in this steel coffin. I'm the man! You clear on that?"

Kolnikov slapped him. Just a quick open-handed slap as hard as he could swing his hand. Rothberg went off the chair onto the tiled deck. Quick as a cat Kolnikov reached for Rothberg with both hands, pulled him half erect, put his face within inches of the American's.

"The only way you can stay alive is to obey my orders. Disobey me just once and I'll put your silly ass in a torpedo tube and you can make like a fish. Maybe you can swim back to Boston."

He opened the door to the passageway and threw Rothberg through it. The man bounced off the passageway bulkhead and fell heavily to the deck.

Kolnikov was all over him. "Do you tolerate pain well, Rothberg? Should I break an arm, smash some fingers? You are here for the money. Now you will earn it. Maybe you'll think better with only one hand."

Kolnikov smelled feces. The American had shit his pants.

CHAPTER SIX

The director of the CIA was a tall, balding, sixtyish man with a portly frame. His smooth, round face wore a perpetual frown; he looked as if he hadn't smiled since he got out of diapers. He scowled now at the copy of the letter Jake Grafton handed him, inspected the letterhead, read every word, grimaced at the signature—which was that of the president of the United States—and reluctantly laid it on the desk. Then he read the second sheet of paper Jake had handed him, another letter, this one an original. He laid it on the desk next to the first, arranged the edges so that they touched each other.

This morning Jake was decked out in his blue uniform. He got a look at himself in the mirror in the foyer as he was shown into the director's office. The thought occurred to him that the uniform with its gold rings on the sleeves and splotches of color on the left breast looked incongruous, out of place among the gray men in this gray building. He had shaken off that thought and looked the director straight in the eye as he said hello and passed him the letters.

When the director had read both documents twice, he looked again at Jake.

"Okay," said the director, whose name was Avery Edmond DeGarmo. He was one of those men who routinely used all three names. No doubt even his pajamas were embroidered with all three initials. "The president appointed General Le Beau to investigate this submarine mess and he sent you over here with full authority to ask questions in his place. So ask."

Jake Grafton took his time responding. He crossed his legs, flicked an invisible mote of dust off his trousers. "I have been told that the CIA was training a team of Russian and German expatriates to operate a submarine with minimum manning."

"That is correct."

Jake waited. When nothing else was forthcoming, he asked, "Why?"

The CIA director picked up the letters, studied them again. "The answer to that question is classified above your security clearance."

"Oh?"

"You have only a top-secret clearance, according to my staff."

"Mr. DeGarmo," Jake shot back, "those letters are all the clearance I need to ask any question I choose."

"These letters are not clearance to violate the security laws. If you think this"—he fluttered one of the sheets—"grants you carte blanche to stroll willy-nilly through that building asking any question that pops into your head, regardless of its bearing on the matter you are investigating, you are sadly mistaken."

Jake Grafton had been in Washington long enough to know that you got only as much respect as you demanded. "General Le Beau and I will decide the relevance of the information I receive," he replied smoothly. "If you're in the mood for a pissing contest this morning, sir, I'll be delighted to get the commandant on the telephone and you can take it up with him. If you wish, he will call the White House and get someone over there to discuss the fine points with you."

"The responsibility for security breaches will be on your head, not mine." First and foremost, Avery Edmond DeGarmo was a bureaucrat. "I want that clearly understood."

Jake gave a curt nod.

"What was the question?" said DeGarmo.

"The CIA trained this crew?"

"What crew?"

"The crew that hijacked *America*."

"I don't know who hijacked that ship. Do you?"

"The FBI agent in charge has informed us that these were the men."

"But you don't know for a fact."

"I am not going to split legal hairs with you this morning, sir, or debate the meaning of 'is.' Did or did not the CIA train a team to run a sub with minimum manning?"

"I have answered that question. Yes."

"Why?"

"The operation was properly authorized and funded. We did what we were told to do."

"What was the objective of the operation?"

"To steal a Russian submarine."

"Was that Operation Blackbeard?"

"Yes."

"Why did the CIA want a Russian submarine?"

DeGarmo shifted his weight in his chair. He leaned forward, played with the letters, tapped his fingers on them. Both men were well aware that this information was available elsewhere. Finally DeGarmo said, "For several years the Russians have been working on revolutionary new torpedoes. The technology, we believe, uses supercavitation and rocket propulsion to drive a torpedo through the water within a bubble, reducing drag dramatically. Our theoretical physicists think the technology might ultimately yield a torpedo capable of a thousand knots. The Russians aren't that far along yet. We hope. They have produced a torpedo that uses the first generation of this technology, we believe. They call it the 'Shkval' or 'Squall.' The Kursk was testing this torpedo when the thing exploded, fatally damaging the submarine."

Jake had seen classified summaries speculating that this was the case. So far, DeGarmo hadn't told him anything he didn't know. "We are doing similar research and having our problems," DeGarmo added. This Jake didn't know. "We wanted to see what the Russians really have, if anything."

It went on like this for five minutes before DeGarmo agreed to make the complete, raw files on the men the CIA trained available that afternoon for Commander Tarkington to study. "We'll need copies of those files," Jake added, "and I would appreciate your staff making them and sending the copies over. For now, however, a look at those files will be sufficient."

It took another minute to persuade DeGarmo to have his staff run the copy machine. Then Jake asked who authorized the operation to steal a Russian sub.

"The national command authority, of course."

"Who wanted this information?"

"The navy, primarily. The planning people at DOD. My staff. Everyone was interested."

"Admiral Stalnaker?"

DeGarmo nodded.

"Why a team of Russians and Germans? Why not Americans, who presumably would have been more trustworthy?"

"The committee thought that the difficulties involved in getting Americans onto a Russian naval base where they could get access to a submarine with *Shkval* aboard lowered the probability of success to an unacceptable level. If the Russians caught these people, the fallout would be manageable if they were former Soviet-bloc sailors but damn near catastrophic if they were Americans. And of course there was the deniability issue, which I think was crucial to getting it approved."

"How were these men recruited?"

"We went after ex-submariners who spoke Russian. The Germans served in the East German Navy and spoke fluent Russian."

"Were they reliable?"

DeGarmo's habitual frown deepened. "In my opinion, Blackbeard was flawed from the start. The minutes of those meetings will prove that I was against it from the get-go. These people couldn't be trusted. That risk was significant." He went on, explained how the crew was isolated, held incommunicado during training.

"The operation was ultimately scrubbed."

Another nod.

"Why?"

DeGarmo shrugged, shifted his weight while he considered what to say. The thought occurred to Jake that this was one of the least loquacious men he had ever met.

"I am not going to respond to that. Suffice it to say that Blackbeard was canceled. The reason is not germane to your investigation, in my opinion."

"Who canceled it?"

"The intelligence committee."

"Did the Russians find out about it?"

"I'm not going to comment." DeGarmo looked at Jake as if he were an obtuse child. "Ask someone else."

Jake studied DeGarmo's face. "If someone else can tell me, why not you?"

A low growl. The CIA director pursed his lips. "That fact couldn't conceivably be relevant to your investigation."

Jake Grafton stared into the director's eyes, unwilling to break contact. "How good is your information?"

The director leaned forward and waggled a finger. "You are in an area that . . . is . . . not . . . relevant to your investigation."

"But the operation was canceled for a credible reason? Or reasons?"

"Obviously."

"Why didn't the CIA seek other ways to get information on the *Shkval* and supercavitation?"

"We tried, obviously. And continue to try. The difficulty is that credible intelligence about Russian research is practically impossible to obtain. Under the Communists, Russia was a society as closed as a locked bank vault, with half the population employed in watching the other half. That's changed since the collapse of communism. In Russia today there are countless people anxious to sell all sorts of technical information. Everything is for sale. You can buy boxes full of secrets on Moscow street corners. Criminals and con artists are busy as beavers. Since the Foreign Intelligence Service can't plug all the real leaks, they are also busy selling bogus stuff. Apparently creating classified files to sell to credulous foreigners is the only growth industry in the country. So you negotiate like hell and fork over and take home your nifty treasure map and add it to the pile you already have.

"Consequently, stealing a submarine looked like a risk worth taking. If we could pull it off, the payoff would be real hardware that could be properly evaluated, not boxes full of fiction. The decision makers thought that, all things considered, the potential payoff justified the risk." He stopped speaking, yet since he looked as if he might say more, Jake remained silent.

After a moment's thought, DeGarmo added, "In an era of tight defense budgets worldwide, those countries doing research are trying to make every dollar count. It isn't enough merely to improve weapons, to spend billions for five or ten or twenty percent more capability; the dollars are too hard to come by. This reality forces us to search for technologies that have the promise of leapfrogging whole generations of weapons development. The *Shkval* is a quantum leap in torpedo technology, five times faster than any other existing torpedo: If it becomes operational we have no defense against it. Whoever possesses it will have a huge military advantage. Perhaps an overwhelming one, unless we can find out exactly how it works and develop defensive countermeasures."

Here DeGarmo leaned forward. "This isn't a game, Admiral. We can't take the risk that potential opponents might bring weapons to a future battlefield that give them a winning military advantage. The atomic bomb was such a weapon; jet fighters would have been if Hitler could have deployed a sufficient quantity. Our way of life is on the table, Admiral. The stakes are too high."

"And Revelation? Is it a quantum leap? A new paradigm?"

"I think so, yes."

"Did the Russians steal it? Is that why *America* was hijacked?"

"I don't know."

"What do your Russian sources say? The ones who told you the Russian government knew about Blackbeard, about your sub-stealing team?"

DeGarmo didn't even glare. He merely waggled a finger at Jake. "Don't leap to conclusions. Blackbeard was canceled for reasons that do not touch on this investigation."

Jake Grafton refused to be intimidated. "If the Russians didn't swipe that boat, who did?"

"I don't know," Avery Edmond DeGarmo said bitterly. "I wish to Christ I did."

Jake Grafton stood up. "If there is a mole in the United States government, sir, we are going to discover that fact. Then I'll be back to see you with more questions. A lot more."

DeGarmo let out a roar. "Goddamn it, sailor. You are in way over your head. I feel like I am explaining the facts of life to Inspector Clouseau." He sprang from his chair with a grace that surprised Jake. "It's not just torpedoes! Supercavitation could revolutionize naval warfare. Antisubmarine bullets fired from airplanes, two-hundred-knot submarines . . . Think of it! A two-hundred-knot submarine! A half dozen of those might well obsolesce the entire world's fleet of surface combatants. What the hell do you think Stuffy Stalnaker worries about in the middle of the night? Everyone wants this! Everyone! The British, the Chinese, Germany, France, the United States . . ."

DeGarmo sat down and leaned forward in his chair. "And it is not just submarines. There is a parallel technology that might have aerodynamic applications. There are rumors that the Russians are working on plasma research, firing a beam of microwaves ahead of an aircraft, ripping the air into a plasma of ions and electrons. Flying in plasma would dramatically reduce the drag on an aircraft, allow hypersonic speeds, kill the sonic boom. And yes, plasma absorbs radio waves, so plasma fighters would be invisible to radar. Think stealth at Mach five." Words failed him and he fell silent.

"Tell me what you think," Jake Grafton prompted. "Is supercavitation real? Or magnificent fiction? Complex, fascinating disinformation?"

DeGarmo took a deep breath, gathered himself, and levered his bulk out of his chair. He came around the desk, casually took Jake's elbow, and began steering him toward the door. Jake had run out of questions, so he was willing to go.

"Maybe there's hope for you after all, Admiral. Good luck with your investigation. Keep me advised on what you find out."

With those parting words DeGarmo eased Jake through the door and pulled it firmly closed.

Out in the hallway Jake remembered that he had wanted to ask the director about Janos Ilin. Too late now, but he would be talking to DeGarmo again soon.

"Yes, Carmellini, what is it?"

Two floors below and a light-year away from the director's office, Tommy Carmellini stuck his head into his department head's office and asked if he might have a few minutes. Now he stepped inside, pulled the door shut, and seated himself across the desk from the great man, whose name was Herman Watring.

"Mr. Watring, I wanted to discuss the reasons why you didn't give me a performance bonus this year. I think I deserve one and so did my supervisor, who gave me the highest recommendation in the department."

"I saw his recommendation. Ridiculous!"

Carmellini wrapped his hands around the arms of the chair he was seated in and squeezed. "I have done an outstanding job all year. In addition, I invented the energy grenade, got a classified patent and assigned it to the agency. If I hadn't invented the thing and financed the prototype, they wouldn't exist."

"The agency is reimbursing you for your expenses," Watring said without enthusiasm. "I don't think you are entitled to anything else."

"I think I'm entitled to reimbursement and a performance bonus for my efforts, and so does my supervisor."

"Energy grenades! Pfft! You read classified summaries about the research into directed energy weapons. Your so-called invention was nothing new. The patent office should never have granted you that patent."

Tommy Carmellini struggled to keep his voice under control. "I'm not going to argue with you about what the patent office should have done. They did grant a patent, and I did assign it to the agency."

"As the law requires."

"Yes, sir. And the regulations contemplate that I will be rewarded for my industry and diligence. After all, I could have just sat on my ass like most of the people around here, swilling coffee and waiting for the eagle to shit me a paycheck." Watring's fondness for gourmet coffee was legendary.

Now Herman Watring leaned forward in his chair and a finger shot out, one pointed at Carmellini's chest. "I'm not going to take any more insubordination from you, foul mouth. Your supervisor made the bonus recommendation and I turned it down. That's the way it was and the way it's going to stay. I don't think you deserve a bonus. You aren't a team player, Carmellini. You're a thief. A burglar. A criminal. You are fortunate that you aren't in jail. Personally I find it difficult to understand why the agency keeps you on the payroll."

"So fire me! Send me out into the big wide world to starve on the sidewalks, to beg for quarters from employed civil servants on their way to their offices to earn their daily crust. Fire me! If you have the guts."

"As much as I'd like to, you know I haven't the authority."

"Okay, okay! I'm the cross you have to drag through life. My heart bleeds. Let's cut through the personal animosity, shall we?

What about the energy grenades? Surely you see how valuable they are?"

"Valuable to thieves and terrorists, perhaps. Not to an agency of the United States government."

"You say that like the CIA was the post office." Keeping himself under tight control, Tommy Carmellini rose from his chair and headed for the door. "You're a foolish, incompetent, vindictive knave, Herman."

"You can't call me names! Who the hell do you think you are? You can't march into this office and insult me!"

Why was he wasting his life conning women and picking locks for these pinheads? "Fire me!" he told Watring again. "Knave, varlet, fathead, toady, gossip, brownnoser, nincompoop—"

"Out!" Watring shouted, pointing toward the door, his face beet red and jowls quivering. "Out! Don't ever come through that door again unless I send for you. Understand?"

Carmellini went. He was in the hallway when the thought occurred to him that perhaps he should try quitting. Just turn in a letter of resignation and wait to see what happened. After all, this is America, he reminded himself. You gotta admit, it's a helluva country—people quit jobs every day. The CIA had had its pound of flesh: They wouldn't prosecute him for those old burglaries. Would they?

When he was a young man, Flap Le Beau never went anywhere without two knives secreted under his clothes, a throwing knife that he liked to keep in a sheath hanging behind his neck, and a fighting, or slashing, knife that he often wore behind his belt or up a sleeve. "Without the knives I feel sort of naked, you know," he had once explained to Jake Grafton, who met Flap and flew with him after the Vietnam War when Jake had the misfortune to be sent to a marine A-6 squadron aboard an aircraft carrier. That was long ago, Jake reflected ruefully as he shook hands this morning with Flap and lowered himself into a stuffed leather chair at the end of the commandant's desk.

Of course the room was outrageously decorated in red and gold, with the marine's globe and anchor emblem plastered on everything, from the paperweights to the carpet and furniture. Jake related the substance of the conversation with Director DeGarmo. Flap tapped a pencil on the desk as he listened, asking no questions. When Jake was done, he said, "Come on," and bolted for the door. Grafton trailed along in his wake as Flap strode through the outer office, not even breaking stride to talk to his executive assistant, a colonel. "We're going to see Stuffy Stalnaker. Be back in a bit."

Stalnaker was in a meeting, but he stepped into an adjacent meeting room to spend a few minutes with the marine general. "We need some background on this CIA operation that didn't fly, Operation Blackbeard. Why was it canceled?"

Stalnaker looked at each man, then pulled a chair around and dropped into it. He glanced at the door to ensure it was closed before he spoke. "The Russians got wind of it," he said.

Flap glanced at Jake, then pulled a chair away from the table and sat in it. Jake dropped into one against the wall.

"How do you know that?"

"DeGarmo told me. Apparently he told the intelligence committee too. They canceled the operation."

"Any idea how the CIA learned that fact?"

"Of course not. DeGarmo would never share that kind of information. We have no need to know."

"What," Jake Grafton asked, "if he was lying?"

Stalnaker ducked his head, swung it ponderously from side to side as he considered his answer. He looked up, eyed Jake. "There are some rocks sailors can't look under, and that's one of them."

General Le Beau asked, "How valuable is supercavitation technology?"

"Until we see where it is, Flap, what's involved, I can't answer that. I can tell you this, the Russians have successfully launched at least one of those *Shkval* torpedoes. That's classified top secret, by the way. The thing ran straight as a bullet for about twenty miles, did two hundred and eighty knots, as near as we can determine. We had two subs close enough to record this on sonar."

"Thing make a lot of noise?"

"No, it didn't. That is the intriguing part. Some noise, yes. If they shot it at you, that's the last thing you'd hear before you died."

"So you are still interested?"

"Very."

"DeGarmo said supercavitation might lead to two-hundred-knot submarines, which would obsolesce conventional navies."

"I don't know where it would lead—far too early to tell. That's what's so tantalizing about it. But sure as God made Viagra, two-hundred-knot submarines would make scrap iron of every existing antisubmarine weapon and ship."

At this point, Flap glanced at Jake Grafton and raised his eyebrows in invitation.

"Admiral, if I might," Jake said, "let's talk about the technology aboard *America*. Who would want it?"

"Everyone," Stalnaker shot back. "Everyone will want it unless they got all the juice from the people who built the systems. In America that is the usual course of events. Espionage, industrial espionage . . . whatever you want to call it, someone buys the technology from someone in government or private industry while it's still in the blueprint stage. Or some twisted little bastard gives it away to save the human race from the evil military-industrial complex. The Russians, or Chinese, or Japanese, or Koreans—whoever—are usually a few years behind us turning the new tech into hardware, which is due more to manufacturing capacity and budget restraints than anything else. Anyone who thinks that competent, determined foreign intelligence services can't discover the secrets of Revelation is living in a fool's paradise. The circle of people with access is too darn big. All big secrets leak—in America that's a universal law."

"What about Russian technology? I have heard that since the collapse of communism, all the really great innovations that their research institutes were working on are for sale. For the right price."

"If *Shkval* is for sale, I haven't heard about it," Stalnaker replied. "Ask DeGarmo."

"He would know, wouldn't he?" Flap said, glancing again at Jake.

"The problem is buying blueprint tech." Stalnaker scratched his head. "It's so damned tricky. You have to know a lot in order to evaluate what the seller is offering."

"Revelation. Does it work?"

"Oh, yes."

Flap asked, "If Russia didn't have it, would they steal a sub to get it?"

Stalnaker weighed the question. "Maybe. But as I said, stuff leaks. I would be amazed if the guts of Revelation are still an exclusively American secret."

Jake asked, "If not Russia, then who?"

"Make a list. A long list. Every country with a high-tech defense industry could make money with the guts of Revelation, which is nothing more than software that runs on high-speed computers. But you should be talking all this over with Navarre." Vice-Admiral Val Navarre was the navy's head submariner. "He knows *America* inside out."

Le Beau and Grafton thanked Stalnaker and left.

In the hallway the two flag officers were met by Captain Killbuck. He handed Jake a sheet of paper. "Here is the *America* weapons loadout you asked for, Admiral."

Jake glanced over the list. "Flashlights? Ten of them?"

"Yes, sir. First operational cruise."

"Thank you, Captain."

Back in Le Beau's office, Jake showed the list to Flap. "Flashlight is the new warhead on the vertically launched cruise missile, the Tomahawk."

"I've read about it," Flap responded after scanning the list. "Maybe they wanted Flashlight more than Revelation."

Jake's lips compressed into a firm, straight line. He thought for a moment before he spoke again. "The Russians assigned a so-called technical expert to the SuperAegis liaison team last month, a couple weeks after the satellite was lost. Guy's name is Ilin. CIA says he's a spook with SVR. He's been playing me for a sucker." Jake told Flap about Ilin's solo talking and the transmitter in his belt. "The FBI is assembling a serious surveillance team to watch this guy, but . . ." Jake shrugged. "I don't know what he could be telling the Russians except what he is seeing and hearing."

"Okay," Flap Le Beau said.

"We've also got a Brit, a Frenchman, and a German on the liaison team. All are intelligence professionals and freely admit it. I don't know why we do this to ourselves, but we're stuck with these people. The question is, who stole that submarine? If any of those countries are behind the theft, then it stands to reason that their rep knows or has orders to report anything he hears about submarines, etc. In any event, I want to give them something to report. I want permission to take them to the war room this evening for the Joint Chiefs brief."

Flap eyed Jake. "You want to let them see what we are doing to find the sub?"

"Yes, sir."

"The Russian too?"

"Especially him."

"He'll ride the subway across town to the Russian embassy and tell them all about it."

"I expect all four to make beelines to their respective embassies. If one doesn't, well, that would be interesting. It would be doubly interesting if we could read some of the intel codes these folks use to communicate with the folks back home."

"Beats the hell outta me," Flap said slowly, eyeing Jake.

"My suggestion, sir, is that you talk to the appropriate people at NSA and the White House, see if you can get permission. And we'll see what happens."

"The White House doesn't want *America* to slip through our fingers."

"We aren't close to finding that sub," Jake shot back. "We couldn't be. *America* is state of the art. We might stumble across her by accident, but we're not going to hear her on the SOSUS or find her with P-3s. The Atlantic is a damned big ocean. We lost a satellite in that pond two months ago and still haven't found it, and everyone was looking right at it when it disappeared."

"How did that happen?" Flap asked. "NASA and the FBI haven't told us anything."

"They haven't told the liaison office anything either," Jake said slowly. He ran his fingers through his hair. "It may have been one of those things, the software hiccupped or the rocket burped, whatever, and at the same time the tracking stations' power supply failed temporarily. Far more likely, someone arranged for all that to happen. They haven't found that someone, nor have they found the satellite. And they aren't talking."

"Do you think the loss of the satellite and the theft of the sub are related?"

"Yes, sir, I think so. But I can't imagine how. The only reason I can point to is the little lecture I got this morning from DeGarmo, the CIA director, all about high tech and quantum leaps. And the fact that the only people who want SuperAegis in the sky and functioning are the Americans. In every direction, as far as the eye can see, are people who don't want the United States sitting comfortably under an ABM umbrella. The Americans twisted arms in Europe, got them to go along. Very reluctantly. But the Chinese, the Indians, the Arab world were left out."

"Thank God the missing satellite isn't our problem," Flap said with a wave of his hand.

"The missing satellite and sub may both be faces on the same Rubik's cube," Jake replied. "If we could figure out how they are related, we'd be a whole lot closer to laying hands on that boat than we are now."

Flap Le Beau grinned at Jake Grafton. "I'll make some calls," the marine said, "tell them we want to take tourists to the war room this evening. I'll call you at your office."

"Yes, sir."

The marine commandant added, "Talk to Navarre and the FBI this afternoon, then brief me in the war room."

"Yes, sir."

As Flap started back to his desk, Jake added, "General, I'm curious. Do you still carry any of those knives you used to pack?"

The motion was almost too quick for the eye to follow. Flap Le Beau reached behind his neck inside his blouse with his right hand, then lunged forward, sweeping his hand down. Jake caught a glint of polished steel flying through the air, then the knife stuck in the far wall with an audible thunk. As it quivered there, Jake could see that the weapon was small, with a handle and blade about six inches long.

Flap straightened, shot the cuffs of his blouse. "The grunts expect it. I hate to disappoint 'em."

"Yes, sir."

Vice-Admiral Navarre was on the telephone when Jake was shown into his office. He was in his shirtsleeves, his tie hanging over his blouse on the back of a chair. He motioned for Jake to sit, then concentrated on listening to what the other person on the line was saying.

"We can't sit on them, sir," Navarre said. He was on the phone to the CNO. "Sure, we can keep the *America* crew isolated in debriefing for another day or so, but the families have a right to talk to the press."

He paused, listening.

"We had to level with the families. We have to keep faith with our people or we lose our credibility with them."

After another pause, Navarre snarled, "The White House doesn't send submarines to sea. The navy does. We do. I do! The families had a right to be told what we know, so by God I told them! If the chief of staff and national security adviser don't like it, I'll clean out my desk anytime they want. I'm ready for the golf course. Tell those clowns that I can turn in my ID card and building pass and be on the first tee by five o'clock...."

He toyed with the cord of the instrument he held, then said, "We can't stop the families from talking to anyone on Earth. And we'd be fools to try."

The pause was longer this time.

"We'd look like flaming idiots, trying to hide ten pounds of shit under a cocktail glass."

He talked in monosyllables for another minute or so, then muttered, "Aye aye, sir," and tossed the phone on its cradle.

He glared at Jake Grafton. "The families are talking to the press. Some of them are on television. The White House is upset."

Jake showed him the letters from the president and General Le Beau. Navarre scanned them and handed them back.

Navarre's finger darted out, pointing at Jake's chest. "Stealing a submarine was an act of war. Yet the White House approved the theft of a Russian sub—that's the big secret that the politicians don't want anyone to know. Now the fucking Russians have done it to us. Sooner or later this is going to explode in the newspapers and television news shows. Hell, for all I know it's already on the Internet. Congress is going to crucify those silly sons of bitches at 1600 Pennsylvania Avenue."

"DeGarmo, the CIA director, said that the navy wanted the Russians' supercavitation technology."

"You bet your ass we did. We do. But the idea of stealing a Russian sub to get it didn't originate in this building, and that's a goddamn fact. I didn't know a thing about it until this morning. The idea was absolutely moronic. Those incompetent spook sons of bitches just got fourteen American sailors killed. Or sixteen."

"Sir, that's a hell of a stretch."

Navarre took a deep breath, then exhaled convulsively. "You're right. I withdraw that comment. But you've listened to me fulminate enough. What do you want to know?"

"You've answered most of my questions. Why was Flashlight on ten of the Tomahawks?"

"Because it's ready to go to sea and *America* was designed to launch it. That's our job: take the best technology we can devise to sea to defend our country."

"Was Flashlight always scheduled to go to sea on *America*?"

"Yep. We tested it on the operational evaluation workup. On this cruise we were going to launch two of the missiles on the Pacific missile range, ensure the software is bug-free and the warheads work as advertised. *America* was going to transit around Cape Horn submerged, shoot the missiles, then work an antisub exercise in the Caribbean on the way home."

"How many people knew Flashlight was on that boat?"

"Jesus, I don't know. The program is classified, of course, but the number of people who knew it would be on *America* would be in the hundreds. The people in the company that made the thing who weren't told it was being deployed could certainly make an educated guess. I would estimate that the number is a couple of thousand."

Jake had a few more questions, but the telephone rang and the admiral snatched it up, so he mouthed a thank-you and slipped out.

"Ship up there," Turchak said, tapping Vladimir Kolnikov on the shoulder. He had been watching Rothberg construct mission profiles for the Tomahawks, check the coordinates, the firing checklists. Fortunately, as they had been told, the targeting computer database was indeed universal; North America was in there so that missiles carrying dummy warheads could be shot at targets on stateside bombing ranges.

Kolnikov glanced at the horizontal tactical display, then checked the sonar displays on the bulkheads, which were essentially windows on the sea. With the sonar display enlarged as much as possible the screen was dark, gloomy, illuminated from within by a faint light, a light that signified the noise generated by a ship's propellers and machinery and the hiss of the hull cutting the swells. As he watched, the light assumed a faint shape, the hull of a ship as seen from underneath.

"It's about fifteen miles, bearing zero one zero relative." Only ten degrees off the starboard bow, the destroyer was almost dead ahead.

"What do you think?" Kolnikov asked Heinrich Eck, who was manning the primary sonar console.

"A destroyer with a towed array. He's got a helicopter dipping. I've heard it, but it's too far away to pick up. If we streamed our own towed array, we could triple the range of our system."

Kolnikov didn't want to stream the sonar array, a raft of hydrophones that could be towed along in the submarine's wake. The array would limit his speed. He looked at his watch. Hours yet.

No, the thing to do was turn north and get away from this destroyer, then come back to a westerly heading in a couple of hours. He gave the order to Turchak, who was at the helm.

"Do you think the Americans have heard us on SOSUS?" Turchak asked.

"No. I think they are just searching." Addressing Eck, Kolnikov asked, "Have you heard any patrol planes?"

"Two."

"Did either of them cross directly overhead?" He wasn't worried about sonobuoys but about the magnetic signature of the boat, which the magnetic anomaly detectors, MAD, in the patrol planes could pick up if they flew close enough overhead. Theoretically, under ideal conditions the MAD gear could detect a submarine as deep as three thousand feet, but that was theory. The practical limit, Kolnikov knew, was much less. And conditions were never ideal.

"No," Eck whispered, shaking his head. He was listening to the raw audio on his headset, verifying with trained ears what the computer was telling him.

"They are engaged in a random search pattern. They haven't heard us."

"Lidar?" The Russians and Americans were experimenting with

blue-green lasers mounted in aircraft to search shallow water for submarines. *America* had lidar detectors mounted on the sail and hull. Kolnikov didn't think the lasers could detect a sub at this depth, five hundred feet, but one never knew.

"Not a chirp."

The Russian skipper smoked a cigarette as he monitored the display, watched Rothberg, kept an eye on Turchak and Eck.

"Are we below the surface layer?" he asked Turchak.

"I don't know."

The bottom of the surface layer in the Atlantic should be between three and six hundred feet deep, depending on weather conditions. The surface layer was an area of relatively uniform temperature as the water was mixed by wave action. "Let's go deeper for a while. Go down to a thousand feet. Watch the water temp gauge."

"A thousand feet," Turchak echoed. "Aye aye, sir." He opened the appropriate flooding valves and eased the stick forward a trifle, letting the boat sink deeper as it took on more water. Passing 575 feet there was a temperature drop, which Turchak mentioned to Kolnikov.

The destroyer had almost faded from the display when Heydrich came into the control room. He glanced at the heading indicator.

"What are you doing?" Heydrich demanded. "Where are we going?"

Kolnikov swiveled the captain's stool until he was facing Heydrich. "There has been a change of plans," he said coldly. He removed his automatic from his trouser pocket and examined it. Heydrich stiffened a trifle.

The pistol's safety was on. The Russian captain held it up, clicked the safety off.

"A double cross! I should have known."

"No double cross," Kolnikov said. "Willi Schlegel will get exactly what he paid for. But we have plenty of time, so Turchak and I thought we would make some money in the interim. Hope you don't mind."

"How?"

"We are going to shoot Tomahawks at some targets we selected. Mr. Rothberg has kindly agreed to help. I explained that you wouldn't mind, that this small project wouldn't interfere with our main mission. So he agreed."

Heydrich didn't take his eyes off Kolnikov. "I cannot understand," he said conversationally, "why you haven't killed me."

"Don't tempt me. I'm very close."

"Perhaps you worry that the men are loyal to me, not you. The Germans know who supplied the money. They will do as I say. Even Eck, he works for me. Tell him, Eck."

Heinrich Eck's eyes widened and he sat up very straight. He looked from Heydrich to Kolnikov, then back again. "Don't get me in this. I do as I'm told. I just want to live to get paid, start out in a new life with a new passport and real money."

Kolnikov never took his eyes off Heydrich. "Willi Schlegel likes you," he said. "And Willi is paying the bills. Or some of the bills. Still, I do not think he would suffer unduly when this is over if I · tell him that you didn't make it. An accident at sea, perhaps. Or a tragic incident with a loaded weapon. Maybe I'll just tell him I killed you because I didn't enjoy looking at you. Schlegel understands the uncertainty of life. You might be the shit that is going to happen."

Heydrich eased himself into an empty chair in front of an unused console.

"Don't sit," Kolnikov said. "You aren't staying. The captain's cabin has a keyed lock on the door. You will stay there for a few days. There are books on seamanship and navigation for you to read. I'll feel better knowing you are there improving your mind."

As the two men were going down the passageway with Heydrich leading, the German shifted his weight, spun, and kicked with his right foot. Kolnikov had just enough warning. He grabbed the foot and pulled. Heydrich crashed to the deck. Two of the Germans heard the commotion and came running.

"Back to your stations," Kolnikov said, glancing at them. He had the pistol in his hand pointed at Heydrich. "Heydrich isn't hurt."

"What is this all about, Captain?"

"Later. Back to your stations."

They went. Kolnikov locked Heydrich in the captain's cabin and pocketed the key. He was under no illusions about the strength of the lock, which was designed merely to allow the American captain to ensure that his private papers remained private. If Heydrich wanted out of that cabin badly enough, he was coming out. But that, both men knew, would lead to a final showdown. And Heydrich needed Kolnikov. At least Kolnikov hoped he did.

When he got back to the control room, he sat down on the captain's stool and lit another cigarette. "Let's run through the launch sequence, Rothberg. Right up until we shoot the first missile."

Turchak put the boat on autopilot and came over to stand by Kolnikov. He whispered in his ear, "Why didn't you kill him?"

Kolnikov pretended that he didn't hear the question, and after a bit Turchak went off to the head.

At the end of the day, after everyone else had left, Zelda Hudson reviewed the E-mail messages Zip Vance had culled for her attention. Tonight there was quite a collection. These were classified, encrypted E-mails, messages sent from one department of the government to another, or to other persons within the department.

The government's new encryption protocol, developed by two Belgian software designers, was good, very good, but had several small flaws. Zelda's field was computer security, encryption standards, barriers to entry, trapdoors, backdoors, worms, etc. One of the foremost experts in the field, she had worked with the FBI, NSA, CIA, and Pentagon converting to the new protocol. And she had added on a few wrinkles of her own. In effect, she had developed wormholes that allowed her access to the U.S. government's deepest secrets.

Her colleagues here at Hudson Security Services were also experts, expert hackers, as she was when she was young. Her hacking had got her thrown out of her first college. She didn't get caught again but learned everything the universities could teach about the new science of computer systems.

Out of college she began consulting, applying her expertise for a fee. Soon she was swamped and began recruiting other hackers, people like herself who came to her attention when their hacking feats landed them in the news or in jail. When the furor died down or they were finally released from prison, she was there with a job offer that topped all others.

Of course, her company had been strictly legit for years and, as far as her employees knew, with the sole exception of Zip Vance, still was. The expertise of the hackers revealed the vulnerabilities of government and industry information systems, and she was in the perfect position to sell her services reducing those vulnerabilities. "Expensive and darn well worth it," was the phrase she used in her presentations to win contracts. So she had grown her business and her reputation, made millions, paid huge salaries . . . and one fine day discovered that it wasn't enough.

Tonight she left her monitor and walked through the loft, remembering. She checked the elevator; the last person to leave, Zipper, had left it in the down position. She pushed the button to bring it up, waited as it rose clanking and groaning, and when it reached the top floor, threw the switch to disable it.

There was a trapdoor under one of the tables, and coiled beside it, thirty feet of knotted rope. That was the only emergency exit in case of fire. Still, in her mind the risk of unauthorized entry was potentially more devastating.

She had earned a hundred million from the Europeans for putting the SuperAegis satellite in the water. If EuroSpace could ultimately recover it, the corporation would owe her another hundred million.

Her deal with Jouany was more complex, with incentives based on the exchange rate between the dollar and the euro. She thought again about the possibility Jouany would refuse to pay. Obviously, if he stiffed her she couldn't sue to collect. What she could do was prove to the world that he had been in a deal to devastate the American economy. A revelation like that would ruin him.

No doubt Jouany had thought of that. His best move to counter that possibility was to destroy this computer center. Which would work if this were the only computer center she had.

Tomorrow she would go to the backup location and have Zipper send her the updated critical files. She would back them up and hide the disks.

Oh, the irony. The CIA had named Kolnikov and his crew the Blackbeard team. Kolnikov! Now Jouany and Willi Schlegel, those two were *pirates*! Two of the blackest scoundrels God ever made, and both wore business suits, pontificated to the press, made flashy charitable donations, and took their wives to the opera.

And she was going to take huge piles of money from them!

CHAPTER SEVEN

Jake Grafton walked from the Pentagon to the SuperAegis liaison spaces on the eighth floor of a Crystal City office tower. He paid little attention to traffic or anything else—he had too much on his mind. Tom Krautkramer, the FBI agent, was waiting in his office with Toad Tarkington.

"I've been talking to General Alt, Admiral Stalnaker, and Vice-Admiral Navarre," he said. "I thought I might as well drop by and fill you in on what we have." Krautkramer looked as if he hadn't gotten any sleep last night.

"We've got a number of leads to check. We are working with the phone company to get the long-distance records for the telephones where these people stayed, we're talking to neighbors, going over the apartments with forensic teams, basically pulling out all the stops."

"Cut to the chase. What have you got right now?"

"A civilian technician who worked on the holographic simulator is missing, guy named Leon Rothberg. His supervisor says Rothberg has been asking for lots of unpaid time off—apparently his private life is a mess. The supervisor said that sometimes bill collectors call wanting to talk to him. Anyway, his landlord says he hasn't been around for several days." He produced a photo and passed it to Jake, who glanced at it and handed it back. "He may be one of the two men who wasn't on the Blackbeard team."

"This guy know the *America*'s system?"

"According to his supervisor, Rothberg was a computer Ph.D. candidate who dropped out of MIT before turning in his dissertation. We're checking that out. The supervisor says he is a certified genius who knows every line of software code in *America*."

"Bullshit," said Jake Grafton.

"I'm quoting the supervisor," Krautkramer replied.

"Sorry." Jake felt like a jerk. Krautkramer was probably as tired as he was.

"One of the missing Americans is a petty officer named Callahan. The general opinion of the others is that he is dead, but no one knows for a fact. Callahan could be alive and well and on that ship. He was a reactor specialist."

"The man who prevented the SCRAM."

"Perhaps," Krautkramer admitted. "It is possible. Callahan is or was in the midst of a nasty divorce and had a pregnant girlfriend. He was an above-average petty officer, but he may have been tempted. Or he may have been as honest as the day is long and killed by the hijackers because he didn't jump fast enough. We don't know."

"Okay."

"The leader of the Blackbeard team was Vladimir Kolnikov. Here is a copy of his file." The FBI special agent passed a red folder to Jake, who glanced through it. Most of this stuff he had already seen. "We're doing our best here and in Paris," Krautkramer continued, "to come up with more information on this guy, who his friends are, where and how he lived, what he drinks, what he reads, essentially the works. It's going to take a few days."

"Who knew him best in Connecticut?"

"The simulator training officer. He spent up to eight hours a day with him for several weeks."

"Let's fly him to Washington. I want to learn everything he knows about Kolnikov. Toad, see what you can do."

"Yes, sir."

"When you get more, Mr. Krautkramer, day or night, call me. Commander Tarkington will give you some phone numbers."

When the FBI man was gone, Jake said to Toad, "Okay. How is it going in the office today?"

"If anyone here knew that the submarine was going to be stolen,

I didn't get a hint of it," Toad said gloomily. "They've talked of nothing else today. The general assumption is that the sub will attack the Goddard launch platform with a Tomahawk."

"Ilin and the other spies?"

"The only time they've been outside is to go to lunch in the Crystal City mall. We went as a group. I stuck with Ilin like chewing gum on his shoe. He was not out of my sight. I even went to the men's room with him. We talked about submarines, baseball and football, politics, economics, the euro . . ." Toad shrugged.

"Any chance Ilin did a drop?" In other words, was Ilin given enough rope to leave something—anything—somewhere for a Russian courier to retrieve?

"The FBI had three agents watching us every second. They even bused the table after we left. I don't see how he could have. They had a video camera and directional mike aimed at us every minute. I felt like I was surrounded by the Secret Service, but they were so unobtrusive I don't think anyone else noticed."

"Bet they all did," Jake muttered and glanced at the stuff in his in-basket. "And tonight?"

"A covert surveillance team for each of them. The agent I talked to said there are fifty people involved. No one will tail these people, yet they will be under surveillance every minute. They've bugged their hotel rooms and installed video cameras in the lobbies, hallways, stairwells, and bars. The FBI has been damned busy. I don't know what priority you asked for, Admiral, but you got the highest one they have."

After the war room session that evening, the foreign liaison people would undoubtedly go straight to their embassies to report to their governments. And yet, why was Ilin wearing a mike in his belt? He could go to his embassy and talk face-to-face with his colleagues any time he wished. Was he dirty?

Waiting for Flap Le Beau to call was difficult. Jake thumbed unenthusiastically through the paper in his in-basket. He signed several letters that Toad placed before him, then stared out the window at the jets coming and going at Reagan National Airport. He was lost in thought when the intercom buzzed. The secretary said, "General Le Beau, sir."

"The White House bought it," Flap said. "The Joint Chiefs will be there. We'll get a complete briefing on the efforts being made to find *America*. If anyone asks a question that I think is out of line or not germane, I'll stop the show."

"Thank you, sir."

When Jake hung up, Toad dashed through the door. "Bring in the spies," the admiral told him.

He greeted them by name: Jadot, the Frenchman; Mayer, the German; and, of course, Barrington-Lee, English as strong tea. All of them had spent a large portion of their careers in military intelligence, as they freely admitted.

All except the Russian, Janos Ilin, tall, reserved, taciturn. He was a bureaucrat, according to his cover story, even though he made no pretense of knowing anything about missiles or defense systems. Jadot had asked him which directorate he worked for and had received a blank stare to reward his curiosity.

When everyone was seated, Jake brought them up to date on the stolen submarine. For the first time he told them the identities and nationalities of the thieves and the fact that they were being trained to operate a submarine with a minimum manning level.

"Trained by whom?" asked Barrington-Lee.

"The United States Navy."

"Guess you Yanks are really getting serious about shrinking your navy," Barrington-Lee commented when he realized Jake was not going to give an explanation for the team's training. "And then the blighters swiped your submarine. First you lose the killer satellite, now this. The press will eat you alive."

"Typical British understatement," Toad Tarkington remarked.

"So difficult to find honest people these days," Helmut Mayer said with a straight face.

"Certainly it is," agreed Maurice Jadot, who flashed a quick grin at Jake. "I am still waiting to meet my first one."

Jake continued with the briefing, detailing the salient facts as he had learned them that day. Jadot asked about *America*'s weapons load out. "A dozen Tomahawks and six torpedoes."

"What kind of warheads, please?" asked Mayer.

"All conventional. That is all I can tell you at this time."

Hyphen knew a thing or two about Tomahawk, which was a mainstay of the Royal Navy. "Certainly these people can't properly target this weapon, can they? Do the mission profiles and all that?"

"It would be extremely difficult. One suspects that they couldn't do it without help."

"Do they have help?"

"They might. Several Americans are missing and may be on the boat with these people. One of them is a simulator instructor, a software engineer, highly knowledgeable about the ship's systems. On the other hand, he might not be there. We just don't know yet."

"This missing engineer—does he know enough to program and fire the weapons?"

"According to the FBI, yes."

"It gets worser and worser," was Hyphen's benediction.

They sat silently for several seconds, thinking about that, trying to control their faces. Actually they did a good job of it—they were ready for the poker tables of Vegas, Jake thought ruefully.

Finally one of them, Mayer, asked the obvious question: "What is the United States doing to find this submarine?"

"Everything we can," Jake replied. "A briefing is scheduled for the Joint Chiefs of Staff in the Pentagon war room two hours from now. We are invited. I am sure all of you will be making reports to your governments about this matter, but I ask you to inform them firmly that the United States government does not want the information you learn here disclosed to the press."

"Speaking for myself, I can give you no guarantees on what my minister will choose to do," Barrington-Lee said. The others nodded their concurrence.

"I understand the realities of the situation," Jake replied. "All I ask is that you inform your governments of our wishes. The U.S. wants to keep a lid on the identities of the hijackers for a few more days."

On their way to the Pentagon, Toad Tarkington walked alongside the admiral. He spoke softly so that only his boss could hear. "It's the Frenchies. I got this feeling."

"Right."

"Everyone talks about the French, but no one does anything about them. After all, those people eat snails."

"A black mark against the whole race, I'll admit."

"Just wait. You'll see I'm right."

"There's been a change of plans," Kolnikov told his crew. He spoke loudly, so everyone could hear. With the exception of Heydrich, they were crowded into *America*'s control room and surrounding spaces. Kolnikov didn't want to use the ship's loudspeaker system for fear that the sound would be picked up by the American SOSUS system, a fear ingrained in him from his days at sea in the Soviet, then Russian, Navy.

"We are going to fire three Tomahawks tonight, probably three tomorrow night, then three the following night. After that we are going to lay low for a while, as planned."

The men were surly. They were submerged in a stolen American submarine, surrounded by technology they didn't understand, with the entire American navy hunting for them. And Kolnikov had shot Steinhoff and locked up Heydrich. Why they didn't know. They were frightened and Kolnikov could see it in their faces.

"Our primary mission has not changed," Vladimir Kolnikov said now, keeping his voice as matter-of-fact as possible. "All of you will still be paid the agreed amount. However, since we are launching nine Tomahawks, you will each be paid an additional one hundred thousand dollars American per weapon as compensation for the additional risk."

"What are the targets?" One of the East Germans asked that question.

"You are from?"

"Berlin."

"The targets are not in Berlin."

A chuckle swept the crowded compartment. The promise of more money was working on their misgivings. All of them could multiply by nine.

"What about Heydrich? Why is he locked up?"

"I do not trust him."

No one said anything to that. They looked at each other, at the overhead, at the large computer displays, the windows on the sea. Finally Boldt asked, "How long are you going to keep him locked up?"

"Until he learns to behave himself."

"I think you should tell us more," Steeckt said flatly. "You are asking us to risk our lives on faith and a bald, unsupported promise to be paid later. That isn't much."

"Precisely how much is your life worth, Steeckt? What were you going back to when this little adventure was suggested?"

"You should level with us," the East German insisted.

"What you do not know you cannot tell later. You will be paid. You have my guarantee. If you get money, do you care where it's been, eh? As long as it spends."

That remark seemed to break the tension. Some of them chuckled.

"Steinhoff died about an hour ago." Gordin spoke flatly, without inflection, as if he were reporting a temperature or depth reading.

"He pulled a pistol on me," Kolnikov explained. "I had to shoot him. Shipmates must trust each other and defer to their captain, who looks out for all of them. Steinhoff failed to do that. He thought his primary loyalty was to Heydrich, a great mistake, and made it him or me. Perhaps he thought Turchak could sail the sub without me." And Turchak could, probably. "Perhaps he realized how easy this submarine is to operate and thought he could handle it himself." That ridiculous remark drew several smiles. Kolnikov continued: "Perhaps Steinhoff hadn't thought that far ahead. Whatever. He made a very stupid mistake and paid the price."

"What shall we do with his corpse, Captain?"

"Wrap it in a sheet and put it in the cold-storage locker. We will dispose of it when the time comes. Not now."

When they had filed back to their stations, Turchak whispered to Kolnikov, "They are scared. They don't know what to think."

"In this day and age, who does?"

"Will they obey, do you think?"

"If the Americans leave us alone, we will be okay."

Yes, as long as everything went all right, they would be fine.

As he waited at Dulles Airport for his flight to London to board, Tommy Carmellini reread a copy of the letter of resignation from the CIA that he had submitted that afternoon. He went in to see his boss after he drafted his composition.

"I gather that your meeting with Watring went badly."

"He's a shit. What can I tell you?"

The supervisor frowned. His name was Pulzelli, and he was a bureaucrat to his fingertips. "I find the use of foul language at the office offensive," he intoned primly.

"Yes, sir," said Tommy Carmellini. After all, Pulzelli had recommended him for a performance bonus. "It just slipped out. Somehow that word seemed a perfect fit."

"He didn't think you were entitled to compensation for the invention?"

"He says the patent office screwed up and I'm a crook. Wouldn't approve it."

Pulzelli had sighed. He knew who and what Watring was and had made the recommendation on Carmellini's behalf anyway, which would no doubt cost him some grief in the near future. Carmellini felt sorry for the man.

"I've decided to resign," Carmellini said, handing Pulzelli his essay. As Pulzelli read it, Carmellini said, "I've given the standard two weeks' notice. It's time to get on with my life. I've done my time with the government. I want out."

"Do you have any plans?"

"I was thinking of the British crown jewels and maybe the czar's jewels in the Kremlin museum."

Although Pulzelli didn't often allow himself to smile, a hint of amusement crept across his features.

"I know what you're thinking," Carmellini said breezily. "You think I should start in the minor leagues, which is probably true. Perhaps I'll do some jewelry stores and museums as a warm-up."

"I'll pass your letter along. While you are still on the government payroll, however, less lucrative chores await. Here are your round-trip tickets to London and the itinerary." He glanced at his watch. "If you get a move on you can catch the van to Dulles."

Sitting now in the waiting area on the international concourse at Dulles Airport, Tommy Carmellini carefully folded the copy of the resignation letter and put it back in his attaché case. A ball game was playing on the television mounted high in a corner of the area, a scout troop was seated against a wall sharing music CDs and snacks, and two rows over a couple sat necking amid a group of dressed-for-success businessmen and -women who were studiously ignoring them. He automatically scanned the crowd to see if anyone was paying any attention to him. Apparently not.

He probably shouldn't have made that crack to Pulzelli about the British crown jewels or jewelry stores, he thought. He'll probably just laugh it off and forget it. Still, if and when, Pulzelli might remember and feel duty bound to call the police.

Oh, well. He couldn't take back the words. He would have to cross that bridge when he came to it.

In the Pentagon war room the overstuffed chairs of the Joint Chiefs were arranged in a semicircle facing a large multimedia screen that formed the wall of the room. A podium stood off to one side so it wouldn't obstruct the view of the screen. Jake's group of liaison officers seated themselves in empty chairs two rows back, behind a cadre of senior captains and one-, two-, and three-star flag officers. The briefing officer was at the podium consulting her notes when a staff officer called the room to attention and the four-stars walked in. As they dropped into their seats the chairman, General Alt of the army, grunted something and everyone sat back down.

The briefing officer, an army colonel, didn't waste time. Immediately a graphic of the North Atlantic appeared on the screen at the front of the room. "*America* has not been located," she said. "Here is a semicircle depicting where she might be if she had made good a twenty-knot speed of advance since she submerged alongside *John Paul Jones* sixty hours ago." The semicircle appeared, twelve hundred miles in diameter, centered near Martha's Vineyard. It covered a huge chunk of the North Atlantic. "And here is the ten-knot circle." That too appeared, in a different color, a fourth the size of the first one.

The briefer listed the U.S. Navy's available antisubmarine assets, including attack submarines, and showed their locations, whether or not they were ready for sea, how long it would be before they sailed. She discussed SOSUS arrays, P-3 patrol plane antisubmarine patrols, then national assets such as satellites with radar and infrared sensors, etc.

Finally the briefer showed the location of all known submarines of other nations, including two Russians. Seated beside Jake Grafton, Janos Ilin didn't turn a hair when his nation's submarines were pinpointed as if the coordinates had been published in the morning newspaper.

The Joint Chiefs interrupted the briefer to hold a discussion among themselves about a destroyer about to enter the Norfolk Naval Shipyard. Could the maintenance be postponed and the ship sent to sea to join a task group?

"Can the satellites see a mast if *America* sticks it up above the surface?" Flap Le Beau asked.

"Yes, sir. If a mast is run up with the submarine at speed in daylight, with no cloud cover."

"At night? Under a squall?"

"Yes and no, sir. Sea surveillance radars would be more likely to pick it up from space in real time."

"Stuffy, don't they have to stick that thing up occasionally to update the inertial?" General Alt asked that question.

"For ordinary navigation, no," Stalnaker replied. "A wise man would want an update before he launched Tomahawks, so he would run up the communications mast. An update might take from one to two minutes. Most of the time would be taken up with the system locating the satellites."

"If they do launch a Tomahawk, will we pick the missile up on radar as it comes out of the water?"

"Uh, no, sir. Not unless a task group is close."

"Airborne surface search? Will they see it?"

"Perhaps."

"A satellite?"

"Sir, it would depend on the sensor and the satellite location. Perhaps is the only possible answer."

"How long until we hear of it?"

"After a launch is detected, a few minutes, sir."

"Okay, with a Tomahawk in the air, flying toward the Goddard launch platform or Yankee Stadium, what are our options?"

The air force was not sanguine. Although Tomahawk was subsonic, it was small and flew low. It would be difficult to intercept and difficult to kill.

"We need to get some destroyers around the Goddard platform, with orders to shoot down anything incoming." The Joint Chiefs discussed that, how long it would take for three destroyers to get into position. Twenty-two hours, they were told.

"How about antimissile defense of Washington, New York, Philly? Can we get Patriot batteries into position to provide some protection?" The chairman asked that.

"Won't do any good," the army chief of staff said disgustedly. "Patriot can't engage a target that flies that low."

The four-stars discussed it. There was a PR issue here—the public needed to see the military doing *something*. It turned out that staff had already given the order. The first batteries around Washington would be in place within six hours. Everything available would be in position within twenty-four hours, but there weren't enough batteries to cover all possible approach directions. Staff was assessing where the batteries could be placed to have the greatest likelihood of intercepting.

And so the briefing went, detail by detail, for over an hour.

When it was over, Jake Grafton huddled with Flap Le Beau while Toad escorted the liaison officers back across the parking lot toward Crystal City.

After Jake had told Flap all he had learned since he had seen him last, he remarked, "I would still like to know why the *Paul Jones* was not authorized to sink *America* while she was still on the surface in Long Island Sound."

"That decision was reached at the White House, not here in the Pentagon."

"Were any of the Joint Chiefs there?"

"Not to my knowledge."

"Sir, I'd like to see the transcript. I know it will be classified to the hilt, but I would like to see it before Congress gets involved and lays their hot little hands on it. And that is going to happen. There is no way on earth that the White House can cork this volcano."

"You want to go look at that transcript this evening?"

"Yes, sir."

"I'll call over there, see what I can do. Keep me advised."

"Aye aye, sir."

The submarine rose slowly from the depths. Almost all of the small crew were in the control room, watching silently as Turchak conned the boat and Kolnikov walked back and forth, taking it all in. They were drinking coffee and the U.S. Navy's orange bug juice—Kool-Aid. They had earned the drinks—that afternoon ten of them had loaded all four of the torpedo tubes and run all the electronic checks to ensure that the weapons were ready. Just in case.

Now Eck was on the sonar, and Leon Rothberg, the American, was at the weapons control console. As usual, Boldt was at the main systems panel. Kolnikov was pacing and smoking, slowly and deliberately.

Eck had streamed the towed array over an hour ago to help clarify the sonar picture as the submarine rose through the thermal layers. The computer-derived pictures of the world on the other side of the steel bulkheads and ballast tanks mesmerized the crew, whose eyes were drawn to that hazy, indistinct horizon. If there were a ship out there, that is where it would be, at the sonar horizon or just beyond.

Kolnikov ignored the horizon. He looked below it, into the depths, trying to see into the constantly changing, swirling darkness. He was looking for submarines. If an American attack boat was hunting *America,* it would be hidden in the depths, listening.

Nothing. He saw nothing.

"Airplanes, Eck?"

"There is a jet running high and fading. Nothing close."

After dark, with the ship running at three knots and stabilized just below the surface, Turchak raised the electronic support measures (ESM) mast. The antennas on the mast were designed to detect radar energy across a wide spectrum of frequencies. Kolnikov and Turchak studied the signals detected by the ESM computer, looked at the relative strengths of the signals, warily eyed the computer's estimate of ranges. Nothing seemed close.

Kolnikov pulled down the ESM mast and ran up the com one. A receiver on this mast would update the global positioning system, or GPS, which would in turn update the ship's inertial navigation system, or SINS, and the inertial navigation systems in the Tomahawks waiting in their vertical launching tubes.

An accurate position was essential for firing the Tomahawk missiles, which lacked terminal homing guidance. As originally designed, the missile flew to a point in space guided by its onboard inertial system, which used terrain-following radar to provide updates from prominent landmarks on the missile's flight path. The latest versions of Tomahawk, which were carried in *America,* also used GPS to update the onboard inertial, if GPS signals were available, but still the missiles lacked terminal homing systems, which were in the research phase but had been delayed in the 1990s for budgetary reasons. While the missiles still could not be guided into perfect bull's-eyes, neither could they be jammed or defeated by decoys in the final stages of their flight.

Rothberg had spent hours at the universal targeting console planning the route of flight of each of the three missiles Kolnikov wished to launch, looking for prominent way points that the missile's sensors could detect and use to update the inertial. The seven-hundred-fifty-pound warheads of conventional high explosives would be totally wasted if the missiles missed their targets by more than fifty feet. Incredibly, the missiles usually flew to within ten feet of the designated aiming position, the target, after flights of up to one thousand nautical miles.

This level of accuracy was absolutely extraordinary, Kolnikov thought as he savored the smoke of his unfiltered Pall Mall cigarette. The quality control and precision manufacturing required to achieve those tolerances in a mass-production weapons system would never have been attempted in Russia. Only in America, he thought. Only there.

The sea and sky were empty in every direction.

"Have you got your GPS update?" Kolnikov growled at Turchak.

"Yes, sir." At least he sounded professional.

"Rothberg?"

"I am ready. Anytime."

"Depth of water?"

"About seventeen thousand feet, Captain," Turchak said.

"Eck, reel in the towed array. Report it stowed."

"Aye, Captain."

"We will launch our three missiles one at a time, one after another, expeditiously. Then we shall turn to a heading of one two zero magnetic and dive to fifteen hundred feet. We shall proceed at twelve knots on that course until just before dawn, when we will slow and rise so that we can raise the mast, receive some American commercial broadcasts. Any questions?"

"What if we encounter American antisubmarine forces? Will we defend ourselves?"

"We will evade. Any more questions?"

There were none.

"Let's run up the photonics mast for a quick squint, just for the fun of it."

The sensor head was raised above the surface of the sea for about ten seconds, just long enough for the visual light sensor to make one complete circuit of the horizon and the sky, then it was lowered.

Now Kolnikov and his crew began the leisurely study of the images projected by the computer on one of the bulkhead-mounted flat displays. They found themselves staring at what appeared to be a television picture of the ocean's surface. With the camera in low-light operating mode, the picture looked as if it were daylight above their heads. Boldt slowly rotated the image in a 360-degree circle, then tilted it so the control room watchers could see straight up. No stars visible under the overcast, Kolnikov noted, then told Boldt to again run the image by, only this time much slower. "Enhance it, let us see if there are any boats or ships on the horizon," he added.

Nothing. The surface of the sea was empty, just as Revelation said.

Thirty-five minutes passed before Eck reported the array in and stowed. During that time the men drank coffee, water, and the U.S. Navy's ubiquitous orange bug juice and whispered among themselves. The tension grew with each passing minute.

And was released when Kolnikov said, "Let us begin. Rothberg, the countdown checklist, if you please." He eyed the clock and the ship's position on the tactical display. The old technology in Tomahawk required that the time of flight to each navigation checkpoint on the route be programmed in before launch, which meant that the missiles had to be launched from precise prechosen locations, so the distance and time would work out properly.

As Rothberg worked the checklist aloud, Kolnikov told Turchak to slow one knot.

Fifteen minutes later the outer door of the first vertical launching tube selected was opened hydraulically. A cap over the missile kept the seawater from reaching it. Seconds later, the encapsulated missile was ejected from its launch tube in a welter of compressed air that generated a subsurface noise that could be heard for a thousand miles. As the missile reached the surface, the booster rocket fired. Seconds later, when the missile's velocity was well over a hundred knots, the turbojet engine lit off, and the first Tomahawk was on its way.

A minute later *America* launched a second missile, and a minute after that, a third. When all three birds were in the air, Kolnikov had Turchak turn the submarine to the 120-degree heading and began a descent. The power lever by the helmsman was full forward now, asking the engineering plant computer for full power. The submarine accelerated with surprising rapidity. When it reached fifteen hundred feet below the surface, Kolnikov would push the boat hard for a half hour to clear the area, then decelerate to twelve knots. He would like to go faster, but the Americans would be closing and he worried about the noise.

After he shooed the spectators from the control room, Kolnikov checked his watch, carefully scanned the sonar displays, then lit another cigarette.

The secure telephone rang in the Pentagon E-Ring office of the chief of naval operations, Admiral Stalnaker. Despite the hour, he was still there, working on a summary of the weekend's events that the president had requested. He picked up the telephone.

"Sir, Space Command reports that a satellite picked up the launch of a missile in the North Atlantic about one minute ago. Apparently a cruise missile."

"Where?"

"From the coordinates, the location appears to be about four hundred miles east of Ocean City, Maryland."

"What are our nearest assets?"

"A patrol plane can be over the area in fifteen minutes. We have an attack submarine two hours away and an ASW destroyer four hours away."

"Keep me advised."

"Aye aye, sir."

The telephone rang twice more, at two-minute intervals. After the third missile launching, the telephone stopped ringing, but Stalnaker couldn't concentrate on his writing. As he waited for the telephone to ring again he went to the window and looked at the lights of Washington glittering in the velvet night.

His days as CNO were numbered, Stalnaker reflected. Within a few days, a week or two at the most, the president would ask him to file retirement papers, and of course he would have to do it. A stolen submarine, missiles raining down on America . . . It was conceivable that a board of inquiry might someday say he was derelict in his duties. No wonder captains often elected to go down with their ships.

He shouldn't be thinking of himself and his career at a moment like this, but hell—he was only human. Damnation! That all those years of work and sweat and achievement should have to come to *this*!

The silence was oppressive.

Stuffy Stalnaker grabbed his hat and walked out of the office, headed for the war room.

Aboard *America,* Eck heard the throb of the P-3 Orion's engines as it approached the area and reported it to Kolnikov, who looked at his watch. Fourteen minutes had passed since the last missile was launched. Maybe the crew of the Orion saw the missiles come out of the water. Or a satellite did. Or maybe they were just flying by.

"Sonobuoy," Eck said when he heard the splash.

Okay, the patrol plane wasn't just flying by.

Kolnikov checked the tactical display. The computers displayed the sonobuoys, which went in on a general search pattern.

The sub was descending through twelve hundred feet, making twenty-two knots.

The patrol plane would put buoys in a circle around the launch site, hoping to pick up the sub as it went under one of them. Well, we will find out just how quiet this boat is, Kolnikov thought.

"All ahead one-third," he told Turchak, who adjusted the power lever.

"Level at fifteen hundred feet," Kolnikov added. "I want to motor straight out of the area. If they hear us they'll tell us all about it. Rothberg, be ready to launch decoys if they put a weapon in the water, but don't do anything until I tell you. They may drop something to panic us."

"Like a fake torpedo," Boldt suggested.

"That would panic me," said Turchak.

"No, it wouldn't," Kolnikov replied. "You're tough, like the steel of a Soviet hammer. All the men of the submarine forces are tough. Isn't that what the politicians always said?"

"Those assholes who had never even been out on a park pond in a rowboat?"

"Those are the ones," Kolnikov agreed.

The foreign liaison officers were gone when Jake got back to the office. Toad Tarkington was there, waiting for him.

"They went out of here like their underwear was on fire," Toad told him. "I think Ilin ran for the subway."

"I've got a car and driver waiting outside," the admiral told the commander. "The commandant has called the White House for me. They'll let us through the gate over there if we go now."

In the car on the way over, Jake didn't say anything of importance. The driver, a navy petty officer, didn't need to hear any of this.

At the White House the gate guard examined their ID cards and Pentagon building passes and waved them through. A military aide met them in the driveway and led them to a small office in the basement. The walls were painted government puke green. It could have been an office in the basement of any government building in the country. Fifteen minutes after they arrived, Jake was handed a classified transcript.

He signed the disclosure sheet and passed it to Toad, who also signed his name. The transcript was so highly classified that the aide sat in the room and watched them read it, to be sure they didn't make notes or steal pages.

Jake opened the file and began reading. It took him twenty minutes to read the entire transcript, which covered the events of Saturday morning, from the notification that intruders were boarding *America* until she submerged two hours and forty-one minutes later. When he finished he passed the transcript to Toad and sat lost in thought while Toad read the pages.

"What is Cowbell?" Toad asked when he finished the transcript.

"I don't know," Jake replied. He opened the transcript to a page he had dog-eared and read it again. After he had studied the page, he returned the transcript to its classified folder and handed it to the aide. He glanced at his watch. Nearly ten o'clock. God, what a long day!

When they were in the driveway behind the White House waiting for the navy sedan to be brought around, Toad said, "Admiral, it seems to me that the national security adviser recommended that the submarine not be destroyed because it had Cowbell and he thought we could find the thing later."

"Umm," Jake Grafton grunted.

"The fact that there were an unknown number of Americans still aboard was certainly a factor in the decision not to tell *Jones*'s skipper to shoot, but as I read that transcript, the critical factor was Cowbell. They thought they could find that boat anytime."

" 'Anytime.' He used that word, didn't he."

"Yes, sir."

"Well, Cowbell or no Cowbell, it seems to be lost now."

"Apparently," Toad said slowly.

"Oh, it's lost, all right. If the chairman of the Joint Chiefs, the chief of naval operations, and the commandant of the Marine Corps don't know where that pigboat is, believe me, nobody in uniform does."

"So what is Cowbell?"

"Beats the hell outta me."

"Whatever it is, it's probably so classified no one will tell us squat."

Toad stood silently for several seconds, letting the sound of the airplanes going into Reagan National wash over him, before he spoke again. "If they hadn't thought they could find that boat again, what do you think the president would have done? After all, he knew there were Americans still aboard."

"Would have been a hell of a dilemma. Sometimes all your options are bad."

"Ignoring Cowbell—because we have no idea what it is—if you had been on the hot seat and had to decide, you would have ordered *Jones*'s skipper to shoot, wouldn't you?"

Jake Grafton nodded. "Bad options and all, I thought that was what the president should have done. I wondered why he didn't."

The navy car pulled to a stop in the driveway, and Jake Grafton walked behind it to get in on the other side. That was when he heard a small jet engine running hard. The noise was higher pitched than the rumble of the airliners in the Reagan National Airport traffic pattern over the Potomac, which was the only reason he noticed it, because while the volume was increasing, it was not loud.

Instinctively Jake Grafton knew what it was. Without conscious thought he looked up into the darkness, although of course there was nothing there that he could see.

Now the pitch of the engine changed dramatically.

"Incoming!" he roared and threw himself forward onto the concrete of the driveway.

He heard a whoosh, then the concussion of an explosion rocked the car and pummeled his back. He felt heat.

As pieces of burning wood and a snowstorm of masonry and plaster and other debris cascaded down, Jake turned and looked. The air was filled with flying debris and dirt. Many of the lights in the building were out. Still, he could see that the missile had smashed into the topmost story of the White House, blowing out a huge hole and tearing off a major chunk of roof. An inferno of hot yellow fire burned in the hole now, so bright it was almost impossible to look at.

"Holy shit!" shouted Toad Tarkington.

The hot fire cast a flickering, ghastly light upon the lawn and the two naval officers, who were still crouched beside the car, frozen in place, staring at the shattered building. The guard by the door was on the ground, apparently unconscious. As pieces rained down, Jake glanced at the car. At least the glass of the windows was still intact.

"A Tomahawk!" Toad whispered in the silence that followed the blast.

"Quick," Jake said to the petty officer behind the wheel as a fire alarm began sounding. "Haul ass! Get that thing out of here before the fire trucks arrive. We'll meet you down the street. Step on it!"

As the car sped away, Jake stripped off his blouse and hat and tossed them on the grass. The guard by the door had a bump on his head—apparently he had been knocked down by the concussion and hit his head on the concrete.

Jake sat the man against the wall, then ran into the White House. Toad Tarkington was right behind.

CHAPTER EIGHT

Jake Grafton and Toad Tarkington met two dazed Secret Service agents inside the door.

"What the hell happened?" one of them shouted over the raucous blaring of the fire alarm.

"A missile hit the upper story and set it on fire," Jake replied. "Let's check if there is anyone up there injured."

He and Toad were running up the main staircase in the White House when a light flashed in the sky. Each man felt a transitory jolt of energy, as if he had inadvertently touched a hot spark plug just for an instant. Simultaneously, every light in the building went out and the siren died abruptly.

"What was that?" the first agent asked.

"Transformer somewhere blew out," the other one called. "Let's check for people." The words were barely out of his mouth when the dull boom of an explosion echoed faintly through the building.

"Flashlight!" Toad said bitterly. "Kolnikov fired a Tomahawk with a Flashlight warhead."

Flashlight was a highly classified warhead, an electromagnetic bomb, or explosive flux generator, mounted on the nose of a Tomahawk. When the warhead detonated a few hundred feet over a city, the explosion generated an intense electromagnetic current in the coil that surrounded the explosive. In the tenth of a microsecond before the explosion ripped the warhead apart, the energy wave was directed into an antenna and broadcast. A trillion watts of microwave energy raced away at the speed of light to fry every electronic circuit they hit, which was all of them. Electrical power switches, telephone switches, the chips in computers, cars, toys, calculators, servers... everything! In a fraction of an eyeblink, 150 years of technical progress were wiped out for several miles from the epicenter of the explosion.

As he ran up the staircase in the unnatural silence, Jake Grafton faintly heard the engines of an airplane moaning in the darkness. "Oh, my God!" he whispered.

Victor Pappas was the captain of an Airbus A-321 on final into Reagan National, flying past the Lincoln Memorial, right down the river, when the E-bomb detonated a few hundred yards from his right wingtip.

Everything in the cockpit went black. At first he thought he was flash blind, and he blinked mightily, trying to clear his eyes. He knew exactly what had happened—lightning!

Then he realized that the city below him was dark, coal black. Even the airport. Everything had disappeared!

"Jesus," he said into the mike at his lips, but it too was dead, without the usual feedback tone that told him it was working.

This is more than just a power failure!

He keyed the radio mike. No sound at all in his headset.

The moon was still there, the stars. He could see the reflection of the night sky on the Potomac, see the empty area that must be the airport....

To land without lights at a blacked-out airport is crazy! What has happened?

The copilot was shouting in his ear. Something about the generators. He reached for the emergency generator and deployed it, a little wind-powered device that popped up from a wing root into the slipstream. He had never in his career had to deploy one before now—only in the crazy emergencies of the simulator—but he had never before had a complete, total electrical failure. The entire glass cockpit was dead ... even the goddamn batteries had bit the big one.

But the emergency generator didn't pick up any of the load.

Holy . . . !

Time to add power, get the hell out of here, and figure this shit out over an airport with lights!

That decision made, he pushed the power levers forward and pulled back ever so slightly on the control yoke. And got the shock of a lifetime.

Nothing. No response.

This isn't happening! Not to me, not with 183 people on board! Please, God, not this!

He pushed the yoke forward a smidgen, reduced power. Nothing. The engines were still running—he would have felt it had he lost one—but the inputs to the controls had absolutely no effect.

Ten seconds had passed since the flash, no more than that.

A total power failure, he thought, one chance in a zillion and by damn it's happening! That flash must have been lightning—it must have fried everything in this plane! The computers are cooked. Lightning! The plane is fly-by-wire, with computers that move the flight controls, that regulate fuel flow to the engines, that—

The plane began a slow roll to the left. A few degrees a second. Victor Pappas felt the plane roll, saw the moon and night sky and barely visible river move. Without conscious thought he twisted on the yoke, turned it to the right and pulled back slightly, trying to counter the nose-down drift that instinct told him was coming.

Oh, Jesus, there it was, the nose was dropping . . . twenty degrees angle of bank, turning toward the Anacostia Naval Station . . . the nose dropping . . .

He slammed the throttles full forward. Nothing.

In slow motion the airliner continued to roll, the nose dropping toward the Earth. Behind him someone screamed.

Victor Pappas released the controls. One hundred and eighty-three people! He closed his eyes and began praying.

The airliner had reached ninety degrees of bank, thirty degrees nose down, when it slammed into the Earth.

At D.C. General Hospital, Dr. Apollo Ice had two patients on ventilators. One of them, an eighteen-year-old male, had been shot in the head earlier in the evening during a gang-related fracas outside a district bar. The other, a fourteen-year-old girl, had taken thirty sleeping tablets, all that remained in a bottle containing a prescription for her mother, after her first boyfriend told her she was ugly and he didn't want to be her boyfriend anymore.

Dr. Ice was in the ventilator room checking his patients when the power failed. He stood in the darkness waiting for the emergency generator to kick in. As the seconds passed, he counted.

When his count reached ten seconds he knew he had a decision to make. He didn't know why the emergency generator hadn't come on-line, supplying power—he didn't know that the switches in the circuit were fried—but he knew for an absolute fact that both his patients would die without air, which the machines had been providing.

The girl, he thought. The boy may have permanent brain damage.

He pulled the girl from the ventilator and began artificial respiration. He glanced at his watch. The liquid crystal display read 10:58.

He got into the rhythm, working slowly and steadily, trying for about twelve breaths a minute. After a bit the sweat began dripping off his nose.

Okay, people, let's get the goddamn emergency generator going here. The boy will die in minutes if we don't get juice to his machine. I can do this for only one person.

"Help!" he shouted. Maybe a nurse will hear. "Damn it all to hell, somebody come help me or we're going to lose this kid!"

How long had it been? The boy's brain would begin to die if he didn't receive some oxygen soon.

Apollo Ice looked at his watch. The display still read 10:58. He couldn't believe his eyes. Two or three minutes had passed, at least. He didn't know that the E-bomb's electromagnetic pulse had toasted the watch too.

"Help me," he shouted, unwilling to leave the girl. "Help me, for God's sake, somebody help me."

Moving carefully along the unfamiliar dark hallways, looking for people in the light of burning drapes and smoldering carpet, Jake Grafton found he had his cell phone in his hand. He jabbed the button to turn it on, waited for several seconds for the small display to light up. It didn't. The thing was dead as a rock.

Before his eyes a wall burst into flame. Unless the firefighters got on it quickly, the entire building would soon be involved. Missile warheads were designed to set aluminum and steel warships ablaze— the effect of a direct hit on a large building with a high wood content by a warhead containing 750 pounds of high explosive was awe-inspiring.

Satisfied that he could do nothing here without protective clothing and breathing apparatus, Jake found a window with the glass blown out and leaned out to get some fresh air. Behind him were the sounds of flame consuming everything it could reach, yet over that he could hear another airplane.

When the dull boom of the explosion from the crash of an airliner several miles away reached him, Jake Grafton left the window and made his way along the hallway, opening doors and searching for victims. He shouted over the noise of the fire, the rush of air, and crackling as dry wall and plaster and wood and steel burst into flame.

"Anyone here? Sing out!"

He was coughing when he found someone, a man in civilian clothes on the floor of one room. He heard the groan and found him by feel. Something had fallen from the wall or mantel and knocked the man unconscious. He was coming to now, but Jake grabbed him by the armpits and dragged him off. If they stayed here without protective clothing or breathing apparatus, they were both going to be victims.

Out on the lawn he found other people who had somehow made their way from the building, the entire top story of which was now ablaze. He pulled the man across the drive and put him under a tree, well away from the building. The man was breathing, with a regular heartbeat, when Jake left him.

Jake walked directly away from the burning mansion, toward the Mall. The Washington Monument should have been prominently visible, lit by floodlights, the city alive with lights and the streets with cars, even at this hour. But not a single gleam of light was visible beyond the garish light from the fire behind him. The noise of the fire was the only relief from the silence. There were no fire sirens, no fire trucks, no police sirens, no traffic noise of any kind.

Several of the people behind him were sobbing. He could see shadowy figures running across the driveway and lawn near the south entrance to the building . . . and from here and there, shouts, calls, curses . . .

Jake heard another airplane, the engines howling. It swept over, apparently descending toward the river. It too crashed in a welter of fire and light, a glow that lit the horizon beyond the trees and buildings. Somewhere near Arlington National Cemetery, Jake thought.

Then he heard that unmistakable sound, a small turbojet engine traveling low and very fast, probably about five hundred knots.

"Another Tomahawk," Toad said in a hoarse whisper. He came up behind Jake.

The missile seemed to cross from left to right, from east to west, directly over the Washington Monument or very near to it. It literally flew down the Mall, over the Capitol, over the Washington Monument, and over the Lincoln Memorial. And that route made sense. All three of those huge man-made objects would make excellent points for position updates as the missile began its final run-in to its target.

"Where is it going?" Toad muttered, speaking more to himself than to his boss.

"West," Jake Grafton replied.

The stench and smoke brought him back to the here and now.

In the darkness the fire in the White House continued to burn. The fire had taken most of the upper stories on this side now. There were people in the driveways flaking out hoses, cursing about water pressure, issuing orders. But of fire trucks, he saw not a one.

"The whole thing is going to go," Jake said under his breath.

Although he waited and waited, he heard no more Tomahawks.

Crossing the Capital Beltway westbound, the last Tomahawk fired that evening from USS *America* pitched up into a climb. Then it nosed over into its final dive.

The E-warhead in the nose of the missile detonated fifty feet above the roof of the main America On-Line technical facility in Reston, Virginia.

The terawatt of energy just five hundred picoseconds long generated by that warhead burned out every computer chip and switch in all of AOL's servers, routers, and computer banks, one of the largest collections of computer equipment on the planet. Fortunately much of the telephone network that fed this massive complex was fiber optic and unaffected by the energy jolt that passed through it. However, the miles of copper telephone wiring that led to and from the fiber-optic system acted like giant antennas, soaking up energy and frying every electronic switch for miles, switches that had not been zapped by the first E-warhead explosion over the Pentagon.

This warhead effectively destroyed a huge chunk of bandwidth throughout the world. The Internet wasn't dead, but it was severely crippled.

All over Washington, Metro trains coasted to a stop as electrical power ceased to flow. Even if power could have been quickly restored, the computers that directed the operation of the trains were toast. Elevators froze in whatever position they were in, trapping people by the hundreds; escalators stopped; the computers at banks, airlines, travel agencies, and in every hotel in the downtown area died instantly. Hotel doors that were controlled by computer chips could not be unlocked, preventing people from getting into hotel rooms. Every motor vehicle or ignition key that contained a computer chip was inoperable. Radio and television stations were turned off in midsyllable.

In five hundred trillionths of a second the heart of this major city of more than four million people had been reduced to an artifact, unable to sustain human life. Reston was similarly affected. All refrigerators, stoves, ovens, and food storage and preparation machinery, all public and private transportation, all electronic communications devices, all automatic teller machinery were kaput—everything.

From the White House, Jake Grafton and Toad Tarkington walked south on Fifteenth Street, across the Mall, toward the Fourteenth Street Bridge that spanned the Potomac. People were rushing in the other direction, toward the flaming White House, which was lighting up the dark city like a bonfire.

The rising moon was just bright enough to reveal the Washington Monument, which stood like a giant Stonehenge megalith against the darker night sky. Off to the south the fire in the wreckage of the Airbus that crashed at Anacostia was dying as the last of the jet fuel was consumed.

An old man stopped them on the Fourteenth Street Bridge. He got in front of them, forced them to stop and address him. Only then did he see their uniforms and looked relieved.

"It's my wife. She needs help. Won't you help me, please?"

The woman was sitting in the passenger seat of the nearest car, staring fixedly at nothing at all. Jake took her wrist, felt for her pulse. There was none.

"She's having a heart attack, I think," the old man said. He was so nervous he trembled. The night wind ruffled his white hair. "Her defibrillator went off. There was this explosion right above us—right over our heads—and the car stopped dead. The engine just quit all of a sudden. Like bang! And she grabbed her chest. The damned defibrillator just whacked the hell out of her for a while, then it stopped."

"How long ago was this?"

"Oh . . . when the lights went off. I've been talking to her, but she hasn't replied."

"She's dead."

"Dead?"

"Her heart has stopped." Jake replaced the woman's wrist in her lap and closed her eyes. "The defibrillator isn't working. She's gone."

"Dead?" His eyes widened. "My God, she can't be—"

"This happened what? An hour ago? Hour and a quarter?"

Despite himself, the old man nodded affirmatively. "What happened?" he demanded. "What went wrong?"

Jake Grafton didn't know what to say.

The old man thought about it, looked at the dark, silent city, letting it really sink in. Finally he said, "A plane crashed over there." He pointed at Anacostia. "Big plane. Rolled over and dove into the ground. Boom. Just like that . . . I was telling my wife about it. You can still see some of the flames. No one fought the fire or rescued the people. Anyone who survived the crash and couldn't get away from the plane on his own hook was left to die. It's like no one cares."

"Maybe no one could get there," Jake Grafton said gently, trying to calm the man.

"Our car just up and quit on us. Like everybody else's. They all quit at once. Our Taurus never did that before.... We live in Bethesda and decided to drive down a while ago to see the city at night. Now ... the lights in the city are off. All of them. My wife's dead. That plane crashed. It's like the world is coming to an end."

"Yes."

"This is America," the man said, grasping Jake fiercely by the arm. "America!"

"Yes," Jake Grafton said again. He used his left hand to gently pry the man's hand away from his arm, grasped and shook it.

Then Jake and Toad walked on across the bridge.

Callie was at the apartment in Rosslyn, across the river from Georgetown. He wondered if she was okay. There was no way to get in touch with her, of course, unless he walked home. Like the old man, he studied the dark, dead city. At least during the nineteenth century the people of Washington had lanterns, candles, and horses, then gaslight.

He stopped in the middle of the bridge and watched the dying flames from what must be the wreckage of the plane that crashed in Anacostia. Unlike gasoline engines in automobiles, which require an ignition pulse for every piston power stroke, jet engines are continuously on fire, so the electromagnetic pulse of the E-bomb warhead would not cause a flameout. It would play havoc with the fly-by-wire flight controls, however, and all the computers that control the airplane's other functions, for example, those that regulate fuel flow. The pilots of the sophisticated modern airliners, Jake Grafton knew, must have lost all control. In a way the vulnerability of the airplanes was a horrible irony: The more modern the jet airplane, the more computers were incorporated into the design to increase the efficiency and maintainability, the more vulnerable the design was to electromagnetic-pulse weapons.

There was a fire in Arlington National Cemetery and another south of the Pentagon. Both, Jake suspected, were crashed airplanes.

Kolnikov. The missing American, Leon Rothberg ... they had done this. Presumably for money.

"Money," Jake whispered to himself as he contemplated the dim reflections in the dark water. Or perhaps something else.

Toad broke into his musings. "Wait until the reporters find out the CIA trained those sons of bitches to steal a Russian sub,"

Tarkington said. "Tomorrow morning, I figure. It'll be a feeding frenzy. They're going to rip the president a new asshole."

Jake merely grunted. He was thinking of Callie. He wanted to go home, see her, hold her in his arms. He wasn't going to do that, though, not with that submarine out there. The pirates had fired two Flashlight warheads and had eight more in the launching tubes. And one more conventional explosive warhead—enough to create a great deal of havoc. No, he needed to go to the Pentagon.

Yet try as he might, he couldn't keep his mind on the submarine. As he walked through the darkness of a city under siege, he found himself thinking of his wife.

There were four of them, all Germans. Steeckt seemed to be the unofficial spokesman. Kolnikov was eating when they came into the control room and lined up in front of him. Two hours had passed since the missiles had been launched. They had hit their targets or crashed. The submarine was at fifteen hundred feet, so he wouldn't know until he could once again raise the communications mast and listen to a commercial radio station. That wouldn't be for hours. There were ships up there, and planes. Until then . . .

"We want to know what is going on, Captain. Why did you launch those missiles?"

"We are being paid. I explained all that." Boldt, he noticed, turned away from his console to look at him.

"You launched one of those missiles at the White House." It was a statement, not a question. Of course Rothberg had whispered to them.

"That is correct." Kolnikov finished scraping his plate with a spoon and laid it on the maneuvering monitor. He turned to face them squarely and looked from face to face. Two of them lowered their eyes.

"You are goading the tiger. We did not bargain for this."

"You think they did not look for this boat after we stole it? That they weren't looking before we fired the missiles? They could not look with more fervor if we threatened to destroy the entire planet. The entire American navy is hunting us."

"But we tell them where we are when we launch a Tomahawk,"

Müller explained. "The satellites see us. We are not somewhere buried deep in the great wide ocean, hopelessly hidden. We are right there, in that one little finite place, right where those missiles leap from the water. Right, precisely, there! And we must run and hide all over again."

Kolnikov nodded.

"How many times can we get away with it, I ask you?"

"Twice more, I think."

"We think once was more than enough. Dead men don't spend money. That is an inarguable fact."

"People who don't take chances don't have money to spend," Kolnikov replied sourly. "I'll try to keep us alive. You have my word on it."

"Do you care if we live or die?" Steeckt asked.

Kolnikov was suddenly at full alert. "We? You four?" he asked softly. "Or just you and me? Precisely what is it you are asking, Steeckt?"

"Who gave you the right to risk our lives? We didn't vote or anything. We don't know what you agreed to."

"You men agreed to sail with me. I told you that it would be dangerous, that all of us might die. I offered you a chance to make some serious money. Every mother's son of you freely agreed to sail with me. You asked to go, worried that the chance would be denied you. Now you stand here whining about the risks. Let there be no mistake, no fuzzy thinking, no sea lawyer talk in the engine room: The lives of all of us—you, me, Turchak there, all of us—are on the line. We are betting everything. We did that Saturday morning when we killed the tugboat crew. We did it again when we fired the first shot at the American sailors on this vessel. And there is no going back. We cannot wipe out a jot of it even if we wanted to. We are totally, completely, absolutely committed. We—all of us. Every swinging dick."

Vladimir Kolnikov paused a moment to let his words sink in while he checked the depth gauge and the compass. Then he continued: "I do not want to see any of you in the control room again unless you obtain my permission before you set foot through the hatchway. This is a ship of war and I am the captain. Those are my rules. Now get back to your duty stations."

Once they determined that there was no electrical power in the Washington metropolitan area, the television professionals quickly solved the problem. Generator trucks were driven into the city from Philadelphia and Baltimore, and broadcasts were sent via satellite elsewhere for rebroadcast.

As Toad had predicted, by the following morning the fact that a CIA crew trained by the U.S. Navy had stolen *America* and photographs of the still-smoking ruins of the White House were playing all over the planet. Thirty minutes after the crew story broke, the president's staff, operating out of the Old Executive Office Building, confirmed that two Tomahawks armed with electromagnetic warheads had exploded over the Washington area. They refused to confirm the exact locations of the warhead detonations, citing military secrecy, but the press had a field day with maps and experts who narrowed the possibilities down to a few blocks.

As Toad also had predicted, the reporters were in a savage mood. So was the Congress, if the statements of random senators and representatives that were aired were an accurate sample. Accusations and recriminations were tossed back and forth like live hand grenades. Hearings and investigations were promised.

This circus played on television to the rest of the nation; the people in Washington were without power, so they didn't hear it. Within several miles of the trillion-watt supernovas, even battery-operated devices had been rendered inoperative. Since newspapers couldn't be composed or printed, Washingtonians didn't read about the attack either.

The Pentagon was a small oasis of civilization inside the devastated E-bomb desert. During the Cold War the Pentagon's electrical system had been hardened to protect it against the electromagnetic pulse of nuclear detonations. Now emergency generators were supplying power for lights. The telephone system worked within the building, and communications with U.S. military units worldwide were unaffected. However, the personal computers and noncritical mainframes in the building had arrived after the end of the Cold War; no one had thought it critical to harden them—no one wanted to beg for the money from a parsimonious Congress—so they were junk.

The Joint Chiefs were again meeting in the war room when Jake Grafton found Captain Sonny Killbuck at his desk in the outer office of the submarine commander, Vice-Admiral Val Navarre. They were the only two people in the office. "No one else could get in this morning," Killbuck said. "I live far enough south that I could get my car started but decided today would be the traffic day from hell, so I rode my bicycle in."

"How far out do you live?"

"Fifteen miles, sir. Great morning for a ride, but not under these circumstances."

"Yeah," Jake said and pulled a chair around. "Tell me what you know about Cowbell."

"Cowbell?" His voice dropped to a whisper. It was instinct, Jake thought. "Sir, even the code name is so highly classified that it can't be mentioned outside of a secure space."

"In light of the special circumstances, I think we're safe," Jake said dryly. "Cowbell."

"Admiral, that program is very tightly held. Very. Less than two dozen people in the world know about it. As it happens, I am one of the two dozen. I don't think you are, sir."

"I read about Cowbell in the National Security Council transcript of this past Saturday morning," Jake Grafton replied, "when the council was reacting to the theft of *America*. Regardless of how highly classified this program is, when Congress gets their hands on that transcript, there are going to be a lot more than two dozen people in the know. I'll take the responsibility for any security violation today if you'll answer my question. What is Cowbell?"

Killbuck automatically glanced around at the empty room, then said in a low voice, "It's a beacon. We put one on every submarine after we lost *Scorpion*. The beacons can be triggered by a coded transmission from the submarine communication system."

"And once activated, the beacon transmits?"

"That's right. Transmits acoustically. Then it's a simple matter of homing in on the transmission to find our submarine."

A homing beacon! If the Russians ever found out ... This was the ultimate secret, the knowledge of which would profoundly alter the rules of the game.

"Unbelievable," he whispered.

"Cowbell wasn't a navy idea," Sonny Killbuck said bitterly. "The risks are incalculable. The politicians didn't want any more lost submarines."

Jake Grafton ran a hand through his hair as he considered the implications. If the upper echelons knew where the submarine was, why hadn't they sunk it? What in the world is going on here? After he had taken two deep breaths, he asked, "So where is *America* now?"

"That's just it, sir. The president didn't order *America* sunk after she was hijacked because he was told we could find her anytime. We should have been able to, but we can't. We're transmitting, and her Cowbell isn't answering."

The worker bees at Hudson Security Services were glued to the television monitors, in awe of the breaking story. Zelda Hudson and Zipper Vance watched their reactions. If they knew that anyone there had anything to do with the Washington attack, they never let on. Of course, Zelda knew they didn't know, so she didn't pay much attention. Vance was not as sure, so at one point she called him over to her desk and told him to quit watching everyone else.

As bad as the attack on Washington was, the workers' bitterest reactions were directed at the White House, which approved the Blackbeard operation, and the navy, which trained the perfidious bastards. The secretary, Zelda's only nontechnical employee, summed up the mood best. "Who the hell do they think they are, training people to steal submarines? Why, that submarine could blow up the whole East Coast, kill millions of innocent people. My God, people have a right to know!" After stating this opinion, she looked up at the ceiling, almost as if she expected a missile to come crashing through.

So Kolnikov had pulled it off. Zelda was never sure if he would really do it. When she had told him what she wanted, he had just sat staring at her. "You're crazy," he said finally. "We can't get away with it."

"Why not?"

When he didn't reply, she said, "You think the United States Navy is going to look more diligently because you launched missiles?"

"No," he admitted. He didn't think that. After a bit he asked, "Why?"

"For thirty million dollars."

"For you? Or me?"

"You. I'll make a lot more."

Kolnikov laughed then. "You should have been a Russian. You would have fit right in. The people at the very top are stealing the foreign aid, the money the IMF sends, washing it and accumulating vast fortunes and putting those fortunes in their pockets. Communism was nice, with all that crap about everyone being in the same boat, but it didn't make them rich. Now they are getting rich."

"They're trying to catch up all at once."

"Yes," he said.

"So. Will you do it?"

"You don't know what you are asking. Rothberg will be the only man who could program the missiles. They aren't like a rifle, just aim and shoot. It's a bit more complicated."

She resented being talked down to, but she bit her tongue.

"No promises," Kolnikov said finally.

"Thirty million. You can split it up among the crew any way you like."

"Willi Schlegel is not going to like this. The man in Paris wanted a satellite."

"I'll handle Willi."

"If you succeed, you'll be the very first. Rumor has it that three or four others who tried are dead. No one ever found the bodies."

"Willi Schlegel wants something very badly. As long as he thinks he has a chance to get it, he'll behave."

Kolnikov refused to promise anything. He wouldn't even say he would try.

But the missiles flew.

As the CNN talking heads went through the Washington disaster one more time, Zelda thought about Kolnikov. He was hard to fathom. A Russian, willing to fight and risk death in that steel coffin. For money, of course. Dead men can't spend money, though.

Ah, who knew what drove him? Doubtlessly he didn't understand her either.

She was sitting at her desk, staring blankly at the computer screen, when she realized that she had an encrypted message. She called it up, verified the encryption protocol, then decoded it: "An explanation is in order. Missiles were not part of our agreement. Willi."

She took a deep breath, then typed her reply: "Kolnikov obviously has his own agenda. Let's hope he hasn't forgotten ours."

She stared at the message, weighed it, then encrypted it. She got up, walked to the refrigerator and took out a Diet Coke. Sipping it, half listening to the CNN broadcast and the comments of her angry, frightened colleagues, she walked back to her computer and fired the message to Willi into cyberspace.

When General Le Beau made it in to work, Jake was waiting in his outer office.

Flap motioned with his hand that Jake was to follow him into the office. He told Flap about Cowbell, but the marine didn't seem too interested. "I've got to go to a Joint Chiefs meeting in a few minutes that General Alt called. This fucking submarine..." He dropped into a chair. "Gonna be a helluva day, any way you cut it. What can we do to make tomorrow better?"

"Induce a four-mile error in the global positioning system," Jake Grafton replied. GPS, as they well knew, allowed anyone on Earth with a little black box to receive signals broadcast by a small constellation of satellites and thereby fix their position within several meters. The satellites' signals, however, could be tweaked, subtly altered, thereby fooling the little black boxes.

Flap looked startled. "I hadn't thought of that."

"An accurate position is essential to launching a successful Tomahawk attack. The pirates will use the GPS to update their inertial. Let's lead them down the primrose path."

"And mislead every airliner and ship in the world?"

"The stakes are high, General," Jake acknowledged. "Real high."

"Why not just shut the system down?"

"Then they will update their inertial position with a star sight. If the GPS works, there is a good chance that these guys will merely push the update button without checking to see how much the inertial position disagrees with the GPS position. That's an easy mistake to make, and this equipment is new to all these guys. They're feeling their way along."

"What if an airliner full of people goes into a mountain?"

"That's the risk," Jake acknowledged.

"Jesus, you are a hard-ass."

"Sir, I've been told that more than four hundred people died here in Washington last night. They were killed. Murdered. It's time to take the gloves off. If the pirates put a four-mile error into their inertial, their Tomahawks will miss their targets. The latest versions of the missiles will self-destruct or dive into the ground when the computer determines that the missile is lost. Sometimes we must risk lives to save lives."

"You are assuming they will shoot more missiles."

"These guys didn't steal a submarine just to wreck the Lincoln Bedroom."

"I'll suggest it," Flap Le Beau said. "The decision will have to be made by the president. Just between you and me, I don't think the folks at the White House have the cojones for a move like that."

In London, Tommy Carmellini awakened from a nap to find the American media circus on most of the channels of his television. He watched the White House burn, horrified and fascinated at the same time.

He left the tube on while he showered and shaved, dressed, hung up his clothes in the closet, checked the attaché case the CIA man who met him at the airport had handed him when he dropped Tommy at the hotel. After looking over the contents of the case very carefully, he closed and locked it.

He turned off the television only when dusk had fallen and he was ready to go find something to eat. He took the attaché case with him.

At ten o'clock he walked two blocks to a pub. He ordered a cider and was sipping it in a booth against the back wall, making it last, when the door opened and Terrell McSweeney walked in. He saw Tommy, ordered a pint, then brought it over to the booth.

"Good to see you," McSweeney said. "What's it been, three months?"

"Something like that."

"Seen any television today?"

"A little, before I left the hotel."

"Holy damn. Sounds as if somebody declared war on the guys in the white hats. They shot the shit outta Washington last night. A stolen submarine, no less. Beats the hell outta me what the world is coming to."

McSweeney was CIA, of course, attached to the London embassy. He was over fifty, balding, porking up, with a braying voice. If the Brits didn't know he was a spook they were complete, utter incompetents.

"Maybe terrorists, you think?" Carmellini asked.

"Iraqis, I bet. Before it's over we'll find Saddam had his eye glued to the periscope."

"I always wondered, McSweeney. Tell me, do the Brits know you're a spook?"

McSweeney snorted. "Of course they know. I go to conferences with them all the time. When they want something from us, they call me. Every Brit spook has me on his Rolodex."

"Umm."

"I know, you're thinking that maybe we should have had a covert officer contact you. Well, hell, I know what the book says, but this is the real world. I mean, who in the hell are we fooling anyway."

"I saw the barkeep give you the high sign when you came in. You ever use this pub before?"

"I have a pint here a couple times a week, sure."

"You're a real horse's ass, McSweeney, a professional joke. I've half a mind to walk out that door and grab the next plane back to the States."

"Don't give me any of your shit, Carmellini. I'm in charge in London. Me! This is my turf."

"You're compromising *me,* asshole!"

"Hell, we're only doing burglary tonight, not espionage."

"That's a relief. I was so worried! But if I get caught and charged with anything, I'm taking you down with me. I'll squeal like a stuck pig. I'll even make stuff up."

"I've got immunity, man, and three years to go to retirement. Tell 'em any goddamn thing you want."

Tommy Carmellini rubbed his forehead. Why, Lord, why?

"Every other guy in the company is some kind of asshole," he said to McSweeney. "Does this work appeal only to assholes, or did working for the company turn you into one? Has there ever been a study on that?"

"They got you, didn't they?"

Carmellini drained his cider and slid out of the booth. He reached for the attaché case. "I'll be outside when you get finished swilling that beer. Take your time. I don't want to talk to you any more than absolutely necessary."

"Fuck you."

"Thanks, but I've been fucked before."

"And a good job they did of it, too."

Working with idiots, he thought. They have me working with flaming idiots. It's been like that on and off since the day I got into this outfit. Oh sure, there are a few good people, and every now and then you find a gold nugget in a pile of dirt.

Almost an hour passed before Terrell McSweeney came strolling from the pub. From the smell of him, he had had a couple more beers. "I thought the bobbies would get you out here for soliciting." He led the way to his car, which he unlocked with a button on his key ring.

Once they were in, McSweeney said, "Let's cut the friendly crap and get serious here. The target is the computers of the Antoine Jouany firm. Washington wants to know how big this guy is betting against the dollar and who is behind him. Anything you can get that answers that question will be appreciated. Get it and get outta there. And use one of those E-grenades in the attaché case on the security computer."

"I got a brief in Washington."

"I don't know why they always say Jouany's betting against the dollar," McSweeney continued. "What he's really doing is betting on the euro. He probably just thinks euros are gonna pop. I do. Stuff ain't cheap over here, but Europe is jumping. Euros got nowhere to go but up. France and Germany aren't going in the crapper."

"Thank you, Chairman Greensweeney."

"I'll just find a spot to park this buggy and wait for you."

"This an embassy car?"

"Yeah."

"Why don't you get a couple of those magnetic signs for the doors that say CIA in big bold letters? Or maybe a logo, an eye peeping through a keyhole?"

"We already got a bumper sticker."

Jake Grafton didn't expect to find anyone in the liaison offices in the Crystal City Tower, across the parking lot and street from the Pentagon. Many of the commuters had driven in from the suburbs—a trek from hell, avoiding disabled vehicles—only to find that without electrical power or telephone service, nothing could be accomplished in the inner city. Jake went to the office to change clothes and think about the entire situation before he walked home. Toad had already set out for his house, worried about his son and the nanny. Jake hadn't heard from Callie—without telephones he was not going to— and he was exhausted and anxious to go home and sleep. Still, he thought he should check the office.

It wasn't empty. He found two secretaries and a staff officer in the warm, stuffy spaces. No one else. They were debating emptying the refrigerator of leftover lunches before things started to rot. Blevins, they said, hadn't been in.

In the closet of his office Jake kept a jogging outfit. It was cleaner than his uniform, which he had worn for two days and a night. He put it on, yet was so tired he had to sit to tie the laces on the tennis shoes. He didn't know if he had the energy to jog the three miles home.

He was trying to work up energy to get started when the door opened and Helmut Mayer walked in. "Are you still here, Admiral? I was expecting no one."

"Getting ready to run home."

"I will drive you, if you wish. A friend in the suburbs brought me a car earlier today."

Jake was genuinely grateful. He put his feet up on the desk and talked over the situation with the German. While they were talking Janos Ilin arrived. He too had a car. "I am a believer now," Ilin said. "You must have a car in America. Everyone."

The foreigners were full of news. Power in Washington would take at least ten days to restore, the telephone system perhaps a week, the men reported. Their embassies had hardened electrical systems and emergency generators, so they had been listening to the cable news networks.

"The networks have learned the name of the pirate captain who stole your submarine," Ilin said, making a steeple of his fingers. "Vladimir Kolnikov." He said it in the Russian way. "The reporters are besieging our embassy, wanting to know whatever it is we know about him, which is of course nothing at all."

"Did your government know that Kolnikov was being trained by the CIA?" Jake Grafton asked conversationally.

"So the story is true?" Ilin replied.

"Today we deal only in the truth, the whole truth, and nothing but. You knew that before the news broke, didn't you?"

"Ah, Jake, you overestimate the capabilities of my government. Once we were very capable, there is no argument about that, but now, with the political situation such as it is and the destitute condition of the government, we are not so capable."

"What a storyteller you are, Ilin," Mayer said in his flavorful Germanic English.

"So answer me a question," Ilin continued, looking at Grafton and ignoring Mayer. "Did the CIA really intend to steal a Russian submarine, or is that only a tale for the children's hour?"

"Is that what the television dudes say?"

"Yes."

Jake Grafton spread his hands and shrugged. "I don't go to meetings at that level. I have heard a rumor to that effect. I cannot swear to its veracity."

Ilin went to the window and looked out. There were other cars on the street now, almost as many as they usually were, and most of the disabled vehicles had been pushed up onto the sidewalks or towed. "There are many accidents at intersections," he told the two men behind him. "Americans need traffic lights."

"Let us call it a day, gentlemen," Jake said. "Herr Mayer, I will accept your kind offer of a ride home. But before we go, let me leave you two with something to think about. May I do that?"

Mayer and Ilin nodded.

"The White House was the target of a guided missile last night, with our head of state in residence. The Secret Service hustled him and his family out of the building, so they weren't hurt, although at least two people were killed by the fire. Several airliners crashed, killing all aboard, and people died all over the city when pacemakers and defibrillators and hospital equipment were knocked out.

"Gentlemen, the attack on this city last night resulted in at least four hundred deaths at last count. Four hundred twenty-nine was the last number I heard. That attack could well be construed as an act of terrorism. Or war! Perhaps both. The blood of innocent people is on the hands of the people behind this attack and cannot be washed off. Prophet that I am, I foretell a bad end for the people responsible for last night's atrocities. They will pay the ultimate price."

Neither man said anything.

Jake continued: "A threshold has been crossed. There is no going back. Regardless of what the politicians say later, the public will demand that those responsible pay in blood."

"I will pass your views to my government," Ilin said.

"You do that," Jake Grafton shot back. "I don't make American policy, but you can take it to the bank: When the identity of the culprits is known, the pressure on the politicians for revenge will be irresistible."

"I hope no government is behind this attack," Mayer said. "That would be a great tragedy."

"Indeed it would," Jake said. "Indeed it would."

The guard in the lobby of the Jouany building in the old City of London had been bought, according to the Langley briefer. Just say the magic words and he'll let you by and forget you ever existed.

Carmellini had winced when he heard that. After a suspected security breach, the lobby guard was the very first person an investigator would question. Any decent investigator would wire the guard to a lie detector. And giving a guard a wad of cash before the entry . . . of course the guy was going to spend it and attract attention. It was almost as if the agency didn't care if Carmellini got caught.

Two weeks. Then he would bid this silly band of paper-pushing bozos good-bye and be off to bigger and better things. If he wasn't in jail somewhere awaiting trial.

The guard was reading a newspaper when he walked in. There was a security camera behind him aimed across the desk at Carmellini, another above the arch over the elevator, and a third above the door where he had entered.

Carmellini nodded at the guard and spoke: "Someone told me you are a fan of American baseball."

"I like the Yankees," the guard replied as he looked Carmellini over.

"I'm a Braves fan myself," the American said. He noted that the monitor behind the desk was automatically cycling from one camera to another every ten seconds. No doubt there was a recorder somewhere, probably in the basement security office, capturing this gripping drama on videotape.

"The bank of elevators on the left. Ninth floor."

"Thanks."

"All the bigwigs are on the trading floor tonight," the guard added, but Carmellini just waved a hand as he headed for the elevator.

No cops eyeing him from behind the potted palms, no wailing sirens . . . just the cameras catching my handsome criminal mug on videotape, he thought bitterly. I'm going to spend the next ten years eating macs and cheese off a plastic tray.

He pushed the button to call the elevator and tried to look slightly bored.

The ninth floor was the upper balcony level. The eighth floor was the lower balcony. The seventh floor, just visible through the floor-to-ceiling bulletproof glass that shielded the offices from the elevator waiting area, was the trading floor, the pit. Amid the computer workstations two floors below, Carmellini could see a crowd of people—at least a dozen—staring at screens, talking animatedly, sipping drinks. The people in the pit traded currencies and currency futures around the clock worldwide, according to the Langley briefer. None of the traders seemed to pay any attention to him standing here at this entrance. They were engrossed in their business.

Hot night tonight, Carmellini thought, with the mess in Washington. The dollar was probably getting hammered worldwide.

The security station that controlled the heavy glass door was on the wall at his left. Two security cameras were in the corners, one aimed at the elevator door, the other at the security station. As Carmellini approached the wall-mounted unit, he took two objects from his pocket and glanced at them. A left and a right. They looked like marbles.

The security panel had a slot about six inches across and three inches high in the face of it, about belt high. Left or right hand? Sarah was right-handed, so he put his right hand into the slot. A light illuminated inside the device. He held his hand very still as the scanner read the fingerprints chemically embedded on the flexible plastic sleeves that covered his fingers and thumb. He had sleeves on the fingers of his left hand too, just in case.

A message appeared on the liquid crystal display at eye level. "Step closer please."

Right eye, he thought, and used his left hand to hold up the marble labeled "R" about four inches in front of the scanner. He held it as still as he could.

Three seconds passed, four . . .

"Thank you, Ms. Houston," flashed on the LCD display, and the main door unlocked with an audible click.

Carmellini went through the doors, then checked his watch. 1:12 A.M. local time.

Her workstation was in an office halfway along the balcony on the south side of the building, about as far away from a corner office as one could get, Carmellini noted wryly. She had a lot of corporate ladder left to climb.

There was a small finger scanner beside her computer. He used his right forefinger. After a few seconds her computer screen hummed and came to life.

Now all he had to do was type in her password and get to work. Alas, no one at Langley knew her password. Neither did Tommy Carmellini.

He sat staring at the blinking computer prompt, flexing his plastic-encased fingertips, reviewing everything he knew about Sarah Houston one more time. He had been dreading this moment for days, and now it was here. He had, he thought, no more than three bites of the apple before the computer would lock him out. Then his only option would be to disassemble the main computer and steal the hard drive.

On the flight across the Atlantic he had decided on the three keywords he would try, but now, at the moment of truth in front of her computer, his confidence deserted him.

He looked around her desk, at the photo of her parents and the cup full of pencils and pens. He opened the desk drawers, glanced at the contents, stirred the nail file and photos and paper clips and candy bar wrappers around with one finger while he thought it through again. Four of the photos were of Houston and a man, sort of a smarmy guy, Carmellini thought.

He had gone through the items in her purse very carefully when she had been lying drugged in the bed of the New York apartment. What had been in there? Think!

He flexed his fingers carefully, then typed "houston" and hit the Enter key.

No. He was still at the password prompt.

So, what could it be? This was a woman who wrote her four-digit bank PIN numbers on the envelopes that held the ATM cards. A telephone number?

He typed "houston020474." Her birthday.

No.

Okay, Carmellini, you clever lad. Last chance. He bit his lip.

"houston090602." Today's date.

Yes. The computer brought up the menu.

Tommy Carmellini found he had been holding his breath. He exhaled explosively.

CHAPTER NINE

"Oh, Jake, I've been so worried." Callie hugged him fiercely when he walked through the door into the candlelit apartment. He held on and hugged her back.

Finally she led him onto the balcony. "I made soup on the barbecue grill. Can I warm up some for you?"

"Sounds great."

"Tell me, was it the submarine that did this?" She waved a hand at the dark city.

"Yes."

"But I thought they didn't have nuclear weapons."

"They didn't need them. They have ten Tomahawk cruise missiles carrying electromagnetic warheads, called Flashlights. We think two of them exploded over Washington and knocked out the power. A Tomahawk with an explosive warhead hit the White House."

As she lit the grill, he explained how the warheads worked. "The warhead is basically a flux generator. A coil is wrapped around a metallic tube full of explosives, and an electrical current is run through the coil, creating a magnetic field. The explosion is more of a fast burn than a one-time boom; as the explosive burns, it creates a pressure wave that flares out the tube holding it and pushes the tube into the coil, which creates a short circuit that diverts the current into the undamaged coil that remains. As the explosion progresses, the magnetic field is violently squeezed into a smaller and smaller volume, which is the coil ahead of the explosion. This creates a huge rise in the current in the remaining coil. Just before the warhead destroys itself, the current flows into an antenna, which radiates the pulse outward. The whole process takes about a tenth of a millisecond and pumps out about a trillion watts of power from a seven-hundred-and-fifty-pound warhead."

"A trillion watts!"

"Yep. Fries switches and blows transformers and generally obliterates computers and telephone systems."

"Why did they shoot these things at Washington?"

"Guesses are two for a quarter. I don't think anyone in government knows for a fact."

As he ate his soup by the light of four candles, she asked, "So what is going to happen next?"

"I don't know."

"Have you any idea where the boat is?"

"Oh, yes." He gestured to the east. "Out there somewhere."

"Isn't this the new superstealth submarine?"

"That's right. *America.*"

"What if the navy can't find it? What then?"

Jake Grafton finished the last spoonful of his soup. "I've been thinking about that. The fact is that we probably won't find the sub. Let's see if we can come up with some ideas." He studied her face in the candlelight. "Those guys can't stay submerged forever. True, they might be suicide commandos, but that's extremely doubtful. Russians and Germans rarely indulge in that kind of thing."

"They have a plan," Callie murmured.

"Yeah," Jake Grafton said. "And they've bet their lives that we can't figure it out."

His CIA superiors had sent Tommy Carmellini to London because a certain key network of the Antoine Jouany firm was completely shielded from the Internet. Without outside or dial-up access even the best code breakers could not read the information contained on the databases of these machines, which were at the very heart of the Jouany operation. Carmellini's task was to find the software that prevented Internet access and disable it, then type in certain keywords that allowed CIA researchers to access the network database. Or to steal the hard drives.

Once he was on-line, the job took about five minutes, and because he was naturally curious, Tommy Carmellini lingered to examine the information that the CIA wanted to see. The menu listed dozens of files, mostly lists of names of investors, their addresses, and the amount of their account. Files setting forth how much money each fund was worth—well, they were mutual funds, weren't they—and files that accounted for the trading activity, profit and loss of every trade, in each fund. No doubt a competent researcher could quickly learn everything there was to know about Antoine Jouany and Company from studying these files.

Carmellini went to the window, looked down onto the trading floor. The dozen people had swelled to twice that number. They were laughing and drinking champagne. The silver lining of America's black cloud was being celebrated.

Carmellini returned to the computer. Numbers, names, addresses, was that everything?

He was flipping through the files, looking at names, when one leaped at him. Avery Edmond DeGarmo. The director of the CIA?

He stopped scrolling rapidly and began reading every name. Floyd Hoover Stalnaker? Wasn't he the chief of naval operations?

Jacob L. Grafton?

Now wait a minute. Tommy Carmellini stopped scrolling and stared at the screen. The problem was that he knew Jake Grafton. If his Jake Grafton was this Jacob L. Grafton. Had helped him rescue his wife in Hong Kong. Had spent almost a month running errands for him when he was named consul general in Hong Kong.

Grafton's account was worth . . . $3,489,922? As of the close of business yesterday?

What is going on? Rear Admiral Jake Grafton?

Carmellini dashed to the window, looked again at the crowd on the trading floor. Having a party down there.

He went back to the computer screen.

Jesus, this is pure bullshit. They sent me all the way to London to . . .

He rubbed his head, tried to get his thoughts in order.

Wow, had he been lucky or what? Houston and today's date.

Slowly he worked his way through the layers of dialogue boxes to get out of the program and shut the computer down. When the screen was dark and the machine off, he placed his right forefinger in the reader and booted it up again.

He paused to scratch his head, then eased over to the window for another look.

Shitty security . . . DeGarmo hated his guts . . . he hated the CIA . . . and here he was.

He typed "Houston" and hit the Enter key.

No.

Typed "Houston" and hit the Enter key again.

No.

Did it a third time and pushed Enter.

Voilà! There was the menu.

Oooh boy!

He escaped out. Shut down the machine while he tried to think.

Booted it up a third time. This time he typed "xxxxx" and hit Enter. The first and second time the computer refused to take it. The third time he was admitted to the inner sanctum. The menu appeared.

Someone had set him up, made absolutely certain that he could get in. Carmellini the computer whiz. Yeah.

He turned off the machine and checked the trading floor one last time. One of the men had apparently had too much champagne and was asleep under a computer stand.

He eased the door shut behind him, made sure it latched, and went looking for the emergency exit. The stairs. Required by the building code, the stairs were always the weak point in the security system.

The door into the stairwell was unlocked, of course, although there was a switch on the door that was undoubtedly wired up to the security desk in the lobby. And, perhaps, in the security office.

Carmellini went down the stairs two at a time.

The door to the lobby was probably unlocked—as required by the fire code—but Carmellini didn't open it. He continued down one flight to the upper level of the basement. The stairwell continued on down to loading docks and various levels of underground parking.

The door out of the stairwell was locked. Carmellini set to work with his set of picks. Again, an alarm might sound at the lobby security desk, but . . .

It took about thirty seconds to find the right way to open the lock, then Carmellini pulled the door toward him and entered the hallway. Sure enough, there was the door marked "Security." Presumably the main security computer was in there.

No fancy high-tech lock on the door, just one for a key. Carmellini was in in two minutes flat.

The computer was on and running, with banks of monitors showing the views from various cameras. All this was apparently being recorded digitally on the computer's hard drive.

Carmellini sat down at the keyboard. He used the icon to find the list of persons who worked for the Jouany firm and scrolled to find Sarah Houston's name. He liked her, thought maybe he might take the time after he left the agency to really get to know her. What he would really like to ask her was why her computer let any Tom, Dick, or Harry in on the third attempt. Let's see . . . Houston, Houston, Houston. Her name wasn't there.

Wasn't there?

But he had gotten in using her finger and eyeprints. No, no one by that name on the list.

So who was the woman he had taken to bed?

He glanced at his watch. McSweeney was outside, and he had said not to waste time.

Tommy Carmellini closed his eyes for a second, trying to sort things out.

No time for that now.

From his pocket he produced an E-grenade, one of his own manufacture. His E-grenade was constructed entirely of explosive and superfast primer cord that he had hardened so that it had the consistency of smooth plastic. All of it would be consumed, leaving only a residue for the forensic experts. He looked the computer over, found the place he wanted, pulled the pin on the grenade and twisted the cap. With the thing armed, he laid it gingerly on the table beside the computer and walked from the room. He was outside the room when he felt the jolt of energy produced by the explosion. So much for the security computer's hard drive.

On his way out of the building he flapped his hand at the lobby guard, who was working with the controls of his television monitor, trying to bring the thing back to life. McSweeney was parked seventy-five feet from the entrance, with the car pointed away from the Jouany building. Carmellini got a glimpse of the man's head behind the wheel.

He walked away in the other direction.

That evening in America the footage was played over and over on every news channel as the chattering class offered running commentaries. The public mood, if the media coverage was any indication, was becoming increasingly shrill. The one thing the chatterers could agree upon, however, was that the administration had made a severe mistake concealing the identity of the hijackers from the public. "They tried to suppress it," were the words commonly used to describe the government's misguided attempt to keep the secret. An administration spokesperson explained that since the stolen warship carried no nuclear weapons and nothing was known of the motives of the crew, a disclosure of a canceled CIA operation would not have been in the public or national interest.

In any event, the existence of Operation Blackbeard was a secret no longer. Every sentient person on the planet had an excellent opportunity to learn of it by late that evening. And every person with a telephone had an opportunity to comment on the news on the endless local, regional, and national radio talk shows. Many were doing just that.

With or without nuclear weapons, the power of the submarine pirates to cause havoc was beyond dispute. Power company executives predicted that it would take ten days to two weeks to restore electrical service in the heart of the capital and in Reston. The damage to the telephone network was still being assessed, but the one fact all the engineers agreed on was that massive banks of switching units were damaged beyond repair. Computer equipment that had been subject to the electromagnetic pulses of the E-warheads was also junk and would have to be replaced. The immobilized vehicles that littered Washington and Reston were being towed away for repair, which would take weeks, perhaps months, due to the sheer numbers that had been damaged.

The government declared a state of emergency and announced that it would use the army to feed the populace of the affected area, which had no way to prepare or store food. Mobile generators were flown in from all over America to provide emergency power to hospitals and police radios. People who needed urgent medical treatment were being flown from the affected area by military helicopters.

All of this was expensive inconvenience salted with occasional personal tragedies, such as the folks wearing defibrillators and pacemakers who went into cardiac arrest or died when the warheads detonated. However, the crashes of the two airliners and two business jets on their way into Reagan National gave the incident a horrifying, visceral dimension. In an age when air travel was an unavoidable, unenjoyed part of life, the specter of being a passenger in a doomed airliner plummeting to earth out of control gave most people the cold sweats. The FAA quickly canceled airline service in the danger area, which the bureaucrats decreed was anywhere east of the Mississippi River. Aircraft on emergency missions or not carrying paying passengers for hire and private aircraft could fly—at their own risk, the bureaucrats said—but few did. Cautious CEOs called their attorneys, who told the executives bluntly that they could not afford to pay the judgments that would be rendered against them if they ignored the FAA's warning and lives were subsequently lost.

When Kolnikov brought *America* up from the depths well after dark and raised the communications mast, he picked up a few of those commercial radio broadcasts and soon had the gist of it. The first Tomahawk, the one with the conventional warhead, had struck the White House. The other two had played havoc with the Washington, D.C., electrical system, inconveniencing millions and killing 439 persons, at last count.

After updating the GPS, Kolnikov lowered the mast. Rothberg was eyeing him. Kolnikov nodded matter-of-factly. "Three hits," he said.

"I told you they were good birds," Leon asserted, jutting out his chin.

"Get busy on the next three."

"When do you propose to launch them?"

"I don't know. I'll have to think about that."

"What should I use as the starting position?"

Kolnikov thought before he answered. He studied the tactical presentation on the horizontally mounted display, looked at the map of the North Atlantic, took the time to rub his eyes. He had slept for three hours this afternoon, but he was still tired.

Finally he made a small mark on the chart and showed it to Rothberg. "Here. That position is as good as any. Just leave the time open."

The sea seemed noisy this evening. Kolnikov had Eck deploy the towed array so he could see and hear better. When it was out he listened to the computer enhancement of the raw audio and watched the presentations on the big wall screens. "Let's go back down to five hundred feet, below the surface layer," he told Turchak, who was back from his bunk and the head.

At one point Kolnikov thought he heard pinging, or echo ranging, but the sound was from a long way away, very attenuated. On the screen the noise was converted to light, of course, but the flashes were so dim he wasn't sure they were really there. The computer, which could discern a pattern that the ear could not hear or the eye detect, verified the sound and gave a bearing.

They are looking, he thought. They are looking hard.

Well, let them look. We are safely hidden below the thermal layer and too quiet for the SOSUS. As long as we don't have a close encounter with an American *Seawolf* submarine, all will be well.

Jake Grafton had just taken a cold-water shower and lain down on his couch when he heard someone knocking on the apartment door. He was wearing jeans and a sweatshirt, so he answered it.

A marine corporal was standing there. "Admiral Grafton? General Le Beau sends his compliments, sir, and asks if you would accompany me back to the Pentagon."

"Are you on a horse?"

"No, sir. The marines at Quantico sent every vehicle on the base."

"Give me five minutes to get on a clean uniform. Come on in."

Callie talked to the corporal while Jake dressed. Of course the young marine stood tongue-tied, unable to think up a single comment in the rarefied air of a flag officer's powerless apartment. He was from Tennessee, was a fan of the Titans, thought the marines were a lot of fun, a comment that drew a grin from Jake Grafton in the next room.

As Jake puckered up to kiss his wife, she handed him a handful of candles.

"Use these to put a little light on the subject."

"Very funny," he said. "Ha, ha, and ha." But he took the candles. He kissed her and followed the corporal out the door.

In the Pentagon war room, Sonny Killbuck and Vice-Admiral Val Navarre were the center of attention. The Joint Chiefs were in their usual chairs and tossing questions. Behind them sat the senior members of the staff. The session had just started, apparently, Jake thought as he dropped into an empty chair in back.

Sonny was in the front of the room holding a pointer, using it on the map that was projected on the screen. He pointed out where the U.S. Navy submarines and antisubmarine patrols were located. Now he overlaid the patrol plane tracks on the screen. The navy had indeed been busy. Still, none of the searchers had found *America*.

Space Command was on full alert, watching for cruise missile launches in the North Atlantic, the air force had AWACS planes aloft, looking for incoming missiles, and fighters on five-minute alert all along the Atlantic seaboard, ready to attempt to intercept incoming cruise missiles. Two carriers were at sea, using their aircraft to search areas that the antisubmarine patrol planes were not covering. There was no doubt—the United States military was exerting itself to the maximum. Everything that could be done was being done.

When Sonny finished his canned brief, the Joint Chiefs began discussing the military's worldwide response to the new defense condition set a few hours ago by the president, DEFCON ONE, war alert. The senior officers of the Joint Staff fielded questions as fast as they were tossed. Some of them made notes.

No one mentioned Cowbell.

Or the fact the *America*'s Cowbell wasn't working. Was that an unfortunate coincidence, or did Kolnikov and company know about Cowbell and disable it? And if they knew, where did they acquire the knowledge?

Well, Jake Grafton thought, Cowbell was history. If he had not already done so, the CNO would have to order that all the Cowbell beacons be disabled and removed from the submarines they were installed on. To do otherwise was to risk the entire submarine force, all of them, in the event of war. Or, Jake thought, in the event that the submarines are *America*'s primary target now.

What if *America* was hunting them?

When the brief was over Sonny came back and sat down beside Jake Grafton.

"I have a question for you." Jake spoke so softly Sonny had to tilt his head to catch the words. "Can *America* detect a Cowbell beacon?"

Surprised, Killbuck glanced furtively around to see who was listening, then eyed the admiral. "Yes, sir," he acknowledged. "All our submarines can detect the beacons. It would be a high-pitched noise, very loud."

"Have you tried to trigger *America*'s beacon?"

"Yes, sir."

"Why isn't it working?"

"I don't know, sir. It could be a software problem. Or a problem with the transmitter. Or the satellite."

"Or it could be," Jake Grafton said, "that someone somewhere told Kolnikov about the beacon and he disabled it. We'd better find out which it is. The answer to that question might be the key that opens a lot of doors. Has the FBI been briefed about Cowbell?"

Killbuck squirmed in his seat. "Not to the best of my knowledge."

"Hadn't we better find out?"

"Sir, you are trespassing on Vice-Admiral Navarre's turf."

"Like hell!" Jake Grafton snarled. "That stolen submarine is *my* turf, shipmate. We've got subs manned by American sailors at sea right now with those beacons on board. And the news may be out! Worry about *that*, mister!"

Killbuck looked ill. "You're right, sir. I apologize."

"When the crowd clears out, let's talk to the heavies. The FBI needs to be told about this, and now."

Flap Le Beau listened to Jake without comment, without a question. He glanced at Sonny Killbuck, who tried to keep his stomach from flip-flopping. A tip-top secret, and he had spilled it to Jake Grafton in violation of every reg in the book. And General Le Beau didn't even ask Grafton where he got his information! He merely crooked a finger at Stuffy Stalnaker and said, "We've got a big problem."

After Stuffy listened to Jake's explanation again, he said, "I wondered why those clowns at the White House didn't order that thing sunk. I guess Cowbell just slipped my mind."

When Jake looked mildly surprised, Admiral Stalnaker added, "The politicians demanded Cowbell years ago and we installed it. And promptly forgot about it. Captain," he said, addressing Sonny Killbuck, "if Cowbell isn't working we certainly need to know why.

Let's get the FBI working on this. Then have the system disabled in every sub we have as soon as possible. Draft an Op Immediate message for my signature. The course of human events seems to have handed us an excellent rationale to rid ourselves of this albatross. Let's take advantage of this gift from heaven."

The chairman of the Joint Chiefs, General Alt, nodded his concurrence. He had tossed out his share of questions this evening, but as he had listened to Jake explain Cowbell earlier, he had seemed in a pensive mood. No doubt, Jake thought, he is as horrified by this mess as everyone else. More so, probably. It happened on his watch, and the ax is probably already falling.

Jake looked around the room at the four-stars there. The chairman, CNO, Navarre—those three at least would get the chop. And soon.

He was under no illusions: If the submarine wasn't found soon, Flap Le Beau was going to soon be playing golf every day. With Jake Grafton.

Vladimir Kolnikov was eating a piece of apple pie and drinking a cup of excellent coffee in the submarine's control room when the faintest flicker of light caught his eye on the big sonar displays. He froze in midbite, staring at the display . . . and saw nothing. Kolnikov swallowed the last bite of pie and put down the dish.

As he sipped coffee he glanced from display to display. Nothing seemed out of the ordinary. And yet . . .

There. He saw it again. A momentary flash. He picked it up from the corner of his eye. Yes, he could pick up the flash with his peripheral vision, yet when he looked straight at the screen he saw nothing.

Now he checked the computer display of the tactical situation.

"Eck."

The German was drinking coffee and munching a roll. He came over to where Kolnikov was sitting, his cup in his hand.

"Out of the corner of your eye, watch the display. No, look at me. Just be aware of the display."

"A flash," he said. "I see it."

"What is it?"

Eck went to work on the computer, his coffee forgotten.

"It's a sound from within the boat," he said after a bit.

"Internal?"

"Yes. A knocking, sounds like to me. Listen." He put the sound that he had distilled from the hydrophones onto the loudspeaker.

Now Kolnikov heard it, an irregular clicking. Something metallic.

"Okay, Eck. Go find out what in the hell that is and let's get it fixed. Start back aft."

Eck went, striding purposefully.

Kolnikov sipped coffee as he listened to the sound on the sonar speaker. Finally he turned off the speaker, the net effect of which was to magnify the sound for transmission away from the submarine. He wondered how close the nearest SOSUS hydrophone was.

He finished his coffee, forcing himself to sip slowly and leisurely for Turchak's benefit, because he was watching.

"You are a fake, you know," Turchak said finally. "You are going to break that cup if you squeeze it any harder."

"Go aft with Eck, will you, Turchak? Check on him. Tell me about that noise."

Turchak touched Kolnikov's arm lightly, then nodded and went.

Twenty minutes passed before Turchak returned. He was wiping oil or grease from his hands on a rag, which he disposed of in the trash. "I think a bearing has gone out in an oil recirculation pump. It's clicking irregularly."

Vladimir Kolnikov took a deep breath. He waited for Turchak to continue.

"I recommend that we go dead in the water and repair the bearing."

"The towed array is out," Kolnikov objected. The array was trailing along twenty-five hundred feet behind the sub. If the sub went dead in the water, the array would slowly sink until it was hanging straight down at the end of its cable. Automatically Kolnikov glanced at the tactical display to check the depth of the water. More than ten thousand feet.

"Reel it in. Then we'll go DIW."

Kolnikov unconsciously tapped a finger on the tactical display. "Any idea how long this will take?"

"I looked at the bolts in the housing. Perhaps three or four hours if we have a replacement on board. They're checking that now. But it could be longer."

"Okay," Kolnikov said. He shrugged. The good news was that the submarine would generate almost no noise as it lay drifting fifteen hundred feet below the surface. Working on the machinery would cause some noise, of course, but not much, and anyway, there was no one close to hear it. They would be safe enough.

Tom Krautkramer of the FBI looked alert but tired when he sat down in Jake's office in Crystal City. The hour was past midnight. Jake had lit his candles from home. They flickered bravely in the small office and reflected their tiny glow in the black windows.

Jake talked for twenty minutes, telling Krautkramer everything he had learned about Cowbell. When Krautkramer ran out of questions, he said, "We can't find hide nor hair of Leon Rothberg, that missing New London simulator expert. We think he's one of the two extra men on that sub."

"Okay."

"He was one of the lead engineers programming *America*'s holographic simulator. He knows how every system in that sub works and how to operate the weapons' systems. He's up to his eyeballs in debt—he has judgments against him and every credit card company has shut him off."

"Any family?"

"Single. An ex-girlfriend getting a grand a month in child support. His parents in Michigan that haven't talked to him for months. The last time he was home he hit them up for a five-grand loan."

"Okay. Who's the other guy?"

Krautkramer took a deep breath and squeezed his nose before he answered that one. "We aren't sure. Rothberg is apparently the only American who knew enough about *America* to be useful who can't be accounted for. Other people are on vacation or sick at home or whatever. One guy who is supposed to be on a fishing trip with his buddies is actually shacked up in Florida with a female co-worker."

"So the other person isn't an expert on this submarine."

"Apparently not. In fact, we're looking into the possibility this person isn't American. We're trying to sort out immigration entry information, build a list of possibilities. That's complicated. We're running the computers and talking to huge numbers of people . . . it's going to take a while. This massive power outage didn't help. The computers at headquarters here in Washington are history. We're using machines in St. Louis and Chicago, but"—he slammed his fist on the desk—"goddamn it, Admiral, it's going to take time. I doubt if we have enough. Those bastards could be shooting more missiles this very minute."

"Antoine Jouany. Could that last person be someone who works for him?"

"We're trying to determine if that is a possibility."

"A Russian or German official?"

"Government?"

"Why not?"

"Let's hope not," Krautkramer said. "They'll be covered too well for us to dig them out without moving heaven and earth."

"I thought you *were* moving heaven and earth."

"We can only shovel so fast, Admiral. I'm being fully supported with top priority, but there are lots of rocks to peek under."

"I understand."

"I'll put people to work on Cowbell."

"Let's start with the list of people who had access. There couldn't be more than a couple dozen."

Krautkramer made a face. "In government, maybe. But you can't manufacture anything these days with only two dozen people. There's a factory somewhere, engineers, executives, assembly workers... Even people with superclearances who work on black projects have spouses and sweethearts and occasionally talk too much. And everybody uses computers, puts everything on them. Everything! Engineers use computers to design circuits and parts and you name it. E-mail, spreadsheets, contracts, specs—you heard about that fourteen-year-old kid who broke into the Pentagon computer system?"

After the FBI agent left, Jake got out a legal pad and turned it sideways. He sat for several minutes staring into the flame of the candles, then drew a small submarine on the pad. He put the sail well forward, made it long and slender. It looked like a man-made fish.

Or a shark.

The door to the captain's cabin aboard USS *America* opened inward. Vladimir Kolnikov knocked politely, then used the key from his shirt pocket to unlock and open it. Standing well back with his pistol in his hand, he pushed at the door with his foot.

Heydrich was sitting on the bed in his underwear.

"Ah, the jailer."

"We need to have a little chat," Kolnikov said, keeping the pistol down by his leg.

"Same thing you said to Steinhoff?"

"That is up to you."

Kolnikov closed the door behind him and sat in the chair by the small desk so that he was facing Heydrich. He laid the pistol in his lap.

"I confess, I don't understand what you are doing or why you are doing it," Heydrich said, watching Kolnikov's face. "When this is over, we will need Willi Schlegel's help to permanently disappear. The Americans will be looking for us in every hotel, hut, and whorehouse on this planet. If you think you can hide in some backwater that has no extradition treaty with the United States, you are going to be severely disappointed."

"I figured, taking these risks, why not maximize the return?"

"So you went looking for business."

"Not really." Kolnikov grimaced. "I was approached by a woman. She knew about Blackbeard. Don't ask me how she heard it, because I don't know. I almost died of fright. After she got me calmed down, she introduced me to Schlegel's man. And another person."

"You jeopardized Schlegel's mission."

"If we had been arrested before we stole this boat, one suspects that the Americans would have done nothing. Schlegel, the man I knew—all of them would have denied everything and hidden behind a phalanx of lawyers. The CIA would have been grossly embarrassed—there was really little risk. They would have hustled us out of the country and told us to never come back."

"Schlegel would have killed you."

"We all have to die and, thankfully, only once. Everything worked out, the men and I will get you to Schlegel's treasure trove in the pink of good health, ready to apply your expensive skills in a cunning and industrious manner for the greater glory of Schlegel and friends. A few days later Herr Schlegel and the people I know will each pay us several million apiece. On that glorious day we shall set forth with wallets bulging to live in the happy ever after. You have been thinking of the happy ever after, haven't you?"

"Something like that, I suppose."

Wondering if he was going to get there, Kolnikov thought. The fate of his shipmates was of no concern to Heydrich; it would never occur to him.

"Predicting the future is always tricky," Kolnikov said thoughtfully. "The slightest unknown can destroy the finest calculations. If nothing goes wrong, we will launch Tomahawks on at least one more occasion, perhaps two. There is no double cross. Everyone will share in the proceeds."

"All these promises—I sincerely hope there is some real money in them."

"Precisely my point. I recall saying that very thing to Schlegel the last time we met, that evening we ate at the Hotel George V."

Heydrich yawned. "Willi doesn't like surprises. I think they offend his orderly mind. He is not a man to mislead or leave with a false impression."

"Fact is I sent Willi a letter above your signature, told him we were going to rob enough ships to either make some serious money or get killed doing it."

The possibility that Kolnikov had a sense of humor had never before occurred to Heydrich. He said lightly, "Did he write back?"

"No. Apparently he doesn't waste ink on the hired help."

CHAPTER TEN

When the sun crept over the rim of the sea, *America* was still drifting fifteen hundred feet below the surface of the North Atlantic, dead in the water. Every minute or so, in response to the movement of people inside the hull, water was automatically and silently pumped into or out of the tanks to maintain the boat's trim. Kolnikov knew the pumps were working because lights flickered on and off on the control panel. Still, the way the computers kept the boat level and maintained its depth within inches seemed almost magic. The control room lights were very dim . . . in fact, Kolnikov concluded, they were off. The only illumination came from the sonar displays, computer screens, and LCD readouts.

Kolnikov studied the computer screen that monitored noise being manufactured within the boat. Every thump and click of metal on metal from the engineering spaces registered here, although the level of noise was far too low for a human ear to detect. Nothing else. He wondered about that oil pump. Why did it fail now? The trim pumps were oh so quiet, with new, well-lubricated bearings. The air circulation fans, the condensers . . . the boat was like a giant Swiss watch with a million moving parts.

Eck's face appeared green in the reflected light of his screen as he experimented with the Revelation computer. The large display screens on the bulkhead were quite dark, not because the sea was very quiet but because most of the natural noises of the sea had been filtered out. The system was waiting, listening, for a noise that should not be there. Still, an occasional flicker or momentary illumination showed ill-defined, ever-changing, fantastic shapes. They are nothing, Kolnikov decided, nothing at all. Or were they?

"This is an extraordinary system," Eck said when he realized Kolnikov was watching over his shoulder. "The computer can detect frequencies and wave patterns that are too faint to be presented optically. Ships at hundreds of miles, planes, whales calling for their mates—it's a fantastic piece of gear."

"Skip the whales. Find me a submarine."

"They are out here," Eck said with conviction. "I hear screw noises, gurgles . . . much too faint and momentary to get a bearing on. But they are real. I hear them. *Revelation hears them.* They are out there."

"Umm," Kolnikov said. He too thought the American submarines were in these waters hunting *America,* and perhaps also British and French boats, but he didn't choose to discuss it with Eck. Eck, on the other hand, was not reticent. "I thank my stars," the German continued, "I am not out there in this sea in one of those noisy old East German boats with this thing hunting me. God, it gives me chills just thinking of it!"

Kolnikov was idly watching the compass and monitoring the opening and closing of trim valves when Georgi Turchak came into the control room. He took Kolnikov aside and spoke very softly so that Eck wouldn't hear. "It's the bearings in that pump. It's in a tight space and difficult to work on."

"So . . ."

"It's a bigger job than I thought. Three or four more hours, at least. We must drain the oil from the housing and rig a hoist to handle the pieces when we break it apart. And if we screw up the gaskets, we're out of luck: The spare parts inventories don't show any aboard."

"So what happens if we can't get it back together?"

"We are out of luck. The pump forces oil into the main bearings. Without it—" He left the sentence unfinished.

"Can we limp along as is?"

Turchak nodded. "If you are willing to tolerate the noise. And we proceed slowly."

"An oil circulation pump . . ." Kolnikov tilted the stool and put his feet up on the tactical presentation. He studied his shoes.

"The men are worried," Turchak said. "They know the thing will make noise. They talked of little else while we worked."

"What do you think?" Kolnikov asked and eyed his friend.

"We have done all we can, Vladimir Ivanovich. You must weigh the risks and decide how to proceed."

"I must decide?"

"You." Turchak sat heavily in the chair in front of the helm controls. "My wife is dead, I haven't talked to my son in years—hell, I don't know where he is, and I guarantee you he doesn't know or care where I am. We are expendable, you, me, all of us. No one cares whether we live or die, whether we go back to France or Russia or wherever." He jerked his head toward the rear of the boat. "Those men back there helping me. They have no one. Oh, they want money, a chance at life. But they have nothing in this world. So you decide. Is the risk worth it?"

"What have we got to lose, eh?"

"Only our lives."

"And they are worth precisely nothing."

"Nothing at all," Turchak said heavily.

"Okay," said Vladimir Kolnikov. "Let's crack the pump housing, replace the bearings. Try not to screw up the gaskets. If we can get it all back together more or less the way the shipyard had it, we'll get under way. Slowly."

"What if we can't?"

"You are a good submariner, Georgi Alexandrovich. Do the best you can and we'll all live with it."

"And then?"

"And then," Kolnikov said, trying to sound optimistic, "we will get under way and motor merrily toward the programmed launch point. If the tactical display is correct, we are only twenty-three miles southwest of it. We will head for it at five knots. Begin a gentle ascent so we get as little hull popping as possible as the pressure comes off. We will poke our masts up, get a GPS update, shoot, then run like hell."

"It will be broad daylight. Midday."

"That's right."

"The Americans will be all over us."

"We will go deep. I think this boat might take two thousand feet. We will find out, eh? That's below the depth any *Los Angeles*–class boat can reach. With a smidgen of good fortune, there will be some kind of thermal or salinity incongruity below a thousand feet. We will run awhile, clear the area, then go dead in the water and drift. They won't expect that. Deep and dead silent, we will be devilishly difficult to find. We'll drift for days if necessary. We'll outwait them. We've got plenty of time. The Americans will get impatient and eventually leave."

"Drifting . . ." said Turchak, thinking about it.

"I've been watching the compass. The boat has turned about eighty degrees in the last two hours as we drifted. The trim pumps have had no trouble controlling our pitch attitude, and they are brand-new, dead quiet. If necessary, we could use the screw a little to give the planes some bite. A knot of way at the most, I think." He thought about it a moment, then added, "I have never seen a boat so quiet. I can hear my heart pounding. Drifting like this, we almost cease to exist."

"The American subs will be looking for a quiet place in the sea," Turchak objected. "A black hole in a noisy universe. You know that as well as I."

"Old boats are too noisy, this one is too quiet—what would it take to please you, good friend?"

"What if an attack boat shows up in the neighborhood and goes active?"

Kolnikov got out his lighter and played with it. "I don't think an American skipper will take that risk. If he goes active, he's a beaconing target."

"We'd better have a couple of fish ready," Turchak advised. "And we'd better be ready to run like hell. Just in case there's an American skipper out there with a bigger set of balls than you normally see in the woods."

In Washington that morning Jake Grafton found that Flap Le Beau had sent a car and driver to pick him up. As the car carried him the two miles to the Pentagon, he scanned an intelligence summary of the previous day's events. He also glanced out the window, watching the traffic, which seemed to be almost back to normal. Most of the commuters lived in the suburbs, so their automobiles were far enough from the blast of the E-warheads to escape damage. There were no traffic signals in Washington this morning, of course, but police officers directed traffic at every major intersection. Heaven knows what the commuters would do when they reached work—perhaps add columns of figures by candlelight in buildings with windows that could not be opened.

The old mansion at the center of the White House complex had burned completely to the ground. Fortunately the East and West wings had been saved, but between them was a smoldering heap of rubble. Two people had died; one person had been critically burned.

The intelligence summary contained some specific assessments of damage caused by the two E-warheads and rough estimates of how long the repair efforts would take. And how much they would cost. The price tag was in the billions. Insurance lawyers were telling the press that the "act of war" exclusion clauses present in every insurance policy meant that none of the damage was covered. Other lawyers were disputing that conclusion, arguing that unless it could be shown that a foreign power was behind the theft of the submarine that had launched the missiles, the act of war clauses should not apply. What was obvious was that the insurance companies had no intention of paying anyone but lawyers a solitary dime unless and until they were ordered to do so by final judgments of appellate courts, a position that was certainly in the finest traditions of American business. Make the bastards sue.

Yesterday the nation's financial markets were open less than an hour before the major indexes had dropped so much that authorities suspended trading. Selling pressure, reported the nation's financial press, was strong and building. The prognosticators thought that when the markets opened later this morning, they would fall to the limit in less than twenty minutes. The authorities had appealed to the SEC to suspend trading altogether. Around the world the American dollar was taking a severe beating.

As usual, most of the items in the intelligence summary looked as if they were taken straight from the news wires, Grafton thought as he replaced the summary in its envelope.

The United States was under attack. Even though they didn't know who or why, the reality of the attack was obvious to the investing public, which had panicked. And who could blame them?

A stolen state-of-the-art attack submarine, a missile attack on the presidential mansion, E-warheads causing electrical meltdowns, apparent cover-ups by the administration, outrageous rumors thick as bees in a hive, a military powerless to catch the perps...and of course, there was the missing satellite. Everything these days seemed to exude a faint odor of incompetence.

Several senators predicted spreading anarchy and the collapse of civil government—even in this age of failed dreams, that kind of talk rated headlines. Several more prominent lawmakers had appealed to the president to declare martial law.

And yet, Jake Grafton thought, the police are directing traffic and the streets are full of people going to work.

Surrounded by his staff, General Flap Le Beau was in his E-Ring office at the Pentagon preparing for a Joint Chiefs meeting when Jake arrived. "What should we do that we haven't done?" The commandant tossed out that question as Jake headed for an empty chair.

"Induce a four-mile error in the global positioning system," Jake Grafton promptly replied.

Flap sighed. "The White House shot that one down."

"That was yesterday. This is a new day. Let's try it again."

"Yesterday they said that the pirates might not shoot any more missiles. And they haven't. Until they do, the politicos will look like savants."

"Has any terrorist group claimed credit for kicking the imperialists?" Flap's chief of staff asked.

"Four, so far. The FBI says none of them are credible."

"What's the weather this morning?"

"Clouds over the East Coast, General, but several hundred miles at sea the clouds dissipate and the visibility is excellent. We'll know about a cruise missile launch within two minutes."

"That's one small positive," Flap Le Beau admitted. "The air force and navy will have everything they own out there looking."

"Any ransom demands, General?" Another staff officer asked this question. "Any demands to release political prisoners, anything like that?"

"Not that I know of." Flap eyed Jake. "What's the story on the FBI?"

"They are still working on the problem of identifying the last person who went aboard *America,* sir. We assume the fifteen members of the Blackbeard team went aboard and one Leon Roth-berg, a civilian engineer from the sub base simulator department. That leaves one more man. The FBI is working on that tape that the Boston television station shot from a chopper of the Blackbeard team stealing the sub, seeing if there is a face on there that they haven't seen before." The tape had been running almost continuously in America and on cable stations around the world. The people in Washington hadn't seen it, of course, since they had been without electrical power for almost thirty-two hours. The television with-drawal would have been merely inconvenient anywhere else in the wired world, but without the benefit of instant feedback, the Wash-ington politicians were operating in a painful new world.

"The FBI is checking on the disclosure list for Cowbell," Jake said. "Krautkramer is supposed to get back to me this morning. He will have to interview those people."

Flap looked glum. "If there has been a leak, the FBI will need months to find it, if they ever do. Man, we don't have months."

"The pirates must have known about Cowbell, sir. Be a hell of a coincidence if they didn't. Right now that's the only lead we have."

Flap threw up his hands in frustration.

"In a few hours NSA may have something from the Brits," Jake concluded. "All over the world people are talking and the spooks are listening."

"Give me a minute alone with Admiral Grafton," Flap said to his staff. The commandant led Jake back into his office and closed the door. "I had a little oral scuffle with the national security adviser yesterday evening, told her that they had given me a fool's errand. I was tired of people not leveling with me—all the usual stuff."

"And?"

"One item. Blackbeard was canceled because the Russians found out about it. Want to know how we learned that happy fact?" Flap's eyes narrowed. "The director of the CIA was attending a reception for the Russian trade delegation when Janos Ilin dropped the bomb over a glass of Chablis."

Vladimir Kolnikov was sitting in the control room watching the sonar displays when the chief German engineer and five other men came in, following Georgi Turchak. They had been working on the oil circulation pump for seven hours. Behind them came Heydrich, lean and cadaverous as always, carrying a cup of coffee.

"We have it back together," the chief engineer said. "No oil leaking, so the gaskets appear to be all right."

"We worked as quietly as we could, used rags to try and deaden the sound," Turchak told Kolnikov.

"Well, it's fixed now."

Kolnikov studied the tactical display. "Rothberg, reprogram the missiles. We will launch in two hours. We will be two miles north of our current position. Then we will dive to two thousand feet, run at twenty knots for an hour, then go dead in the water and wait for the Americans to get tired of looking. We will not do any eating or moving around, no going to the toilet. I think this would be an excellent time for everyone not needed in the control or engine room to take a nap. Fortunately we have plenty of bunks. Everyone pick one, close your eyes, and check for light leaks."

"You're crazy," Rothberg said flatly. "The Americans will see the missiles come out of the water and come charging out here like they're going to a fire. They'll be armed to the teeth and ready for anything. Dead in the water, unable to maneuver or fight, we'll be sitting ducks."

From the look on their faces, it was obvious the others agreed with Rothberg.

"The screws of this boat are as quiet as technology allows. Still, unavoidably, they do put low-frequency noise into the water. All of you know that. That is the only noise this boat generates, so it will be the one noise the Americans will be looking for. We must do the unexpected."

"Jesus!" Rothberg exclaimed. "You think the U.S. Navy is some kind of third-world yacht club? They ain't the fucking Russian Navy, Jack! They're—"

Kolnikov backhanded him across the mouth. The slap sounded loud as a shot in the control room.

"Now all of you, listen to me," Kolnikov snarled. "You volunteered for this. Every one of you swinging dicks."

"You never said—" Steeckt began.

Kolnikov cut him off. "I won't listen to your whining. I told you the U.S. Navy would hunt us, I told you the odds were against us. Heydrich told you if we made it we would all be set for life, with three million American dollars for every man. And you bought it. Each of you. Yeah, for that much money we'll risk our lives. Yeah. And all of us fools began planning where we would go and how we would live, the women, the cars, the good life . . ."

He saw several smiles now and knew he had them. "Even you, Rothberg. Money for women and gambling, money to be somebody. You were tired of being a short, fat, nerdy slob working at the sub base. *This* was your chance. And it still is!"

He let the silence build. Heydrich's face was impassive, impossible to read. "I'm not suicidal," Kolnikov continued. "I know what I'm doing. You men do your jobs, obey orders, and I'll do my level best to get us through this alive. No guarantees, no promises. I'll do my best."

Kolnikov searched Steeckt's face. "There's no way to undo what we have done, no way to bring those dead American sailors back to life, to return their submarine and slip away into the crowd. We're halfway across the abyss on a tightrope. Our only choice is go forward."

Heydrich stood in the back of the compartment sipping silently on coffee. Steeckt turned to him. "What do you say?" he asked respectfully.

"If any of you can run this boat in Kolnikov's place, say so now." Several of them glanced at Rothberg.

"He's a simulator man," Heydrich said dryly. "This is the first time he's ever been to sea. Turchak?"

"Not me. I trust his judgment, not mine."

Heydrich drained the coffee cup. "It seems our only alternative is to do it Kolnikov's way." Without waiting for a reply, Heydrich went down the ladder to the mess deck.

Technicians working around the clock had gotten the SuperAegis liaison office in a Crystal City office building back in business. Emergency generators had been brought in and connected to the building's main circuit breaker panel. All the circuit breakers had been replaced, as well as most of the light switches in the building. Every portable electrical device in the building had been carried away to be disposed of, and new computers had been carried in. New telephones had been installed, new typewriters, copy machines, electric staplers, new card readers for the building's security system, new switches to operate the door locks, new security cameras and smoke detectors. The liaison staff—with their small office suite—certainly didn't rate the priority, but the building was full of other major military commands, which did. The small army of technicians who had accomplished the impossible were now gone, moved on to another government building.

Jake Grafton found Toad Tarkington opening new packages of software and installing them on the new computers. After he had greeted his boss and reported all that had been done, Toad remarked, "We're almost ready for another Flashlight. If they pop another one over Washington, I thought I might take a month's leave while you folks go through this drill one more time."

"Promises, promises," Jake said. He picked up a new telephone and held it to his ear.

"The telephone system is still dead, sir."

"I knew that," Jake said with disgust as he tossed the instrument back onto its cradle. He sat on the edge of a desk and watched Toad for a moment. "They won't shoot another one at Washington," he said after a moment's thought. "New York probably, maybe Boston or Philly. A long shot would be the National Security Agency at Fort Meade."

"No pun intended."

"Umpf."

"So what are the pirates accomplishing, sir?"

"They're wrecking the American economy. Intentionally or unintentionally. The bottom has fallen out of the market, every missile causes billions of dollars in damage, the prestige and sovereignty of America are diminished with each passing day, with each warhead that explodes. And they've fired only three missiles. There are nine more on that damn boat."

"The lawyers can argue about intent," Toad said. "As far as I'm concerned, that isn't a question. It's obvious that they intend the warheads to cause damage."

"The only thing that is obvious is that the missiles were aimed and fired intentionally," Jake Grafton replied. "Each warhead that explodes sets off a chain of events, some of which are predictable, some of which aren't. Once an avalanche starts down a mountain, where it goes and what it hits are events beyond anyone's control."

"They must intend to hammer the economy," Toad insisted. "That's what's happening."

"And a great many things will flow from that," Jake said. "Fortunes will be made and lost, careers ruined, careers built . . . tens of millions of lives will be affected, which will cause profound reactions to these events in the years to come. My point is simply that once a missile is launched, no one can predict or control the consequences."

"Where does that train of thought take you, Admiral?"

"Damned if I know," Jake Grafton said and threw a pencil at a photo of a submarine hanging on the wall of a cubicle eight feet away.

He was staring at the submarine when Krautkramer walked in. "Since the telephones are out of whack, thought I should drop by and let you know how we're doing."

"Uh-huh." Jake threw another pencil at the sub. The point of this one went into the soft soundproof cover of the cubicle panel and stuck.

They talked about the state of affairs in Washington for a few minutes, relating stories about life without electricity. Toad and Krautkramer did most of the talking, with Jake listening. Every so often he selected a pencil from a coffee cup on the desk and threw it at the submarine on the cubicle wall. The first one that stuck in the wall was apparently a fluke. The others struck at the wrong angle and fell to the carpet.

"We've identified the unknown man, the last one, we think," Krautkramer said finally, when the rehash of the missile attack had run its course. He opened a cheap attaché case and extracted a file, which he passed to Jake. The photo in the file was of the unknown man boarding the submarine, glancing up. That look straight into the videocamera had been blown up on regular film. Jake glanced at it, then consulted the other documents the file contained.

"He's an underwater salvage expert," Krautkramer explained. "Name of Heydrich. Works for the European aerospace consortium, EuroSpace. In the past he's reported to a vice president named Willi Schlegel. In addition to his salvage abilities, we think he does general smoothing work."

"Smoothing."

"Uh-huh. Whenever there is a problem he is brought in to smooth things out."

"How does he do his smoothing?" Toad asked.

"Any way at all."

"Amazing that you can identify people from pictures," Jake said as he looked at Heydrich's photo.

"The computer age is truly here. Everyone is wired up together. Sharing databases was one of the antiterrorism initiatives."

"I remember when the privacy people jumped up and down about it."

"That's why it gets zero publicity. The idea of government databases scares some people silly. But there's no way to stop it. The information is there, it's on computers, no one wants airliners or trade centers or government buildings bombed by wild-eyed maniacs with a righteous cause. Ergo, government agencies share databases."

Jake glanced at the other items in the folder, then handed it back to the FBI agent. He went to the window, stood staring out. The view here was to the north. He could see a corner of Reagan National Airport and most of the Pentagon. In the distance the Jefferson Memorial and the Washington Monument were prominent. The sky was empty.

"The Europeans," Toad mused. "Underwater salvage. They must know where the SuperAegis satellite wound up."

"We're trying to find a link between the European aerospace consortium and someone on the SuperAegis launch crew. So far we've had no luck."

"Are you checking bank accounts?" Toad asked.

"Can't do any of that foolishness until we get a warrant."

"Hmm."

"Strictly by the book."

Jake Grafton turned from the window. "I need some help on a project," he said. "Won't lead to a prosecution, so nobody will have to testify about it."

"Sounds like something immoral, unethical, and illegal," Krautkramer said with enthusiasm. "Ought to be right down my alley."

"Is there any other way?" Toad asked and sniffed self-righteously.

Twenty minutes later Jake was standing by the window looking down into the street when he saw Janos Ilin get out of a limo. At least it appeared to be Ilin—from eight stories up it was difficult to tell.

"Could the Russians have gotten another limo from someplace?"

"Probably. More than likely their UN mission drove a few down for the embassy staff to use. The French and Brits did that, I heard. Maybe they rented one from one of the services out in the suburbs."

Ilin crossed the sidewalk toward the entrance. It looked like him anyway, the way he walked.

"Is the car that picked me up this morning still downstairs?"

"Yes, sir. Driver should be there."

"I'll take that car and send the driver upstairs. Wish me luck."

"Be careless," Toad said.

Jake snagged his hat and walked for the front door. He met Ilin climbing the stairs.

"Zelda, I think you should come look at this."

Zip Vance was at the computer near her. She could see what was on his monitor, but no one else could. She and Zip had purposely arranged the office that way. "So no one can see you play FreeCell," the secretary said knowingly. Everyone laughed dutifully, but rank has its privileges, privacy among them.

She got up from her desk and went over for a good look at Zip's monitor. The display was a photo of a man, a single frame. He was in his early thirties, tall, with wide shoulders and craggy good looks. The camera was looking at him almost full face, but he appeared to be paying no attention to it.

"It's Tommy Carmellini. You asked to be notified if and when he returned to the country. This shot was taken early yesterday evening at the immigration office at Champlain, New York. He came in from Canada."

Scanners to read the numbers of passports had been installed in immigration offices all over the nation for years. Now the data from the scanner and a photo taken simultaneously was sent to the INS, which could compare the information to the info in the State Department's passport database. And photographs of known terrorists, criminals, and fugitives.

Carmellini was a sore spot. After all that work setting him up to get Jouany's file and bring it home in triumph to the CIA, he had taken a look and bolted. Disappeared. Leaving McSweeney infuriated and pounding out furious E-mails to Langley.

Zelda Hudson wouldn't have thought it possible. She had spent hours in Carmellini's company on repeated occasions. He was a nice hunk, with an A+ smile, C+ brains, and a D– character.

Back at her desk, she logged on to one of her computer terminals. In minutes she was looking at rental car records. Yesterday, the Montreal airport . . . There he was! Carmellini, Tommy A. Virginia driver's license.

While she was at it, she typed in another string of numbers. Up popped a face of a man she had never met. She recognized his name, however: Heydrich. The FBI had identified him from the television video taken during the hijacking.

He should not have boarded *America* in New London. The presence of a television helicopter was predictable. He would be photographed, the FBI would eventually identify him . . . and like prophecy, the event had come to pass.

So Jake Grafton and Tom Krautkramer knew Heydrich was aboard. From Heydrich the trail would lead to France, to EuroSpace. Willi Schlegel just didn't understand the cyberage.

What would Grafton and Krautkramer's next move be?

The sea was empty. Nothing visible on sonar in any direction. The towed array was stowed, so the range and definition of the Revelation system were degraded, but even so, it was better than any sonar Vladimir Kolnikov had ever dreamed of. Yes, the American navy was hunting its lost submarine, but the North Atlantic was vast indeed.

With the boat stable and trimmed and making three knots, Kolnikov raised the electronic support measures, or ESM, mast, studied the frequencies of the energy detected by the WLQ-4 gear that processed the signals. He knew only enough about the gear to get the most basic frequency readouts. At least there didn't seem to be a P-3 twenty miles away. He then raised the communications mast to get a GPS update. When he had that, he raised the photonics mast a few feet above the wave tops for a ten-second look around. With all the masts retracted he studied the photonics image on a bulkhead-mounted screen. A fair day, some high cirrus clouds, not much wind. He had known that the swells weren't breaking before he raised the mast.

"How much do the positions differ?" Kolnikov asked Boldt, who was studying the GPS input.

Boldt made another input into the computer before he answered. "Twenty-five feet, the system says."

"You always check that before you update, don't you?"

"Aah . . ."

"Our lives are the wager, Boldt. Don't do anything without thinking."

"Aye, Captain."

"We are ready to shoot," Rothberg announced.

"Whenever you wish," Kolnikov said.

At a nod from Rothberg, Eck turned off the sonar so the noise of the launch wouldn't destroy the system . . . or his eardrums.

"Number six," Rothberg said. "Open the outer door."

When the door had been opened hydraulically, Rothberg pushed the firing button. The missile was ejected upward with a roar that was loud even with the sonar off. The rush of incoming water helped balance the loss of the weight of the departing missile, but still the bow bucked upward a little, almost like hitting a speed bump.

"Open the outer door on number seven."

A minute later he fired the missile.

The Tomahawk in tube ten went a minute after that.

"Close the outer doors," Kolnikov said. When the panel showed green, Turchak pushed the power lever to all ahead two-thirds and pushed the joystick forward a quarter inch. Kolnikov opened the valves to the ballast tanks, began letting water into the boat. Turchak's control input rotated the bow planes down and the stern planes up. As the submarine accelerated and gained weight and dropped her nose from the horizontal, the thrust of her screw drove her down into the dark, silent sea.

Sonny Killbuck was standing in the main SOSUS processing center when a North Atlantic operator called, "Missile launch." In seconds the computer triangulated data from three different sets of sensors and displayed a probable launch position on the graphic of the North Atlantic.

The duty officer was already busy, issuing orders to navy P-3s and

ASW hunter-killer task groups already at sea. Contacting the attack submarines hunting for *America* was more difficult. Only radio signals with very long wavelengths could be detected underwater. To communicate with the submarines, a signal had to be transmitted on an extremely low frequency (ELF) array that the submarines could receive on an antenna wire that trailed behind their sail. The signal told the submarines to come to periscope depth, where they could raise their communications antenna and receive an encrypted burst transmission on a UHF radio frequency. This process took time. Still, Killbuck noticed, the display depicted a *Los Angeles*–class submarine, *La Jolla,* only forty-five miles from the launch position. Of course, it could be dozens of miles from that position. Still, he thought, *La Jolla* might have heard the missile launch on its sonar.

USS *La Jolla*'s senior sonar operator was Petty Officer First Class Robert "Buck" Brown. He recognized the unmistakable sound of a missile launch. He had called it to the OOD's attention and notified the commanding officer. He knew from message traffic that *America* had fired three Tomahawks thirty-six hours ago, so he had been listening for another one, just in case. He punched the buttons to put the raw sonar audio on the control room loudspeaker. Everyone in the room heard the second launch. The rumble silenced conversation. The sailors stood frozen, listening, silently speculating, when the noise of the third missile being ejected from *America*'s vertical launch tubes arrived through the water.

The bearing to the launch noises was plain enough. What wasn't plain was the distance that separated *La Jolla* from the launch site.

"Whatd'ya think, Buck?" the skipper asked. His name was Jimmy Ryder, Jr. He was several inches over six feet and had unusually large hands. Behind his back the sailors liked to call him Junior.

"At least thirty miles, Skipper. Maybe twice that."

"Okay," said Jimmy Ryder, who glanced at the screen to get the bearing. "Let's go find this guy. Chief of the Boat, steer three zero five. Let's try to get there quick. Flank speed."

Flank speed in *La Jolla* was thirty-two knots. Of course they couldn't hear anything at that speed, but they could dash toward the launch site, then slow down and begin listening.

When they heard the order, several eyes widened in the control room. The name of this game was finding the other fellow before he found you. Rushing to the scene of the crime was a risk. A calculated risk, but a risk nonetheless. Everything depended on how long Ryder was willing to keep the boat at speed before he slowed.

Buck Brown wondered about that as he tried to concentrate on the sonar. He could feel the boat accelerating, knew that he wouldn't hear much, but he wanted to stay busy. *America* was out there, the quietest, stealthiest submarine in the world, and it was manned by a group of ex–Russian submariners. According to the scuttlebutt, those guys knew their shit.

Anyway you cut it, Buck Brown thought, we're in for a gunfight with real bullets.

He wiped his forehead, then wiped his hands on his trousers.

The skipper seemed to read his thoughts. He leaned over, whispered, "I want you to stay on the panel. If you need to take a head break, do it now, before things get interesting. Do your job, tell us what's out there, and let me do the rest."

"Yes, sir."

Ryder slapped one of those big hands on Brown's shoulder, then went to the back of the compartment where a sailor kept a manual running plot on a maneuvering board. Like *America, La Jolla* had a computerized tactical presentation, but Ryder merely used it to back up the manual plot. The computer could crap out—and when it was desperately needed, probably would—but the manual plot could be kept with dead reckoning, if nothing else, and would be there when all else failed.

Ryder was well aware that he was rushing to a position that would be more than an hour old when he arrived. Worse, he was just following a bearing, not going to a known location. In all likelihood, *America* was leaving the launch site at a good clip right now. But where was she going?

He was thinking that problem through when the com officer brought him a flimsy of an ELF message. It consisted of a single letter of the alphabet. Without consulting the code book, Ryder knew what it meant. The message was an order to ascend to periscope depth to receive an encrypted UHF message transmitted via satellite.

He was tempted. The UHF message would probably give him the exact location of the missile launch. Yet he would have to slow to rise and receive it, and even if he knew the exact location, the basic problem remained: He was rushing to a position where *America* had been, not where she would be when he arrived.

So where was the stolen submarine?

CHAPTER ELEVEN

An air force E-3 Sentry AWACS aircraft on patrol two hundred miles east of Atlantic City, New Jersey, was the first to spot the Tomahawk missiles after launch. The crew picked up the first missile on radar just seconds after it came out of the water, then the second and third as they rose from the sea. The coordinates of the launch site and a rough intercept heading were broadcast to a navy P-3 Orion patrol aircraft, which was approximately a hundred miles to the south.

The Orion commander turned as soon as he heard the heading over the radio. In the back of the Orion, the tactical coordinator, or TACCO, typed the coordinates into the computer and called out a new bearing. The pilot made the correction, three degrees, and set the bug on his horizontal situation indicator (HSI).

At his console in the main compartment of the plane, the TACCO began planning his search and programming the sonobuoy panel. While the TACCO worked, the pilot and copilot restarted the number one and four engines, which they had secured earlier to save fuel. Only when both engines were developing cruise power and the temperatures were stabilized in the normal range did the pilot key his intercom mike. "How long until we get there?" At the time he was level at 200 feet above the water, making 250 knots.

"Twenty-three minutes," the TACCO told him.

The pilot was Duke Dolan, a graduate of Purdue University. His ambition had been to fly fighter planes from aircraft carriers, but the needs of the navy and his standing in his flight school class had conspired to put him in P-3s. There were worse fates, he often told his wife. "At least I don't have to go on a cruise on the big gray boat."

So now he was hunting one. USS *America*. She had gotten the name, he recalled, after the *Kitty Hawk*–class carrier named *America* had been scrapped. Rumored to be the quietest thing in the ocean, *America* would take some finding. The way to do it, he thought, was to actively echo-range, or ping, the sonobuoys.

But wasn't there another submarine out here someplace? No doubt the TACCO knew where it was, so the pilot didn't need to worry about it.

Indeed, the TACCO did know about *La Jolla*. He didn't know her exact position, of course, but he knew she was in this operating area. Which frosted him more than a little. With a friendly boat down there, he would need absolutely certain identification before he strapped on the pirate ship with a Mk-48 torpedo. Finding the damned boat was going to be tough enough, but an ironclad positive ID? And he wasn't going to be able to use active sonar because he might illuminate *La Jolla* for the bad guys. Hoo boy!

"Where did they say those missiles were going?" the copilot asked Duke.

"Probably don't know yet."

"Didya see the White House on TV after the bastards whacked it? Smoking hole, man."

"Yeah. I saw it."

"I hope they don't hit the O-Club, anything like that."

The copilot was an idiot, no question. How in the hell did he get in the navy, anyway? And by what twist of evil fate, the pilot wondered, did he wind up in my right seat on what is probably the only day of my naval career that I will hunt a submarine for real? Why me, God?

Five minutes after the first missile was launched, a pair of F-16 fighters, which had been on alert status at the end of the Dover Air Force Base runway, with their pilots in the cockpits, lit their afterburners and rolled. They made a section takeoff, raised their gear together, and punched into the overcast that blanketed the East Coast of the United States at about twenty-three hundred feet. Two minutes after takeoff they switched to the operational frequency of the E-3 Sentry aircraft, which was a Boeing 707 with a thirty-foot radar rotodome mounted atop the fuselage.

"We have three Tomahawks in the air," the mission commander aboard the Boeing told the F-16 section leader, whose name was Rebecca Allison. "Your vector to intercept is zero six zero. Estimated distance to intercept is four hundred twelve miles, recommend you use a max range profile."

"Roger that," Rebecca Allison said and noted the info on her knee board. She dialed the heading bug on her horizontal situation indicator (HSI) to the recommended heading and engaged the autopilot, which could keep the fighter in a smooth, steady climb while she punched the intercept data into her computer and checked the symbology on the heads-up display, or HUD. Each plane was carrying two six-hundred-gallon aux tanks, one under each wing, and each had a Sidewinder on each wingtip missile station.

The planes were climbing through cloud. Allison checked her wingman, Stanley Schottenheimer, who was tucked in nicely on her right wing.

They topped the clouds at ten thousand feet and continued their climb. Schottenheimer increased the distance between the planes so that he too could attend to cockpit chores.

"Anvil One, Eagle Four Two," Allison called on the secure UHF radio. "Do you have a projected destination for the bogies?"

"Looks like New York. Unfortunately, all three are on different flight paths. We'll put you down on the closest one."

"Do you have any other interceptors, over?"

"None that can intercept prior to the target area. You two are it."

"Why don't you split us up, give us each a target, over?"

"Okay. Wingman, state your call sign."

"Eagle Four Seven," Schottenheimer replied.

"Both of you stay together for now. We'll separate you in a bit, try to give you each a missile."

Three missiles, two planes. Uh-oh. And the missiles were Tomahawks, which flew right in the weeds. Allison tightened her harness straps and reached for her master armament switch. She would try for a Sidewinder shot, if she could get a lock on the missile's exhaust. If not, she would have to use the gun.

The control room was packed as *America* descended toward the depth Vladimir Kolnikov wanted, two thousand feet. Boldt was wearing the sound-powered telephone, so it was he who reported leaks in the engine room passing eleven hundred feet.

Kolnikov turned and glared at the crowd. "Have you never been on a submarine before? Check for leaks. Everyone should be at his post wearing sound-powered phones. Find 'em and fix 'em. Check every compartment." The control room emptied, leaving only Eck, Boldt, Rothberg, Turchak on the helm, and Kolnikov. And Heydrich, who sat in the back at an unused sonar console doing and saying nothing.

Two thousand feet was three hundred feet below her certified depth, and everyone in the room seemed to be holding his breath. When the boat's hull creaked and groaned a bit from the stupendous pressure passing eighteen hundred feet, Kolnikov said, "That's deep enough. Take it back up to seventeen hundred and let's get the giggles and bangs out of it." When she stabilized at seventeen hundred feet, her certified depth, the noises stopped. Boldt reported that the boat had leaks here and there, but the crew was working on them.

"This isn't a dinner boat on the Seine," Kolnikov growled. Leaks were the bane of a submariner's life. They could develop at any moment.

"We'll not go lower than this unless we have to," Kolnikov said aloud, to no one in particular. "We must stay as silent as possible, or believe me, the Americans will find us." Kolnikov had not streamed the towed array. He planned to drift with no way on, so the array would end up hanging straight down on its half mile of cable, of little or no use.

At a nod from Kolnikov, Turchak let the submarine drift slowly to a stop. About two minutes passed before the inertial readout stopped going slower. The final speed was half a knot, which was probably the speed of the current at this depth.

The pumps that kept her trimmed seemed to work fine. She lay motionless in the sea, steady as a rock. Kolnikov put his head against the metal of the bulkhead to listen, then checked the computer screen that analyzed the ship for noise. Almost nothing. The ship was as silent as the sea itself.

"Just in case," Kolnikov said to Boldt, "while we are alone, have everyone make a head call, then secure the head until further notice. And let's flood tubes one and two and open the outer doors."

Turchak, at the helm, was also wearing a sound-powered telephone headset. He concentrated on monitoring the trim of the boat. He would ease the power lever forward for a few turns to establish steerageway—and plane effectiveness—if that became necessary. Eck and Boldt were busy with the computers, with Rothberg supervising, running from one to another, looking over shoulders, offering little explanations. Kolnikov stood mesmerized by the large, flat bulkhead-mounted sonar displays. Once again the impression that the displays were mere windows in the hull and he was actually looking at the ocean struck Kolnikov powerfully.

The screens were dark just now, for the sea at this depth was very quiet. Yet the darkness was not total—there were gleams of light here and there from the grunts and calls of sea creatures, fish and whales and dolphins, very faint and far away. The muted symphony also gave them tantalizing hints of hull and machinery noises, no doubt from distant ships and planes. And every now and then they were teased by low-frequency rumbling noises, perhaps from earth-quakes or landslides, maybe deep-sea volcanoes.

He reluctantly left the sonar displays and was looking over Boldt's shoulder, studying the navigation data displayed there, when out of the corner of his eye he saw Eck press his earpieces tightly against his head. After a bit Eck held up a hand and said in almost a whisper, "I think I hear screw noises. Low-frequency beats." He removed the sonar audio from the control room loudspeaker so it wouldn't be returned to the sea.

Kolnikov donned the headset and listened. Meanwhile Eck was typing on his keyboard, initiating a track, labeling it. A symbol appeared on the horizontal tactical display and on one of the bulkhead screens. The men stared mesmerized at the symbol, which almost obscured a faint gleam of light hiding amid the darkness.

Turchak, wearing the sound-powered headset, told Kolnikov, "Tubes one and two flooded, outer doors open."

Kolnikov climbed onto the captain's stool and lit a cigarette. He was staring at the dim gleam that Eck said was the noise of a submarine when a tiny light flashed on the surface in the other direction some distance away, perhaps six or seven miles.

Five seconds passed before Eck said softly, "Sonobuoy. We have a P-3 overhead."

There were eight sonobuoys in the water when Eck gestured toward the submarine symbol on the panel display. "That isn't where it is. There's a thermal layer distorting the sound."

"Can you identify it?"

"We need a little more noise. He's closing, that's certain."

Three minutes later Eck said, "*Los Angeles*–class, according to the computer."

"Which one?"

"Still working on that."

A half minute later he said, "*La Jolla*. Her signature is in the computer."

"Jesus fucking Christ," Leon Rothberg said bitterly and sagged into an empty chair.

Toad Tarkington was at his desk in the Crystal City SuperAegis liaison office when the intercom buzzed. The unexpected sound made Toad jump. Without telephones ringing, the office was abnormally quiet, pleasantly so. The security officer in the lobby was calling. "Sir, there is a Mr. Carmellini down here asking for Admiral Grafton."

"Carmellini?" Toad drew a blank for several seconds, then he remembered. Oh yeah, the CIA guy from Cuba. "I'll be down to escort him," Toad told the guard. Carmellini. He was in Hong Kong with Admiral Grafton last year, Toad remembered, when the revolutionaries kidnapped Callie.

The building elevators were still out of service, so Toad took the stairs to the lobby. He recognized Carmellini and shook hands. "The admiral isn't here, but come on up," Toad said and led the way to the stairs. "Anything you'd tell him he'd refer to me, so you might as well eliminate the middleman."

"What floor are you fellows on?" Carmellini asked.

"Eight. I'm in training for the Boston marathon."

When they reached the office, Toad sank gratefully into the chair behind his desk and tried not to look bedraggled. He eyed Carmellini without enthusiasm. Several inches over six feet, with wide shoulders, impossibly narrow hips, and hard, callused hands, the guy looked to be in terrific physical shape. The eight-story climb hadn't made him draw a deep breath. His forehead wasn't even damp.

"Bet you don't get a lot of visitors up here with the elevator out," Carmellini said conversationally.

"You got that right. When most people drop by, I tell them to come back when the Redskins win their next home game. I hadn't been up the stairs in over an hour, so I made an exception in your case. To what miracle do we owe the honor of your presence?"

"I was in London. After the FAA grounded all the planes arriving on the East Coast, I was stuck. Flew to Montreal and rented a car, just got in."

"You came straight here?"

"Yeah. I have a story to tell the admiral, but since you're sorta his alter ego, I'll tell it to you, just in case my former employer figures I'm here and sends someone looking for me before he gets back."

"I'll let that alter ego crap go by if you'll tell me why the agency might be looking for you," Toad said.

"Let's put it like this. The folks at Langley don't know where I am and may or may not be in a sweat about that. I resigned Monday before I went to England, effective in a couple weeks, then I decided to quit early."

"I hope the bank doesn't repossess your car," Toad said, eyeing Carmellini skeptically. It was almost as if the man were too glib, too smooth. One half expected him to pull three walnut shells and a pea from a jacket pocket and ask if you wanted to make a friendly wager.

Tommy Carmellini casually glanced around to see who might be in earshot—there was no one—then began. "Antoine Jouany. The company sent me to England to raid his computer." He went on, telling Toad about it.

Captain Rebecca Allison's F-16 was pushing against Mach one when she dropped out of the overcast over the southern beach of Long

Island. Try as she might, she couldn't get her radar to pick the Tomahawk out of ground return. She shallowed her dive and began scanning ahead and below for a glimpse of the small missile.

The thick haze under the clouds limited visibility to about three miles. Finding out a tiny cruise missile was going to be extremely difficult, she thought, and wondered if she had already missed it and flown by.

"Should be dead ahead," the Sentry controller told her, "about two miles. The speed readout is five oh six." Oh, man, 506 knots. Right against the Earth.

She kept the fighter descending, glanced at her indicated airspeed—550—and quickly scanned her instruments. All well.

She concentrated on the view through the HUD.

"One mile, at your twelve."

She was down to three hundred feet on the radar altimeter now, and into the city suburbs. Streets and houses and schools flashed under the speeding fighter, giving her a sensation of speed that was sublime.

There!

Oh, so small! She was overrunning, so she picked up the nose and chopped the throttle, then dropped a wing to keep the missile in view. It was a hundred feet above the ground, maybe less, just clearing the highest obstacles as it roared along. Allison matched the missile's speed, then dropped down behind it into trail. It was so tiny, almost impossible to keep in sight.

She had never in her life flown so low and fast. The buildings were right there, she was barely clearing the roofs. Somehow she found the courage to glance at the weapons panel to verify the switch settings, then she squeezed the trigger on the stick to the first detent.

The Sidewinder gave her a tone, then dropped it as a cell phone tower whizzed past, only yards from the wingtip.

That rattled her for a second. She was right against the city, suicidally low.

Come on, Allison!

As she was trying again to get a heat lock-on, she realized that the missile was crossing over an airfield. It must be JFK! Without thinking she pulled up slightly, and in the blink of an eye was at five hundred feet. Below she saw the huge mat, runways, the control tower, the terminal with airplanes at every gate—she forced the stick forward and went rocketing by the control tower so low that she felt she could almost reach out and touch the thing.

The tower must have been a discrete navigation fix for the missile, she realized. Gritting her teeth, trying to ignore the blur under her, she added throttle, began closing the distance to the hard-to-see missile.

Stanley Schottenheimer found a missile, although unknown to him, it was not the one the Sentry controller had pointed out. Not that it mattered. There were three missiles, and if any of them could be shot down before they hit their targets, that would be a small victory.

The borough of Queens spinning beneath him unnerved Schottenheimer who, like Allison, had never flown so low and fast. No one did training like this—the risk was too great.

Schottenheimer gritted his teeth, forced himself to stay down on the rooftops and add throttle to close on the racing missile. With all the heat sources immediately below him, his Sidewinders also failed to lock on to the Tomahawk's exhaust, so he planned on using his gun.

Now the missile shot over LaGuardia Airport, the fighter only two hundred yards behind.

Closing, closing, he squeezed off an experimental burst from the twenty-millimeter Gatling gun mounted in the port wing root. And missed the tiny target.

The land fell behind as the missile shot out over the sound, then laid into a port turn. The radar altimeter went off, but the damn thing always did over smooth water.

He could see the missile plainly for the first time, unobstructed by haze and a cluttered background. And he wouldn't be hammering Queens with the twenty-millimeter. This was his chance!

He steepened his turn, tried to pull lead on the missile as the radar altimeter deedled insanely. He could see the shore coming up ahead, knew he had only seconds.

Over smooth water on a dark day it is always difficult to accurately judge one's height; in any event, Schottenheimer had too many things shrieking for his attention. Inevitably he slid inside the missile's turning radius. As he tried to nudge the pipper in the HUD onto the missile, the left wingtip of the F-16 kissed the dark water.

Still traveling at a bit over five hundred knots, the wing of the fighter tore off as it cartwheeled along the surface of Long Island Sound. As the fighter decelerated, spinning like a Frisbee, the eyeballs-out G ruptured hundreds of tiny blood vessels in Stanley Schottenheimer's brain, killing him instantly. He was dead when the fighter disintegrated. The engine made a mighty splash. The cloud of jet fuel and pieces that had been the rest of the plane grew and grew as the components of the cloud decelerated at different rates. The pieces of metal and sinew, wire and fiber and bone struck the water gently, almost like snowflakes, amid the rain of fuel droplets.

Tearing across the rooftops of Brooklyn at almost full throttle, Rebecca Allison succeeded in placing the HUD pipper on the tiny exhaust of the Tomahawk missile ahead of her and hesitated for a heartbeat. Some of her twenty-millimeter cannon shells were going to hit buildings and cars, doing God knows what in the way of damage. And if she succeeded in damaging the missile, it was either going to crash into a building or detonate immediately.

She certainly didn't have time to think about it as she streaked across the city, trying to keep the pipper on the missile and not smear herself across half of Long Island. They sent her to shoot down missiles—that was the mission when she and Schottenheimer manned the alert fighters. "Intercept and shoot down."

Someone else had made the decision. Someone who was paid a lot more than an O-3 fighter jock.

She squeezed the trigger, held it down. A stream of twenty-millimeter shells vomited from the six-barreled cannon. For some reason, the stream was a few inches low, going under the Tomahawk. Instinctively Rebecca Allison moved the stick back a tiny fraction of an inch . . . and the river of cannon shells slammed into the missile.

The missile exploded in a blinding flash. A trillion watts of electromagnetic energy raced away at the speed of light.

Even though the electronics in Allison's fighter were hardened against the electromagnetic pulse from nuclear blasts, the close proximity of this one burned through the protection and fried every

208 ★ STEPHEN COONTS

circuit in the airplane. Then the airplane overran the cloud of decelerating bits and pieces of the missile and swallowed a hatful. The pieces went through the various stages of the spinning compressor in a thousandth of a second. Blades ripped loose and were flung through the skin of the airplane, fuel lines were severed, the unbalanced engine began tearing itself apart. All this happened in the third of a second after the missile exploded.

Before Rebecca Allison even realized what was happening, her fighter exploded. The fireball of fuel and pieces splashed into the buildings of Brooklyn with devastating effect. In a dozen seconds twenty city blocks were on fire. A giant column of black smoke formed as the raging fire sucked in air from every direction. Soon the fire became so intense that the asphalt in the streets caught fire. The inferno blazed without sirens or alarms of any kind, because every electrical circuit within three miles of the blast was destroyed.

The other two Tomahawks, the one that Schottenheimer had died trying to shoot down and the one that had not been intercepted, crossed the East River and exploded over Manhattan. One detonated over the New York Stock Exchange, the other over Rockefeller Center. The missile that Allison destroyed had been targeted to detonate over the Empire State Building. The fact that it didn't get there made almost no difference to the damage caused by the attack: Almost every electrical switch, circuit, and microchip on the island of Manhattan was destroyed by the two stupendous pulses of electromagnetic radiation.

Kolnikov fully appreciated how the presence of the *Los Angeles*–class attack submarine *La Jolla* complicated the search problem for the P-3 overhead. No doubt before long other P-3s would be arriving. If *La Jolla* weren't there, the P-3s would go active, echo ranging or pinging with their sonobuoys. They had little chance of finding *America* if they listened passively, he suspected.

And that was a wonder. As quiet as *La Jolla* was—and it was quieter underway than a Soviet boomer tied to a pier—the Revelation sonar could still detect it. There it was on the bulkhead-mounted vertical displays—*he could see it!* It was a ghostly form in the gloom, illuminated by the sound of its hull moving through the water.

And *La Jolla* couldn't see him. His boat was too quiet for her sonar to detect passively. *America* was the ultimate stealth ship, so silent it was invisible to anyone without Revelation's ability to make sense of the massive data flows from the hydrophones.

Well, he reflected, *America* was invisible until someone went active, began radiating noise into the water and listening for echoes. She was deep, perhaps so deep that the radiating beams would be deflected before or after they echoed off her hull. Then again...

If he sank *La Jolla,* removed her from the problem, the P-3s would be free to ping. Still, finding a deep-running boat this quiet under the thermal layers would be very difficult. With luck, they might pull it off. And Kolnikov and Turchak and their colleagues would be dead. Of course, with *La Jolla* out of the problem, Kolnikov would be free to maneuver *America* to the extent of her capabilities and use the built-in tricks, such as the noisemakers and decoys.

La Jolla was much shallower than *America,* perhaps eight hundred feet deep. She was making four knots, hadn't altered course. She was, Kolnikov concluded, running up a bearing line that she had established when she heard the Tomahawk launches. She undoubtedly had her towed array deployed, maximizing her listening capability, although of course he couldn't see the array on the sonar displays. Perhaps if he were closer...

Or went active.

What if...?

"Let's find out how quiet this boat really is," he said to Georgi Turchak. "Ahead one-third, begin an ascent, then turn in behind *La Jolla,* staying at least a hundred feet below her wake so we won't get tangled in her array."

"Are you crazy?" Turchak hissed.

"Sooner or later this guy may go active. He won't see us unless he does. If he does, we want to be below and slightly behind him. And we want to stay there. Now let's do it."

"Why don't you just torpedo him now?" Heydrich asked conversationally, "before he knows we are here. Escaping this P-3 afterward should not be difficult."

"I signed on for the money, not to kill sailors."

Turchak looked at him askance. "Vladimir Ivanovich..."

"I have to sleep nights, goddamn it! Ahead one-third."

Without another word Turchak pushed the power lever to the one-third-ahead setting and began the process of ascending as the boat accelerated. *La Jolla* was at one o'clock, crossing from left to right at a forty-five-degree angle, so he should be able to rendezvous without exceeding *La Jolla*'s speed. Apparently she had not detected the beat of *America*'s prop. If he had to speed up to catch her, the frequency would change, and detection might follow.

Let's be realistic, Turchak thought. *America* was going to be right behind her! He didn't know whether to laugh or cry. In all the years he had known Kolnikov he hadn't realized that the man was willing to bet everything in one wild, suicidal gamble.

Both men were watching the computer presentation in front of Turchak, and the forward-looking sonar display, so they didn't see Rothberg staring unblinkingly at their backs.

The explosion of the two Flashlight E-bomb warheads over Manhattan caused a complete, total, massive power failure in the heart of the most wired city on the planet. At the NASDAQ and New York Stock Exchanges the indexes had already fallen the maximum amount allowed in one day and the authorities had suspended trading minutes before the trillion-watt electromagnetic pulses destroyed the computers and communications equipment that made trading possible. The television and radio broadcasting network nerve centers in Manhattan were destroyed, leaving people all over the globe wondering why the video and audio of their program had suddenly disappeared.

Telephone switching units, Internet servers, mobile telephone transmission towers, heat and air-conditioning units, office equipment—the devastation was as total as that which had struck Washington, but affected more people since New York was a larger, denser city and the hub of so many of the world's networks.

Of course the power grid in the affected area failed. The fused switches and massive short circuits dragged down the power grid throughout the northeastern United States. All of New England temporarily lost power, as well as upstate New York, New Jersey, and much of Pennsylvania.

Electric trains all over the area coasted to a stop. Within a three-mile radius of the blasts, the electric motors in subway trains and regular locomotives were destroyed.

Fortunately the FAA administrator had grounded non-emergency private and commercial flights east of the Mississippi River—visiting a financial disaster upon the airlines and their employees and stranding and outraging a large portion of the traveling public—so no airliners packed with people fell from the sky. The electrical systems and navigation gear in the airplanes parked at Newark and JFK were totaled by the E-warhead blasts. The electromagnetic pulses from the blasts were sufficiently weak by the time they hit the aircraft parked at LaGuardia that they only damaged them, destroyed some delicate avionics, and left better-grounded or -shielded boxes unharmed.

Two police helicopters, airborne when the warheads detonated, went into uncontrolled autorotations, killing all aboard when they screwed themselves into the ground; a medevac helicopter transporting a heart attack victim crashed on final approach to a hospital landing pad; and a private jet descending into the New York area with a cargo of human organs for transplant went nose-first into the Hudson River.

In the minutes following the blast, millions of Manhattan office workers waited impatiently for power to be restored. Of course, the recent attack on Washington was common knowledge, so many immediately assumed the worst. As people discovered that even battery-operated devices no longer worked, the realization that New York had been attacked by E-warheads from USS *America* spread like wildfire.

When emergency generators failed to restore any level of electrical service—the emergency generators were themselves dead—the dimensions of the disaster began making themselves felt as people tried to exit their buildings. Elevators were stuck where they had been when the pulses arrived. Those in transit were hung up between floors. Emergency crews began working to extract the passengers, a task that would take as long as twenty-four hours in some cases. The vast bulk of the people trapped in the office towers of Manhattan began trekking down endless dark staircases.

On the street they found that the sound of the city had completely changed. Not a single gasoline or diesel engine was running. The sounds of the streets were voices, angry, unhappy, some panicked, as everyone stared at streets crammed with dead vehicles. The gridlock nightmare extended from the Battery to Central Park and beyond. Many vehicles contained people trapped by electronic door locks that wouldn't open. Policemen used gun butts to shatter the safety glass of vehicles with people trapped inside. Since there were not enough police, volunteers attacked windows with anything handy.

Times Square, the beating heart of the city of New York, that pop-art cathedral to tacky outdoor advertising, was dark and strangely quiet. Theater and movie marquees and the giant electronic billboards were blank, the human energy gone. Under an overcast sky, New Yorkers and pilgrims alike stood stunned amid the ominously dead buildings, unsure what to think or do.

Endless columns of frightened, claustrophobic people trudged through stygian subway tunnels to escape stalled trains and climbed the stairs from dark stations. They formed unmoving crowds at the subway exits, trapping those still underground, as they stared disbelievingly at the traffic jam from hell that blocked the streets.

Reports trickled in via messengers to police stations and City Hall. An absolute electrical failure—even water had ceased to flow through many of the city's supply pipes since the pumps that moved it were disabled. Without water, the sewage system would stop carrying away waste products.

The authorities quickly realized that they faced a catastrophic disaster of the first order of magnitude. Approximately eight million people were trapped in the affected parts of Brooklyn, Queens, Staten Island, Manhattan, and New Jersey, unable to escape from a city that in one terrible moment had been rendered incapable of sustaining human life. Worse, getting outside help to the people who would need it would be extremely difficult; in fact, in many places, getting food and water in would be impossible for days to come—perhaps even weeks. Eight million people would need a lot of help. The usual disaster assistance organizations were going to be totally inadequate.

Gradually the authorities came to the realization that New York City, the beating heart of high-tech America, had become a death trap.

The warehouse in Newark that housed Hudson Security Services was far enough away from the epicenter of the two Tomahawk blasts over Manhattan that most of the computers inside escaped damage. Surge protectors and backup batteries worked as advertised, soaking up excess voltage. Two hard drives crashed, only two. Zelda grabbed the telephone, felt relief wash over her when she got a dial tone. Then the power failed. Although the Hudson employees feared the worst, seven minutes later the electricity came back on.

As the crew divided their attention between diagnostic efforts and the television monitors, Zip Vance told Zelda, "That was too damned close."

Indeed, had they known when the Tomahawks were coming, Vance could have had all the equipment shut down and grounded. And immediately inflamed the suspicions of everyone in the room. Coincidences like that don't just happen. So it worked out for the best, Zelda thought. She picked up the telephone, checked again for the dial tone. Still there, although the switches would soon be overwhelmed with people calling relatives.

It took several hours to verify that the main storage units were unaffected, with their files intact. Only when that was done did Zelda shoo out the employees. They charged for the elevator, anxious to go to their homes and ascertain the damage there.

When the last elevator load was out the front door, Zip brought the elevator back up and killed the power switch. "So far so good," he said and dropped into a chair.

"I thought we were going to have to use the rope," he added. "Always wondered if Freda could make it down." Freda was forty pounds overweight, the heaviest woman in the crew. "She always said she wouldn't try. Guess you would have had a roommate for the duration."

Zelda didn't want to talk about Freda or the rope.

"With incentives, Jouany owes us more than four hundred million," she said lightly. "Or did before those Tomahawk missiles hit. By tomorrow the number will be over five. Think of it! A half a billion dollars!"

"Money? Is that all you think about?"

"In America money is how you keep score. We're winning big, baby."

"There's more to life than money," her partner shot back, meeting her eyes.

"Zip, we've been through all this before. I just never thought of you that way."

Vance got out of his chair and headed for the elevator. He talked as he walked. "In two or three weeks this will be all over, one way or the other. We'll be in jail or filthy rich."

He threw the switch to power up the elevator, opened the door, and climbed in. "What are you going to do with the rest of your life, Zelda? Have you even thought about it?"

He didn't wait for an answer. The elevator hummed, and down he went.

CHAPTER TWELVE

The wide road ran on and on toward the distant blue mountains, until it rounded a far curve or topped a rise and disappeared from view. Even then the road was still there, even if out of sight. It would faithfully reappear when you rounded the curve or crested the hill. That was the promise of America. In America there was always the road.

Jake Grafton was thinking of the road as he drove along in the government sedan with Janos Ilin in the passenger seat. Neither man had much to say. Ilin had readily agreed with Jake's suggestion of a drive for lunch when he intercepted him on the fifth-floor landing of the office building stairs. He looked almost relieved as he spun around and descended the stairs that he had just trudged up.

Jake headed west on Interstate 66. They were passing the Beltway exit when Ilin asked their destination.

"I thought we might have lunch in Strasburg," Jake said, "the hotel there."

"Fine," Ilin replied and asked no more.

They drove with the radio off. They had no audio cassettes or disks, so the only sounds were the hum of the engine and tires and the snore of truck diesels. As they passed Manassas the interstate narrowed to two lanes in each direction, the traffic thinned, and they were left with the September day, with its dissipating overcast and mild breeze, and the road. Always the road.

Jake knew what he wanted from Janos Ilin. He wanted to know what the Russian knew about the theft of USS *America*. He wanted to know who was behind the theft and what they hoped to accomplish. If they were Russians, he wanted to know. If they weren't, he was even more curious. Alas, he didn't know how to go about getting what he wanted.

The guy was so foreign! Oh, he spoke decent English, could understand and be understood, but Jake Grafton had been to Moscow and seen the place. Ugly, inhospitable, polluted, filled with people speaking an incomprehensible language and fighting like rats for the bare necessities, Moscow was as foreign to Jake Grafton as any spot he had ever been. Thinking about Moscow as he drove this morning, he remembered that sense of hopelessness that he had felt when he visited there years ago, immediately after the collapse of communism. At that time the population was still living in the shadow of the absolute dictatorship, an oppressive tyranny from which humanity and common sense had long ago been squeezed, if indeed there had ever been any. A more cheerless place he couldn't imagine.

And Moscow was Ilin's home, his national capital, the place where he had spent his life learning and pulling and climbing the ropes.

What, exactly, did he and Ilin have in common? Explain that, please.

"Your embassy," Jake said, breaking the silence, "does it have electrical power?"

"Oh, yes," Ilin said, grinning ruefully. "We Russians have worried for years about American intercept methods, so we hardened the wiring inside the building and installed extra generators. The lights will be on there even if the sun burns out."

"One assumes that contingency is extremely unlikely."

"No doubt, but if it happens, we will be ready. The ambassador will be able to see to write his report to Moscow: 'Today in America the sun burned out.' That is the way of a bureaucracy. When someone somewhere predicts a possible crisis, that prediction assumes a life of its own. Regardless of the likelihood of that crisis occurring, regardless of the cost in effort or money to guard against it, someone will build a career minimizing the damage that crisis could cause, if it ever happens."

"I see."

"The bureaucracy rules."

"And the microphone in your belt buckle? Was that hardened against electromagnetic pulses?"

"Alas, no. It is history, as you Americans say."

"Why the microphone in the first place? All the liaison officers were free to return to their embassies whenever they wished and presumably reported everything that they saw or heard."

"Always the bureaucracy. By listening to what I heard, the bureaucrats could guard against incompetence or betrayal by me."

"Don't they trust you?"

"They trust me within reason. But the bureaucrats know that the world is a tempting place and people are weak."

"Are they listening now?"

"No," Ilin said and grinned. "I am free as an American, at least for a little while."

"And those little soliloquies outside my house in Delaware? What were they about?"

"Sol—what? Excuse me. I do not know that word."

"Soliloquy. A conversation with yourself."

Ilin grinned. "I tease the listeners, who cannot talk back."

Grafton smiled. At last he had a glimpse of the human being.

"So who stole our submarine?"

"Vladimir Kolnikov and Georgi Turchak and the rest of your CIA Blackbeard team."

"How did the Russian government find out about the Blackbeard team?"

Ilin grinned again. "Now I ask you—is this car wired? Are *your* people listening?"

"I don't know," Jake said. He drove in silence for about a minute, then when a place offered itself, pulled over to the side of the road and got out of the car. Ilin did likewise. They were alongside a cow pasture. Jake and Ilin climbed the fence and walked fifteen or twenty yards.

"They are not listening," Jake said. "I guarantee it."

Ilin laughed. "Your guarantee only means that you do not know if they are listening. I must factor in the possibility that you have a pure heart and an ignorant head."

"The world is never as it seems," Jake murmured.

"Occasionally it is," Ilin said.

"You are evading the question. How did the Russian government find out about the Blackbeard team. Answer it or refuse to do so, your choice."

"One of the members of the team told us."

"But the CIA vetted them," Jake pointed out. "None were SVR."

"A Russian cannot get out of Russia without the approval of the SVR. He can't get an exit visa. The bureaucracy knows something, always something, about everyone. They never let go. A Russian can never escape them. One of the members of the team worried that the SVR would eventually find out about his participation in the scheme and retaliate against him or his relatives. So he reported it."

"Who turned the team, told it to steal a U.S. sub?"

"I don't know." Ilin shrugged.

"The SVR?"

"That is a possibility. I do not know."

"Would a matter like that be routinely shared with you?"

"Never. Unless I was a part of the operation."

"How did you learn of the Blackbeard team?"

"I was assigned the job of making contact with one of them."

"Did you?"

"Yes. The one who betrayed their mission."

"But you told the director of the CIA of the team's existence?"

"Yes."

"Why?"

As Ilin weighed his answer, Jake added, "Were you told to do so by your government?"

"No."

"It was your idea?"

Ilin nodded, as if examining that reality for the first time. "Yes."

"If you had not told, what would have happened?"

"Presumably the team would have been captured in Russia, interrogated, perhaps tried publicly. It is difficult to predict because the decision about what to do with them would have been made at the highest levels based on what the leadership wanted from the United States at that time. It is possible they would have been executed secretly." He raised his shoulders a millimeter and let them fall.

"But you spilled the secret?"

"Yes."

"Wasn't that a risk? Isn't it possible the SVR will learn that you betrayed the service, betrayed your trust?"

"Life is full of risks," Janos Ilin said flatly. "Discussing this with you is one of them."

Jake Grafton tried to read the Russian's face. Was that statement true? Or magnificent fiction? "I can understand betting your life now and then, but you are putting it at risk rather freely, wouldn't you say? And for what? To save the lives of rogues you don't know?"

"In a country as poor as Russia, lives aren't worth much. Theirs or mine."

"Did the thought occur to you that the CIA might not be happy that you threw a monkey wrench into their plans?"

Janos Ilin's eyes narrowed. "Are you suggesting that the CIA wanted the Blackbeard team to fail?"

"That is a possibility," Jake Grafton said innocently, glancing at Ilin's face. "There are others."

"Did they want a Russian submarine, or would any submarine do? Is that where you are going?"

"A CIA team trained to steal a submarine stole one," Jake said, weighing his words. "The team fired missiles at an American city. That is the reality we must somehow explain."

Before Ilin could reply to that comment, Jake heard the buzzing of a light plane. It was the first one he had heard all day, so he automatically looked up. The plane was no more than a thousand feet above them, a high-wing Cessna with fixed gear, a Cessna 182 perhaps. Jake got a glimpse of two heads in the front seat.

"That's the first plane I've heard today," Ilin said, glancing up. "I thought only emergency aircraft were authorized to fly."

"He's probably gotten permission from someone," Jake responded slowly. The Cessna rolled into a turn, pointed its left wing at the two of them. As the Cessna held the turn, Jake realized the men in it were looking at him and Ilin. It flew away to the north, toward a low hill, descended gently, then turned steeply. Down to about a hundred feet, the plane came racing back toward the two men in the pasture.

Jake saw one of the men lean out the passenger window opening—obviously the glass had been removed. He had something . . .

A weapon.

"Jesus, he's got a gun!"

Before they could run more than two paces, a burst of automatic fire went over their heads and kicked up dirt.

As the plane went over, Jake Grafton darted north toward the nearest trees, away from the road. He heard Ilin puffing along behind him.

The four-strand barbed-wire fence along the tree line was old and rusty. Grafton threw himself flat and rolled under the bottom strand as he heard the airplane coming back. Ilin went under headfirst, digging wildly with his arms and legs. Both men managed to roll behind trees as the engine noise crested and a burst of submachine gun bullets beat a tattoo on the tree limbs and trunks over their heads. The white plane with faded blue trim swept on by with its wheels just above the grass, then began rising gently to clear the tree line to the east.

Ilin's chest heaved as he fought for air. His face was gray. Too many cigarettes.

"What was that comment you made about risks?" Grafton asked.

Unlike *America,* the control room in *La Jolla* was brightly lit. The room was directly under the submarine's sail. The computer consoles and control stations were arranged around the periscopes, which were so long they ran from the keel of the boat to the top of the sail when stowed. There were no Revelation panels on the bulkheads because the new sonar system with its massive computers for processing the raw audio data was not installed in *La Jolla,* or any other American submarine for that matter. At the forward bulkhead were two cockpitlike control stations, complete with airline-type control wheels. One of the stations controlled the planes, the other the rudder. The chief of the boat stood behind the two helmsmen, watching the analog depth gauges, compass, and trim indicators and checking them against the information presented on a computer display.

Petty Officer First Class Buck Brown sat at the primary sonar control station studying the displays, sampling frequencies, and designating tracks for the computer to follow and plot. Beside him sat three other sonarmen. There were actually eleven sonar consoles, but only four were necessary for full operation of the system. The others were there in the event one of these consoles had a maintenance problem, or to use for training purposes.

Brown had heard the sonobouys hit the water and correctly designated them as bouys. The fact that the tracks failed to move was the giveaway. The computer kept a running tactical plot, but to back it up, two sailors stood at identical drafting tables in the rear of the control room plotting the bearings and connecting the dots. The navigator checked them constantly. Junior Ryder, the skipper, also liked to glance at the charts as they drew, ensuring that the tactical picture he carried around in his head matched the picture that unfolded on the computer display and the plotting tables.

Ryder left his stool in the center of the room and walked the three steps aft to the plotting tables with his usual quick stride. He was a large man full of nervous energy, and it showed. Now he checked the boat's progress along the bearing line that Brown had laid down two hours ago when he first heard the Tomahawk launch.

He tried to decide what he would have done had he been the pirate captain aboard *America* after he launched the cruise missiles from the vertical launch tubes. Clear the area as fast as possible would be one's first instinct, he knew. However, the faster *America* left the area, the more likely it was that someone would hear her. Perhaps the Russian skipper had dashed a few miles, then slowed to minimize his noise signature . . . and listen.

Who was this Russian, Kolnikov, whom SUBLANT said stole *America*? An experienced submariner, obviously, but how experienced? How knowledgeable? Was he one of those Russians who knew how to think for themselves, or had he spent his life saluting and doing precisely what he was told?

After he launched the missiles, in which direction did he leave the scene? At three knots his boat would travel only a hundred yards in the minute that it took to get the three weapons airborne. One minute, a hundred yards . . . of course Brown had been unable to determine any change in bearing from the first launch to the last and thereby get a hint of *America*'s course.

But afterward . . . Kolnikov had launched missiles at Washington thirty-six hours ago from a position about 160 miles south. These missiles today could have been aimed at New York or Boston, maybe even Philadelphia. Did he intend to go northeast, toward Nantucket? Or east, out to sea? Perhaps south?

If he went west he would soon get into shallow water. . . .

"Captain?" That was Buck Brown, on the sonar.

"Yes."

"I'm hearing something funny . . . well, sir, I just don't know. It shouldn't be there and darn if I know what it is."

Was it possible, Junior Ryder asked himself? Have we met *America* leaving the area?

Junior Ryder slipped on a headset and adjusted it to fit. He pressed the earpieces to create a tight seal as he closed his eyes and concentrated. He heard . . . something, some kind of a gurgle maybe . . . nearly inaudible.

"Can you enhance it?"

"Yes, sir." Brown twiddled a few knobs.

Now the commanding officer could hear it better. Definitely a gurgle. "Is that us?"

"I don't think so, Skipper."

"What is it?"

"Sir, I'd just be guessing."

"Guess away, Buck."

"The problem is that I can't resolve a bearing. The array seems to say it's coming from dead ahead, and the flank sensors seem to indicate it's coming from behind. Does that make sense? Could it be between us and the array?"

Junior Ryder stood very, very still. "How long have you been hearing this noise?"

"I noticed it about three or four minutes ago, sir. But it's so faint, it may have been there for quite a while."

"Hours?"

"Oh no, sir. Maybe fifteen or twenty minutes. Maybe less. I'm sure if it had been there longer I would have noticed it sooner."

"So what is it? Take a guess."

"I'm probably way off base, sir. It kinda sounds to me like water swirling around an open torpedo tube. Or a couple of them."

The changing tone of the Cessna's engine drew Jake's attention. He put his head around the tree, looked for the plane. There it was, descending, turning, lining up on the pasture.

"Damn! They're going to land! Let's get the hell outta here."

He turned and charged into the woods, Ilin following.

The Russian was quickly winded. As they ran through the brush and second-growth timber, slapping limbs out of the way and being slapped by them, he managed to ask, "Who—? Who wants you dead?"

Grafton paused for a moment to let Ilin catch up. "I thought they were after you," he said, searching the Russian's face. At least it was no longer gray. Now it was bloodless, the color of old paper. "Maybe the SVR has found out about your chat with DeGarmo, the CIA banana."

Ilin leaned against a tree, trying desperately to get air. "Oh, no . . . They . . . would never . . . have let me . . . walk out . . . of the embassy." He took a huge breath and exhaled dramatically. "They would have sent me back to Russia . . . or executed me in the embassy. . . . Not this . . ." he waved a hand at the men behind.

Jake Grafton could no longer hear the hum of the aircraft engine. Presumably the killers had shut off the plane and were now coming through the woods, searching for their quarry.

"C'mon," Jake said and led off.

Unless the gunmen were expert trackers, and this wasn't the Wild West, they were going to have to come slowly through the woods, looking carefully. Maybe he and Ilin had a chance.

Unfortunately they were going up a slope, which slowed them down, and Ilin was panting like a sled dog, which must be audible for a quarter mile.

After what seemed like a quarter hour, but was probably half that, they crested the ridge and found a trail along the top. Right or left?

Jake opted for right because the direction seemed to take them away from the highway. He felt like running but forced himself to walk. If he ran, Ilin would never keep up. As it was he was holding his side. Still, he too walked as quickly as he could.

They had gone a quarter mile or so when the trees ahead thinned.

A house. Jake glimpsed the brick. White trim. Big house, with chimneys.

Across the lawn, looking for signs of life.

No people, no cars in the driveway, no one visible in the windows.

He rang the doorbell on the entrance nearest the garage. He tried the knob. Locked, of course.

Felt around in the mailbox, looked under the doormat. Nothing. A flowerpot on the window ledge. He took it down, looked in.

"What are you looking for?"

"A key. Unless you want to run through the woods like a rabbit."

Now he heard the engine of the airplane, revving . . . taking off.

A light fixture . . . no. A box for milk deliveries . . . And there it was, taped to the bottom of the milk box.

Please, God, no alarm! *Please!*

He unlocked the dead bolt, then found he had to do the doorknob too. Finally the door swung open.

No alarm.

He relocked the door behind them, then looked around. They were in the foyer of a large house, ten or twelve rooms, well furnished. The place reeked of serious money.

"Stay away from the windows. And look for guns. Any kind of guns."

He went looking for a phone. The kitchen was to the right of the foyer, overlooking the parking area. There was a telephone there, of course. Dial tone. He punched 911.

As it rang he heard a popping outside. Muffled shots . . . then the line went dead.

"Bastards."

He threw down the telephone and charged through the house looking for a gun cabinet. He found Ilin on the second floor, in a den, trying to open the gun cabinet with a key. "It was in the drawer." Shelves filled with books lined the walls, soft leather chairs were arranged around a fireplace, a blowup of a thoroughbred hung over the fireplace.

Grafton picked up a book from a coffee table and broke the glass of the cabinet. "They shot out the telephone line," he explained. The cabinet held half a dozen shotguns, all expensive double-barrels.

Grafton grabbed two—twelve gauge—then rummaged through the drawers in the bottom half of the cabinet.

He found a box of shells. Birdshot. What the hell!

He passed Ilin a handful of shells and pocketed the rest.

Someone was working on the door downstairs. He could hear it. He could also hear the buzzing of the light airplane, which sounded as if it were flying back and forth near the house.

He loaded the gun and went to the head of the stairs, where he could see the door. "Look out the windows, see if you can get a shot," he told Ilin.

Several minutes passed. He wiped the perspiration off his face, tried to calm down. He had a gun in his hand, everything was going to be okay. They were going to live through this. Yeah.

The shotgun felt heavy, solid, good.

He eased down the stairs, trying to see out the windows.

There, at the window in the living room, someone looking in. He flipped off the safety, raised the shotgun, and fired both barrels as fast as he could pull the trigger. The glass in the window exploded outward.

Too late! The face had disappeared just before he fired.

He reloaded as quickly as possible, then eased over to the window and looked outside, ready to duck if someone out there decided he was enough of a target to be worth the effort.

No one in sight. No blood, either, which filled him with relief.

He got a glimpse of the plane, up there under the clouds.

"Did you wound him?" Ilin asked. He was on the stairs, his shotgun at the ready.

"I was too late."

"So who wants you dead?"

"Nobody. I'm a junior flag officer in the navy. I don't know anything about anything. Nobody in his right mind would have any reason to want me dead. They must be after you."

"No."

"Think what you like," Jake said. He checked the doors coming from the basement and garage—all locked.

"If they try to get in again, this is the way they will come," he told Ilin and left him to keep an eye on these doors while he searched for food in the kitchen. He was hungry and thirsty.

There was little in the refrigerator. Jake checked the freezer, then the cabinets. Finally he filled a glass of water from the sink tap and took it to Ilin, who accepted it gratefully. Back in the kitchen he stood at the sink and drank two glasses full.

More exploring followed, with both men carefully avoiding windows. Fortunately the lawn fell away on the front of the house, which had huge windows looking toward the Blue Ridge Mountains.

Taking his time, Jake unlocked the door to the garage and gently pushed it open, half expecting someone to be in there. There wasn't.

He flipped on the light. . . . A pickup. Four-wheel drive. Unlocked but no key. "Here's our way out if we can find a key," he told the Russian.

Back upstairs he went to the den, rooted through the desk drawers. Plenty of keys, but none that looked like it might fit the pickup.

"Look in the kitchen," he advised the Russian, who left him in the den.

After a bit Jake went downstairs and met Ilin heading for the garage with a key ring in his hand. "They were in a drawer with batteries and flashlights," Ilin said over his shoulder.

When they were satisfied they had the right key, Jake held up a hand, stopping Ilin from turning on the truck. "If we drive out now, they'll follow. We'll have a better chance after dark."

"That's hours away."

"We've got shotguns, water, and toilet paper. I'm in no hurry."

Ilin nodded and climbed out of the truck.

They sat on the stools at the kitchen counter, well back from the windows, shotguns on their laps. The Cessna was still up there, circling. On the walls were family pictures, teenage girls at the beach, girls with boys, a photo around a Christmas tree. Several of the framed pictures were of a couple in their fifties, the owners, probably.

"Who are these people?" Ilin asked. "Who owns this house?"

"The guy is a car dealer, I think. Maybe retired. There were some old awards from Ford Motor Company up in his office, a framed picture of a dealership."

"A capitalist."

"Yep. A leech. Sold cars to anyone who wanted one. Sucked the blood of the proletariat. The proletariat liked it, apparently, which is why America is full of cars and millions of people make an excellent living in the auto industry."

"Too bad Karl Marx didn't sell cars."

"And Lenin," Jake said, flashing a grin.

"I think after dark would be best," Ilin said, leaning back on his stool and making sure the shotgun was handy.

"There's food in the freezer and a television. Maybe even liquor. And a loaded gun at hand. What more do you want?"

"What I want is a cigarette." Without another word Ilin lit one. There were no ashtrays, of course. He found a saucer in the cabinet and used that.

Seated in the left seat of the P-3 Orion, Duke Dolan checked his watch. The sonobuoys were in the water, the TACCO and his troops were trying to sort out the undersea noises . . . and the copilot was talking to Scout One, the E-3 Sentry AWACS that was somewhere nearby, directing aerial traffic. The four-engine patrol plane was low, only two hundred feet over the ocean, so Duke was working hard as he hand-flew it.

Clouds were moving in from the west. The high overcast would come down during the day and showers would develop this evening, according to the weather briefer when Duke discussed the forecast with him this morning an hour before dawn. That was the thing about the military—the working hours were truly terrible. Up at three in the morning, brief and fly for twelve hours, debrief, sleep a little, then get up and do it over again. At least his crew was flying days. He hated flying all night and trying to sleep in the middle of the day.

This contact was a welcome break from the boredom of long patrols. The people in back were pumped, the copilot was energized, Duke was working hard. All this over an ocean empty in every direction as far as the eye could see, which was about eight or nine miles; then the sea and sky merged in a bluish haze.

Duke turned the selector knob on his intercom box so that he could listen to the crew in back as they sorted out the undersea sounds. The sonobuoys were set to reel out their hydrophones to different depths, so *America* couldn't hide under a temperature or salinity discontinuity. Not that the boat really needed to hide, Duke Dolan thought ruefully. It was so damned quiet that the P-3 had little chance of hearing it.

That thought had just crossed his mind when he heard one of the operators tell the TACCO, "I've got something here."

After a moment the TACCO began giving Duke heading changes. He brought him around in a fairly tight circle and had him fly toward an area he wanted investigated.

Duke Dolan was amused by the whole business. Didn't these people understand that they weren't going to hear *America*? That damned pirate, Kolnikov, was down there right now laughing at the U.S. Navy. Maybe that was the sound they heard, Kolnikov laughing.

The TACCO had him make a turn and come back over the area that he thought might have something.

Time passed as the plane droned along, turning this way and that, the pilots following the TACCO's orders. After about twelve minutes of this, the radar operator, who also ran the magnetic anomaly detector, or MAD gear, sang out, "MAD, MAD, MAD." He had a contact! "The needle pegged! Clear to the stop!" the man shouted over the ICS at the TACCO.

"Back around for another run," the TACCO told Duke. "We'll put a sonobuoy in on this pass, then work out his course and speed."

"When you get it all figured out, then what are you going to do?" Duke asked.

"Report it all to the heavies, I guess. They aren't going to let us shoot if there are American boats within a hundred miles. You know that as well as I do."

"Yeah," Duke said disgustedly and laid the P-3 over in a turn.

"P-3 went directly overhead," Eck said softly, just loud enough for Kolnikov to hear. There were still a few kibitzers in *America*'s control room, including Heydrich, and for some reason Eck felt they were intruders.

"Tell me if he comes back," Kolnikov said. He kept his attention on the ghostly shape of *La Jolla* on the flat-screen display. The noise generated by the prop pushing water shone like a floodlight on the presentation. Eck had softened the gain somewhat on the presentation to keep the light from overpowering the rest of the submarine. All sonar images were fuzzy, of course, but the computer cleaned up this one and gave it a tangible reality that made it leap at the viewer.

"The P-3 probably got us on MAD," Eck said. Kolnikov was too calm. The man just didn't seem to understand that their lives were at stake here.

Eck glanced at Kolnikov, was nodding affirmatively, a tiny up-and-down jerking of the head. Then it stopped. He was intent on *La Jolla*.

Two minutes ago he had picked up the sound of water passing around the array cable. After Eck designated noises on that frequency for the computer to sort out and display, the cable was visible on the port Revelation displays, a pencil-thin line that stretched from the port side of the submarine, above *America,* and disappeared astern. The thought struck him that the cable looked like a power line along a highway.

"He's turning and moving away," Kolnikov said to Turchak, who was at the helm control station. "Stay with him."

"I'm going to have to add a few turns."

"Okay."

"He knows we're back here," Turchak said softly, trying not to alarm Eck or the kibitzers. "He's started the dance to see if we'll stay with him."

"Surely not. We're too quiet. Turn on the sail lights, poke the photonics mast up a few feet and turn on the camera. Let's see if we can get this guy on television."

Rothberg scurried aft and raised the mast. Turchak flipped on the sail's floodlights, used primarily to light the gangway at night when the sub was against a pier.

Yes. After the image was enhanced by the low-light illuminator, there she was, *La Jolla,* on the forward screen, dim and ghostly.

"Try the blue-green illuminator," Kolnikov said over his shoulder to Rothberg, who was still at the photonics console.

"That might set off alarms," Turchak objected. Blue-green was often used by airborne and space-based sensors for submarine detection.

"Okay, ultraviolet," Kolnikov muttered.

In ultraviolet the American attack boat was slightly clearer. Kolnikov, Turchak, and Rothberg discussed frequencies for a bit, then Rothberg changed the freq of the blue-green illuminator slightly, taking it off the freq they thought most likely to be expected, and tried that. *La Jolla* leaped clearly into view.

Several minutes passed. *La Jolla* turned again, five or six degrees back to the right.

"Stick like glue. He can't hurt us from that position, and no one else will shoot with him there."

"And if he manages to break away?"

"He doesn't know we're here," Kolnikov assured his friend. "We'll stick with him until the P-3 leaves, or any other antisubmarine forces that enter the area, then drop astern and break away."

"I think he knows we're here."

"So. What can he do? We are within the minimum range of his torpedoes, they wouldn't travel far enough to arm, and he can't turn them back across his wake due to the safety interlocks. And if he tries to break away we'll gun him the instant he crosses our minimum range line."

Aboard *La Jolla,* Junior Ryder was examining his options. He had turned his boat fifteen degrees to the right and put in turns for six knots. He and his XO, Commander Skip Harlow, were listening to the raw sonar audio. As the boat's speed increased, it seemed to Junior that the gurgling noise got louder. He asked Harlow and Buck Brown what they thought.

Both nodded. Yes.

Then he turned the boat five degrees back to the right, to see if the noise would follow. It did.

"That fucking Russian has his nose up our ass," Harlow murmured. Sweat glistened on his forehead and ran down the crevices of his face. He swabbed at his face with his hand.

"He can't shoot us from there," Junior said thoughtfully, "but if he breaks away . . ."

"If he breaks away, we can shoot too."

"He didn't shoot us when he had us cold," Junior Ryder said slowly, thinking out loud. "He heard us, probably even knows what boat this is, knows we're hunting him, and he didn't shoot."

"He isn't hunting us," Harlow said without conviction. "We're hunting him."

"Oh, man!" Combat wasn't supposed to be like this, Ryder thought bitterly.

"So what do you want to do, Skipper?"

"I sure as hell don't want this asshole killing my crew. That's for damn sure. I want a high-percentage shot and I want to give him a low-percentage one."

Harlow leaned over to speak softly to Brown. "Is this contact *America*? Are you sure?"

"I don't have positive verification from the system," Petty Officer Brown explained. "I'm not sure of anything, sir. We have the signature of *America* in the computer, but they're going too slow for me to get anything but this gurgle."

"What if it's some Russian boat?" Harlow asked his commanding officer. "Some Russian skipper who thinks he's cute?"

"If that boat were Russian we would have heard him. Russian boats aren't this quiet. What do you suggest? You want to give this guy the first shot, just to be sure?"

Skip Harlow thought about it. The lives of everyone on this boat were on the line. So were the lives of everyone on the submarine following *La Jolla*.

One thing was absolutely certain: If *La Jolla* made it back to port, every decision made aboard her was going to be weighed by a board of senior officers seated around a long green table. Good judgment was absolutely essential at all times, yet there were always a host of unknowns in every combat situation. Harlow well knew that in the United States Navy the system was biased in favor of those captains who acted aggressively in the face of the enemy. Much would be forgiven a man who waded in swinging. The legacy of John Paul Jones was alive and well. Still, sinking an allied submarine would not be career enhancing.

"Stealing *America* was an act of war," he said finally, hoping this commanding officer would get his drift. Ryder did. He nodded once, seeming to make up his mind as he did so.

"Go back to our base course, slow to four knots," Ryder said to the chief of the boat, who gave the appropriate orders to his two helmsmen. "XO, let's set up snapshots on four torpedoes. Quietly. Any shot we get will be minimum range, point and shoot."

"Do you think he'll give us a shot, Skipper?" the chief of the boat asked.

"Oh, yes. Eventually. He didn't shoot when he had a free shot, when we didn't know he was there. He could have, but he didn't. In my opinion, he thinks that boat he's in is undetectable. He's going to let us be his shield while that patrol plane is in the area. Sooner or later those guys are going to leave. When we're all alone, Kolnikov and friends are going to try to sneak away. When they cross our minimum range line, we'll let 'em have it."

Shooting someone in the back who declined to shoot at you wasn't very sporting, but that thought didn't even cross Junior Ryder's mind. Buck Brown thought of it, but he bit his tongue. Those guys stole *America,* they killed six sailors. They had earned their tickets to hell.

CHAPTER THIRTEEN

Jake Grafton and Janos Ilin learned of the missile strike on New York City when they turned on the television in the kitchen of the house they were in, somewhere west of Manassas and a half mile or so north of Interstate 66. Grafton and Ilin had walked the halls, looked at the doors and windows, concluded that there was just no way for whoever was chasing them to enter the house without making noise, then they went back to the kitchen.

Jake found peanut butter in the cupboard. Ilin touched his finger to the peanut butter, tasted it experimentally, and made a face. They were eating it on crackers and drinking water when Ilin finally reached for the television and flipped it on. Some of the channels were off the air, so he flipped around until they found one that was on, CNN.

New York! The sub had E-bombed New York!

They started with the volume off so they could hear the sound of glass breaking, but eventually they turned it up so they could hear the audio. The television types were confused and besieging the military authorities for answers, which weren't forthcoming. At least two Flashlight missiles had struck New York City, perhaps three, maybe four—no one seemed to know. A fighter had crashed, perhaps several, perhaps there had been an air battle in the skies over the city, blocks of buildings were ablaze, firefighters couldn't get to the scene.

Manhattan and Brooklyn had been surgically removed from modern America. The power had failed. Lights, heat, elevators, and telephones didn't work, the subways didn't run, the streets were filled with cars, trucks, taxis, and buses that were no longer operable, the television and radio networks that originated there were no longer on the air. Eventually Grafton and Ilin learned that the television crews on the air were from New Jersey.

The whole scene reminded Jake of Baghdad during the Gulf War, with camera crews on rooftops looking at columns of smoke rising in the distance.

After a half hour of watching the breathless reporting and the guesses, good and bad, Jake turned the television off and walked through the house again with the shotgun in his hand. Standing well back from the windows, he looked out, trying to see if anyone were still out there.

And saw no one.

"What do you think?" he asked Ilin, who was doing the same thing.

"I think they may still be out there," the Russian responded. "I have nothing more pressing on my calendar."

"Maybe they are waiting for us to come out."

"That is possible. One wonders if the owners will come home this afternoon."

That, Jake suspected, wasn't in the cards. The house looked like it had been vacant for weeks, perhaps longer. There were no perishables in the refrigerator or cupboards. He pointed this out to Ilin.

They were trapped. The circuits in Jake's cell phone were fried the night before last—he had almost thrown the thing away, but Callie suggested he retain it to show to the insurance company if there were problems. She was confident their household insurance would pay their losses. A forlorn hope, Jake suspected, but he put the telephone on his dresser and left it there.

Now he wandered through this house looking for a cell phone. He checked the bedrooms and the owner's office area, looked in the drawers. He found a charger for a cell phone, but the instrument was not there.

New York!

Well, at least they had the pickup. Tonight.

"Are you married?" he asked Ilin.

"She died. Cancer."

"I'm sorry."

"It was years ago. Life cheated her. She loved me, she loved life, she loved her country. Then she got sick and died young."

Jake thought of his wife. He and Callie had been lucky, extraordinarily so, and they both knew it. That realization dusted every day of their lives with magic. He didn't say this to Ilin, of course.

"People change," Ilin mused, "the world changes. When I finished school I was recruited by the KGB. My father was prominent in the defense department, his father had been a hero of the war against fascism. The KGB seemed the path of least resistance." He shrugged. "In those days we knew who the enemy was. America. And what a fine enemy you were, too. Rich, powerful, strong, at times stupid and heedless. We looked for cracks, for chinks in the armor, prepared for the final battle between good and evil, Armageddon. It didn't come. The Soviet Union was always a geopolitical oxymoron, an empire that tried to be a nation. It collapsed, finally, stunning us all."

They sat, each with his own thoughts, listening to the silence.

"So everything changed," Ilin continued after a while, "and nothing changed. Russia remained what it always was, poor and backward in so many ways, isolated, afraid of foreign ideas, struggling to keep up with the outside world, not sure it wanted to. Today the enemy is still America . . . and Europe and China and Japan. And given the state of affairs in Russia, that is good. When Armageddon comes we will be on the sidelines."

"Maybe it's here now," Jake Grafton said.

"The struggle has no beginning and no end. It is ongoing and everywhere. You comfortable Americans, you have never understood that basic fact. Change brings new challenges. That is the fallacy of SuperAegis. Regardless of how much money you spend or how clever you are, technology cannot give you security. Checkmate happens only in chess, not in human affairs. Man has been looking for a magic weapon since he first picked up a club. And hasn't found it yet."

"Nuclear weapons worked," Jake objected. "They prevented World War III."

"Nuclear weapons forced the struggle into other channels. And Russia lost. But the struggle never ends. As long as life continues, the struggle continues." Janos Ilin gestured at the silent television set, then picked up a dead telephone and pointed it at Grafton. "And America is losing."

"Skipper, what if the navy sends another boat into this area?" Skip Harlow, executive officer of *La Jolla*, asked that question of his commanding officer, Junior Ryder. Two hours had passed since Buck Brown had told them of *America*'s presence behind them. The P-3 was still searching the area, dropping sonobuoys periodically, apparently searching in vain for the stolen submarine.

Ryder had been thinking of the message advising him to rise to periscope depth to receive an encrypted message via satellite. He had elected not to waste time or give away his presence by that maneuver. Now he wondered if he had made a mistake. There were a variety of things SUBLANT could have thought urgent enough to justify that maneuver, and Harlow was right, another sub entering the area was one of them.

If another boat entered the area, he thought Kolnikov aboard *America* would probably hear it first, at maximum range, before Ryder knew it was there. What if he elected to fire a torpedo at the oncoming boat while he was still too close to *La Jolla* for either him or Ryder to launch a torpedo at the other?

Oh, man! This could get crazy! Ryder looked around the control room, looked at the sailors on the consoles, his XO, the chief of the boat, the watch officer.

"We must be ready for anything," he said. "I want everything ready to go, torpedoes, decoys, bubble makers, everything."

All the action stations were already manned, and mentally the skipper took stock. Even if his boat lacked *America*'s capability, he would stack his crew up against any crew in the world. The two torpedo control consoles were manned, all four of the sonar consoles, the computers, the helm, the chief of the boat watching everything, the guys on the plot backing up the automatic systems. . . . They were ready to shoot as soon as the boat's sensors found a target within the torpedoes' operating envelope. The torpedo control consoles automatically monitored the attack-director function and generated preset data on a continuous basis for two torpedoes, which could be fired instantly. The attack director received its data from the central computer complex, which integrated inputs from sonar, the ship's inertial nav system, underwater log, and analog dead-reckoning analyzer/indicator.

"Buck," Ryder said, placing a hand on the first class petty officer's shoulder, "if another sub comes into the area, I want to know it as soon as possible. If *America* shoots a torpedo, it will be at one of our guys, so the instant it leaves the tube, sing out."

"Aye aye, sir."

In a whisper in the exec's ear, Ryder asked him to go through the boat, check that all watertight doors were properly secured, that every station was manned and ready, and to say a word to everyone. Then he turned to the com officer. "Encrypt and transmit a message via the underwater telephone. Tell that P-3 that we have found *America*. Tell them to clear the area and keep everyone else away."

"Aye aye, Skipper. But the pirates have *America*'s codebooks. They can decode the message."

"Indeed, if they know what to do and how to do it, they can. I bet they won't bother. Go."

"Yes, sir."

Vladimir Kolnikov was standing behind his helmsman, Turchak, monitoring the bulkhead-mounted vertical displays when he caught the faintest flicker of light from the massive, shimmering shape of *La Jolla* on the Revelation display. Automatically he glanced at the photonics image, the computer-constructed image derived from television and inputs from the sensors on the photonics mast, which was elevated several feet out of the sail so it could look ahead. *America*'s sail floodlights were still illuminated, which helped give the image clarity but . . . no, the flickering light was not present on that image.

"See that light!" he hissed at Turchak, who looked up from the screen where he had been monitoring the performance of the sub's autopilot. Like Kolnikov, Turchak's eyes went from display to display.

"*La Jolla* is using her underwater telephone," Eck announced softly. "It's encrypted, I think, but I'm recording it if you want someone to try to decode it."

"Who—?" asked Turchak, obviously mystified.

"The P-3," Kolnikov said, disgusted with himself that he didn't realize instantly what the energy source was. "He's talking to the patrol plane. They'll pick up the audio on their sonobuoys."

"He knows we're behind him," Turchak said, as if he were a judge pronouncing a sentence.

Aboard the P-3, the sonobuoy operators did receive the message. After running it through the decoder, the TACCO took the printout forward for the pilot to see.

Duke Dolan read the message, then passed it back. "That's certainly clear enough," he said.

"Yeah, it is," said the TACCO. His name was Ruben Garcia. "I think we should indeed clear the area, but let's stay where we can hear the sonobuoys. If *La Jolla* doesn't get this guy, we can come back and look some more."

"This message says *America*'s following close behind *La Jolla*. You hear her?"

"Well, no, but—"

"Hell!" said Duke Dolan and threw up his hands. "We got plenty of gas and nothing better to do today, so why not?" He motioned to the flight engineer for climb power. As the props bit more deeply into the atmosphere, he lifted the Orion's nose and began a climb to the west. He said over his shoulder, "Better tell the Sentry to relay the message to SUBLANT. *La Jolla* waved us off."

"The P-3 is leaving," Eck told Kolnikov and Turchak. "His noise is fading."

"Which way?"

"He went out to the west."

"If this guy knows we're back here," Turchak said, "he'll torpedo us as we break off contact."

"I've been thinking about that," Kolnikov said.

"You should have sunk this guy when we had the advantage of surprise."

"*I* should have! Just killed them all and nuked off into the sunset. Yeah. Isn't that right, Heydrich?"

Heydrich got up from his chair and wandered out of the compartment.

In the Pentagon the secure telephone on the desk of Vice-Admiral Navarre rang. He answered it and found himself talking to SUB-LANT, a two-star admiral. "Sir, I thought you should know. We have received a message from a P-3 sent to investigate the area where the cruise missiles were fired from this morning. *La Jolla* heard the firings and went to investigate. She put a voice message in the water that the Orion picked up. She reports that she has contact with *America* and asked the P-3 to leave the area."

"When was this?"

"Just moments ago, sir. The P-3 asked to remain close enough to monitor the sonobuoys in the water, just in case, and I agreed. He is going to pull off about fifty miles and orbit high."

"This wasn't the way we planned to hunt for *America*. What went wrong?"

"Sir, the message directing our boats to come to periscope depth went out as an advisory, not mandatory."

"I'm going to tell you again, just this once. We will never find *America* with passive tactics: She's too quiet. I want P-3s to get there as soon as possible and echo-range with those sonobuoys. When they have her illuminated, they can call the attack subs in. Not before."

"Yes, sir. But that didn't happen this time. We didn't get the plan out. Now *La Jolla* says she has a contact on *America*. We have another boat in the vicinity that can reach the area in several hours at high speed. *Colorado Springs*. She was at communications depth to receive our original situation update . . . so I authorized her to proceed into the area."

"Did *La Jolla* ask for help?"

"No, sir. In fact, the skipper requested that everyone stay out. But *America* is so stealthy, I just don't feel it wise to bet everything that *La Jolla* can sink her."

Navarre didn't know what to say. A hell of a day . . . American submarines hunting American submarines.

"I've got a real bad feeling about this," he said finally. "We're after a rogue grizzly bear. I think the only safe tactic is to let P-3s illu-

minate *America* and our boats shoot from long range. If we do it
any other way we're going to lose boats."

"Sir, the problem is, *La Jolla* says she's on her. We have no way
to pull her off, even if we wanted to. The question is what is the
best way to help *La Jolla* prosecute this contact."

"You're the man on the hot seat," Navarre said. "Keep me advised," he added and hung up the phone.

SUBLANT was going to pile in the forces until *America* went
down. And damn the cost! What else could he do?

On one of their trips to look out the windows, Jake thought he saw
someone across the lawn, at the edge of the woods. He paused and
waited. Ilin joined him eventually and they both watched. After five
minutes they saw a moving figure—perhaps the same one, perhaps
someone else—well back in the trees.

"If they crash in here with guns blazing they'll kill us both," Jake
said. "You realize that?"

"I've watched your television shows."

"On the other hand, if it's you they're after, they can pot you any
old time going into or out of the embassy. Heck, they can just go
back there now and wait for you to show up."

"If they were after me," Ilin replied dryly, "they could have shot
me this morning when the limo drove out of the embassy gate. It's
you they want."

"You are a real ray of sunshine."

"Just explaining why I don't think they will teargas the house and
knock down the door. I saw that on television last week. California
must be a marvelous place. Three beautiful women with gorgeous
hair, magnificent chests, and submachine guns. They didn't even
bother with body armor. Only cretins would shoot at women like
that."

There were half a dozen cans of beer in the kitchen fridge, so
Jake thought, Why not? He passed one to Ilin and opened one for
himself.

"After the SuperAegis satellite was lost, why did your people send
you to the liaison team?"

Ilin snorted. "To keep an eye on Mayer, Jadot, and Barrington-Lee."

"So what have you decided?"

Janos Ilin shrugged. "I look for a gesture, a glance, a wrong move. I listen for a slip of the tongue. So far, nothing."

"Who put the satellite in the water?"

"I don't know. The FBI may find out, but not by questioning people. Someone will retire to a life of leisure. Or spend too much money. A spouse seeking a divorce will voice suspicions. Something like that."

"I think you know a lot you aren't telling me," Jake said, making contact with Ilin's eyes and holding them.

Ilin searched Jake's face, then reached into his pocket for cigarettes. He took his time getting one out, lighting it. "Knocking out the tracking stations at precisely the right time and putting the rocket in the water—someplace—was a sophisticated operation. Several people were involved, perhaps a half dozen."

Jake nodded.

"Running a covert operation like that would be extraordinarily difficult for a foreign intelligence service. Difficult for anyone, but essentially impossible for a foreign service. Funding, covers, cut-outs, it would be a huge undertaking. As a rule, the larger the operation, the more likely it is to be affected by random chance, by the friction of normal life."

"So it wasn't Russia."

"I doubt it. My directorate wouldn't handle it."

"No one but the Americans wanted SuperAegis," Jake said thoughtfully, scrutinizing Ilin's face. "Europe and Russia went along only when their tails were twisted."

Ilin nodded. "They ceased active opposition only when they were backed into a corner, with no other options. America is the only superpower. With an antiballistic missile shield in place, America will be even less inclined to listen to other nations' concerns."

"I thought expanding the shield to cover Europe and Russia made the system politically palatable?"

"It made the medicine impossible to refuse, but if the system never becomes operational, Europe will not be unhappy."

"Europe?"

Ilin smiled. He dropped the stub of his cigarette into his beer can, then went to the refrigerator and helped himself to another can. "You

Americans! You sit here in your prosperous paradise, with your beautiful houses and stables of cars and supermarkets full of cheap food and think the unwashed hordes in China and India and the Middle East are your enemies. Not so. Your enemy is your largest economic rival. Europe has a larger economy than the United States; in fact, it's the largest economy on Earth. They have slashed taxes, jettisoned massive overregulation, kissed socialism good-bye, embraced capitalism, and adopted one currency. Europe is on the road to becoming a federal state. Europe is the next superpower."

"Not Russia."

"Not Russia," Ilin agreed flatly. "An academic economist I met at a Washington cocktail party told me that Russia will never be able to accumulate capital as rapidly as Europe or the United States. She was right, of course. The place is too large, with a harsh climate and relatively few people. The Russians will always pay more for the infrastructure upon which a modern economy rests. Roads, factories, bridges, food, electrical grids, pipelines, all kinds of distribution systems ... everything costs more. Always has and always will. The problem with capitalism is that it is a game Russia cannot win."

In the silence that followed that remark he lit another cigarette.

"Europe is Russia's natural enemy," Ilin continued finally, musing aloud. "Has been for centuries. Russia's foreign policy since the Middle Ages has been designed to protect itself from the European powers. As along as they were divided and could be played off against each other, Russia, with its vast spaces and thin, poor population, had a chance. With Europe united, Russia's future looks grim."

"I see."

"Today the bulk of our intelligence efforts are directed against Europe. More of them should be."

"I suppose the Europeans resent that."

"What they resent is *American* intelligence efforts against them. With the collapse of communism, they directed their efforts against the United States, sought to use their intelligence services to provide an edge for their industrial efforts. Naturally the Americans reacted." He grinned tightly. "It is a different game these days. Without the ideological bogeyman to frighten people, they can more easily convince themselves that betrayal of their company is not betrayal of their country. After all, they tell themselves, it's only money. Most people want more of it. Want the good life that their neighbors have." He gestured at the room in which they were sitting. "They want this."

"And you, Ilin? What do you want?"

"Are you asking my price?"

"No," Jake Grafton said. "I don't think you have one."

"Thank you," Janos Ilin said. A smile lit up his face. "That is the nicest compliment I have ever received from an American."

CHAPTER FOURTEEN

Three hours after the P-3 Orion left them, USS *La Jolla* was still making six knots, still running at eight hundred feet. *America* was a hundred yards behind her, about one hull length, stepped down slightly to stay out of *La Jolla*'s wash and clear of the towed array cable. An hour ago *La Jolla* had made a gentle turn of ninety degrees to a course of three four zero. If she stayed on this course for another fifteen minutes, then turned left again, she would be making a perfect square search pattern with the launch site at the approximate center.

Kolnikov had kept the lights on *America*'s sail illuminated. With the aid of the blue-green illuminator and the visible light sensors, he had a relatively clear image on one of the vertical displays. He stood staring at it, mesmerized by the gently turning prop, trying to read the mind of *La Jolla*'s commander. Did he know he was being followed?

Kolnikov was inclined to believe the American didn't know, but how do you explain those two minor course changes in the minutes after *America* joined behind her? It really looked like he had some noise from the stealth sub on his gear and was checking to ensure it wasn't a false signal. If he knew *America* was behind him, he was pretending just now. Would he let *America* fall back and disengage?

Or would he shoot the instant the range opened enough for his torpedoes to arm, which was about one thousand yards?

A hell of a problem.

Turchak was right, of course, Kolnikov mused. And Heydrich, though he hated to admit it, even to himself. He should have fired two torpedoes at the attack boat as soon as she got within the torpedoes' envelope, before the crew even had an inkling that *America* was near.

Fighter pilots kill fighter pilots, submarine captains are supposed to kill submariners—isn't that the way it goes? Sneak up, launch a torpedo or missile before they see you, shoot 'em in the back. Escape before their friends can take revenge. That is the essence of modern war.

God knows Kolnikov had spent enough years training for it. He knew what it was and how to do it.

But this isn't war, he told himself. We stole a submarine for money. If we had stolen a car no one would have gotten very excited. On the other hand, shooting people while you are stealing things is a bad business. Yeah, we had to shoot some people to get aboard the sub, and we killed that American traitor. Thinking about the dead, he waved irritably, as if he could banish them from his memory.

Too many things on your conscience, Kolnikov. Far too many. A dangerous luxury, a conscience, beyond the pocketbook of a poor man like you.

If *La Jolla* makes the ninety-degree left turn—in what? ten, no, eleven minutes—Kolnikov mused, then I'll break away, slow to barely maintaining plane effectiveness, let him motor on until he's increased the separation to a mile or so. Then I'll turn ninety degrees to the right and sail away, staying in his stern quarter, where his sonar is the least effective. In the event he does anything aggressive, I'll be in a perfect position to launch from the port tubes.

That decision made, he descended the ladder to the galley and poured himself a cup of coffee. He sipped the hot, black liquid, savored it, stared at his reflection in the plastic that covered the coffeepot operating instructions, which were mounted on the bulkhead. After several sips, he topped off the cup, then climbed back to the control room, where he perched on the captain's stool and lit a cigarette.

On the proper minute, *La Jolla* began her port turn. Vladimir

Kolnikov sighed with relief. He had Turchak follow her diligently around the turn, then as she steadied on her new course, two five zero degrees, he told Turchak to slow to two knots. "Watch out for that towed array," he warned. "It's right above us."

"I'll avoid it."

Kolnikov nodded. He could rely on Turchak, which was a good feeling.

"Rothberg," he said, glancing around to locate the American. "Check the torpedo control panel. I want to ensure the panel is continuously updating the presets in the torpedoes. I hope to sneak away from her without anyone the wiser, but we must be ready, with our finger on the trigger. I want to let the towed array go by before I turn and point our prop at it. Putting those pulses right into the towed array and expecting them not to hear is asking too much. When we are well aft of it, then we will turn."

He paused, examining their faces, then continued: "If they put fish in the water we must shoot back and get out decoys while we accelerate. Turchak, be ready if I call for power. Alert the engine room. Eck, pay attention to that sonar. Boldt, I want you to continuously monitor the torpedo firing solutions that the torpedo control machine is generating. Sometimes these idiot savants can garble the data coming in and turn out truly amazing, useless solutions. If we must shoot, it will be our asses if we miss. Do you understand?"

"Yes, sir."

"Rothberg, Eck?"

"Aye, captain," they each said, one after another.

As *La Jolla* faded from the photonics screen, Kolnikov had Turchak kill the sail lights. He walked aft to the mast control panel. He personally eased the mast down and waited until the green light came on, indicating it was completely stowed. Then he waited until the watertight door closed over the opening, sealing it to prevent flow noises.

The sound from *La Jolla*'s prop still beaconed from the darkness of the sea on the Revelation screen, even though the hull had faded from sight. If she maintained a four-knot speed advantage, Kolnikov calculated, it would take her fifteen minutes to open the distance between them to a nautical mile, a smidgen over six thousand feet. That would be enough. Then he would begin his turn. On the other hand, if this guy was going to punch off a minimum-range shot, he would be far enough away in about seven and a half or eight minutes. Allowing for the fact *America* was decelerating, call it ten minutes.

Ten minutes . . . *La Jolla*'s towed array . . . When the bitter end of the array went by, the distance would be precisely a half mile. Anytime after that.

"He's definitely slowing, dropping back," Petty Officer Buck Brown said to the control room crew aboard *La Jolla.*

"Mark the time," Junior Ryder said, and glanced at the clock on the forward bulkhead.

"Don't lose him," the chief of the boat said to Brown.

The XO, Skip Harlow, mopped his forehead again with a sodden handkerchief, even though the room was not overly warm.

The commanding officer, Junior Ryder, glanced at the inertial navigation computer. Six knots. That speed agreed with the dead-reckoning plot. One nautical mile every ten minutes. Say the Russian slowed to two knots . . . no, make it three. In twenty minutes at three knots the distance between the boats would be one nautical mile, which is two thousand yards. Even if he only slowed to four knots, in twenty minutes the distance would be two-thirds of a mile—call it thirteen hundred yards. That was enough for the torpedoes to arm, but not enough to get the decoys out far enough to be effective in the event Kolnikov instantly returned fire. No, the idea here is to kill the other guy and not get killed yourself. Point-blank torpedo shots were too risky, damn near suicidal, if the other guy was also ready to shoot.

Of course, once *America* faded from the sonar, the circle of probability where she must be began expanding. The more time that passed, the larger the circle. At some point the circle would be so large that a spread of torpedoes would have to be fired to achieve an acceptable probability of a hit. Eventually the circle would become so large that the probability of a hit would shrink toward zero, even firing a spread. If *America* were in range.

Junior Ryder considered all these things and made his decision. "Forty minutes, folks. In forty minutes the range will have opened to at least twenty-six hundred yards. We'll give her the gun and put some noise and bubble makers in the water. When the decoys are out, we'll turn. Then we'll shoot two fish."

The crew had trained for years for this moment and everyone knew his job, so there was little to say. People swallowed hard and tried not to look at one another. All highly qualified submariners, they knew that the pirate crew in *America* would undoubtedly hear the oncoming torpedoes and try to fire torpedoes of their own. Each crew would then try as best they could to evade the torpedoes seeking them. The winner of the battle would be the boat that survived what might be multiple salvos of torpedoes.

If there were a survivor . . .

"The frequencies on those gurgles are almost too low for the towed array," Buck Brown said. "Not getting much help there. I'm losing him. When he goes aft of the towed array, we'll lose him in seconds."

"Where is he now?"

"Dead aft, Skipper."

Ryder glanced at the clock. "Thirty-seven minutes from now. Remember, this guy may have changed his mind and shoot us as soon as the separation reaches minimum range. Buck, listen up."

Brown concentrated on the computer display before him and pushed his earphones more tightly against his ears.

"Which way will he turn, Skipper?" The OOD asked that question.

"Starboard, I think. Based only on the fact that a port turn would take him right back to the exact position where he launched the Tomahawks. I suspect he will instinctively turn to get away from that location. Of course, he could turn port just because he thinks I think it probable that he'll turn the other way."

"Two torpedoes?"

"That's right. We'll turn ninety degrees starboard and fire both from the starboard tubes. I think he'll probably turn starboard. Fifteen seconds between fish." At these close ranges, the torpedoes would begin an active sonar search for their target immediately after they left the tubes, while accelerating to their attack speed of forty knots. As they ran they would send sonar data back to *La Jolla* via fiber-optic cables that would reel out behind them. If the fiber-optic wire remained intact, the sonar operator in the firing submarine could help the torpedo differentiate between decoys and its real target during the attack phase and issue steering commands. If the wire broke, the torpedo was on its own, guided by the logic programmed into it.

"If the first torpedo finds him," Ryder said, "we can ensure that the second fish turns that way. One of these things should get a hit." He said that for the benefit of the control room crew, trying to radiate confidence. Alas, he was gambling all their lives. Try as he might, he didn't see any other choice. Kolnikov and his men had hijacked *America*—Ryder and his crew had been sent to find and sink it.

It was as simple as that. Really. Junior Ryder and his men were obeying the orders of their lawful superiors. If they died doing their duty . . . well, a great many good men wearing American uniforms had gone before them.

Vladimir Kolnikov carefully explained to his control room team what he wanted each man to do and what the execute commands would be. "Don't do anything without orders," he concluded. "Doing the wrong thing is usually worse than doing nothing at all."

He was briefing them just in case, he told himself, hoping against hope that the Americans didn't know that the stealth submarine was anywhere around and that they would disappear into the dark wastes, searching futilely. If the commander knows we are here, he will probably shoot, Kolnikov silently acknowledged.

"The Americans watch too many John Wayne movies," Kolnikov muttered.

"That they do," Heydrich replied, just loud enough for Kolnikov to hear.

He checked the torpedo presets, made sure the computer was properly calculating the angles. It seemed to be. He was studying the horizontal tactical plot when Eck said, "There's another submarine out there. Forty degrees forward of our port beam, I think."

Kolnikov took a deep breath and checked his watch. Seven minutes had passed since *La Jolla* began pulling away. She was just a fading light on the bulkhead Revelation screen. "What kind?"

"Don't know yet. The computer is trying to match the screw and flow noises."

Eck had already designated a track, but of course, with passive sonar there was no way to quickly determine the depth of the other sub or the range, the distance to it. The control room crew would have to take a series of bearings over time, plot them, then average to eliminate errors, to establish a probable distance, course, and speed on the other sub. Fortunately a torpedo data computer, or TDC, helped with this chore. The same technique could be used for depth, with less accurate results since the angles from the horizontal were so small.

"Another *Los Angeles*–class attack sub," Eck reported.

"I've lost him completely," Buck Brown said to the skipper of USS *La Jolla*, Junior Ryder. "That gurgle wasn't much, and it's completely gone now, faded into the background noise."

Ryder glanced at the tactical plot, then his watch. Nine and a half minutes. Allowing for the deceleration, the Russian was down to about two knots, slower than he thought. That meant the distance was opening quicker than he'd estimated. He was going to wait until the distance had opened to at least a mile and a half, giving the decoys sufficient time to deploy and the torpedoes more time to acquire their target. Still, it was going to be a minimum range, down-the-throat shot. Another fifteen minutes.

Sweet Jesus, into your hands I commit the lives of these men who sail with me.

"If *La Jolla* takes a crack at us, this new guy may decide to strap us on too," Turchak said to Kolnikov. Both men knew that decoying and evading torpedoes was a noisy affair, sure to be heard for many, many miles, depending on the location of the temperature and salinity discontinuities. And like blood in the water, attract sharks.

"Port torpedo, from number two tube," Kolnikov said, addressing Rothberg, "target the newcomer. Starboard for *La Jolla*. Just in case."

"Only one torpedo for each," Turchak whispered hoarsely. "What if one malfunctions?"

"We only have six. We may damn well need the last four."

"I just want you to know that I'd be most unhappy dying with four torpedoes still aboard."

Kolnikov resented Turchak's melodrama. "You're not going to die," he scoffed, "unless food poisoning nails you."

A sweating Rothberg was all thumbs changing the setting for the port torpedo. Kolnikov watched him, made sure he did it right.

Then he waited. Ten minutes came and went. Perhaps *La Jolla*'s commander was waiting for the range to open.

The unbearable tension seemed to get even tighter.

Rothberg began sobbing.

"Shut up," Heydrich snarled at him.

"They're going to kill all of us," he whispered, barely audible. He glanced fearfully at the bulkheads. The other submarines were out there, listening.

"We must shoot now," Turchak insisted. "Before *La Jolla* tells this new contact of our presence.

Vladimir Kolnikov lit a cigarette and smoked it in silence.

The minutes ticked away in dead silence in *La Jolla*'s control room. Everyone perspiring, everyone watching this and that, no one saying a word. Ten minutes since *America* passed the end of the towed array . . . eleven . . .

On the fourteenth minute, Buck Brown broke the silence. "Contact! I have a subsurface contact. About fifteen degrees forward of our port beam."

Junior began doing mental arithmetic. The range between *La Jolla* and *America* had opened to almost a mile and a half, which the torpedoes would traverse in about two minutes after they had made the turn.

"*Los Angeles*–class," Brown said.

Shit! With her Revelation sonar, *America* must have heard the other boat. And there was no way in the world that boat would hear *America*. For whatever reason, that sub had just sailed unsuspectingly into the middle of a shootout.

Should he wait?

If he contacted the other boat on the acoustic circuit, Kolnikov might shoot at both boats. The American could fire back, down the bearing line of the incoming torpedo, but at short range would he have enough time to get his decoys out, accelerate, and evade? While

Junior weighed the problem, the oncoming victim was steadily closing the range.

"Okay," he said, making up his mind. "Let's do it. Right full rudder. Flood tubes one and two."

"Kolnikov, *La Jolla*'s making a funny noise." Eck pressed his headphones tightly against his ears and watched the presentation on his scope. It took him all of five seconds. "He's flooding tubes."

Kolnikov's face was a mask. He took two steps to the torpedo control console, checked the presets going to each weapon one more time. Without knowing the range to the second sub, he was going to have to merely shoot down the bearing line and hope for the best. Not knowing how far the torpedo had to travel made that an iffy proposition. And with a limited number of torpedoes, he couldn't afford to miss.

"Target turning starboard," Eck reported.

"Go active," Kolnikov snapped at Eck. "Give me exact range and bearing to *La Jolla,* then to the port-side submarine."

Eck turned a knob on his console, selected a narrow beam width. Ping! The needle jumped when the pulse went out.

Buck Brown heard the ping from *America* just after the first Mk-48 pump-jet torpedo swam from its tube and raced away, turning toward *La Jolla*'s beam, in the direction that *America* had to be. As he sang out the news, he checked the PPI readout on the scope of the neighboring console, looking for the bearing. "Starboard beam, Captain," he roared.

"Fire two," Junior Ryder ordered, although only seven seconds had passed since the first fish was launched. He couldn't afford to wait. He was counting on the second torpedo guiding automatically, because the fiber-optic wire would undoubtedly break as he accelerated.

"All ahead flank, launch the decoys."

Four decoys were ejected from the housings in the sub's tail planes, two noisemakers and two bubble generators. Bubbles reflect sound, so they acted like chaff clouds that reflect radar energy. The noisemakers and generators would create an acoustic wall, Ryder hoped, which would defeat the active sonar in the nose of the torpedoes he knew Kolnikov would inevitably launch.

Eck sang out the range and bearings to the two submarines as they came up on his display, but the process now was strictly automatic. *La Jolla* was only twenty-four hundred yards away, a little over a mile, while the Johnny-come-lately was at twenty-six thousand yards, about thirteen miles. The information about each contact went to the torpedo data computer, which computed the proper course to those locations and the necessary firing angles, the presets, which were electrically sent to the torpedoes in the tubes. Then they were launched and Turchak slammed the power lever to flank speed ahead. They could feel the acceleration as the turbines accelerated and the prop pushed violently on the seawater. "Watch the temperatures," Turchak admonished the engine room crew.

Each succeeding sweep of the active sonar beam allowed the computer to determine a slightly different range and bearing to the targets. Subtracting the apparent movement of *America,* the computer then calculated the course and speed of both targets. The torpedo data computer updated the intercept bearings and fed that information to the appropriate torpedo via the fiber-optic wires. Meanwhile, the active seekers in the torpedoes were searching for their targets.

"Should I launch the decoys?" Boldt asked. Rothberg was curled in a chair, useless, staring at the Revelation panels. Heydrich was leaning against the aft bulkhead, a cup of coffee in his hand, discreetly bracing himself against the acceleration and any maneuvers Kolnikov ordered.

"No," said Kolnikov. "We'll use the antitorpedo weapons." These were small defensive torpedoes that homed in on the sonars of the incoming ship killers, riding the beam to them and exploding them prematurely. The latest thing in submarine defense, they were going to sea for the first time on *America,* which was the only boat that had them. "Enable two," Kolnikov added, "and I pray to heaven they work."

Four of these missiles were mounted in the sail. When enabled, they would automatically fire in sequence when they received a sonar signal on the proper frequency.

"And the jammer," he added, pointing at Eck, who nodded vigorously.

"Make notes," Kolnikov said to Turchak, who was monitoring the boat's increasing speed and waiting for the order for the violent turn that he knew was coming. "Anything doesn't work, we'll write a hot letter to Electric Boat."

The *Los Angeles*–class attack submarine that had sailed into the midst of the torpedo duel at twenty knots was USS *Colorado Springs*. Her sonar operators heard the thrashing of *La Jolla*'s prop, then the echo-ranging ping of *America*'s sonar. No neophyte, the captain knew precisely what he was hearing—torpedoes had been fired. The sonar quickly provided bearings to the active sonar and the accelerating sub. The problem, of course, was determining which sub contained the pirates and which one held good guys.

Within seconds his leading sonarman confirmed his first deduction. Mk-48s were indeed in the water, several of them. The distinctive sound of the swash-plate piston engine—which burned Otto-fuel, nitrogen ester with an oxidant—driving the pump-jet propulsion system was one he had heard many times before on exercises.

Seconds later the sonarman told the captain that at least one of the torpedoes was closing on *Colorado Springs*.

At least now, the captain reflected, he knew which sub was which.

"Fire two fish on the bearing of the incoming. Quickly now, let's do it, people." Fortunately the integrated sonar/combat control suite performed automatically. As the sonar derived a bearing, that data was fed into the system, which calculated the presets and electrically set the selected torpedoes while the tubes were being flooded.

When the outer doors were opened, the two torpedoes were ejected from their tubes by compressed air, their engines started, and they raced away, accelerating swiftly. The crew of the *Springs* did not elect to let the fiber-optic wires reel out behind them, however. Already the boat was accelerating. The captain intended to maneuver as violently as he could to cause the incoming fish to miss; fiber-optic wires would probably be broken, and they probably weren't long enough anyway.

With both torpedoes gone, *Colorado Springs* laid over in a hard turn designed to put the incoming torpedo forward of the beam, forcing it into a maximum rate turn, which might make it miss. And she launched a half dozen decoys.

Ruben Garcia's screaming voice in his earphones startled P-3 pilot Duke Dolan. "Torpedoes in the water, noisemakers. They're shooting at each other."

The P-3 Orion was orbiting at 25,000 feet, fifty miles from the center of the sonobuoy set. Gauzy cirrus aloft softened the afternoon sunlight, diffused it. Four miles below, the surface of the sea appeared a deep blue. The haze and the sea merged twelve or fifteen miles away, so there was no horizon. The surface of the placid ocean was flawless, unbroken by a single ship or wake. And yet, it wasn't empty.

"Tell SUBLANT," Duke told the TACCO. "Get permission for us to go back in. There may be survivors or something."

"Roger."

"Tell me if you hear any explosions."

"Got it," Garcia snapped and flipped switches so he could talk to SUBLANT on the radio.

Aboard *America,* Eck and Kolnikov heard the high-pitched pinging of the incoming torpedoes as they locked onto their target. *La Jolla's* decoys were pouring noise into the water, but Eck's sonar was so advanced that the decoy noise was easy to filter out. The Mk-48 Kolnikov had fired, however, lacked Revelation's sophistication.

Although he had ordered *America* to increase her speed drastically, Kolnikov had not ordered a turn for fear of breaking the fiber-optic wire unreeling behind the war shot aimed at *La Jolla.*

Eck studied the torpedo sonar data displayed on a separate screen.

He had too many targets. He couldn't tell which was the real one, so he made the assumption that all the targets were false and the submarine was behind them. Eck turned the torpedo to go around the targets he could see and come in behind, where he hoped the forty-knot fish would find *La Jolla.* He was so intent on his task that he didn't hear the antitorpedo weapons being fired from the sail and accelerating away, though the sonar faithfully captured the event.

Kolnikov glanced up at the bulkhead-mounted sonar panels and stood frozen, mesmerized. He could see the decoys, like newborn stars, and the river of disturbed water that was *La Jolla*'s wake, which appeared as a luminescent flow of gases in a darker universe. The sight that captured his attention, though, was the streaks left by the wakes of the speeding torpedoes—both his going away and *La Jolla*'s incoming.

He couldn't take his eyes off the two incoming fish, racing toward him like tracer bullets.

Out of the corner of his eye he caught the streaks that were the antitorpedo weapons. The one on the right went straight as a flashlight beam for the incoming warhead—and hit it. The detonation of shaped charge rocked the submarine slightly and appeared on the screen as a brilliant flash of white light.

The second antitorpedo weapon missed.

Involuntarily he grabbed for the table, braced himself, unable to tear his eyes from the screen.

Now a series of strobing lights flashed across the screen as more than 150 transducers buried in *America*'s anechoic skin began emitting sound in a pattern that was designed to confuse the acoustic receivers in the nose of the torpedo and cause it to turn.

Racing in at forty knots, the incoming death ray seemed to turn away from the center of the screen at the very last second and disappear out the side.

The torpedo had missed!

Vladimir Kolnikov exhaled convulsively.

Over the noise of the incoming torpedo, Buck Brown heard the explosion caused by the premature detonation of *La Jolla*'s first torpedo and assumed it had struck *America*. He also heard the active sonar countermeasures of *America*, but the reality of what he was hearing didn't register. He was too busy tracking the incoming torpedo and ensuring that the tactical plot was correct.

Junior Ryder also heard the first explosion and thought for a fleeting instant that he had torpedoed *America*. That thought died when he heard the active countermeasures. Although he had never heard it before, he had been briefed about it and recognized the sound for what it was. Still, these thoughts occupied only a corner of his consciousness—his attention was devoted to the tactical plot, a two-dimensional computer presentation of the tactical situation. His submarine was in the center of the plot. *America* and the *Springs* were depicted in their relative positions ... as was the track of the incoming torpedo.

He could see that the torpedo was being steered around the acoustic decoy cloud. He ordered more decoys deployed and called for a hard turn into the oncoming torpedo to try and force an overshoot.

If his boat had been going faster, the maneuver would have worked.

Ryder's eyes widened and he involuntarily grabbed the table as the torpedo track merged with the center of the plot.

The explosion rocked the boat.

Aft! It hit aft!

Then the lights went out and the computer screens went blank.

The explosion of the shaped charge in the warhead of the Mk-48 ruptured the hull of USS *La Jolla*. The enormous pressure of the ocean did the rest. The engineering spaces were crushed. The watertight hatch leading forward held for a long moment ... as the steel carcass that had been a sub settled deeper into the sea. Down she went, slowly, the pressure building inexorably.

"Emergency surface. Blow the tanks!"

Junior Ryder shouted the order over the groans of steel being twisted and deformed under the enormous pressure. They heard the compressed air being released, heard the rumbling of water being forced from the ballast tanks.

The generators had failed. In the glow of the battery-operated emergency lantern, Junior watched the depth gauge. If he could get the sub to the surface he could save some of his men—the ones still alive. If not ...

Behind him the talkers on the sound-powered circuit were trying to raise the men in the engineering spaces. One of them was sobbing.

The needle on the depth gauge quivered as the boat tilted, the aft end sinking and the bow rising. There was too much water aft.

"Shit!" shouted the chief of the boat over the voices and the noise of tortured steel. "It ain't gonna work."

He was right. The needle on the depth gauge began moving clockwise. The boat was going deeper.

"Oh, Jesus," someone exclaimed. Then the sea crushed the bulkheads aft and the air pressure increased astronomically, rupturing every eardrum, collapsing lungs and eyeballs in the microsecond before the wall of water hit them like a flying anvil.

And then they were dead.

Kolnikov recognized the ripping, tearing, crushing noise after the torpedo detonation for what it was. He immediately turned his attention to the *Springs*. He had one torpedo on the way, which the attack sub might well avoid.

He checked the combat computer to ensure that the remaining torpedoes in the tubes were getting presets. One was receiving range and bearings to *Colorado Springs,* the other to what was now the wreck of *La Jolla*. He flooded the tube, opened the outer door, and launched the torpedo that was tracking the *Springs*. Then he set up the remaining fish to track her too.

He turned away from the combat computer and stood in the center of the room looking at the Revelation panels. Noises were still coming from *La Jolla* as metal tore and she was crushed, compartment by compartment. Revelation displayed her agony as random flashes and smears of light that were brighter than the general glow of the acoustic decoy area, which was beginning to cool off.

The torpedoes fired at the *Springs* were two streaks that led away into the darkness.

Twenty-six thousand yards, about thirteen miles, the torpedoes would need a little over nineteen minutes to traverse that distance. And no doubt that sub had fired torpedoes in this direction that would require about the same amount of time to arrive.

America was still accelerating. Kolnikov directed Turchak to turn to ninety degrees off the bearing to the *Springs*. With a lot of luck he might run out of the detection cone of the incoming torpedoes, for undoubtedly there was more than one. He didn't expect to succeed in this maneuver, but he thought it worth a try. In any event, he would have the torpedoes in his stern quarter. When they were close enough, he would begin turning into them, tighter and tighter, trying to bring them forward of the beam and force an overshoot.

At the same time, he would trigger the active acoustic defense. He had only two more antitorpedo weapons, and he didn't want to use them here unless forced into it. On the other hand, as Turchak pointed out, it is silly to die holding a loaded gun you refused to shoot.

"Let's pray there are no more than two torpedoes inbound," he said aloud.

"I didn't know you prayed," Turchak muttered, and wiped his hands on his trousers.

"SUBLANT says to go in," the TACCO told Duke Dolan. "And we have explosions. Breakup noises."

Duke Dolan turned his attention to the autopilot. He studied it carefully, gingerly turned the heading control to bring the big plane out of its turn and steady on the proper heading. Then he retarded the throttles and lowered the nose several degrees.

He did everything slowly, trying to concentrate, trying to block out the thought of dying men.

To die on such a day.

God forgive us.

"I can hear torpedoes running," Eck said as he worked feverishly to get accurate bearings. Kolnikov could hear them too through the sonar headset he was wearing, but mainly he was listening to the sounds of *La Jolla* being crushed. The noises had about stopped. There was nothing left to crush as the wreckage sank slowly toward the ocean's floor, here about sixteen thousand feet below the surface.

More torpedoes were running. Life or death?

The deciding factor, Kolnikov hoped, would be the antitorpedo countermeasures. *America*'s were two technological generations beyond the countermeasures in the *Los Angeles*–class boats. *Seawolf* was the generation between them. If he encountered *Seawolf* he would shoot fast and first.

Perhaps he should not have fired at the *Springs*. The other boat might have been unable to resolve a firing solution.

Well, it was done. Perhaps the *Springs* would successfully evade and he could slip away.

Or perhaps he and Turchak and Eck and all the others would die right here in just a few minutes when the torpedoes arrived.

Kolnikov didn't really believe in God, not as He was depicted by organized religions. He believed that there was *something* bigger than man, bigger than life, but he didn't know what. He hadn't thought about it much, either. He would learn all the answers soon enough.

He could hear the incoming torpedoes now, pick them out of the background noise . . . part of which was the *Springs*'s noisemakers and bubble generators. The devil of it was that he couldn't tell how far away they were. He glanced at the clock.

Eleven minutes had passed. Running time should be a bit over nineteen if the *Springs* had fired at a target with a known range. Probably she hadn't. The Mk-48 torpedo was probably cruising at forty knots, searching as it came. That would make the running time . . . what? He tried to do the mental arithmetic and couldn't. He did it on a piece of paper lying nearby.

Nineteen minutes, forty seconds.

Twelve minutes gone . . .

Heydrich was sitting negligently in one of the chairs at an unused sonar console. He was watching Eck, the Revelation displays, Boldt, and Kolnikov. Just taking it all in, like a man whiling away the remainder of a lunch hour.

Kolnikov felt a rush of anger. He turned his back on Heydrich so he wouldn't have to look at him.

Thirteen minutes . . .

Boldt was chewing his fingernails, tearing at them. Sweat ran in rivulets down the cheeks of Georgi Turchak; the few remaining strands of hair on top of his head were sodden. He had the boat under perfect control, right at twenty knots, which was about as fast as the boat would go and still remain reasonably quiet. Eck was working like a madman at the sonar control panel, resolving the bearing, tweaking it, ensuring that the information was being fed to the computer-driven tactical plot. And Leon Rothberg, the American? He was staring listlessly at the bulkhead, his eyes apparently unfocused. Perhaps he was the only sane one among them.

Kolnikov studied the tactical plot. The torpedoes were curving in behind in a tail chase, one trailing the other. Alas, he had not managed to get outside their acquisition zone.

"Ten degrees left rudder, Turchak . . . Little more rudder . . . A

little nose down, a few more turns ... Boldt, fire off the hull transducers, let's see if we can make the torpedoes pass behind."

He looked up from the tactical plot to the Revelation screen on
the port side. There was the first torpedo, a luminous streak curving
in, growing larger, closing ... And the second, well behind, following
the first. The distinctive high-pitched noise of their seekers squealed
in his earphones; on the Revelation screen it looked as if the incoming
torpedoes were sporting a single headlight each.

Should he launch an antitorpedo torpedo? Both of them?

"Full left rudder, Turchak. Wrap it up tight."

At these grazing angles, the hull-mounted active acoustic coun-
termeasure should be effective—the antitorpedo weapon probably
would be the best choice for a torpedo coming in on the beam. Might
get one of those tomorrow, he thought. Or in an hour.

Closer and closer came the rushing torpedo ... and at the last
instant turned to go behind the ship. He turned and saw it going
away on the after starboard screen.

Back to port. One to go.

Racing in, tighter than the last one.

"Give me all the turn that's in her," he roared at Turchak, who
tilted the boat with the planes. Kolnikov had to grab something to
keep from sliding on the deck.

As the second torpedo streaked past, he heard Rothberg sobbing
again.

"Right full rudder," Kolnikov commanded. "Take her down to
sixteen hundred feet, put the *Springs* dead astern, and run like hell."

After the boat rolled out of the turn with her bow down, Heydrich
rose from his chair and stretched. "That was certainly an education.
You are very good at this, Kolnikov. Very good." Then he walked
out of the compartment and went down the ladder to the galley.

Aboard *Colorado Springs,* the crew deployed decoys to build an acoustic wall between the incoming torpedo and the sub. Without a human brain to help it find a way through or around the decoy, the
first torpedo picked out the strongest signal and went for it. Unfortunately that signal was well above and left of the submarine, and
once it had missed, the torpedo ran on, vainly searching for a target.

It was only when the noise from the decoys began subsiding that the crew heard the second incoming torpedo, which had been fired several minutes after the first.

They put noisemakers in the water, but a bit too late. The torpedo struck the upper starboard tail plane a glancing blow and detonated. The force of the blast did not hole the pressure hull, but it blew the seals in the main propeller shaft and actually bent one of the blades. It also made a mess of the upper starboard tail plane.

When it became obvious that there were no more torpedoes inbound, the leaking, vibrating shaft convinced the captain the time had come to get to the surface. As quickly as he could. He gave the order to blow the tanks, emergency surface, and the submarine began to rise from the depths. Under control, still intact, but in no shape to hunt further for a stolen *America*.

SUBLANT called Vice-Admiral Navarre in the Pentagon war room. He was standing there with the CNO, Stuffy Stalnaker, going over the tactical situation, figuring out what ships were where, what could be done with them.

"Torpedoes were fired, at least four. One submarine was hit and sunk. Another was hit and damaged and began an emergency surface maneuver. That is the evaluation of the P-3 TACCO from the sounds on his sonobuoy. We don't know which subs were hit."

"Can SOSUS confirm?"

"We are working on that now, sir. I'll have more in a few minutes."

"Keep us advised," Navarre said and hung up the phone. He turned away from the CNO for a moment to try to get his face under control, then faced the man and relayed the news.

"I hope to Christ one of those torpedoes hit *America*," Stalnaker said hopefully. From the look on Navarre's face, he could see the submariner didn't think that likely.

A half hour later they heard that Duke Dolan's P-3 was overhead the sub that managed to surface. Dolan said she was a *Los Angeles*–class boat. The sub was wallowing on the surface, down at the stern, unable to make way.

Two minutes later the admirals in the Pentagon learned that she was *Colorado Springs*. She was soon on the air, radioing a report of the action.

As the messages came in, it became obvious that the boat that had gone down was *La Jolla*. *America* had escaped.

CHAPTER FIFTEEN

Jake Grafton and Janos Ilin waited impatiently for darkness to fall. They walked around inside the house they had entered as refuge from the gunmen who pursued them, glanced out of windows, paused to scan with the binoculars Ilin had found in the den, looked at the family albums and knickknacks, talked of inconsequential things.

Several times Jake flipped on the television to learn of the extent of the damage in New York City. The talking heads quickly informed him that billions of dollars in damage had occurred, an unknown number of lives had been lost, and private citizens and the authorities were trying to determine the extent of the catastrophe. Of course the politicians were making promises: aid, investigations, prosecutions, and punishment. General Alt also appeared for a sound bite, promising to find the stolen submarine in short order. How that was going to happen, he didn't say. He also didn't mention the fact that the commandant of the Marine Corps, General Flap Le Beau, had been given orders to find that sub by the president himself, who was more than a little put out with the navy.

Depressed, Jake could listen for no more than a few minutes before he turned off the idiot box.

"They are out there," Ilin said gloomily, peering between drapes at the great outdoors, lawn and trees and sky. "They'll set up a roadblock."

"You saw that on a television show."

"We do roadblocks in Russia. A roadblock on a lonely road, then the car and the bodies go into a hole in the ground. The permanent disappearance, neat and tidy, with no witnesses, no evidence, and no bodies to wail over. People are left to speculate over the sins of the decedents and their fate. Stalin raised it to an art form."

When the last of the twilight had faded and he couldn't see the trees through the binoculars, Jake led the way to the garage. He used a shovel to break the lightbulbs in the automatic door openers, then turned off the light in the garage and engaged the truck's starter. It had been sitting there awhile and didn't want to start, although it cranked strongly.

After a bad moment the engine came to life.

Unfortunately the truck was parked with its tail to the door, so the backup lights would illuminate as he backed out of the garage. With the engine running, he turned on the truck's lights, then got out of the vehicle and used a hammer from the workbench on the backup lights. The taillights remained lit.

He tossed the hammer on the floor and climbed back into the vehicle, buckled his seat belt. Ilin had already done so. Ilin's shotgun was in his hands; Jake's was wedged beside him with the muzzle pointing down. He turned off the truck's lights and pulled the lever that put the vehicle in four-wheel drive, felt the small thunk of the transmission going in.

Now he pushed the remote opener that was tucked into a drink holder. As the door rose, both men rolled down their windows.

"Ready?" he asked, looking out his window, trying to see the lower edge of the rising door.

"Go."

He backed out carefully, turned the truck, then started down the drive. As soon as he cleared the retaining wall around the house, he turned hard right up onto the lawn. The truck's front tires spun on the sod, then gripped hard.

He could barely see what lay before him.

Hell, they're probably watching with night-vision goggles. They must hear the engine! He flipped on the headlights.

Around the house he went, trying to avoid the shrubbery, running over several bushes anyway.

"How are you going?" Ilin asked.

"Same way we came in. We'll go through the fences, see if we can get to the interstate."

They made it to the woods without any shots being fired. Finding the gate and the path through the forest took some backing up and swerving to scan with the headlights.

When he saw the gate, he gunned the truck, rammed the posts, knocking them over. They went along the path at about the speed a man could jog, knocking over saplings and being raked by low-hanging branches. Once a tree intervened, so Jake stopped, backed up, and maneuvered around it.

They couldn't find the spot where they had climbed the ridge, and the hillside was covered with trees anyway, so Jake stayed on the path, which was little more than a seasonal hiking trail.

He had gone at least a mile and a half when they came to a dirt road. Jake turned left, heading westward, parallel to the interstate, he hoped.

"This is probably our host's driveway," he muttered. "That'd be just our luck."

The road descended slightly. When they reached the bottom of the grade, the trees ended and they had a pasture on their left. They could see the headlights of the interstate beyond it.

"Are you game? Through the pasture?"

"Yes," Ilin said. He was gripping the handle on the doorjamb tightly with his right hand and the shotgun with his left.

Jake turned hard, jumping the truck over the little embankment that lined the road. He rammed a post in the barbed-wire fence and kept going.

Thumps and scraping sounds. "We're dragging half that fence with us," he told Ilin.

On the other side of the pasture was another fence, which he rammed. The truck nosed over sickeningly toward the ditch that separated the highway from the farm.

Desperate, afraid he was going to bury the nose of the truck in the ditch, Jake swerved right violently. The left front wheel went into the soft ditch bottom, and he floored the accelerator.

After the first gut-wrenching deceleration, the truck picked up speed. Jake sawed at the steering wheel, then the left wheel found purchase and the truck shot through the ditch throwing mud and went up the embankment toward the highway shoulder. And almost collided with a semi.

He jammed on the brakes, waited until the traffic went by, then floored it again. With a roar the truck accelerated on the pavement, dragging several fence posts and gobs of wire. At sixty miles per hour the mess under the truck tore loose and went under the wheels in one final thump.

"Amen," he said fervently.

"Amen," Janos Ilin agreed.

"Armed and dangerous, driving a stolen truck. A rear admiral and a Russian spy. I can see the headlines now." Jake laughed so hard he wheezed.

"The real American experience," Ilin said. "You made my trip to the States complete. I can never thank you enough."

"You'd better come look," Boldt told Kolnikov. "I don't know how he did it without me hearing anything. I was in the next compartment."

Vladimir Kolnikov took a last look at the computer screen above the helm. Turchak was still there in the chair, the joystick in front of him, monitoring everything. He had said little in the hours since the engagement with the two American submarines. *America* was deep now, fifteen hundred feet, running at fifteen knots to the southeast. The computer showed that she was making little noise at this speed. It was almost as if she were a black hole in the ocean. Above and behind they could hear pinging from sonobuoys. Due to a salinity discontinuity, apparently the P-3's TACCOs could not find *America* below the layer. The echo ranging appeared as flashes on the Revelation screens, almost like heat lightning on a far horizon.

"I'll come too," Heydrich said from his chair in the back of the control room. He had been there most of the afternoon, watching silently. Now he heaved himself to his feet, shook down his trouser legs, and walked forward.

"Go ahead," Turchak said, turning his head to glance at Boldt, then Kolnikov. "You have to go."

So Kolnikov followed Boldt with Heydrich trailing along. Through the passageway, around the corners, into the berthing compartment.

Leon Rothberg dangled from the overhead. He had stood on a box of oranges from the galley, wrapped his belt around a pipe, stuck his head in the noose, and kicked away the box. How long he had dangled there, silently strangling, was anyone's guess.

He was dead now, of course, his tongue black and protruding, his eyes wide, white, bulging, staring fixedly at nothing at all. Looking at him was hard, so after the first glance, no one did.

"Let's get him down," Kolnikov said, and wrapped his arms around the dead man's legs. He lifted while Boldt and two other men who were there extracted Rothberg's head from the belt noose. They lowered the corpse to the floor.

"Put him in the meat locker."

"I didn't hear anything," Boldt said. "Honestly. I would have—"

Kolnikov waved him into silence. Boldt and the other two carried Rothberg's corpse away, leaving Kolnikov alone with Heydrich.

"What now, Kolnikov? Can you and Turchak run these computers, make them do their magic things?"

"Don't be a fool."

"Speaking for myself, there were times this afternoon that I thought we would soon be dead. Without Rothberg, we won't survive another afternoon like the one we just had."

"Let's hope that was the only one."

"We had better." Heydrich searched Kolnikov's face. "You genuinely regret killing those men in that other submarine, don't you?"

Kolnikov turned his back and went along the passageway toward the control room.

Turchak looked at him as he entered.

"He's dead, all right. Hung himself with his belt from a pipe in the overhead."

"Aah . . ."

"Boldt was in the next compartment and didn't hear a thing, he says. Rothberg managed the perfect silent strangulation, so no one came to rescue him. Finally, he successfully accomplished something."

"He must have known the men in the other submarines," Turchak mused. "Trained them, perhaps. Then to help kill them . . ."

"Umm," Kolnikov said as he read their position from the ship's inertial system readouts, checked it against the computer database, then checked it again against the paper chart on the plotting table. He checked the bearings on the pinging sources, listened a moment to verify that the faint signals were indeed fading.

"I thought if we had to do it . . . you know!" Turchak said, searching for words. "I thought it would be self-defense."

They were not going to run into an island tonight, or an underwater mountain, not on this heading. Nothing in this direction for at least a thousand miles. Reactor temperatures and pressures normal, nothing close by on the sonar, nothing threatening out there in that great empty universe.

"Go get something to eat," he told Turchak. "Then get some sleep. Come relieve me when you awaken."

Turchak checked the autopilot carefully, ensured all was well, then went.

"You too, Eck. Sleep while you can. I'll call you if I need you."

Vladimir Kolnikov sat alone in the control room with the computer screens and Revelation pictures. He smoked and watched and thought about life and death as the submarine burrowed into the silence of the great eternal ocean.

Traffic was light on the way into Washington. Jake kept the pickup at the speed limit.

"Hungry?" he asked Ilin. "Want to stop?"

"And find out if we are still targets? No thanks. I'll eat in the embassy."

"I have a theory I wish to try out on you."

"A hypothesis?"

"Actually it's algebra. I'm trying to solve for X. Suppose someone wanted to see and test the components of the SuperAegis satellite. Which would be preferable, the blueprints, which I presume are on Consolidated Aerospace's computers, or the actual hardware?"

"The hardware, of course. The blueprints would be nice, but Consolidated has spent billions building and testing the components. Getting one's hands on the hardware would save years of effort and billions of dollars."

Jake Grafton nodded. "Salvaging that satellite is a possible use for the submarine. That SEAL minisub on its back might be used for that, if the water is shallow enough. Airplanes and recon satellites would see nothing, because on the surface there would be nothing to see. It's a possibility, don't you think?"

"So who is X?"

"X is the person who knows where the satellite is."

"It is a theory," Ilin said flatly.

"Would the Russians be interested in that satellite?"

"Beats me. A decision like that would be made way above my pay grade, to quote your Commander Tarkington. And believe me, they wouldn't tell me about it. And if they did, I wouldn't tell you."

"But it is a theory."

"It is that."

Without electrical power, Washington reminded Jake Grafton of a dark, silent graveyard filled with monuments to fallen heroes. It was nearly midnight when he rolled to a stop near the Russian embassy. The lights there were on, of course, powered by generators hardened against nuclear blasts. A legacy of the bureaucracy, according to Ilin.

The two men looked up and down the street and saw no one. The FBI was hidden somewhere nearby, watching of course, filming everything that happened on that street. Ilin knew it and Grafton knew it so they both knew they were home free.

"I'll leave you with the shotgun," Ilin said. It lay on the floor out of sight. The Russian held out his hand and Jake shook it.

"See you at the office," Jake said as Ilin opened the passenger door and got out. He glanced around, ensuring they were alone, then leaned in, holding the door open.

"Thanks for an entertaining day," he said, then closed the door.

Jake Grafton sat behind the wheel watching as Ilin walked across the street and flashed his credentials at the guard.

When the Russian had disappeared into the embassy, Jake pursed his lips, whistled silently, then took his foot off the brake and drove away.

He found a parking place on the street near his apartment building in Rosslyn—despite the lateness of the hour, a tow truck was loading dead cars and hauling them away for repair. The empty parking places were a welcome sight. There were no people about, no one waiting in nearby doorways, no one sitting in a parked car.

He saw light in the window of his flat. Apparently Callie had found a lantern someplace, or three dozen candles.

Two lanterns. They lit the room well as Jake opened the door. Callie rushed him. As she hugged him he saw that Toad Tarkington was sitting on the couch. And someone . . .

"You remember Tommy Carmellini?" she said softly. "Toad brought him here to wait for you."

"Are you hungry?" she asked after the men shook hands.

"Starved. And thirsty. I'd love a warm beer."

Callie headed for the kitchen.

"Well?" Toad said. "How'd it go?"

Jake glanced at Carmellini.

"I told him all about it. I'll explain in a little bit."

"Okay," Jake said, accepting Toad's assessment of the situation without further question. "I think it went pretty good for something arranged on such short notice. The guys flying the Cessna were maniacs and scared the hell out of me with those submachine guns. Then later, up at the house, I got off a couple of shotgun blasts through a window at one guy when he was sneaking around the house, blew the whole window out. Hope to hell I didn't hurt him."

"A couple of minor cuts," Toad said. "Band-Aid stuff. He said it was nothing."

"I worried about that all day."

"Did Ilin buy it?"

Jake grinned ruefully. "I doubt it. He's a sharp cookie, and I did my best to be scared as hell. But I'm no actor. When he got out of the truck a half hour ago at the Russian embassy he thanked me for providing an entertaining day."

"Maybe he just got wise at the end. Did he say anything?"

"He didn't give me what I thought he might, but he said some things I thought interesting. I'll have to digest it. What did your uncle say when you got hold of him, told him we wanted to use his house?"

"Uh, I couldn't reach him, boss. He's in Arizona playing golf, I think."

"I had a few bad moments looking at photos on the wall. You weren't in any of them, thank God, then later Ilin went through the family photo album. If he saw you in any of the pictures he didn't mention it."

"Just for the heck of it," Toad said, "I'll go through that album the next time I'm there, just to see."

"I locked the truck, put the shotguns behind the seat. You'd better get it back there in the morning. Get that window fixed in case it rains."

"Yes, sir."

Callie brought in beer and a sandwich for her husband. She also brought beer for Toad and Carmellini, who gratefully accepted. Then she sat down at the table across from Jake.

"So, Carmellini, what brings you by for warm beer?"

"It's a long story," Tommy Carmellini said. "I got into town this morning and went straight to your office. The CIA doesn't know I'm around, but the immigration guy swiped my passport through the machine at the Canadian border, so they'll get the word pretty soon."

"Tell me about it," Jake said, and took a big bite of his sandwich.

Carmellini went through it all, from the assignment to raid the computer in Antoine Jouany's London office, getting Sarah Houston's eyeprint, the CIA's man in London, finding Houston wasn't in the employee file . . . then he dropped the bomb. "You were on one of Jouany's lists, Admiral, as a guy betting big money with him in the currency markets."

Jake Grafton was stunned. "Are you kidding me?"

"No. I'm not. You, the members of the Joint Chiefs, at least a dozen other high naval officers. Sitting there reading those names, the thought popped into my empty head that I'd been set up. That the people on that list were being set up. I was supposed to return triumphantly to Langley bearing the trophy list, and the smelly stuff would immediately hit the fan big time."

Callie couldn't resist. "But those people are military officers. The only wealthy flag officer I know about is General Alt, the chairman. And he inherited it. He certainly didn't pile it up saving dimes from his green checks twice a month. God knows we didn't."

Tommy Carmellini turned to face her. "No one is going to think your husband invested money, Mrs. Grafton. That looks like a payoff list. Everyone on Capitol Hill will see that in a heartbeat. They know all about that kinda stuff over there."

"When did you start trying to get to know Sarah Houston?" Jake asked.

"A couple months ago. No, make it about three months, since early June. But looking back, man, I gotta wonder, who's zooming who? As Aretha used to ask. Houston was smooth. I never once suspected."

"Then a month ago, around the first of August, Ilin told De-Garmo that the Russians knew of the Blackbeard team," Toad mused aloud, eyeing his boss.

"These events go together, but I don't know how," Jake muttered.

"*America* smacked New York today, Admiral," Toad continued. "Three Flashlight Tomahawks. Two of our attack boats went after her. She sank one, *La Jolla,* lost with all hands. She blew a tail fin off the other, *Colorado Springs,* which managed to do an emergency blow and get to the surface. Then *America* slipped away. Half a squadron of P-3s hunted the rest of the day and never found her, even with echo ranging."

Jake Grafton rubbed his forehead. Half the sandwich remained, but suddenly he had no taste for it. A hundred–plus American sailors dead. "We watched some of the New York news on television," he said. "Were a couple of planes lost?"

"F-16s, I heard," said the Toadman. "The Pentagon was a madhouse today. Philadelphia, Boston, Atlanta, or Miami. Serious money can be made if you can guess *America*'s next target."

A half hour later, when the two men left, Jake and Callie got a few minutes alone.

"This whole mess is a monstrous tragedy," she told him.

He nodded.

"Do you want to listen to the news? Toad left us a battery-operated radio that he got somewhere."

"Nope. The news is all bad. After a while I just can't listen anymore."

"Did Ilin tell you anything useful?"

"Nothing specific. You gotta read between the lines, and it's tough. He talks and talks, sort of like Greenspan; doesn't say a whole lot. If that house was bugged and the Russian ambassador was listening, he can tell Moscow that Ilin didn't betray a solitary secret."

"Did he say anything of substance?"

"Not so you'd notice. He said he thought the theft of the submarine was an inside job. Hell, that's my opinion too."

When Callie went to get ready for bed, Jake sat down in his easy chair and tilted the thing back. He closed his eyes, recalling Ilin's words, how he had said them.

Ilin may have suspected the day was a show for his benefit, or worse, a ploy to trap him into making statements that could be used to blackmail him. Even so, did he point the way?

When Callie came back into the room ten minutes later she found her husband asleep. She spread an afghan over him and left him there.

He awoke several hours later. From the window he looked out at the dark city, silent except for occasional passing cars. The governor of Virginia had ordered out the National Guard to help prevent looting in the Virginia suburbs that were still without power, so occasionally an olive-drab truck or Humvee went slowly down the street.

Billions of dollars in damages in Washington and New York, several hundred people dead here, probably some dozens in New York, a submarine lost . . . for what?

He thought he had the pieces of the puzzle. If he could just put them together in the proper way.

The stakes were huge. That was obvious. Whoever was behind this was betting the ranch, so the payoff must be equally huge.

Think big, Jake. Big.

CHAPTER SIXTEEN

In the days following the attack on New York, Americans held their breath, waiting for the ax to fall again.

When it became plain that months would be required to return electrical service to normal levels in New York and Washington, people abandoned the cities in mass exoduses, overwhelming transportation and human services agencies. The simple truth that everyone was discovering was that modern cities require electricity to function; without it, they are uninhabitable.

The towns and cities that surrounded the dead urban metroplexes were flooded with refugees, many of whom were without a place to live or the means to pay for it. The inability of the authorities to deal with the sheer numbers of people who needed food, water, and a place to sleep resulted in a survival-of-the-fittest attitude that led, in some of the most crowded places, to a breakdown in law and order.

In addition to the emptying of the stricken cities, people in significant numbers throughout the eastern United States fled undamaged cities, choking highways and gridlocking public transportation. There was little panic, but the people leaving the cities had made up their minds and were not dissuaded by urgent entreaties from elected officials, or by less subtle closings of key roads and bridges by state police on orders from governors trying to manage the mess. Determined knots of people ignored and taunted police officers, pushed police vehicles out of the way, and went where they wanted to go.

This massive displacement of people was unprecedented in American history. Some commentators were reminded of the scenes of people fleeing from the advancing Nazi armies during World War II.

It was obvious that armed force was going to be necessary to enforce order, but elected politicians were unwilling to take that step for a variety of reasons, not the least of which, the president told his cabinet, was that the men and women in uniform might refuse to obey orders if those orders required firing on unarmed civilians. This danger was real, General Alt advised.

Huddled at Camp David with his advisers, the president realized that if he lost control of the armed forces, the federal and state governments in America would collapse in the resulting anarchy. What might happen then was too horrible to contemplate. Still, he had already ordered National Guard units to patrol Washington, D.C., and New York City, so he federalized more guard units to patrol the major cities that were being abandoned: Baltimore, Philadelphia, Boston, Atlanta, Miami, Pittsburgh, Charleston, Savannah, Richmond, Norfolk, and a host of others.

He also made a speech, quoting the words of Franklin Delano Roosevelt: "The only thing we have to fear is fear itself." The words did have a quieting effect, but they weren't enough. The economy was coming unwound, businesses were laying off employees by the thousands, the stock market was in free fall, and all over America people realized that the country was on the cusp of an economic depression.

USS *America* was somewhere in the Atlantic, and everyone knew it. Any day, any hour, more Tomahawk E-warheads could burst . . . anywhere.

So everyone waited.

Two days after the strike on New York, Vladimir Kolnikov brought *America* up under a storm system in the central Atlantic and raised the communications mast above the surface. He kept it there for five minutes, just long enough to record a dose of CNN's headline news on the hour.

He and Turchak listened, then erased the tape.

"We can't launch a missile without Rothberg to program the flight path," Turchak said, pointing out the obvious, more to stimulate Kolnikov than anything else.

Kolnikov grunted. He had said little in the last two days, preferring to keep his own counsel.

"They don't know that," Turchak continued, waving generally eastward.

"Umm."

"Of course, we don't know where the attack submarines are, where the Americans have placed their ASW forces."

"I don't want them to catch us shallow," Kolnikov said finally. "Let's go back down, slowly, updating the sonar model."

"Same course as before?"

"Yes."

With that, Kolnikov wandered toward the captain's cabin to try again to take a nap. He hadn't been sleeping well. He hadn't mentioned it to anyone, but he was exhausted. A guilty conscience, he told himself. You'll get over it.

Toad Tarkington brought a television from home—he lived in Morningside, far enough from the locus of the E-warhead blasts that the electronics in his home had not been affected. With a satellite dish on the windowsill and some fancy jury-rigging, the office crowd got it up and running. They kept the idiot box tuned to CNN.

Jake Grafton was at his desk studying the information on the files Tommy Carmellini had stolen from the Jouany firm in London when Toad stuck his head in the door. "They're interviewing Jouany, Admiral. You might be interested in this."

Jake stood in the doorway and watched. Carmellini was there, as was the rest of the staff. Stranded in a dead city, everyone seemed to want to come to the office. To visit, even if no productive work could be accomplished.

Antoine Jouany was a short, rotund sixtyish man with only wisps of hair on his perfectly round head. He spoke excellent English with a French accent.

"Of course I am making a fortune trading currencies on behalf of my investors. I apologize to no one. Our economic models suggested that the American economy was overextended, so we sold dollars and purchased euros. Events beyond our control have left us looking quite brilliant. Today. Had the dice rolled the other way, no one would have shed a tear for us."

The interviewer asked just how many billions Jouany's activities had generated, and he refused to answer. "This is not the time or place for such a discussion."

"What is your prediction? Will the dollar continue to slide?"

"I have no crystal ball. Common sense suggests that the decline is not over."

"You must admit, Monsieur Jouany, that your massive bet against the dollar was fortuitous, to say the least."

" 'Fortune favors the bold.' That is a quote, but I do not know who said it."

"Today your attorneys filed a libel suit against a columnist for an American newspaper who suggested your good luck might be more than fortune."

"Indeed they did. There is not a word of truth to that charge. That newspaper is distributed here in the United Kingdom, so we sued here. British libel law is quite clear. We defend our honor."

There was more, but Jake went back to his desk. The names, Alt, Stalnaker, Le Beau . . . Grafton! And Blevins. All these military officers supposedly had investment accounts with Jouany's firm. Was that the fact that had been leaked to the columnist? If so, it would certainly come out in the libel suit. It was untrue, of course, but it would cast a pall of suspicion over those officers. Would lead to investigations and charges and countercharges in the press and in Congress. A lot of smoke.

He went back to the door and called for Carmellini, who came in to Jake's office. Jake indicated a chair and closed the door.

"Let's do the timetable again. When did your supervisor tell you of the Jouany problem?"

Carmellini consulted the calendar on Jake's desk before he answered. "Fourteen weeks ago, at least, Admiral. We targeted Sarah

Houston and I started working on her about twelve weeks ago, in early June."

"But the Jouany operation predated the loss of the SuperAegis satellite?"

"Well, looking back on it, I guess it did. The Jouany firm had been selling dollars and buying euros for months."

"Was the date for the London break-in set when they first told you to meet Sarah Houston?"

"No. It couldn't be. We had no idea just how fast I could get her into a situation where we could put her out. I'm good, but I ain't James Bond. We knew something about the security setup and knew we needed eyeprints and fingerprints to get access."

"The other night you told me about always getting into her computer, regardless of the password, on the third try."

"Right."

"What if you hadn't gotten in?"

"I didn't expect to. I went there to steal the hard drive. Obviously, if I took it they would know I had it, so I tried to finesse 'em. Whoever set me up didn't expect me to learn that any old password would do. They wanted me to get in, open the door for NSA hackers, then go sashaying home proud as punch about how I played that outfit like a fiddle. So I didn't do it."

"You're a difficult employee, Tommy."

"Thank you, sir."

"The CIA still doesn't know you're in Washington?"

"I suspect they do, but they don't know where. Or if they do, they haven't come after me. I'm doing okay bunking at Tarkington's. He's got beer in the fridge. Hell, he's got a fridge. My apartment is in the dead zone. I hate to think what the refrigerator is going to be like when I get back."

"Tell me again about the CIA's London man."

"McSweeney, a real piece of work. The Brits have to know he's CIA. He might as well wear the black T-shirt with the big white letters. They know as much about his business as he does. Maybe more."

"That's an opinion."

"He makes no secret of the fact he's CIA. He tools around London like he was an earl on an expense account. They know what he eats, where he eats it, when he eats it, who he screws, when he screws, everything."

"So what do you want to do? Go back to the CIA? Tell them you are alive and well inside the Beltway, reporting back?"

"No, sir. I've submitted my letter of resignation. I'd just as soon hang out with you and Tarkington until my time runs out, then sort of sift on out of here. If the Langley crowd never sees my smiling face again, that'll be fine by me. If they get pissy maybe you can tell them you had me sweating in your shop?"

"I don't think the federal personnel regs work just that way," Jake Grafton said. "Why don't you just drop them a note and tell them you quit? I'll even buy the stamp."

"Geez, I would, Admiral, but there are some old felony investigations lying around in various prosecutors' offices. The statute of limitations has run on some of that stuff, but some of it's still hot. To make a long story short, the CIA sorta drafted me a few years back. Now I want to move on to a more lucrative career. A man's got to make his way in the world, seek his fortune, save a little for his old age."

A hint of a smile made Jake's lips twitch. "I see," he said. "Involuntary servitude, in this enlightened age. Who would have thought it?" He made a sound with his tongue.

"Shocking, I know," Carmellini said earnestly. "I normally don't trot out my troubles at the office, but I am in kind of a bind."

"I'll do some research on the personnel regs. It'll take a few days."

"Fine. Anything I can do to help, just say so."

"Well, there is one thing. This list is going to start stinking one of these days. Who is Sarah Houston?"

"I don't know," Carmellini said, his brows knitting.

"If you were going to find out, how would you go about it?"

"I've got her eyeprints and fingerprints. I—"

"Do you?"

"Well, I've got someone's."

"Talk to Tom Krautkramer when he comes in. Get a real name to go with your eyeprints and fingerprints. Let me know what you find out."

"Yes, sir."

Next through Jake's door was Captain Sonny Killbuck. "What is the navy doing to find the SuperAegis satellite?" was Jake's question.

"It's a question of probabilities, Admiral," Killbuck said, rubbing his hands together. "This is pretty neat. I wish I could have taken credit for it, but the engineers at NASA came up with this." He used a pen on a sheet of paper to illustrate. "The trajectory that the missile was to follow is this line, which is also the line of highest probability. Lines are then drawn, say one degree apart, radiating outward from the Goddard platform. Inevitably, the greater the distance from the intended track, the lower the probability that the third stage came to rest there. The distance from the Goddard platform is also a function of probability—we know precisely where the missile was when we lost it on radar. Voilà, with those parameters we drew the chart and started searching the areas of highest probability first, then worked our way down."

"Scientific as hell," Jake Grafton said and whistled softly.

"Left alone, engineers are dangerous," Killbuck agreed.

"How many assets are devoted to this task?"

"Thirty ships, sir. Everything that will carry magnetometers and side-scan sonar. And every area gets searched twice."

It was indeed a neat system, but the searchers had yet to find the missing third stage. Jake refrained from commenting on that obvious fact.

"How about doing a computer study, by tomorrow, if possible. I want you to identify all the areas in the Atlantic between, say, Britain and Natal, with one hundred feet of water or less. Better make it a hundred and fifty."

"I'll do it both ways, sir. Shouldn't be difficult."

When FBI agent Krautkramer came in an hour later, he had a file on Heydrich. An underwater demolition and salvage expert, Heydrich had worked all over the globe. Jake studied the file as Krautkramer briefed him on the state of the FBI's investigation.

"One of the SuperAegis techno-kings is missing. Peter Kerr. Told his wife he was going fishing for a few days and never came back. She called us yesterday, fearing foul play."

"'Foul play.' I didn't know real people used phrases like that."

"Her words, not mine. Kerr is in his fifties, got a daughter in grad school, been married over thirty years. In any event, before he went fishing he cleaned out his savings account and withdrew all the money from his 401(k) plan. We're going through his house and office now."

"SuperAegis and *America*."

"According to the scientists, Kerr could have put SuperAegis in the water. His specialty was software, but he worked on the launch team and had access to everything. It's a break."

"He did have access," Jake agreed. "I know him. I sat in several meetings he chaired. He's one of those guys who knows a lot about everything. A lot of people think they do, but Pete Kerr really does."

Krautkramer scratched his head. "If we can somehow connect the satellite and the submarine . . ."

"Not to change the subject, but your guys did a good job playing assassins the other day."

"They loved it. They want an invite the next time you throw a party. Did Ilin bite?"

"I don't know. He said some things worth thinking about, but he certainly didn't spill his guts. Here, look at this."

Jake tossed Krautkramer the list of military investors from the Jouany computer, then sat silently as he scanned it.

"What is this and where did you get it?"

The admiral explained. Krautkramer looked him in the eyes as he spoke. "So you never invested a dollar with these people?"

"No. My family's stupendous fortune is with an American broker." Jake named the company. "It strikes me that someone has gone to a lot of trouble to slander the senior officers in the American military who might be looking hard for *America*. Or SuperAegis."

Krautkramer nodded.

"My prediction is that this list will surface shortly in London as part and parcel of Jouany's libel suit. Then the American government will be asked if they know about this, and lo and behold, the answer is yes. A CIA agent filched the list from Jouany. If the president or government spokesperson denies it, they will ultimately be branded liars; if they admit it, it looks like the Americans have something to hide. Either way, it's going to be bad. And the people on that list will be under a cloud."

"You included."

"You betcha."

"Why?"

"Whoever put this together wanted a lot of smoke. The more smoke there is, the more difficult it becomes to find the stick that's actually on fire."

"So what do you want to do about this?"

"I want everything there is to know about Jouany and the European aerospace consortium, EuroSpace, and I want it by five o'clock today."

Krautkramer looked at his watch. "I'll do my best," he said. "May I have this list?"

"Not yet."

Jake snagged his hat and the telephone book and on the way out of the office motioned for Toad to follow. Down the endless staircase, then out to the car. Another car. The one Jake drove to northern Virginia and abandoned alongside the road had been quietly returned to a government motor pool so that Ilin wouldn't see it again.

"Where to, boss?"

"Federal Protective Service." Jake flipped open the telephone book and after a minute came up with an address.

He had to use his letter with the president's signature, but he eventually got what he wanted. The copy machines were toast, so he and Toad pored over the records and made notes. It was mid-afternoon by the time the two men left the building, just enough time for Jake to get to the Pentagon to see Flap Le Beau.

Flap looked harassed. "Give me some good news," he pleaded.

Jake dumped the bag. When he finished, Flap frowned. "So you don't have any hard evidence that the loss of the SuperAegis satellite and the theft of *America* are connected."

"They must be," Jake insisted and went over to the map hanging on the commandant's wall. "What are the odds that two major events would happen two months apart? And the connection has been staring us in the face all the time. That satellite is somewhere in this ocean"—he tapped the chart—"*America* is carrying a minisubmersible on her back and she has an underwater salvage expert aboard. The salvage expert is not critical, but the minisubmersible is."

"We're hunting for the satellite," the marine pointed out. "Hunting hard, I might add. We've got thirty ships out there right now towing magnetometers and using every gadget in the book."

"It's a stupendously big ocean," Jake replied. "We may never find the thing. I think the salvage guy on *America* has a huge advantage— I think he knows where it is. Or where it should be. Peter Kerr could have told him. Indeed, Peter Kerr could have put it there."

"One guy in a minisubmersible. He doesn't have the diving gear or enough stuff to salvage the satellite, let alone the upper stage of that rocket."

"I think the sub will rendezvous with a ship—somewhere—get more people and gear, then recover the satellite. If they can find it. That's going to take some doing, but with Revelation . . . I think it's possible."

"Then why is the salvage guy already aboard?"

"Sir, I don't know."

"How deep can the submersible go?"

"On its own, down to a few hundred feet. Attached to the sub, it can go as deep as the sub takes it. The limitation is not the crush depth but the capacity of the ballast system."

"Two hundred feet," Flap said thoughtfully, examining the chart. "That's still a lot of real estate."

"Offshore waters for all of Europe, Africa, and the Atlantic islands," Jake agreed. "And even some of the Mid-Atlantic Ridge."

"And the attacks on Washington and New York?"

"Diversions. Profitable ones." He pointed toward the list from Jouany's computer. "This didn't just happen. Someone planned very carefully, and the plan is working. The American economy is staggering like a dying horse and Europe is doing quite well, thank you. Nations around the world are selling dollars and buying euros. European investors in American stocks are taking their money home. European companies will pick up a lot of international business when American companies have difficulty meeting their delivery dates, for whatever reason. The business that American companies lose will go to European enterprises that can meet the demand."

"So who is the man inside?" Flap Le Beau asked.

"I've got a candidate," Jake Grafton told him.

"Okay."

"The problem is that the timetables don't fit."

Zelda Hudson found the message on one of her regular visits to a hacker's bulletin board. "Butterfly," the caption said. It was encrypted, of course, a meaningless gobbledygook of letters. She downloaded it, got off-line, checked the message for viruses—there were none.

She reached for *Merriam-Webster's Collegiate Dictionary* on the bottom shelf of the nearby credenza and looked up the word *butter*. Then she checked the posting date, added those numbers together, multiplied by another number, and began counting words that began with the following letter, *c*, ignoring words with fewer than six letters. When she found the word she wanted, she typed it into an encryption matrix and pressed Enter. The computer then used that word to construct a complete matrix, which was used to transform the downloaded message into another long sequence of apparently random letters.

Fly. She counted again, carefully, in the compilation for words beginning with *g*, found the word, typed it into another matrix. The computer ran the message through the second matrix, and voilà!

I am writing to express my concern with the course of current events. When you offered me the information about the Blackbeard team, requesting that I reveal it to DeGarmo, thereby killing the operation, I knew then that I was fulfilling some purpose that would benefit you. After consultation with my superiors in Moscow, the decision was made to do as you requested, for several reasons. The current political situation in Moscow would be destabilized by the successful theft of a Russian submarine or by a thwarted attempt. And our relationship has been quite successful—we hope it continues to our mutual profit into the future.

The possibility that you had other plans for the Blackbeard team did not occur to us. I think I see your hand in subsequent events. So does Admiral Grafton, who I suspect is closer to the truth than he realizes. Certainly closer than you thought possible.

My government does not want the SuperAegis satellite to end up in foreign hands. I think your most likely customer is EuroSpace. It must not happen. Russia and the United States have similar interests in this matter. Frankly, do not rely on your relationship with us to protect you in a matter of such gravity.

Zelda Hudson read the message through again, then deleted it and the matrices that had decoded it. Then she purged the trash file and reformatted the disk segment she had used.

Peter Kerr, the fool! His disappearance must have incited Grafton's suspicions.

Like many of Washington's power elite, Avery Edmond DeGarmo
lived in the Watergate apartment complex near the Kennedy Center.
And like many of his fellow residents, he had decamped during the
power crisis. When Jake, Toad, and Tommy Carmellini arrived the
following morning, the building was deserted. There were two
guards at the desk in the lobby but not a resident in sight. Not even
a doorman. Jake and his friends sat in the front seat of the van
looking things over.

"You'd think for all that money the tenants would get a doorman,"
Toad said.

"Where'd DeGarmo go, anyway?" Carmellini asked Toad, who
carried around a surprising store of useless, unimportant facts.

"Bunking with the marines at Quantico, I heard. The grunts de-
liver him and a bunch of others to Washington every morning by
helicopter."

"Simplifies commuting, I suppose."

"They may never move back to town."

"You think you can get into this place?" Jake asked dubiously. He
was in the passenger seat of the carpet company van, Carmellini was
behind the wheel, and Toad sat between them.

"Just watch the master at work," Carmellini said. From the hip
pocket of his coveralls he removed a pack of chewing tobacco, broke
the seal, and helped himself to a man-sized plug, which made his
unshaved cheek bulge nicely. Then he got out of the van and headed
for the main entrance.

Carmellini was wearing a one-piece coverall with the carpet company's name and logo across the back. So were Toad and Jake, who
remained in the vehicle. Last night Carmellini called a fellow he
knew, and the man rented him the van and uniforms for the day
for the magnificent sum of one hundred dollars.

"Are you sure? That doesn't sound like a lot of money."

"You aren't going to get caught, are you? Nothing will come back
on me?"

"You'll hear not a peep from anyone. Guaranteed."

"A hundred is enough, and I'm glad to get it. With the power mess and all, our business has dried up to nothing."

Outside the Watergate, Tommy Carmellini spit on the sidewalk, adjusted his chew, and went in. He went up to the security desk, where the guards had supplemented the light coming through the glass door with a small kerosene lantern. There were two of them, in uniform, a man and a woman.

"Got a carpet delivery for . . . for . . ." Carmellini removed an invoice from his hip pocket and scrutinized it. "DeGarmo. Apartment 821."

The male guard consulted a list on a clipboard. "He's not in today."

"By God, I hope not. Gonna have to pull up the bedroom and living room carpet and lay new. Not many customers want to watch us do it." He glanced at the closed-circuit camera mounted above the guards' desk and at the dark monitor behind them.

"You got a key to his apartment?"

"Why, hell no, I ain't got no key. He said you people'd let me in."

"You're not on the tradesman list." The guard gestured toward the clipboard.

"Umm, you got a place I could spit?"

With a look of disgust, the guard nodded toward a trash can at the end of his desk. Carmellini relieved himself and returned.

"Much obliged."

"Talk about a filthy habit!" That was the woman.

"Yeah. So how'm I gonna get this carpet in there?"

"I can't let you in unless you're on the tradesman list," the male guard said.

"Just curious, but without phones, how is he gonna tell you to put me on that list? Not being smart or nothin', I hear that this guy is some big weenie in government. He supposed to just tell the president to sit tight while he makes a personal trip down here to talk to you about the carpet in his pad?" After delivering himself of this speech, Carmellini took two steps to the trash can to spit again.

He worked his chew into position while he waved the invoice. "Here's his signature on this. Men who buy forty-five hundred dollars' worth of carpeting don't usually like to lay it themselves. But if you don't let me in, he's gonna. We'll offload it right here in the lobby and you can let him have it the next time he wanders by."

"Tell you what," said the male guard, who did take a cursory look at DeGarmo's forged signature. "We'll let you in downstairs. Miss McCarthy will take you up to the apartment and wait while you do your thing."

"Much obliged," said Tommy Carmellini, and gave them both a big tobacco grin. Out on the sidewalk he spit a stream of brown juice over his shoulder, then climbed into the driver's seat of the van.

"We're in," he said to Jake and Toad. "Just let me do the talking."

As they rolled around the building, Carmellini said, "We lucked out. Got a female who thinks tobacco chewing is a filthy habit. After she unlocks the place, I'll fart and spit a bit and she'll find something else to do somewhere else."

And that was the way it worked out. The men put on cotton gloves, then unloaded a roll of carpet from the back of the van and hoisted it onto their shoulders. Miss McCarthy led them to the freight elevator.

The apartment was stifling. "Must be eighty degrees in here," Carmellini complained.

The guard lady took it personally. "We crank and crank on that air-conditioner in the basement and the cool air just never gets up this far. We need some real muscle men to do the cranking."

"I'll bet," Carmellini replied, then spit into a Styrofoam coffee cup that he had brought up from the van.

The men were moving furniture in DeGarmo's bedroom when Miss McCarthy told Carmellini, "Be sure and stop by the desk on your way out."

"This is gonna take awhile. Gotta do it right, I always say. If it's worth doing, it's worth doing right. That's why people buy their carpet from us."

They waited for a count of ten after she closed the door behind her, then Jake said, "Very well done."

Carmellini spit his chew into his hand and nodded. He dashed for a bathroom to wash out his mouth.

They began searching, carefully, meticulously, not trashing the place but searching it as thoroughly as possible.

"What do you hope to find, Admiral?" Toad had asked that morning on their way over in the carpet van.

"Anything at all that shouldn't be there. Occasionally people leading secret lives keep little tidbits or artifacts of that secret life tucked away. Or so I've heard."

288 ★ STEPHEN COONTS

"I certainly do," Carmellini said, nodding a vigorous assent. "You oughta see my collection."

"We're looking for something," Jake continued, "anything that we can use to unravel Avery DeGarmo's secret life."

"How do you know he has a secret life?"

"I don't."

"Probably got a wife and kids in L.A. that he hasn't told a soul about," Toad told Carmellini and winked.

They found that DeGarmo, a lifelong bachelor, had a collection of paper matches bearing the logos of restaurants in which he had eaten. Hotels he had visited. Businesses. Golf courses. All kinds of matches. Drawers full, boxes full.

He kept a loaded nine-millimeter pistol in the drawer beside his bed, he used toothpaste with baking powder, soft toothbrushes, and disposable razors. He had a prescription for an anticholesterol medication, ten pills still in the bottle. He threw socks away one at a time, so he had a nice collection of singles. He wore Jockey shorts and tailored wool suits.

Jake Grafton settled into DeGarmo's chair behind his desk in the den. There were two computers, both with telephone wires leading to them. After the stink about the CIA deputy director who kept classified info on his home computer, one assumed DeGarmo wouldn't be so foolish. But really, when you stopped to think about it, computers were involved in this whole mess. One wouldn't know what was on them until he checked. Jake unplugged the monitors and keyboards, pulled all the wires from the main computers, and picked them up, one atop the other.

He went looking for Tarkington and Carmellini. They were snacking on crackers in the kitchen.

"Nothing, Admiral. Absolutely nothing."

"Did you open the refrigerator?"

"No," Carmellini said brightly. "We thought you should have the honor."

Jake tugged at his gloves and took one last look around. "We'll do the fridge next time. Let's take the two computers and our carpet and make a clean getaway."

Zelda Hudson watched her monitor. The computer graphic ordered by Vice-Admiral Navarre was being put together now by the National Geodesic Survey's main Earth-mapping computer. Areas of the Atlantic with one hundred feet or less of water, then another map depicting 150 feet or less.

Zelda was in a foul mood. Someone, somewhere had figured out the connection between *America* and the missing SuperAegis satellite.

Of course it was there all the time, in plain sight, but no one saw it. Until now. She looked at the authorization. Captain Killbuck, office of ACNO (submarines).

Carmellini. He was turning into a regular pain in the posterior. The FBI had run a fingerprint identification request through the Clarksburg fingerprint database. The name that popped up was Susan Boyer, deceased.

That request could have originated only with Carmellini, who was carrying around the dead woman's eye- and fingerprints. The request was authorized by Special Agent Krautkramer, the agent in charge investigating *America*'s hijacking. Killbuck, Krautkramer—the tracks led to Rear Admiral Grafton.

When Jake arrived at his apartment in Rosslyn that evening, Callie had two steaks and two potatoes ready for the barbecue, which was getting quite a workout since the electric range was useless.

"Do you think *America* will fire any more missiles?" Callie asked as they brought each other up to date on their days.

"No, I don't," Jake replied. "We've got every P-3 we own on the East Coast in the air, loaded with sonobuoys and torpedoes. If anyone shoots a missile we can have a P-3 on site in less than a half hour. We've cleared friendly submarines from the area, so from the moment the first sonobuoy hits the water, they'll be pinging actively. With one P-3 Kolnikov might have a chance. Even two. But not four. When they get *America* located, they'll put torpedoes in the water."

Callie was not her usual self. "I can't get those men aboard *La Jolla* off my mind. Sometimes life just isn't fair."

"Kolnikov's luck will run out," Jake said forcefully, wanting it to be true. "So far he's anticipated every move. He knows what is possible and how long it takes to make things happen. Now that we're ready, I doubt if he'll chance it. Of course, he could prove me a poor prophet and have one on the way to Boston or Atlanta this very minute. If so, the odds are that he and his crew aren't going to be with us much longer. Which would be fine by me."

"So how are they going to escape?" Callie asked. "They must have some plan. They aren't going to cruise around the world forever like Captain Nemo aboard the *Nautilus*."

"That's what we're trying to figure out," Jake said. "If you were Kolnikov, how would you do it?"

CHAPTER SEVENTEEN

Myron Matheny's telephone rang at two in the morning, waking him from a sound sleep. Several seconds passed before he recognized the voice.

"That matter we discussed last week—it's going to have to be handled immediately."

Matheny waited several seconds before answering, trying to clear his thoughts. "You know I don't work that way," he said.

"No choice. I never thought it would come to this, but the world is pressing in."

"Wish I could help you."

"This morning. If I go, you go."

The Man broke the connection, leaving Matheny listening to a buzzing telephone.

He replaced the instrument on the receiver. Oh, boy! He sure as hell didn't need this.

"Who was it?" the woman asked.

"Him." It wasn't really. The voice was a woman's, but Matheny didn't want his wife to know that.

"At this hour?"

"Go back to sleep."

Fumbling in the darkness, he put on a robe and went to the kitchen of the old farmhouse to make himself a pot of coffee.

Way deep down, Myron Matheny had always known that this day would come, that the life he had built for himself might come to a smashing halt. It would, he always thought, be his fault, the client's fault, or some freak twist in the cosmos, some fluke of fate. Random chance or someone's screwup, those were the forces that made the wheels of the universe go around.

When he graduated from high school he had joined the marines, where he had become a specialist on area-network surveillance systems. The CIA recruited him after his four-year hitch was over. The CIA sounded more interesting than Motorola, so he signed on.

About ten years ago in South America, he had been betrayed by a man seeking an entry into the profitable drug business. He escaped before the druggies could kill him, then found the man who sold him out and made him permanently disappear.

You weren't supposed to do that kind of thing in the CIA. There were laws against it, regulations and all that. Still, every now and then, when lives or important national interests were on the line, a quiet disappearance could solve a lot of problems.

Murder became his specialty. Myron Matheny thought of himself as a personnel removal specialist.

Killing someone is ridiculously easy, of course. Getting away with it is much more difficult given the fact that murder is a serious crime in every nation on the planet. The best and safest way to foil the police was to make the victim disappear. If the police couldn't prove a crime had been committed, they never got to the next step, determining a perpetrator. Intense planning and preparation were required to pull off a disappearance, and sometimes, due to the lifestyle of the victim, it was just not possible. Second choice was to make it appear that the victim died of natural causes—also difficult, with preplanning and preparation required. Again, the police must prove a crime had been committed before they got to the next problem, the identity of the criminal. The last option was to kill the victim in such a way that the identity of the killer could not be determined—with only one layer of defense, this option was extremely high risk. A single mistake here could cost you life in the pen, or even, in some jurisdictions, death.

Now comes the call—The Man wants this guy removed immediately. This morning.

So much for planning. So much for minimizing the risk.

Ha!

The thought occurred to Myron Matheny that he should find The Man and remove him! That 'if I go, you go' crap was really unacceptable.

As he looked out the windows at the forests and pastures lit by the dim moonlight, Myron Matheny realized that he wasn't ready to give up his life. He didn't want it to end. He liked living here, liked working part-time at the local tackle shop, liked tying flies and fishing all summer. The best part, though, was the woman.

Oh, man! After all these years, just when he finally figured out what it's all about . . .

Still, The Man wouldn't call if the threat were not real.

She came padding down the hall barefoot, wearing her old blue bathrobe. She read the bad news in his face.

With a cup of coffee in hand, she said, "Why don't you and I leave now? You've got those passports in the safety-deposit box. Let's clean it out when the bank opens and go."

"Leave all this?"

"We wouldn't be leaving anything we couldn't do without or replace."

"There's nowhere to hide. Not in this day and age."

"Myron. Think this through."

"I don't want to run," he said. "I'm too old."

He dressed carefully in nondescript clothes, old tan slacks, lace-up leather shoes, a long-sleeve shirt, and a windbreaker to hide the pistol in the shoulder holster. He dusted his hands with talcum powder, then pulled on latex gloves. Only then did he carefully wipe the pistol and the shells and load it. Silencer, knife, he wiped them carefully. He did the wooden handles of the garrote too.

He should take a rifle, just in case. He went to the basement, unlocked the safe in an old potato cellar under the stairs, and stood looking.

He had three Remingtons standing there, all in .220 Swift, without a doubt the finest small-caliber round ever invented. Years ago he had learned that the rifle he could shoot best was the one that recoiled the least. The cartridge's only drawback was the semirimmed case, which was not a problem in a bolt action. He had built the rifles himself, installed composite stocks and custom triggers, hand-loaded the ammo with the new 55-grain Nosler bullets with plastic, frangible tips. All three were serious weapons—and untraceable. His favorite had a little scratch on the right side of the barrel ... he automatically reached for it, wiped it down, picked up ten cartridges and pocketed them.

He left the house just at dawn. The woman stood in the doorway. She didn't wave, just stood there watching as he got out of the car and loaded it and drove away. At the end of the driveway he looked back, and she was gone. The door was closed.

Traffic was light. He had an address in Rosslyn, had a map. . . .

Jesus, this was half-baked! He had never even been to the address before. For all he knew this guy lived next door to a police station.

He did know what the guy looked like. The Man had given him three photos last week. Just in case. And the guy was in the navy. That meant a uniform, although in that neighborhood there should be a lot of uniforms. He had the best photo with him, if he needed to refresh his memory. He had studied it and shouldn't need it.

Christ, if he were caught! A photo of the intended victim, an unlicensed, loaded pistol, an unlicensed silencer, a rifle ... he would be lucky to draw a sentence of less than twenty years.

He knew the city well enough that he didn't make any wrong turns, but he did have to pull over once and consult the map.

The day was going to be gorgeous—the heat of summer had eased and the haze had blown out after the front went through yesterday. On such a day, why was he taking chances like this?

He parked as near as he could to the guy's building—so many dead cars had been hauled away that there were actually parking places—and sat looking things over. The nearest Metro station was two blocks down the street to the north. It wasn't running these days. There was a bus stop there too, and the city had brought in buses from all over. Of course, this guy could be driving one of these cars. Or have a limo picking him up. Or a car pool.

This is where he should be starting several weeks of observation of the subject, not looking for a fleeting opportunity to do him! Even if he dropped the guy here this morning, how was he going to get away? Walk back to the car and drive off? Into rush-hour traffic? In his own car? He certainly didn't have time to steal one.

Matheny put his head on the steering wheel and took a deep breath.

Relax! Just take it easy, watch, see if this guy gives you an opening. If he does, bang. If he doesn't, you'll learn enough so that you can do it safely in a few days. If The Man doesn't like it, tough shit. The bastard can pop this guy himself.

People were coming out of the buildings, streaming along the street. Traffic was building. Probably not as many people as usual; with the electricity off, many people weren't working or had left the city.

Now or never.

Myron Matheny checked that the pistol was loaded, made sure the safety was on. He screwed the silencer onto the barrel and lowered the pistol into the shoulder holster, which had a hole in the bottom to accommodate the silencer. The garroting wire was in his right jacket pocket. He got out of the car and locked it. He inserted four quarters in the parking meter, then walked up the slightly inclined sidewalk to the entrance of the guy's building.

The lobby was dark. Of course, the elevators weren't working. He began climbing the stairs. He would just wait until the guy came out of his apartment and follow him down the stairs. Shoot him in the back of the head and keep right on going. Out and into the car, drive away.

That was a plan. Baring something freaky, he had a fairly decent chance of getting away with it. Car pool, private car, bus, limo— however this guy was going to work wouldn't matter.

On the second flight of stairs he heard someone coming down, looked up . . . and there the guy was, wearing a white naval officer's uniform.

Two people were following him. Matheny stood aside to let the three men pass. The guy even made eye contact with him. Gray eyes under a naval officer's white hat with black rim, nose a little large. Then he moved by and the next two guys were trooping past. They didn't make eye contact.

Matheny put his hand on the butt of the pistol, trying to decide. All three? Right here?

Then it was too late. The guy in the lead, the guy he wanted to get, went around the landing and disappeared from view. There had been a four- or five-second window of opportunity, and he hadn't been able to make up his mind.

Shit!

There was another flight of stairs! He would do them then. All three. He leaped to follow the trio.

Only at the second floor, more people came through the fire door into the staircase, joined the procession going down. A woman was now in front of the guy, another woman got between the guy and the man behind him, and another man in uniform fell in behind the whole parade.

By the time Matheny exited the stairwell into the lobby, the guy was going through the front door of the building. He had plenty of company. There were a dozen people within thirty feet.

Out on the sidewalk the guy went over to the curb.

Okay, he's waiting for a car pool. Standing there, looking up the street.

This is it! Walk up behind him, gun him in the back. As he goes down put one round into his brain. Then just walk away. Everyone will be looking at him.

Then walk over, get into your car, and drive away.

Myron Matheny was three steps away, his hand on the pistol butt, when a white government pool car slid to a halt on the street, and the guy walked between two cars toward it.

The guy got into the backseat, pulled the door firmly closed, and the vehicle eased away into traffic, leaving Myron Matheny standing helplessly on the sidewalk.

He drove to Crystal City, had a hell of a time finding a place to park. Finally he put the car in a parking garage in a nearby building. He never saw the guy arrive at the building where he worked. Maybe he was there, maybe he wasn't, but Myron Matheny couldn't just climb the stairs and ask.

He stood on the sidewalk out front looking things over. The Crystal City area consisted of a dozen or so medium-sized office buildings, around twenty stories each. Some of them had limited outside parking; most people had to put their vehicles in multistoried garages. The Lee Highway ran north and south along the west side of the area. On the east side was Reagan National Airport. Just to the north was the Pentagon surrounded by several hundred acres of parking lot.

Beneath Crystal City was an underground shopping area, a mall with Metro stops at both ends. Without electricity the underground resembled a coal mine tunnel. The people who were in the buildings—perhaps half the usual number—had to eat somewhere, so one of the underground restaurant entrepreneurs had gotten permission to set up an outdoor eating area.

Myron Matheny watched as a crew of people unloaded two trucks. Barbecue grills were set up, filled with charcoal, and lit. Portable generators to run coolers, folding tables, boxes of food and paper plates, stacks of plastic cups, folding chairs, garbage cans . . . The crew worked quickly and efficiently, setting up shop in a square between four buildings. Four large trees in planters provided a leafy cover over the area.

Okay, if the guy is up in his building, maybe he'll eat lunch here.

Matheny walked back through the area, trying to figure out how he could escape after the hit. If he could park his car somewhere else, steal a car and park it in one of these outside handicapped spaces . . .

Lots of military in these buildings. Eating lunch, this guy is going to be surrounded by military. If I shoot him with the pistol while he's sitting at one of these tables, four or five of them could grab me, and that would be that.

If I use the rifle, shoot from up there, on top of that parking garage . . . well, I might get a shot from there through these trees.

Myron Matheny went up to the top story of the garage and looked down. The tree canopy obscured about half the area. He went down a story. Better, but not good enough. He went down one more level. He was two stories up now. This was about as good as it would get.

Sixty yards or so to the center of the square, an easy shot with a scoped rifle. Hell, at this range he could put one in the guy's ear.

After the shot he'd be standing in this garage with the rifle in his hands. He'd drop the rifle, leave the garage the way he came in, get in the stolen car he had parked in a handicapped spot.

That would work. Maybe.

Hell, that was the only way it could be done.

The alternative was to go back to Rosslyn and wait for the guy to come home tonight. If he came home tonight.

That will be the backup plan, if the guy doesn't come here for lunch.

He walked the escape route out of the garage, then went back upstairs for his car. After he paid the tab on the way out, he headed for Alexandria to steal something wearing a handicapped license plate.

"The minisub can go down to a hundred and fifty feet," Sonny Killbuck said, as he unrolled his chart for Jake Grafton and Toad Tarkington. "I called New London to confirm that."

"Okay," Jake said and adjusted his reading glasses on his nose.

"With that fact in mind, I just ran off the one chart that shows water a hundred and fifty feet deep or less. If you wish, sir, I can do another with any parameters you like."

The three were looking the chart over when Krautkramer came in with the Jouany file. He joined the three naval officers at the chart, a large computer printout.

"If the killer satellite was put in the ocean for eventual salvage with *America*'s minisub, it would have to be in less than a hundred and fifty feet of water," Jake explained. "Heydrich is an underwater salvage dude, he's aboard . . . it fits."

"When I was putting this file together, Admiral, I ran across an interesting fact. It seems that Antoine Jouany is one of the directors of EuroSpace. I don't know whether you knew that or—"

Jake grabbed the file and began digging through it. "Show me," he said.

Krautkramer found the list of Jouany's directorships and showed it to Jake.

"Heydrich? What do you know about him?"

"That's this next file. He worked for years for various salvage firms, pulling up wrecks and cargoes all over the world. Actually got an ownership interest in the company about ten years ago, just before the insurance recovery business boomed, so he's fairly well off. The Nautilus Company. It owns four ships."

The four ships were named.

"Sonny, how about seeing if the satellite intel people can find these four ships? I want to know where they are right now."

Killbuck took the list and left.

Krautkramer talked for a while, then left Jake and Toad to study the map and files.

"An awful lot of the Atlantic is pretty shallow," Toad said dubiously, looking at the thousands of square miles the computer had colored yellow. "If a fellow were picking a spot to plant a satellite, seems like he has a lot of choice."

"Not really," Jake replied. "The missile is coming down without power in a ballistic trajectory. The target area of necessity must be pretty big."

"But how is the pirate crew of *America* going to find the third stage if they can't use active sonar?"

"I've been thinking about that," Jake said. "They're going to need a noisemaker, something that puts a lot of noise into the water so Revelation can pick up the reflections off the bottom and, they hope, the lost missile. Something that looks benign."

"So what is that something?" Toad asked.

"I don't know. I was hoping the recon satellite photos of areas of interest might give us some hints. What you and I need to do is designate areas of interest."

Myron Matheny had a busy morning. He stole a Ford from a hospital parking lot in Alexandria, successfully got it into a handicapped parking space on the street behind the parking garage, and carried the Remington into the parking garage embedded in green plastic garbage bags. He got it arranged inside a trash can at the entrance to an elevator and finished filling the can with trash from a can near the restaurant operation.

He stood back, scrutinized his can. Few people would pass it outside this inoperative elevator. If the trash people came by while he was downstairs, so be it—he would wait for the guy tonight in Rosslyn.

He checked the shooting position on the second deck again, got a cold feeling up his spine because it was so open. He would be semihidden here behind these parked cars, which would just have to do. He certainly wouldn't have time to dawdle.

When he had done all he could, he went down to the square and

walked past the food operation, checking out the customers in line
and seated on the planter retaining walls and at the long tables. The
guy wasn't here yet.

Matheny bought a fountain soft drink, then sat near the entrance
where he could see everyone who came in.

He was nervous. This just didn't feel right—he hadn't done all
the planning, hadn't eliminated controllable variables. So much could
go wrong. Random chance, the friction of life . . . and his life was on
the line. He was betting his life that the stolen car would start, a
cop wouldn't turn up in the wrong place, an accident or construction
project wouldn't block traffic . . . my God, the list of things beyond
his control that could go wrong was almost infinite. Knowing, being
prepared beforehand, that was how he had stayed alive all these
years.

The time was 11:50.

The queue waiting to go through the food line grew steadily
longer. From 12 to 1 was going to be the big rush.

At 12:01 two uniformed policemen walked up and got in the
queue. Terrific. Those two were going to rabbit after him the instant
the rifle cracked.

The queue was moving quickly through the food service line—
this entrepreneur obviously knew the food business—yet it was
growing as all the people on lunch break in the buildings in the area
descended on the square.

And there *he* was, in line with a bunch of other people, a few in
uniform.

Myron Matheny forced himself to relax. He must wait until he
saw where the group sat before he left. He certainly didn't want to
stand up there on the second floor of the parking garage waving
binoculars or the rifle around trying to find this guy.

The knot of people the guy was in talked animatedly among
themselves, enjoying the break from their desks.

They paid for their meals individually, then commandeered the
end of one of the long tables.

Myron Matheny rose, threw away his soft drink as he walked
toward the parking garage. Yep, the guy was going to be visible
from the second deck.

This was it. It was time to kill.

Walking toward the parking garage, Myron Matheny was still

thinking of things that could go wrong. The two cops were still eating nearby. They were wearing bulletproof vests but not their little two-way radios—maybe those had been burned up by the E-warheads. That was a break. At least they wouldn't be calling in before he could even get in the car and start the getaway. Nor were the garage security cameras working. Perhaps the good breaks would cancel out the bad.

After he drilled the guy, maybe he should gun one of these two, slow the other one down. It would take seconds. That might slow the pursuit just enough. Or it might be just the break the survivor needed to get a clear shot at the back of his head as he drove away in his stolen Ford.

He wouldn't think about it, he would just go on instinct.

"So tell me again, Mr. Ilin, about this grand adventure of yours running through the forest the other day to escape assassins." Jadot asked that question.

"I see from the skeptical expression on your face that you doubt the veracity of my previous remarks on that subject," Janos Ilin said.

"You do not," Jadot protested. "The great stone-face, they call me. Recruiters for the World Series of Poker write me passionate letters every year. My face is a mask that shields my innermost thoughts."

"Jake, as our host I appeal to you," Ilin said, raising his voice enough to be heard by every member of the group. "Tell our doubting colleagues I wasn't lying, that those foul assassins lusted for our rich, red, non-Communist blood."

"We decided to play hooky for a day," Jake told Jadot. "We made up the assassins lie while we were fly-fishing the Shenandoah. Ilin said you folks would eat it with a spoon."

No one had blocked in the Ford. The way out to Lee Highway looked wide open. Satisfied, Myron Matheny climbed the stairs to the second floor of the parking garage.

No one in sight on the second deck. That is, no one standing. If there was someone sleeping off a hangover in one of the cars . . . Worried, trying to be supercautious, he scrutinized the cars carefully, then walked to the can that held the rifle. He took a last look around, then pulled out the rifle by the barrel. It was still wrapped in three shapeless green garbage bags, and he left it that way.

He walked to the vantage point, put the rifle on the concrete floor, then looked for the guy.

There he was! And the cops at the next table.

Matheny turned back and looked the parked cars over carefully. He was the only person in sight. He bent down and used his pocket knife to strip the green bags from the rifle. He opened the bolt, took three cartridges from his pocket, and carefully inserted them in the magazine. Then he closed the bolt, making sure a round chambered.

Now he laid down the rifle and stood for one last look around.

Everyone still eating.

Just as he bent for the rifle, someone came out of the stairwell and walked his way. The rifle was partially hidden under the car right beside him, so he left it there.

A woman, walking quickly, the hard material of her heels rapping loudly on the concrete.

She looked at him, nodded, then broke eye contact. Never looked at the rifle or garbage bags.

She dug in her purse, used a clicker to unlock the door of her car.

Myron Matheny turned his back, leaned on the rail, listened as she started the car and backed it out and drove down the ramp toward the exit booth.

The guy was still there, talking to his colleagues.

Oh, man, he was nervous. He just hadn't done enough planning to feel comfortable with the risks involved. Too much was unknown.

The truth was there was no way to pop a guy quick and feel comfortable about it.

He couldn't just stand here all day. . . .

Now!

Myron Matheny bent down, got a good, solid grip on the rifle, straightened, looked at his target, and lifted the rifle smoothly to his shoulder. The crosshairs came right onto the guy's head. He had the scope on three-power magnification, which was as low as it would go.

Automatically he leaned forward, putting his elbows on the rail.

Matheny exhaled, steadied the crosshairs, and squeezed the trigger.

As Jake explained it to Callie much later, his plastic fork slipped from his fingers and fell into his lap. He had been eating baked beans with it, which he knew would stain his white trousers. He pushed his chair back and bent his head to see if the beans had caused a mess ... and felt the whiff of a bullet passing an inch or two over his head at the same time as he heard the shot.

The bullet hit Maurice Jadot in the chest with a loud, meaty smack.

He knew instantly what it was and shouted and dragged Jadot off his chair onto the floor.

As he explained to Callie, he didn't realize then that the shot had probably been aimed at him. He thought the shooter's target was Maurice Jadot, and he had no idea how badly he was hit. Instinctively Jake knew the shooter might try another shot, so with Jadot on the ground, Jake climbed on top of him.

Myron Matheny knew he had missed the instant the gun recoiled. In the millisecond before the gun kicked, the head in the crosshairs jerked back and down. The mild recoil lifted the barrel off target. Matheny had learned years ago to not fight the recoil but to go with it.

As the gun was recoiling he worked the bolt, ejecting the spent shell and chambering another. As the rifle came down he looked again for the guy in the white uniform, his target.

He saw a mass of people, some running, some bending over, someone lifting the table, food flying everywhere ...

Jesus Christ! Where is he?

The cops! He swung the rifle, picked out a blue police uniform, squeezed the trigger again.

Worked the bolt, looked one more time for the guy ...

Couldn't find him.

Holy fuck!

Myron Matheny lowered the rifle, threw it under a car, and walked quickly toward the staircase that would take him down to the stolen Ford.

He heard the shouts and hubbub from the food area ... and the insistent, low moan of a siren.

Jadot said something in French, a phrase or piece of a phrase, and then he was dead. Jake was pumping on Jadot's chest and telling him to hang tough as rich red blood ran from his mouth and nose when Toad finally told him it was useless, the bullet had gone through the Frenchman's lungs and heart.

Jake Grafton sat back on his heels, tried to catch his breath. Blood everywhere, on Jadot, his white uniform, his hands...

"Trying to save him, I probably killed him faster," Jake said aloud.

It was only then that he realized another person had been shot. A cop, someone said. A knot of people were gathered around her, trying to keep her heart beating.

He too heard the siren.

"Toad!" he roared.

"Yes, sir!"

"That may be an ambulance. Run out toward Lee Highway and—" He stopped because Tarkington was already gone.

Staying calm, concentrating on the job at hand, Myron Matheny carefully inserted the ignition key in the stolen Ford, applied the brake, and started the engine. He had found the key in a small magnetic box under the rear bumper when he cased the cars in the hospital parking lot. He had had to do some crawling, but the key meant that he didn't have to hot-wire it.

Looking at the gearshift indicator, he placed the transmission in reverse, looked behind him, backed out.

That siren, coming closer, growing in volume and pitch. Those bastards couldn't have got the cops coming already, could they?

Clear of the parking place, he concentrated on getting the transmission into drive.

Never panic. Concentrate fiercely on the task at hand. Those rules had kept him alive all these years, and he had no intention of abandoning them now. Yes, he had missed the kill, but tomorrow was another day. If you lived to enjoy it.

Feeding gas slowly, braking as he approached the corner, he tried to ignore the swelling howl of the siren.

Around the building. Straight ahead was the stop sign for this little street, then across the access road, the traffic light on Lee Highway, which was of course inoperative. That meant stop, yield, and go. He slowed for the stop sign, ensured that no one was coming, then moved forward to the edge of the highway intersection. Braked to a complete stop.

Siren loud, very loud.

He looked left . . . a large truck was almost stopped, barely moving.

The siren!

Matheny twisted the wheel to the right to turn to the inside northbound lane, took his foot off the brake, and fed gas.

He never saw the ambulance that was passing the large truck in the far right lane, doing at least thirty miles an hour. The right front bumper of the ambulance hit the Ford in the driver's door and snapped Matheny's head back. His body was half out of the seat when the combined inertia of the two vehicles caromed the Ford into a light pole. The impact snapped Matheny forward and threw him toward the windshield on the passenger side of the car. His head smacked into the windshield, breaking his neck. He died instantly.

Myron Matheny had forgotten to fasten his seat belt.

Jake Grafton was watching the ambulance crew load Maurice Jadot's body when a senior police officer came over to tell him about the accident victim two blocks away. "It was the assassin, we think. He had a silenced pistol on him, and this was in the car." He held out a photo. "This is you, isn't it?"

It was one of Jake's file photos, perhaps a copy of one from his personnel file. "It's me."

"Your photo, not this other fellow, Mr. Jadot."

"Umm."

"One assumes he missed."

"Apparently."

"When you're finished here, how about stopping at the morgue and seeing if you can identify him? In this heat, without cold storage, we'll have to start the autopsy in just a few hours." The officer gave him the address.

"Give me a few minutes, then I'll be along."

Janos Ilin found himself looking into the cold eyes of Jake Grafton. The admiral had a smear of blood on his forehead, but the eyes looked like they were frozen. Behind him a doctor was working on the wounded police officer, trying to save her while the other officer herded spectators away, trying to give them some room.

Grafton held up his hands in front of Ilin. They had Jadot's blood on them.

"You think this is all a game, do you?" The admiral wiped his hands on the front of Ilin's shirt. "More than six hundred people dead. Jadot is another. This isn't ink on paper in a Moscow file, this is real blood!"

"I did not kill him!" Ilin said angrily, roughly pushing away Grafton's hands.

"Stolen submarines, spies, lies . . . it's all a game to you, isn't it?" Grafton pressed fiercely. He grabbed a double handful of Ilin's coat and pulled him up short. "Why don't you stop the fucking games and tell me the goddamn truth?"

"I've told you the truth," Ilin protested, grabbing Grafton's wrists.

"No you haven't! You've lied to me. And now, by God, I want the truth!" Grafton shook him like a dog shaking a snake, then pushed him away.

Ilin almost fell. "What lie?" he asked.

Keeping his hands to himself, Grafton moved closer. "You didn't learn about the Blackbeard team from the SVR. That was a lie."

Ilin adjusted his tie, straightened his coat. His face was expressionless.

"I've been checking. Those people were all held incommunicado. You didn't go to Connecticut to chat up one of them."

Ilin straightened his shirt.

"Someone else told you about the Blackbeard team, then perhaps you told DeGarmo. He went to that party, all right. The Federal Protective Service provided a bodyguard. An American betrayed the team to the SVR. Either DeGarmo or someone else. It's entirely possible that you didn't talk to DeGarmo during the party, that he knew you already knew."

Janos Ilin helped himself to a cigarette. He lit it, blew out smoke, then met Jake Grafton's steady gaze.

"Six hundred people dead, a stolen submarine," Jake continued, insistent.

"DeGarmo didn't know I knew," Ilin replied coolly. "I could see it in his eyes."

"Then who?"

"I can't tell you. The identity of that person is a state secret."

"Your state."

"Indeed. My state! That is the only state I'm interested in."

Jake weighed his words before he spoke again. "The problem is that you keep lying to me. The SVR didn't send you here to keep these three Europeans company. That was not a good lie. You could have done better."

Ilin's eyes narrowed. "I have underestimated you," he said.

Jake Grafton was not to be denied. "I think your bosses are worried that EuroSpace is going to get its hands on the SuperAegis satellite. You're here to make sure that doesn't happen."

Ilin dropped his cigarette and stepped on it. "They sent me here to watch you. They were worried that you Americans weren't smart enough to handle it."

CHAPTER EIGHTEEN

The mood was somber at the office that afternoon after Jadot's death. Jake changed from his bloody uniform into his jogging clothes. Two secretaries and one of the junior officers went into the women's room and cried, several of the men felt like crying but didn't, so finally Jake Grafton sent everyone home except Tarkington and Carmellini, who were working on DeGarmo's hard drives.

The boss, General Blevins, was in Florida, huddled with the techies. The software gurus were narrowing down the possibilities of what might have gone wrong with the SuperAegis rocket. Blevins had brought in more experts from Space Command and felt he had to be present while the experts consulted.

Jake walked through the empty office, fingering this and that, trying to put the pieces of the puzzle together.

Washington, the dead city!

The newspapers were back in production, somehow, and people had proudly carried in copies this morning. A small symbol of normal life had returned, and welcome it was. The papers were full of predictions about when power and telephone service would be restored, when life would be "back to normal."

Normal.

And they were full of speculation about Kolnikov, *America,* and Tomahawk missiles. "Where is Kolnikov?" screamed one banner headline. If only Kolnikov had known. With a good lawyer and the right public relations firm, the Russian skipper could probably beat the rap and sell a book for millions, perhaps even get a movie sale. Add in a highly publicized relationship with a naughty pop singer or starlet ... well, the possibilities boggled the imagination.

The question, though, was a good one. Where *was* Kolnikov?

Jake was drinking coffee and thinking about possible answers to that question when Krautkramer, the FBI special agent in charge, came in.

Krautkramer told him more than he wanted to know about Myron Matheny. He grunted occasionally as he listened to the FBI agent, but he had no questions. When Krautkramer ran down, Jake said, "Tell me about Peter Kerr."

"The missing NASA specialist? What do you want to know?"

"Everything you haven't told me. The works."

"When do you want this?"

"Now."

Krautkramer snapped his fingers.

"Tomorrow afternoon," Jake said.

"Must have been pretty rough, seeing Jadot get it like that."

"I think he was dead when he hit the ground. Bullet seemed to go through a lung and into his heart. Actually a pretty good way to go, all things considered."

"Was he the target? Or you?"

"Maurice Jadot was a genuine nice guy who had the misfortune to be in the wrong place at the wrong time. He was sent to the liaison team to learn all he could about SuperAegis and report back to French intelligence. Presumably he did just that. If he knew anything at all about submarines and Tomahawk missiles, he never gave me a hint."

"I heard Matheny had your photo in his car."

"Maybe he was after me, maybe not," Jake said, not willing to label himself worth killing. "If I was his target he made a hash of it. Jadot's tough luck, killed by an incompetent assassin. Hope they don't put that on my tombstone."

"Umm," said Krautkramer, and looked around. "Where's Carmellini? I have some information for him. He asked me to check a fingerprint. Well, actually some prints embedded on latex finger sleeves." He removed a manila envelope from his file and tossed it on Jake's desk. "That guy is something else. Some cock-and-bull story about a sultry wench and knockout drops . . . and the sleeves have a dead woman's prints on them." He told Jake the name.

Grafton went to the door and called for the CIA officer.

Carmellini stared at Krautkramer when he heard the news. "How long has she been dead?" he asked, so softly he had to repeat the question. "How long?"

"She died in a car wreck about a month ago."

Jake jumped in. "This ID is off the FBI fingerprint computer?"

"In Clarksburg. We just scan in the print and they code it digitally and the computer searches the files."

"Has anyone hacked into the files lately?"

Krautkramer looked startled. "Not to my knowledge, but that isn't the kind of thing that lands on my desk."

"Does the government maintain any other fingerprint files?"

"A few agencies still maintain their own. It's a duplication of effort, so we're trying to get them all in-house, but you know bureaucrats."

"Indeed I do. But these databases . . . someone has been manipulating the data they contain. I can tell you for an absolute fact that a collection of career flag officers hasn't invested money in currency futures and hasn't sold out to Jouany. Let's find out who Sarah Houston really is. How about sending an FBI team to the CIA safe house in New York where Carmellini met this woman and have them go over the place for prints. See if these are the prints of the woman he knew as Sarah Houston or if someone at the CIA substituted prints."

"Okay. We can do that."

He waited until Krautkramer was out the door before he tossed Carmellini the envelope. "You and Toad visit some Beltway bandits today. The Reston area is full of small high-tech shops that don't use the FBI master fingerprint files."

Toad was standing in the door. "We're not fingerprint experts," he said, frowning.

"You don't have to be. The FBI has classified the prints, so it's a matter of matching classifications. Not good enough for court, but good enough for us. I want a name and photo of a woman who isn't dead. It's a long shot, I know, but it's possible she is the person who manipulated Jouany's database. If she is, she's a computer expert, and that means she's been around the high-tech industry. If she isn't, she can tell us who sent her to bat her eyes at Carmellini. Let's turn over some rocks and see what's underneath."

Toad nodded. "Nothing on DeGarmo's hard drives is of interest to us, boss. E-mails to nieces and nephews, his brother, a couple women he is apparently mildly interested in, and that's about it. Oh, he does answers to suggestion box questions on one computer."

"Mail the hard drives back to him. Try to do it in such a way that Krautkramer doesn't come charging over here waving warrants for our arrest."

For the first time in weeks, Jake saw a glimmer of light. He told himself not to get his hopes up—but. Somewhere in this mess was someone who knew a whole hell of a lot about computer databases and security systems. And he doubted if that someone was Peter Kerr, the missing NASA software expert.

When Vladimir Kolnikov was convinced that there were no submarines lying in wait, he eased the photonics mast above the surface. The camera looked at the sky, lowered its point of aim, spun through 360 degrees, then automatically eased down into its housing. In the control room, Kolnikov, Turchak, and Heydrich examined the video. After they had run through it slowly, they ran it again and froze the frame on a ship anchored three miles away, at the entrance to the bay at Cadiz.

"That's her, *Global Pioneer.*"

"I see no American ships, no airplanes," murmured Turchak, who was worrying a fingernail.

"We have done it, then," Kolnikov said. He looked around the control room, at Eck, Boldt, and the others, and smiled. "And done it well."

"We're only halfway there," Heydrich growled. "Just you be here when I come back."

"Or what?" Kolnikov demanded harshly. Then he softened his tone. "God, you are tiresome."

"Bring us some beer," Eck said.

"A reasonable request," Kolnikov agreed. "A case, please. Something bitter. A good German beer."

Heydrich turned and went aft. Kolnikov followed him. From the engineering spaces they climbed a ladder to the compartment that housed the airlock. One climbed through it to gain access to the minisub, which was mated to the boat above it. Heydrich went first, climbing the ladder. He settled into the minisub pilot's seat while Kolnikov stood on the ladder with only his head inside.

Heydrich flipped switches, and the minisub's battery brought it to life.

"Don't forget to flood the ballast tanks or you'll bob to the surface like a cork," Kolnikov advised.

"I won't forget, Captain."

"We will cruise back and forth. Use the underwater telephone and your lights. We will have our lights on. You shouldn't have any trouble once you see us. I'll have the boat at three knots to maintain plane effectiveness."

"I understand."

"Good luck," Kolnikov said, dropping down into the airlock. He carefully shut the hatch and dogged it down. Only when he was sure that the hatch was properly sealed did he continue on down the ladder and close the hatch at the bottom of the lock, then dog it down.

He stood listening. He heard water rushing into the minisub's tanks. After a few moments that sound ceased. Finally he heard the minisub's hydraulic latches retract. He heard it scrape along the hull, bump several times, then it was free of the boat, swimming on its own.

Only then did Kolnikov leave the compartment and make his way forward toward the control room.

The minisub had no windows. Closed-circuit video cameras showed the pilot what was ahead and to the sides. Worse, the pilot had to skillfully manipulate the cameras by means of joysticks, adjusting the sensitivity of the light sensors, all while operating the rudder and planes. The task required skill and practice, neither of which Heydrich had ever had.

He immediately realized he was in over his head. For the first time in his life, Heydrich knew fear. When he released the hydraulic locks that held the minisub to *America,* he also engaged the electric motor. The minisub actually slid backward, scraping along the hull, before he gave it enough power to keep pace with the mother ship. Then he found he had too much ballast aboard and slid off the rounded side of *America*. The sub sank, the nose dropping, as he pulled back on the yoke and added power and blew off some ballast.

Finally, he wasn't sure how, he got the craft stabilized. *America* was a dark presence on his starboard side, separating from him in the gloomy sea.

For the first time he looked at the compass. Yes, he realized with a flash of panic, he had not even checked the submarine's base course or whether the minisub's compass jibed with that number. He had no choice; he had to assume all was working properly. If it wasn't, he would soon be on the surface, he hoped, swimming to stay alive.

He bit the bullet, picked up the underwater telephone, and keyed the mike. "What is the course I should follow?"

The answer, when it came back, was ethereal. "Try steering one two zero, which will be a ten-degree crab for the current. Three miles."

Gingerly he turned the sub to that course and concentrated on holding a steady heading and even depth.

Gradually the fear left him. He could do this! He had used underwater sleds before—this was just a larger version, he told himself. Yet he wished he had paid more attention when Rothberg had explained the controls.

With the current running, the minisub took a half hour to make the three-mile passage. It was with great relief that Heydrich saw the hull of *Global Pioneer* materialize in the murky water ahead.

He was getting the hang of operating the minisub now, so he steered under the ship, adding ballast judiciously, until he saw the dark black hole in her keel. That was the hole through which underwater fiber-optic cable was laid. Fortunately there was no cable dangling there just now, so Heydrich inched the sub forward using the maneuvering jets, taking his time. When he got under the hole, he tilted the forward camera up, so he could see into it. And he saw lights.

Reassured, at what he judged was the proper moment he blasted the ballast tanks with compressed air to lift the minisub quickly. She caromed once off the side of the hole, then rose into it.

When he opened the top hatch, a voice spoke to him. "We thought you'd never get here."

Heydrich made two trips between *Global Pioneer* and *America,* ferrying divers and their gear. He also brought two cases of beer and a stack of newspapers that detailed the physical damage the E-warheads had caused in Washington and New York, and the psychological, political, and financial damage, which was, by any measure, stupendous. The administration was in deep and serious trouble, according to the pundits. Congress was in a mercurial mood, demanding the heads of everyone responsible.

Which includes us, Kolnikov thought as he read the stories while sipping beer in the wardroom. At the next table the divers laughed and scratched with several members of the crew, who were delightedly telling them about the battle in the depths.

When the cook brought in food, Heydrich came in and sat down beside Kolnikov. "So how did it go?" Kolnikov asked.

"I made many mistakes," Heydrich admitted. "I have learned much."

"I have heard it said that experience is a mistake you lived through."

"Then I have gained experience."

They discussed the minisub, how it operated, each man learning from the other.

"What are our chances of finding the satellite on the seamount?" Heydrich asked.

"Such a long distance, such a small target. If the missile missed by more than four miles, it will be too deep for us to recover with the gear we have. You will have to return later with one of your salvage ships. If the Americans haven't found it first. Believe me, they haven't given up."

"I understand."

"The water over the seamount is shallow and very dangerous for a submarine. If a submarine comes prowling while you are out, or a patrol plane, my first responsibility will be to save the boat. I will return for you when and if I can."

"I understand."

"These others," Kolnikov indicated the laughing men at the next table, "do they understand the risks?"

"Diving is a dangerous life. They know that. The money for this job is very, very good. No one lives forever."

"So they say," Kolnikov replied.

That afternoon one of the televisions at Hudson Security Services was tuned to a local cable news station in Alexandria, Virginia. By midafternoon the station had the story on the shootings at Crystal City and the subsequent death of the assassin in a traffic accident. Zelda Hudson glanced up when she heard it, watched the footage, most of which was of the mangled remains of the stolen Ford, and said nothing. She was writing a proposal for a company in California and continued working on it, huddling with three or four of her staff, negotiating with a travel agent over train schedules to get two people to the West Coast.

When the staff left for the day, Zipper Vance stayed behind, as he usually did. "I'm worried," he said, "about Willi Schlegel. He sent you that E-mail after Washington. After New York, nothing. Total silence. That's not like him."

"He wants the satellite," she said dismissively. "He'll get it too. He doesn't give a damn about New York."

"That assassination attempt in Washington," Zip continued, "killed a Frenchman. Would you know anything about that?"

"Never heard the name before."

"I have," Zipper said brightly. "Works with Jake Grafton in the SuperAegis liaison office. As I listened to the story, I wondered."

Her face revealed nothing. "Wondered what?"

"Wondered if you hired someone to kill Jake Grafton."

"He's no threat."

Vance snorted. "Hell, he's the only threat. He's got this caper figured out. Doesn't have any proof yet, but he'll get some. Carmellini is working with him now—oh, yes! I browsed through the classified, encrypted E-mails those people are firing around. Why in the world you did that little charade with Tommy Carmellini is beyond me."

"Who else was going to do it? You? Carmellini wouldn't have been interested in your manly charms."

"Did or did you not try to have Jake Grafton murdered?"

"For Christ's sake, Zipper, don't get squeamish on me now." She picked up a newspaper off a nearby pile, one with a front-page, above-the-fold photo of a column of smoke arising in Brooklyn from the crash of an air force fighter, and held it where he could see it. Then she tossed it back on the pile.

"We didn't kill anyone, Zel. Until now."

"Don't give me that *shit!*" she roared. "I won't listen! You and I worked very hard to get this snowball rolling. Now it's an avalanche, and I don't want to hear you holier-than-thou telling me *you* have clean hands."

"We'll go to our graves with those people's deaths on our conscience," Vance whispered, refusing to meet her eyes. "But we never pointed at one person and said, 'You! I sentence you to die.'"

"Oh, there's an important distinction," Zelda said acidly. "I am really not in the mood for this shit. How about taking it down the street."

Standing at the elevator door, waiting while the cage rose, Vance said, "Guess I'd better start watching my back, huh? Like Jake Grafton. One of these days it will occur to old Zelda that Zipper Vance is the only eyewitness who could testify against her. Too bad for the Zipper, but he'll never see it coming. Won't feel a thing! And we all gotta go sometime."

He got into the cage and pushed the button to take it down.

She waited until she saw him walking away from the building on the outside security camera, then went over to raise the elevator and turn it off.

Who did he think she was, anyway, some bleeding-heart flower-power hippie like her mother used to be?

Zip Vance needs to open his eyes. This is the twenty-first century, the age of capitalism. Hudson Security Services exists because the world is full of companies that want to protect their secrets. And they want to buy other people's secrets. She made a fine living selling both stolen secrets and security systems to the same people! Everyone wants to buy! Ethics? Don't make me laugh!

Today it's Europe, Incorporated, versus America, Incorporated. Forget the flag-waving bullshit. Those are the two big dogs and they are vicious. Willi Schlegel, billionaire industrialist, has spent a lifetime making sharp deals and squashing anyone in his way. Antoine

Jouany, financier, has been busy separating people and their money any way he can get away with. He has even invented ways. Regardless of how he got it, he knows that money spends just fine.

Scruples? Ha! Give me a break!

People die every day. Zip knows that. Car wrecks, cancer, lightning, plane crashes, stray bullets from gang-bangers . . . What is the difference?

"Admiral, this is Commander Packenham," Toad said. "He was the officer in charge of training the Blackbeard team in New London."

If Packenham thought there was anything unusual about having a conference with a flag officer wearing a T-shirt and shorts, he didn't mention it. He had driven down from Connecticut, he told Jake, at Toad's request. He began by describing the training program he had constructed for the team, then discussed personalities.

Jake Grafton said little. When Packenham discussed Kolnikov, however, Grafton met his eyes, listened intently.

"Kolnikov was the best of them," Packenham said, "the quickest study. Turchak had as much experience as he did, but Kolnikov was a natural leader. He would have done very well in anyone's navy."

A few minutes later Packenham said, "Nothing bothered Kolnikov. He was the calmest, steadiest man I have ever met. The others worried about safety, about backup systems and emergency procedures and all that, but not Kolnikov. He listened and absorbed the information, but it didn't seem to me as if"— Packenham paused and searched for words—"as if life or death really mattered to him anymore. It was as if he didn't care. About anything! Does that make sense?"

When Jake arrived home that evening, Callie was on the balcony of the apartment washing clothes by hand. She was heating water on the charcoal grill, washing the clothes in a tub, then hanging them on the railing of the balcony to dry. He helped her while he told her about the shot that killed Maurice Jadot and critically wounded an Arlington police officer.

"Why," Callie asked after she had heard him out, "would an assassin shoot Jadot?"

"I don't think he intended to," Jake replied. "I think he shot at me and missed." He hadn't said that to the FBI agent—he didn't know whom he would repeat the comment to—but he always leveled with Callie.

"Jake! You set up that whole thing with Ilin. Those people were FBI."

"I don't think this had anything to do with that little adventure. I was just trying to make Ilin talk that day. I think the shooter today wanted to shut me up."

"Why?"

"Someone told somebody something."

"Who?"

"Ilin, maybe. Maybe not. He told me Russia doesn't want Europe to get the satellite."

"Is that what this is about? That satellite?"

"Maybe. I think so. But hell, I don't know."

He poured the hot water over the tub of wet clothes to rinse them, then began working the soapy water from a pair of undershorts.

Callie sat down abruptly. She stared at the sky, examined her hands, then rose and went into the apartment.

Jake worked his way through the tub, twisted each item to get as much water out as he could, shook it out, and hung it on the railing. When he had finished he went to find her.

Callie was sitting in the kitchen, crying silently.

"Hey," he said. "What's wrong?"

"Like everyone else in this damned city," she said, "I am working my ass off trying to keep body and soul together. Classes were canceled at the university, so I have no job. The dealer sent a tow truck today for the car—the driver said two weeks at least, maybe three. They're swamped.

"I cook on a charcoal grill, wash clothes in a tub, sweep the apartment with a broom, eat canned food by candlelight—I don't ever again want to go to a restaurant that has candles on the table—take sponge baths, and go to bed ten minutes after dark because there is no television or radio or CDs or movies or Internet. *Nothing!* I live like my great-great-grandmothers, reading by candlelight. Then my husband comes home and casually announces that someone tried to murder him today. The bullet missed by an inch or two. No big deal! Ho-hum, just another day in twenty-first-century America." Tears leaked from her eyes and ran down her cheeks.

He reached for her. She pushed his hand away.

"I'm feeling sorry for myself. Okay?"

"That's allowed," he said.

Her voice was hoarse. "I didn't volunteer for any of this. I don't want my husband shot to death. I don't want to be a widow. I don't like get-back-to-nature campouts in the city. I don't want to live a simpler life—I liked it fine just the way it was. Jesus, is this America? What the hell happened to my country?"

After this outburst her tears dried up. She sniffed and swabbed at her cheeks. In about a minute she said, "I'm sorry."

"For what?"

"For being selfish."

He bent over and kissed her. "You aren't selfish. You're human. No apology necessary."

"Oh, Jake!"

"Hey, they didn't get me. We're still alive and kicking."

"Yeah."

"We're still trying to figure it out."

"Figure out what?"

"What happened to our country."

The following morning Jake Grafton was in a thoughtful mood. The police had said that the dead assassin was carrying a silenced pistol in a shoulder holster.

Twice during the night Jake had awakened thinking about that pistol.

Was he really the target, or was that deduction mere anxiety from being so close to a death by violence? Had he really felt the whiff of the rifle bullet? Did his sudden movement throw off the assassin? Or did the assassin aim at Jadot? If he was the target, why didn't the assassin shoot at him with his second shot?

There was no way to know any of the answers, of course. After the rush of adrenaline, there was only a cold memory of the edge of the abyss.

While he was putting on his blue uniform he dug out an old

Smith & Wesson .38 from the bottom of his sock drawer and loaded it. He put it behind his belt in the small of his back. Just in case, he told himself. Then felt foolish.

Foolish or not, he still had the gun on him when he kissed his wife good-bye. She was still in bed. On his way out he pulled the apartment door closed until it locked. Then he tried the handle.

The September air was like wine as he stood on the sidewalk examining the people passing on foot and in cars. The sunlight was brilliant, the shadows crisp.

If he had been the target, someone else might try again. He consoled himself with the thought that only a fool would ignore that possibility.

Still, the pistol felt heavy and hard in the small of his back.

A smile crossed his face. God, it felt good to be alive.

He was still savoring the air and the people and the noise when a car pulled to a stop beside him on the street. Flap Le Beau was in the front passenger seat and a marine was behind the wheel. Jake climbed into the back.

"Good morning, sir," Jake said. "Corporal."

"Good morning, sir," the driver said.

Flap just grunted and passed Jake a newspaper. It was from Atlanta. The headline was the revelation that the top echelon of American military officers was profiting from the travails of the American economy. Someone leaked the list Carmellini had brought back from London.

Jake glanced at the story, which originated in London. So the leaker wasn't anyone in his office. For some reason, that fact made the headline easier to take.

CHAPTER NINETEEN

A television reporter and photographer were waiting outside Jake's building when he arrived. He sat in the car with Flap Le Beau watching them. They hadn't seen him yet. "Uh-oh," he said.

"What are you going to do?"

"If I ignore them it will look like I've got something to hide."

"That's the spirit. This is Washington. Deny, deny, deny."

"I'll go a long way following that advice."

"Don't hold anything up in front of your face. And don't let them see the handcuffs. That stuff prejudices the jury."

"Your name was on that list too. Want to come over and hold a joint conference, tell them how we're going to invest our newfound riches?"

"Out," Flap said, jerking his thumb. "I'll hurry over to my office and watch you on the news."

As Jake got out of the car he adjusted the pistol under the blouse of his blue uniform so it wouldn't fall out.

The reporter was a woman, and she had the drill perfected. He heard her say into the microphone as he walked toward the door, "Here comes Admiral Grafton now."

She shouted, "Admiral Grafton, Admiral Grafton!"

Jake walked over, trying to look innocent. How do you do that?

"Admiral Grafton, this morning a London newspaper printed a

story that said you and a number of other American military officers have huge accounts with the Jouany firm. Would you comment on that?"

"I don't have an account with any of the Jouany firms. I have never invested a dollar with them. There's been some mistake."

"So you're denying that Antoine Jouany owes you over three and a half million dollars?"

"Yep, I'm denying it. He doesn't owe me a penny."

"How about the other officers on the list?"

"I can't speak for them," he said, and turned toward the door to the building.

She asked another question anyway, "Have you been subpoenaed yet by the House subcommittee?"

Jake kept going. Oh, boy! A congressional subpoena. That would get today off to a rollicking start.

Sonny Killbuck was waiting upstairs with a pile of computer-generated maps and photos taken by reconnaissance satellites. Ilin, Barrington-Lee, and Mayer were in the outer office going over software with two NASA experts. They were still trying to determine why the SuperAegis launch went awry. Jake doubted if the reason would ever be determined, but it gave them something to do. Fortunately, telephone service had yet to be restored, so reporters weren't ringing the phone off the hook.

"Two of Heydrich's salvage ships are working wrecks," Killbuck told Jack. "One is in the Maldives, and the other is docked in Nice. Verified with satellite photography."

"That missile didn't make it halfway around the world to the Maldives. It would have had to achieve orbitable velocity to get that far. It went in the Atlantic, someplace."

"I agree," said Captain Killbuck. He pointed out likely ships, ships that had cranes and thrusters and sufficient deck space to be used for salvage work. One of them, a cable layer, was in Cadiz.

"What's it doing there?"

"Who knows? We can find out, but it will take awhile."

"I think the satellite is on a seamount or continental shelf. Without a salvage ship, they can't work helmeted divers in deep water. I would bet it's where scuba divers can get to it, say less than a hundred feet. The divers could come out of the sub, open the missile, take out the satellite."

"They can't get it into the sub," Killbuck objected. "The airlock opening is too small."

"That's right. But maybe they could put a cable on it, tow it, take it someplace where it can be raised by a ship with a crane. At night. What we've got to do is find that ship."

"Why did they need the minisub?"

Jake Grafton took his time with that one. "I don't know that they needed the minisub. It was on *America* when they stole it, but I think the target was really *America*. They needed a sub that a small crew could man. As you know, *America* is more computerized than any other American submarine. And it's stealthy. If they had had any other boat, they'd be dead after a sea battle with two *Los Angeles*–class attack boats."

"I think they'll use the minisub to go back and forth between another ship and the submarine."

"I think so too," the admiral said. "They know all about radar and IR recon satellites. And they know we're looking. What they need is a ship that they can get the minisub into."

Killbuck made a note. Then he asked, "What do you think they will do with *America* after they have the satellite?"

"You know the answer to that. They'll abandon her. Submerged."

"So they'll use the minisub to get the people out?"

"I doubt it," Jake said. "Those fifteen men killed six American sailors and stole a submarine. They fired missiles that killed more than six hundred more Americans. They sank *La Jolla* and killed her crew. They're the most wanted men on Earth. Whoever is behind this doesn't want those men to ever talk to prosecutors or sit on a witness stand. I have this sneaking suspicion that USS *America* will be their tomb."

The foreign liaison types, Ilin included, went to lunch at noon. Jake hadn't spoken to Ilin since immediately after Jadot was killed. He had been avoiding the man. Jake had nothing to use as a lever to pry whatever Ilin knew from him, so there was no point talking. They were past the point of idle chitchat.

He was sitting at his desk staring out the window when Toad and Carmellini came in carrying a pizza. "Want a piece, sir?"

"A couple, if you can spare them."

"Normally we wouldn't, but since you're regular navy . . ."

As they opened the box on Jake's conference table, Toad said, "We got lucky this morning. A Beltway bandit has a former FBI agent as their security guy. He keeps the prints of everyone who gets access to the inner sanctum in a card file. He found this." Toad handed Jake a copy of the access card.

"Zelda Hudson. Hudson Security Services." He read the address in Newark aloud, then put the card on his desk. "No photo?"

"I was saving the best for last." Toad whipped another sheet of paper from his pocket. This was a sheet of copy paper with the photo reproduced on it. A white woman with regular features and a mass of dark hair. She looked as if a smile would transform her face, make her radiant.

"Well?" Jake said, looking at Carmellini.

"It's her, all right. Sarah Houston, Zelda Hudson."

As he worked on the pizza, Jake thought about it. "Maybe we ought to wait to find out what Krautkramer finds in that CIA West Side apartment."

"I don't care what he finds," Carmellini retorted. "We have a name and address. We even called information and got the phone number of Hudson Security in Newark. I called and asked for her. I recognized her voice. Didn't say anything, just hung up."

"What did she say?" Toad asked with his mouth full.

" 'Hello.' "

"That's it? You can recognize women with two syllables?"

"How many does it take before you figure out it's your wife?"

"The degree of familiarity is a bit different, but your point is well taken." Toad turned his attention to Jake. "What say Tommy and I take a car and zip up Jersey way this afternoon. Maybe we can have a little talk with this woman."

"What are you going to say to her?"

"Stolen any submarines lately? Hired any killers?"

Jake finished his slice of pizza before he spoke. "We'll wait for Krautkramer. He might want to put a wiretap on their phones. Maybe he won't want to do anything until he's had a wiretap in place for a while. If he wants to talk to her, perhaps he'll let us tag along."

Toad didn't argue. He knew who called the shots.

Tom Krautkramer showed up at quarter to one. He listened in silence to Carmellini's report, looked at the copies of the fingerprint card and photo, then said, "These were the prints in the West Side apartment. A cleaning service had been in there, but they missed a few prints. Apparently someone put some bum info into the computer in Clarksburg."

"Wonder who?" Toad said innocently.

"I'd like you to tap her phones," Jake said, "as soon as you can get a judge to sign something. And I want to interview her. Today if possible. Will you come?"

"Let's go by my office and I'll dictate an affidavit. One of the guys can fill out the rest of the form and get it to the judge. With luck, we can have her phones tapped in about six hours."

"Maybe we should wait and interview her tomorrow, after the taps are on," Jake said, tugging at his ear.

"That would certainly be normal procedure," the agent agreed, "but I had another blast from the director this morning. Max effort. The president has given us our marching orders. He wants that submarine found and put out of action. That's priority one, so the airlines can fly and the economy can level out. Jailing those responsible is priority two."

"If you put them in the can and they ultimately get off because you don't have a good case, you'll hear about it then," Toad objected. "You know this town."

"Can this woman lead you to the submarine?"

"Maybe," Jake said. "Let's go."

An hour and a half later when Krautkramer came out of the FBI building and climbed into the car with Jake, Toad, and Carmellini, he looked at them with new respect. "Hudson Security Services has forty telephone lines," he said. "I talked to the judge, and he'll sign the warrant, but monitoring forty lines is going to be a major operation. We're going to have to bring in assets from all over."

"We've all been hoping for a break," Jake said. "Maybe this is it." Toad was behind the wheel. Jake tapped him on the shoulder. "Let's go to Newark."

An ambulance and a small sedan belonging to U.S. Customs were waiting when the Gulfstream V taxied up in front of the Teterboro executive terminal and shut down its engines. As the door opened and the linemen maneuvered a stairway against the plane, a customs officer and an immigration officer got out of the sedan and strolled over. They were joined by a paramedic.

A man in a business suit came down the stair with a handful of passports. "Monsieur Schlegel wishes to thank you for your hospitality," he said in a French accent.

The immigration officer flipped through the passports, stamping each of them. "Which one is the sick woman?"

"This one," the man said, indicating a passport. "The ambulance will transport her to the hospital."

"Anything to declare?" asked the customs official respectfully.

"Nothing, Monsieur. We will only be here a few hours. The woman is a relative of Monsieur Schlegel and needs to see a specialist. We will be leaving this evening after the consultation."

The immigration officer nodded at the paramedic, who climbed the ladder and disappeared into the plane. In less than a minute he came to the door and waved at his colleague, who removed a stretcher from the ambulance and carried it up the stairs into the plane.

The group on the tarmac were joined by an official of the FAA. He went up the stairs to talk to the pilots. When he came back down, the immigration and customs officers were driving away.

"Thank you for allowing us to land," the Frenchman said to the FAA man.

"Humanitarian emergencies justify some risks," the FAA official replied. "Your embassy explained everything. We're delighted to be of assistance, but I wanted your pilots and Monsieur Schlegel to realize that there is some danger. If there is another attack by missiles armed with electromagnetic warheads, control of the aircraft could be lost. The consequences could be catastrophic."

"Monsieur Schlegel appreciates the danger. Still, the lady is very ill, and risks must be taken."

Soon the paramedics carried a stretcher from the plane. The man who followed them was in his late fifties or early sixties—it was difficult to say—of medium height, with wide shoulders and a flat stomach. On his right cheek was a faint shadow of a dueling scar. He was wearing an exquisitely tailored blue silk suit, hand-painted tie, and custom-made leather shoes. He looked every inch the billionaire accustomed to command.

Three other men followed him. They waited respectfully while he whispered to the woman on the stretcher, then all of them watched the paramedics place the stretcher in the waiting ambulance.

Schlegel nodded to the FAA man, then, followed by his entourage, walked toward a stretch limo that had pulled up between the plane and the terminal. The four men got into the limo, which followed the ambulance toward the gate in the perimeter fence.

"Did you have a nice flight?" the FAA man asked the Frenchman who remained.

"Very nice. Never has it been so easy to get into the New York area. The controllers let us descend across Manhattan. The sky, it is empty."

A look of irritation crossed the FAA man's face. "Yes," he acknowledged, "completely empty."

"Why do you want out of the CIA, anyway?" Toad Tarkington asked Tommy Carmellini. They had just crossed the Delaware Bridge and were on the New Jersey Turnpike headed north. Carmellini hemmed and hawed, and finally produced a metal cigar canister from his pocket. At least, it looked like a cigar canister, complete with the logo of a well-known cigar company. It was, however, a bit larger in diameter.

"I invented this," Carmellini said, "and they won't give me any royalties or pay me for it. They're just a small-caliber bunch."

Jake held out his hand and Tommy passed it to him. "Don't turn the cap," he advised. "That's the fuse."

"It's an explosive device?"

"That's right. An electromagnetic grenade, or E-grenade."

"And you carry it around in your pocket?"

"Well, yeah. I gotta carry it somewhere. Won't do me any good if it's at home when I need it."

"What if it pops?" Jake passed it on to Krautkramer, who gave it a cursory glance and handed it back to Carmellini.

"That would ruin my day," Carmellini acknowledged. "And put every electronic device within fifty feet out of commission, including this car. We'd be walking. And if that pistol in your pants goes bang, you too are going to have a problem."

"You're not supposed to notice that."

"Right."

"I can't believe this," Krautkramer said, sticking his fingers in his ears. "Here I am riding around with a bunch of guys armed to the teeth with illegal weapons."

"Hey, this is America," Toad said, as if that explained everything.

"That is her building," said the man sitting in the back of the limo with Willi Schlegel. He pointed. His name was Crozet. "Hudson Security Services. Apparently legit. I have made the acquaintance of several of the women who work there, talked to them in bars and gymnasiums. The office is on the top floor. The rest of the building is an open, empty warehouse. The only access to the top floor is an elevator."

"Is she in there?"

"Yes, sir. She went to lunch at noon and returned an hour later."

"Fire escapes?"

"There is a hole in the floor, and a rope. A person using it would end up on the ground floor inside the building. There is a back door made of steel, which can be opened only from the inside; it opens onto a loading dock in the alley behind the building. The building is a flagrant violation of the local building code."

"Access to the roof?"

"Yes, from the offices. A ladder that can be pulled down, then a door allows access to the roof. However, there is no way off the roof, so anyone up there would have to be lifted off by a ladder truck or helicopter."

"So what do you propose?"

"I think some smoke grenades in the adjoining building, which is a warehouse for furniture donated to charity. The fire department would then, I believe, evacuate the adjacent buildings as a precaution."

"She may not come out."

"If she doesn't, I thought that I and one of the men might go in from the roof. A helicopter can land us there while the evacuation is under way. I have made arrangements with the pilot of a television news helicopter. He will earn a fast ten thousand dollars."

"The door on the roof?"

"Plastique. A small charge should do it."

Willi Schlegel looked up and down the street. "And the timing?"

"We will meet the helicopter at three." Crozet looked at his watch. "In thirty-seven minutes. If the smoke grenades go into the windows of the furniture warehouse then, the operation should go off reasonably well. Two of the men should be on the street in case she comes out with the employees, one in back in the alley."

"Is she armed?"

"I could never ask that question of the women. I was afraid of arousing suspicions. It is possible."

"You have the necessary equipment?"

"Yes. I thought this the best plan."

"*Bon.* Brief the men and begin."

"Ms. Hudson, there's a fire in the building next door." The secretary made the announcement, since the main entrance intercom was on her desk. "The fire department wants us to evacuate, just in case."

Zelda Hudson glanced at the security monitor. The fireman was wearing a slicker and the usual fire helmet. The side of a pumper truck and men flaking out fire hoses were also visible.

Fire was one of the hazards inevitable with a high degree of physical security, a fact that Zelda Hudson knew well. She had bribed a building inspector to get an occupancy permit when she bought the building and put in offices. He had wanted an external fire escape installed on the back side of the building, and she refused. If the people in the building could go down it, burglars could come up.

Well, there was no help for it now. "Everyone out," she called over the hum of voices. "Five in the elevator at a time. Zip, would you supervise?"

The employees were already queueing up. In short order the first load went down.

On the monitor she could see smoke billowing from the next building, which shared a common wall. That wall was two-foot-thick masonry and wouldn't burn unless the temperature in the furniture warehouse rose to spectacular levels, but with the fire department at the door, what choice was there?

She looked around at the computers, which were still on-line. Hers and Zip's were the important ones, the ones that they could not afford to lose. On the other hand, better to lose them than to let the FBI get their hands on them. She and Zip had one-ounce charges of plastique inside each computer nestled against the hard drives, with fuses rigged to a battery in case the law cut off the power. All she had to do was push a button under her desk.

She heard the helicopter as the last of the employees boarded the elevator for the trip down. Zip stayed behind. He came over to her desk.

"Aren't you going too?"

"What's the helicopter doing up there?"

"Probably a news chopper getting some footage for the five o'clock news."

"Zip, it could be—"

"Naw," he said. "That place next door is a firetrap. It's a miracle it hasn't gone up before this. What we need is a place in the suburbs. We can afford it."

The whopping of the helicopter was getting louder. It sounded as if the thing were right on the roof.

"Come on," he said. "Let's clear the building, just in case."

"You go ahead." She waved toward the elevator.

"Hell, this isn't a raid!"

"This building is brick and stone. The only thing that could burn is the floor beams, and not unless the fire was downstairs. Go on, leave me here."

Zip went over to the elevator and pushed the button. He was waiting for it to come up when an explosion rocked the office. He looked up, in time to see the door to the roof disintegrate and two men charge through the smoke onto the landing. The noise from the helicopter flooded the room. One of them stepped onto the wooden stairway, which was rigged with counterweights. As the stairway took his weight, the bottom began descending toward the floor.

Zelda pushed the button under her desk and felt the whump as the charges in her computers detonated simultaneously, bulging the boxes. The screens went black, and smoke began oozing from one of them.

"Freeze!" the man coming down the ladder shouted. He had a weapon in his hand.

Zip went for him. The man chopped down with the pistol and dropped Zip in a heap at the foot of the stairs.

"You bastard," Zelda screamed and charged him.

The second man was right behind the first. Together they wrapped her up and put her on the floor. As one man held her down the other produced a small box. In seconds he had a hypodermic needle in his hand. He grabbed an arm, squeezed it, and jabbed the needle in.

Zip stirred, tried to rise.

When he gathered his wits, he saw one of the intruders climbing the stairs to the roof with Zelda draped over his shoulder.

Vance rose, swayed, and went for the stairs.

He didn't even see the karate chop that dropped him like a rotten log. Or the foot that smashed into his ribs.

The pilot of the television helicopter was stunned when he saw one of his passengers carrying a woman toward the passenger door. No one had said anything about another passenger. The guy gently put her in the backseat before he could object. She appeared to be unconscious. The second man came running over and climbed in beside the pilot. "Go," he shouted.

"What's with the woman?" For the very first time, the possibility of being involved in a serious crime occurred to the pilot, and he didn't want any part of it.

"Smoke inhalation. Land us at the hospital helo pad."

Relief flooded the pilot. "Which hospital?"

"Mercy General."

The pilot checked the wind and engine while the rotor RPM rose, then lifted the collective.

There was an ambulance waiting at the helo pad. Two uniformed paramedics came over and unloaded the woman while the helicopter idled. Afterward the pilot wondered why the man sitting beside him didn't use the radio to notify the hospital that a smoke inhalation victim was inbound, but he assumed that someone must have notified them on a two-way radio. Perhaps the police.

In any event, the two men got out and one shook his hand. They went over to the ambulance and were helping the paramedics put the woman on a gurney when the helo lifted off.

At Teterboro the customs and immigration officials were properly respectful. The immigration man flipped through the passports, jotted down the numbers, then handed them back. While he was doing that, Willi Schlegel bent over the woman on the stretcher, ensured she was okay, then motioned for the men of the entourage to carry it onto the plane. The ambulance drove away.

"How is she?" the customs man asked the uniformed flight attendant who had talked to him when the plane arrived.

"I do not believe the prognosis was good," the attendant confided, "but Monsieur Schlegel doesn't tell me much. I merely overheard."

The customs man nodded. He knew about class status among the filthy rich, or he thought he did.

As the plane taxied out, the two government employees got in their car and drove out through the gate.

Five minutes later the Gulfstream lifted off, and when it reached a thousand feet, made a right turn to a northeast heading, on course for the North Atlantic and Europe.

When the carload from Washington arrived in front of Hudson Security Services, the fire department was putting their equipment away.

"What happened?" Jake asked one of the firemen.

"Some smoke in that furniture warehouse," the man replied, nodding his head. "No fire. The captain said he thinks someone fired a couple of smoke grenades through one of the windows."

An ambulance crew was wheeling a gurney from the Hudson building. A man, conscious. Jake looked at his face, which looked like a slab of raw meat. This was where he hit the floor.

"What happened to him?" he asked the attendant.

"Someone beat the hell out of him. He's bleeding internally, got a collapsed lung."

"Zelda Hudson? Where is she?"

"Ask him. He was talking to the cops."

Jake addressed the man on the gurney. "Where's Zelda?"

"They snatched her. Came in the door from the roof. Kicked me."

"Who're they?"

"Schlegel, I think. I don't know. Maybe Schlegel."

"What's your name?"

"Zip Vance."

The security door was propped open, so Jake went in. All four of the Washington crew rode up in the elevator. Eight people, half women, were standing around looking lost. One of them sobbed out the story to Jake and Tom Krautkramer. Two men came in through the door to the roof, kidnapped Zelda, flew away in a helicopter.

"And look," the woman wailed, pointing at Zelda's computers. "They destroyed six of the computers, three on that desk and three on the other one."

It didn't take long for Krautkramer to discover that the computers had been destroyed by a self-destruct system. He whispered his findings to Jake, who just nodded, then he used the telephone.

"Looks like we're a day late and a dollar short," Toad said.

"Maybe." Jake crossed his arms.

When Krautkramer finished his telephone call, he said, "I've called our field office to get people over here. We've had an alleged kidnapping and we're on the scene. Doesn't get any better than that. Maybe you'd better go back to Washington without me."

"I want to talk to Vance," Jake said. "You want to come along?"

"Tell him we'll come by in a few hours. I want to question these employees first, learn just what it is these people really did here."

"You don't mind if we question Vance first?"

"Find the sub, the president said."

Jake shook hands and headed for the elevator.

In the hospital room, Tommy Carmellini was jarred by the crispness of Jake and Toad's blue uniforms and gold sleeve rings against the white of the sheets and off-white walls. The doctor and nurse hovered nearby, adjusting the IV drips, checking the leads on the heart and respiration monitor.

Vance had four broken ribs and a collapsed lung, the doctors said. They were worried about infection. They had given him a painkiller to take the edge off, yet not enough to impair his impulse to breathe.

Every breath Vance took hurt severely. Still, he wanted to talk, to share the load, and Jake Grafton was the man he picked. When Grafton wasn't angry or lost in thought, he looked like your father might have when you were small, a man you could tell things to because he would understand.

With the medical team out of the room, Vance's story poured out a phrase at a time between rasping breaths. Occasionally Jake asked a question when Vance paused, unsure what to say next.

"It was Schlegel, Willi Schlegel, who snatched her. No, I didn't see him, but it had to be. She didn't really double-cross him, you understand, but she had sold the sub's services to Jouany without bothering to tell Willi. I knew that would piss him off—and she did too—but she did it anyway. I told her not to, but she did it because the money was so good.

"Money was the way she kept score. We—each of us—have more money than we can ever spend, but she wanted more. Wanted a huge fortune. Wanted to be somebody, you know?

"Yeah, we got into people's computers, stole stuff, sold it to folks who paid us major money. Then we went back to the people we had ripped off, told them we had been doing a study of their security system, wowed them with a few things we had learned, and got a contract to tighten up their system to keep the common hackers out.

"Of course it was illegal, but it wasn't really wrong. Ideas belong to whoever can use them, not just to the person who was first through the door of the patent office. That's what the Internet is all about. And for whatever it's worth, a lot of the stuff we swiped and sold hadn't been patented. Or copyrighted.

"Yes, we sold some stuff to the Russians. They were always anxious to buy but rarely had the money we wanted. Me, I would have given them the stuff for whatever they could pay, but like I said, Zelda wanted money. Occasionally they would come up with the bucks Zelda demanded, if the stuff we had to sell was cutting edge. Usually it was. But her main clients were the Europeans, EuroSpace. Willi Schlegel. He had money, real money, and he knew the value of what we had to offer.

"I love her, sure. What can I say? You don't always get to pick whom you fall in love with. She is brilliant. Has these magnificent insights. Truly a first-class mind. But wanted money, a lot of it. For some reason money impressed her. Never understood that.

"Yes, she put the satellite in the water. Worked with Kerr on the software, figured out how to do it, hacked into the NASA system and made the changes. Then, when the rocket was in the water, went in and deleted her changes.

"She recruited the Blackbeard team. Kolnikov refused to take her seriously at first, then finally he did. She had been in the CIA computer and knew all about the Blackbeard operation, the plan to steal a Russian sub. She told Ilin and had him tell the director of the CIA that he knew. That made Kolnikov available, after he had had the training.

"She hacked into the navy's communications system and screwed with Cowbell. There is no technical challenge beyond her. Maybe ordinary rules aren't made for people that smart.

"I don't know where she put the satellite. She never told me and I never asked. At some point I realized that I didn't want to know. Maybe I got scared, I don't know. . . .

"Ilin tried to warn her. She decided to eliminate the worst threat, you. She hired a hitman she had used once before when the mob tried to move in on us. They didn't know what we were doing, but they knew we were making major money doing it, so they tried to muscle in. She hired the guy, and he killed the mob guy. You've probably got it as an unsolved someplace.

"I don't want her dead. You understand? Schlegel will kill her. He agreed to pay her a hundred million to put the satellite in the water, and he's paid just ten. He agreed to pay another hundred million when it's recovered. He'll kill her instead, so she can't talk. And he won't have to pay.

"I never really wanted money. I wanted Zelda, and to get her I thought I would have to play her game. She never set out to hurt anyone; it was the game. You see that, don't you?"

Jake Grafton may have looked like a father figure, but Carmellini noted that he didn't nod, didn't say yes just to please Vance.

"Life doesn't often work out the way it should." Even Vance seemed to realize that he had been rationalizing.

The doctor came in then, listened to Vance's chest with a stethoscope. "You gentlemen must leave. He's talked too long as it is. His right lung . . ."

"Thank you, doctor. Thank you, Zip."

"You save her, Admiral. If we go to jail, that will be okay. Maybe when we get out Zelda and I will have another chance at life. We've screwed this one up pretty badly."

There was a pay phone at the nurses' station twenty feet from Vance's room, and Jake used it. "This is Jake Grafton calling for General Le Beau."

"He's in a meeting, sir."

"Get him out of it."

Sixty seconds later he heard Flap's voice.

"We were about an hour and a half too late, General," Jake said. "Zelda Hudson was the brains behind the loss of SuperAegis and the theft of *America*. Someone kidnapped her out of her office this afternoon. They went to a fair amount of trouble to pull it off. Her partner got kicked a time or two and is in the hospital. He confessed to me. He thinks the man behind the kidnapping is Willi Schlegel, the number two at EuroSpace. According to Vance, he paid these two to put SuperAegis in the water."

There was a moment of silence as the marine digested this news. "What now?" he said.

"Well, they didn't kill her. They took her from her building in a helicopter. The FBI will chase the chopper down, but they'll be long gone when they find it. I doubt that she's still in the area. These guys are French. I think it likely she's on her way to Canada by car or plane. Or Europe by plane. I recommend we get the FBI and immigration people involved. Search every car and truck crossing into Canada. Ask the FAA if anything flew out of the northeastern United States headed for Canada or Europe. It's possible they took a plane VFR without filing a flight plan, so we need to know if anything is in the air. Anything at all."

"When will you get back here?" Flap asked.

"As fast as we can drive, sir."

"I'll make it happen."

CHAPTER TWENTY

A few strokes on the keyboard of the FAA computer revealed that the Gulfstream that left Teterboro was registered in France to EuroSpace. As the large corporate jet winged its way across the Atlantic, the U.S. Air Force launched two AWACS planes from bases in Germany.

Night had fallen when the Gulfstream changed its destination from Paris to Lisbon, Portugal. The AWACS Sentrys arrived on the scene as the Gulfstream taxied to the Lisbon executive terminal. Tracking the vehicles that left the terminal with side-looking radar proved a challenge, but when one of the vehicles went to the water-front, Jake and Flap Le Beau grinned at each other. In front of them was a listing of the vessels in Lisbon harbor. One of them was a cruise ship, *Sea Wind,* owned by a German corporation in which the majority stockholder was . . . Willi Schlegel.

"It fits," Flap Le Beau said. "Don't most cruise ships have cranes and dock-level openings for loading supplies?"

"The ones I'm familiar with do," Jake agreed.

"They could pull something aboard at night, perhaps rig an awn-ing so that the activity there can't be observed by anyone leaning over a railing or by a satellite in space."

Flap called a travel agent he knew, got him after dinner, sent him back to his office. An hour later the man called back.

"*Sea Wind* is sailing the day after tomorrow from Lisbon. Her published itinerary calls for stops in the Azores, the Madeiras, Las Palmas in the Canaries, and Casablanca, before returning to Lisbon."

"Is she full?"

"Not according to the computer. There are still cabins available, but they're damn pricey and the damn prices are all double occupancy. This is sorta a gourmet cruise for rich retirees."

"Give me five cabins, five American couples. We'll call you with names in a couple hours."

"How about in the morning?"

"Okay. But reserve them now."

The man wanted a credit card to hold the cabins, so Flap pulled out his wallet and used his own. "Just a deposit," he told his travel agent friend. "I don't have the credit limit to handle that amount."

"Hell, man," Jake told him when he hung up, "you're filthy rich. Use some of that money Jouany owes you."

"Yeah, right."

"You're not really planning on going yourself, are you?"

"I certainly am." Flap gave Jake the commandant's stare.

"Well, you're kinda famous," the admiral told him. "Black commandant and all that. Suppose one of these cruisers is a retired marine. He'll recognize you immediately."

"I'll take care of it," Flap said, in a tone that implied it was time to change the subject.

Jake did. "Maybe we ought to have State call the U.S. embassy in Lisbon. If the CIA could verify that Schlegel is on that ship I would feel a lot better about this."

"Okay." Flap picked up the phone and made the call.

"If he is aboard," Flap said after he hung up, "we'll know in a few hours. That would prove to me that USS *America* is in the eastern Atlantic. If we get that verification, what say we call the president and tell him to turn on American air travel? *America* isn't going to fire any more missiles at the United States from there."

"I hope you're right," Jake said, "because if you aren't . . ."

"Jacob Lee Grafton, we've been betting our heinies for a lot of years. One more big bet won't make any difference."

"You're the man," Grafton said with a grin. "Call Camp David and tell the big honcho it's safe to come home."

"I'll give them an opinion. While I'm at it, you call the air force and tell them I want a plane to get me and nine other fools to Lisbon in the morning."

"Aye aye, sir."

The fishing boat was trawling with three noisemakers. They weren't tremendously loud, but each of them emitted a steady, high-pitched sound. When the Revelation sonar in passive mode picked up the echoes of the sound off the shallow bottom, the effect was the same as if the noisemakers had been searchlights. The multiple noisemakers created a three-dimensional effect, eliminating many of the shadows on the irregular bottom and allowing any man-made item, such as the third stage of the SuperAegis launch vehicle, to be seen and recognized. That was the theory, anyway.

"So where the hell is it?" Heydrich demanded.

"You missed your calling," Turchak told him from his station at the helm, without turning around. "With that tone of voice, you should have been a czar."

"I don't know where the hell it is," Kolnikov replied icily. "If I did, we would simply motor over to it and let you perform your heroics. Now why don't you find a seat in the back of the control room and watch people who know more about it than you do look for your missing third stage?"

They had been looking for a day. Almost ten hours. Kolnikov scrutinized the Revelation screens with care. The sonar wasn't designed for the task he was trying to perform with it, and the computer presentations were often murky, difficult to make out. Heydrich and the divers were there in the control room in addition to the normal crew. They were sitting in chairs or standing, occasionally moving around from pure frustration, all the time concentrating fiercely on the Revelation screens.

The shallow seamount over which USS *America* crawled was the top of an ancient volcano. There was some controversy, Kolnikov recalled, a few years back over whether one of these seamounts was the legendary Atlantis, covered by the sea. The volcano that made this seamount was old when the world was young. The cone had penetrated the surface and been eroded to nearly level by wind, rain, and surf. Then at some time during the geological past, the island sank beneath the waves. Or the sea rose. Whichever, the top of the ancient volcano was today about fifteen square miles in area and submerged to a depth of ninety feet.

Fifteen squares miles was a lot of area. If the SuperAegis third stage had made it here. Vladimir Kolnikov tried to curb his impatience. The noisemakers being towed by the fishing boat could not be heard at any great distance, but if he used active sonar and radiated a pulse, that *could* be heard. For hundreds of miles.

Trying to find the third stage of the rocket was like looking for a needle by candlelight. And other submarines might be out there, sharks angling for a torpedo shot. He could never discount that possibility. He glanced over his shoulder at Eck, who was searching for other submarines and trying to optimize the Revelation pictures. When he tired, this operation would have to be temporarily suspended. Boldt could check for other subs, but he couldn't do two things at once.

Weird shapes abounded on top of the seamount. There were ancient shipwrecks, at least one modern one, fantastic coral shapes, eroded rock.... Here and there the sub passed over the gloom of a deep fissure that was impenetrable to Revelation in the passive mode.

The first problem had occurred when the fishing boat had turned at the end of the first pass and started back. The radius of the turn had been so large that a segment of the seamount's surface would be left unexamined.

Kolnikov decided to risk the underwater telephone, which used sound. It could be heard at about fifty miles by *Los Angeles*–class subs. If there were any out there. But if the missing third stage was in one of the areas that were being missed, it would never be found. Kolnikov bit the bullet and handed Heydrich the telephone headset.

The fishing boat was plodding along now with GPS precision.

"How long to search this entire seamount?" Heydrich asked.

"Since we must rest and sleep, I would say another day, at least."

The weather forecast that Boldt had downloaded when he raised the communications mast said a storm was brewing to the south. An area of low pressure drifting off Africa would become a tropical depression, then perhaps a hurricane.

Fortunately, the storm was well south, and in any event *America* should have recovered the satellite and be gone by the time it got seriously wound up. Storms were tricky. In these shallows the motion of the swells from a serious storm might rock *America*. That wouldn't

be a problem if she were properly ballasted and making enough way
to have full control with the planes, but at three knots she was so
slow that the planes had little effect. No, Kolnikov thought, he didn't
want to be caught at slow speed in these shallows if a serious storm
happened by.

Where was the satellite?

Kolnikov glanced at Heydrich, wondering how long his patience
would last if the satellite didn't turn up soon. He had sat in the back
of the control room since the boat left Long Island Sound—when
he wasn't locked up or sleeping; never a soft and fuzzy type, now
Heydrich seemed to have an edge, an urgency about him. Perhaps
it was the storm to the south.

Yes, the storm. Recovering the satellite. That was it.

The passenger list for the trip to Lisbon presented something of a
problem. Flap's first thought was that he and Jake and eight of the
toughest marines in the corps would go to Europe and kick butt.
Upon further reflection, he realized that in addition to Jake Grafton
he needed Sonny Killbuck's submarine expertise, Tommy Carmellini's knowledge of Zelda Hudson, and of course, Toad Tarkington.
That was five men, and unless they were accompanied by five
women, they certainly weren't going to melt into the cruise ship
crowd.

Jake thought Callie would want to go—he *knew* she would want
to go—and Toad's wife, Rita Moravia, was home. Jake Grafton nodded enthusiastically and said, "You bet," whenever Rita's name was
mentioned. Flap thought his wife might go even though she got
seasick in a bathtub—she and Callie could schmooze their way
through the passenger list. Flap needed two more women, and he
knew whom he wanted. He talked to his chief of staff, and soon
two of the toughest drill instructors in the corps had volunteered.

As the group waited to board the plane at Andrews, a man from
the State Department—or perhaps he was CIA, he didn't say—arrived with ten passports. All brand-new, U.S. government–issue
fakes. Each passport had the proper photo and birthday, but the
name and rest of the information were bogus.

Callie didn't like her photo. Rita didn't like her new name—
Betty—and Mrs. Le Beau was appalled that the fake passport

contained her real birthday. "I don't see why they couldn't have taken five years off," she said to Callie, who shared the sentiment.

The woman marine who was supposed to pretend she was Carmellini's significant other looked him up and down, then told him, "I've got a boyfriend who could break every bone in your body."

"Izzatright?"

"Keep your hands to yourself, lover boy, and think pure thoughts. No funny business."

Her name was Lizzy and she was from Oklahoma. When she wasn't on duty, she worked out in the gym. She had won some amateur bodybuilding competitions and thought she might try professional wrestling when this enlistment was up. Carmellini thought that if bone breaking were on the menu, Lizzy wouldn't need her boyfriend's help.

The airplane that was to fly the group to Lisbon was a civilian Gulfstream, much like the one that EuroSpace owned. Flap thought a military airplane would jeopardize the mission and insisted on a civilian-registered plane. The air force chartered one.

Jake Grafton's first look at the marine general this morning left him agape. Flap Le Beau had shaved his head and wore a large, bushy mustache and a pair of heavy horn-rimmed glasses. The mustache was glued on, of course, but Flap certainly didn't look the way he did yesterday. Part of the makeover was the civilian clothes, which were at least one size too large. He looked like he had lost weight recently. Jake complimented him on the quick change. "Corina shaved my head last night and we went to the mall for a new outfit. The larger clothes were her idea."

As they waited to board, Flap said, "I've got this sick feeling that we're going to be too late."

"The ocean salvage operations I've seen resemble greased-pig contests," Jake remarked. "Nothing goes as planned. These folks are undertaking a tricky salvage operation with makeshift equipment. I wonder if they've even found the thing."

"Surely they know where it is!"

"Zelda Hudson strikes me as a pretty slick operator. So slick, apparently, that Schlegel wanted to get his hands on her."

As they walked out to the plane, Callie said to Flap, "Thanks for including me. This invitation was a godsend. I didn't think I could take another day in that candlelit flat."

"I wouldn't classify this trip as a vacation."

"It is for me! Just watch me enjoy it."

The day was clear as only a September day can be. As the luxury bizjet climbed over the Chesapeake Bay, Jake and Callie leaned against the window trying to spot their Delaware beach. The jet was over New Jersey when it crossed the beach for the first time. It flew over Boston and Nova Scotia before it left North America behind.

Somewhere over the North Atlantic, Callie said to her husband, "I still don't understand why these people are being so sneaky about recovering the satellite. I thought that under international law abandoned ships and things like that belonged to whoever salvaged them."

"You know, I haven't asked the lawyers about that," Jake said. "I'll bet no one else has, either. The satellite was not abandoned—it was lost. Or stolen. And the French government owns some huge minority interest in EuroSpace; they may control it, for all I know. I doubt if the French government wants to go to the edge of the abyss with the Americans over a killer satellite."

The edge of the abyss. Jake thought about that phrase as the jet flew the great circle route to Lisbon. This wasn't, he concluded, a typical hardball business deal for Willi Schlegel. He had been physically present in Newark when Zelda Hudson was snatched—the customs and immigration officers both stated that for a fact. They had seen him and his passport. So Schlegel was betting everything he could steal that satellite and get away with it. Standing trial for kidnapping wasn't on his agenda, either.

Across the aisle, Toad Tarkington was getting reacquainted with his wife, Rita Moravia, who was also in the navy and on leave between assignments. She had arrived home the day before yesterday, hugged the kid and husband, and settled in for a month of domestic bliss. Then Toad informed her he was going on a cruise. "Gotta. It's a nasty job and somebody has to do it."

Rita and Toad were going to spend a week by themselves later that month, so they decided that this would be that week. The baby-sitter had instructions, her mother would arrive by car that evening, so here they were, on their way to Lisbon.

"Glad you could go with me, hot woman," Toad said. "I've really missed you. I told Admiral Grafton that we planned on spending the whole cruise in bed."

"And what did he say?"

"Just laughed."

"I missed you, Toadman," Rita said. "Hold my hand." And she slipped her hand in his.

In the row behind Toad and Rita, Tommy Carmellini was getting acquainted with Lizzy. "What do you like about pro wrestling?" he asked.

"It's my favorite thing," Lizzy replied. "Aren't you a fan?"

"Alas, no. My schedule . . ."

"It's life in microcosm. The story lines make me want to cry and laugh at the same time, you know? They're just so . . . so . . ."

"Story lines?"

"You're not a marine. What do you do for a living, anyway?"

"Civil service. Paperwork and stuff. Pretty boring. Tell me about the story lines."

Lizzy took a deep breath and began.

Flap Le Beau married later than most of his colleagues. When he finally tied the knot he was past forty and had his first star. The woman he married, Corina, was a college professor who ran a home for troubled youth when she wasn't working her day job. Flap had grown up on the streets—he knew the problems she willingly faced dealing with troubled kids. He became her biggest fan, helped her all he could, then decided they should tie the knot and go through life together. She had been married once before and wasn't anxious for another round of matrimony, but Flap persisted. He knew what he wanted, and she was it. Through sheer perseverance he finally overcame her defenses.

On the way to Portugal he sat in the front of the passenger cabin with Corina and told her about the mission. "Just be yourself," he advised. "You're a college professor who runs a home for kids. That will minimize the acting requirements."

"And who will you be?" Corina asked.

"A retired marine, I think. Collecting those retirement checks every month, fishing, and keeping busy helping you with the kids. We needed a little break, so here we are. That story works, doesn't it?"

"When you retire, *are* you going to help me?"

"Woman, did you ever have any doubts?"

"No," she admitted, "I never did."

She laughed then, and Flap Le Beau leaned back in his seat and grinned.

Jake Grafton was looking out the window when his wife whispered to him, "Thanks for bringing me along. I appreciate you sharing your burdens."

He squeezed her hand and grinned.

He had explained last night when he invited her to come. "There is some danger involved. I need your help, but this is no vacation. If you don't want to come, I'll understand. We're going to sink a ship. People are probably going to die."

"What do you and Flap think will happen?"

"*America* will eventually recover the satellite and rendezvous with the cruise ship or a cable layer that's anchored in Cadiz harbor. We have U-2s, Sentry AWACS planes, and recon satellites watching this area continuously. Our job is to call the P-3s on satellite telephones if *America* slips in under this cruise ship. There're more than a dozen P-3s at Rota, Spain. They'll hunt *America* using active sonar, then destroy her with torpedoes. Obviously, we'd like to wait until she has recovered the satellite."

"And the satellite?"

"We'll send it to the bottom with *America*, or thank Willi Schlegel and take it home."

"Why do you think *America* might rendezvous with the cruise ship?"

He explained that Schlegel had kidnapped Zelda Hudson, and they thought he was aboard this ship. "He's at the vortex of this mess."

Callie was silent for a moment, then asked, "And if something goes wrong?"

"There's a carrier battle group in the Med headed west for Gibraltar and one out of Jacksonville transiting east. The president was firm—do whatever it takes to get the satellite and the sub."

Knowing all that, she had chosen to come. "I want to help any way I can."

Today over the North Atlantic, with the sun shining in through the windows of the airplane, he squeezed her hand again.

When Zelda Hudson awoke, she was lying in a hospital bed wearing handcuffs. A uniformed nurse was in attendance. When she saw that her patient was awake, the nurse went to a telephone and made a call.

Her head thumped and she felt groggy. And slightly nauseated. Gathering her strength, Zelda tried to move and discovered that she was restrained on the bed with straps. And that she was wearing a catheter.

As she stared at the strange room and the woman in white whom she didn't recognize, the memories came flooding back. The explosion at the roof door, the stair swinging down, the men rushing in as chopper noise filled the room . . .

She remembered one of the men hitting Zip. Then . . . nothing.

So where was she?

She started to ask the nurse, then changed her mind. Don't say a word to these people.

A strange hospital, with little doors and metal walls and. . . . Oh, my God! She was on a ship!

A man came in, sixty-something, tan. She recognized him from his photos. Willi Schlegel. Two other men followed him in. The one in the white coat had a stethoscope draped around his neck.

"Ah, Ms. Hudson. I am Willi Schlegel. Welcome to my world."

She said nothing.

"You must be wondering where you are. You are aboard *Sea Wind*, which is a luxury liner, or cruise ship, as you Americans call it. We are currently anchored in Lisbon harbor. We will sail tomorrow and eventually rendezvous with USS *America*, which will transfer the satellite to us. The men aboard *America* are recovering it now."

Zelda Hudson looked at the doctor, the nurse, the third man, looked for a friendly face and didn't find one. They're bought and paid for, she thought.

"I thought you should be with us for the glorious moment," Schlegel said, "when the satellite comes aboard. I knew you would want to see it, to savor the moment of our triumph. It was a magnificent operation, and you did it. Of course, you also did many things you weren't supposed to—all those missiles to earn money from Antoine Jouany . . ." He clucked his tongue.

"You are greedy, Ms. Hudson. A greedy, unpredictable, unreliable genius. For all those reasons I thought you should be here with us, rather than sitting in front of your bank of computers in Newark making mischief."

She wondered if Zip was dead. She started to ask, then changed her mind. This asshole would tell her anything. He probably didn't know the truth. Or care.

Schlegel waited for a moment, waited for her to speak, and when she didn't, he turned away. She waited until he was out of the room before she said to the doctor, "I want off this damn bed and I want to go to the bathroom."

The doctor nodded to the nurse, who began removing the restraints. The man who had entered the room with the doctor stood against the wall and watched.

A Gulfstream is the Cadillac of business jets; people who arrive in one get the same courtesy and respect in Portugal as they do in New Jersey. Portuguese immigration and customs waved a friendly hand and the five couples walked to two stretch limos that the embassy had waiting while the limo drivers—CIA agents—unloaded the baggage and stowed it in the trunks. Since a problem at the airport with customs would have ruined everything, the contents of the luggage were completely benign. The weapons, ammunition, and satellite telephones had arrived under diplomatic cover earlier in the day and were already in the limos.

The scene on the dock was the usual hustle and bustle. Buses, taxis, and limos arrived in a steady stream, officers greeted people and handed out cabin and dining assignments, ship's crewmen checked lists and loaded luggage with a crane into a cargo sponson, veteran cruisers greeted each other. While Callie ensured their bags were properly tagged, Jake examined the sponson, memorizing its exact location and the location of the hatches leading from it.

The bags containing the weapons and ammo were not checked. Each of the Americans carried one aboard.

A steward led the Graftons to their assigned cabin, which opened onto the promenade deck. The room had a large double bed and a television. Obviously, rank had its privileges: Flap had gotten the Graftons one of the nicest staterooms. Still, the décor reminded Jake of a Holiday Inn. The steward showed them how the fixtures worked, accepted a tip with a smile, and left them alone.

Callie started to speak, but Jake held a finger to his lips. He mouthed the words, "The place may be bugged."

She nodded and sat on the bed while Jake took off his sports coat and donned a shoulder holster. With the water in the bathroom running and talking loudly to his wife, he inserted the loaded magazine in the nine-millimeter automatic, eased the slide back and chambered a round, then holstered the weapon and put the coat back on.

"What do you think?" he asked when he came out.

"It's been a long day and I'm hungry," she said. "Give me a minute and then let's go find something to eat."

After twelve hours in the control room, Kolnikov called it quits for the day. He made a transmission to the fishing boat on the underwater telephone, then steered *America* off the seamount and submerged to four hundred feet. He took food from the wardroom back to Turchak, who was still at the helm monitoring the autopilot. The rest of the control room crew was eating or in bed—another calculated risk, but they had to have food and rest.

"It may not be on that thing," Turchak said softly, just loud enough for Kolnikov to hear. He nodded in the general direction of the seamount. "Have you considered that?"

"Yes."

"I know the philosophical implications of finding something in the last place you look, but we've covered about sixty percent of the seamount. The third stage isn't small."

"I know," Kolnikov said.

"Heydrich is like a caged lion. After observing him for a week, I think he is slightly insane."

Kolnikov said dryly, "Aren't we all?"

Turchak wasn't amused. "You know what I mean. He's a time bomb with a lit fuse."

The dining area was packed with people eating a late supper. Everyone had been traveling all day, yet the excitement was contagious. Callie looked around nervously—did she know any of these people? Finally she decided she didn't. While she looked for acquaintances, Jake looked for Willi Schlegel and didn't see him, of course. They needed to find the man. That would be a job for Carmellini.

Callie did the talking for the Graftons and only in response to direct questions. They were retired military—like Flap, they thought that cover story fit best.

The woman sitting beside her was from England, cruised all the time. She and her husband had both lost their spouses and met on a cruise three years ago. Cruises were *so* romantic, with the moonlight, the dinners, the dancing!

"And how," she asked Callie in a delightful English accent, "did you and your husband meet?"

"Oh, I picked him up in a bar," Callie replied with a wave of her hand.

Jake choked on something and had to leave the table.

CHAPTER TWENTY-ONE

Sea Wind got under way from Lisbon before most of the passengers were out of bed. Tommy Carmellini was up and strolling the decks when she passed the harbor light and hit her first North Atlantic swell. He wandered along watching the stewards, waiters, sailors, and cleaning personnel bustle about their duties. Fortunately most of these people were men.

The breeze was brisk and the sea was covered with whitecaps—all in all, he thought, another great day to be alive.

The ship itself was something to see, a medium-sized cruise ship about five years old that glistened in the morning sun. It had a rakish bow and stacks, a huge deck pool, and acres of topside deck to stroll. Carmellini covered most of the public areas by breakfast time, strolling, looking, eyeing locks and closed areas, most of which bore the sign, "Crew Only." As the passengers began trickling into the dining rooms to feast on every breakfast food item known to man, Carmellini picked the lock of the ship's laundry. In minutes he was back in the passageway carrying a bundle. He went to his stateroom to change into his new outfit.

Lizzy was sound asleep in the double bed. Carmellini had slept on the floor last night. Lizzy was a bit miffed that he didn't make a pass at her. He had no doubt that she would have turned him down, but for the sake of her self-respect she wanted him to make a stab at it. The air was positively frigid when she turned off the light beside her bed.

This morning he dressed in the bathroom, examined himself in the mirror as he savored the motion of the ship in the sea. *Sea Wind* was equipped with stabilizers, of course, but it still had a subtle motion. Carmellini had noticed that the crewmen habitually walked with their feet wider apart, unconsciously bracing themselves against the ship's motion. He made sure the stateroom door locked behind him and went out on deck practicing that walk.

He walked purposefully, as if he were on an errand, and avoided eye contact with the passengers. One of them, an elderly woman, did put her hand on his sleeve and ask for help with a lounge chair. He placed it where she requested, smiled, avoided her eyes, and walked on.

The first problem, he decided, was finding Sarah Houston. Or Zelda Hudson. Whatever she was calling herself this week. He thought she would be easier to find than Willi Schlegel, who was probably buried in the owner's suite, surrounded by layers of personal staff. God forbid that the owner should have to mingle with common fare-paying passengers.

The crew quarters were the obvious first place to look for Zelda. There were no portholes or personal bathrooms on the decks under the passenger decks. Bunk rooms and lockers. Not many people about because most were busy with ship handling, cleaning, or making and serving breakfast.

Carmellini walked through the passageways as if he owned them, checked likely compartments, finally decided Zelda couldn't be there and left.

Ship's offices? A storeroom? The dispensary/hospital?

He found a guard sitting by the door of the ward in the ship's sick bay, which was equipped to save heart attack victims.

He started to walk by the guard, who stopped him with, "You not go there," in a heavy French accent.

Taking a chance, Carmellini asked, "Has she had breakfast yet?"

"*Oui.*"

"I'm here for the tray."

The man got up, went in. Tommy got a glimpse of Zelda as the door opened. He took the tray from the guard, nodded, and walked purposefully away.

Zelda could see herself in the mirror. She looked old, she thought.

Well, she felt old.

The bastards would probably kill her. Try as she might, she couldn't see Willi Schlegel handing her a plane ticket home and a check for $190 million. Willi didn't look the type.

They wouldn't shoot her. Another injection, probably. This one fatal. They would put her into a bag or something along with some old tools or pots and pans, then toss her off the fantail with the garbage in the middle of the night while the paying customers slept off the food and drink.

That was how it would be.

The truth was she had miscalculated. Played for all the dough and underestimated Willi Schlegel.

She sat listening to the blowers in the ductwork and the muted sounds of doors, people moving, machinery—the sounds of a ship under way—while she thought about dying, about how it would be.

Zip had warned her. The Zipper.

The guy was actually . . . Well, the truth of it was that he was the only man who had ever loved her. Plenty of them wanted her body, and plenty more wanted her money, when they realized she had some, yet few wanted a smart woman around very long. Not in this day and age. If only she had been a blonde with big boobs.

What was it her grandmother said? "Why do you want to be smart? Men are scared by women with brains. Practice being dumb." How do you do dumb? "Ask them how things work—men love to talk about things. Ask them to do things for you. Ask them about themselves. Look interested."

Zip had wanted her, though. He knew how smart she was and liked her for it.

She lifted her arms to the limits of the handcuffs that held her to the chair, then shifted her weight. She sat thinking about Zip, about her grandmother, about everything!

And waiting.

Willi Schlegel also found the waiting difficult. When recovering the satellite had first been proposed seven months ago, he had liked the idea. Heydrich could recover it; EuroSpace could examine and improve upon the technology, perhaps even make a bid for the second generation of SuperAegis. Schlegel knew that there would always be another generation of every modern weapons system, the contracts let long before the first generation was fully deployed. That was the defense business—everything was obsolete in a year or two, research and development never stopped. The demand for new technology meant there were always new profits to be made.

Billions of dollars.

And the people doing the dirty work could be stiffed. Working always through third-party cutouts, putting nothing in writing, he made sure no one had blackmail material.

This time there had been complications. When it became plain that publicly recovering the satellite and keeping it would be unacceptable to the French government, another way had to be found. Ergo, *America*.

He had thought about stealing the technology from the sub too. Then he realized that hot as the satellite was, the submarine was even hotter. Once it was stolen it could never surface again. Ever. Reluctantly, he accepted that reality.

Now the satellite was in the water, the sub was hunting for it, the wheel was spinning . . .

Zelda Hudson was the weak link, of course. She was dealing with everyone! It was merely a matter of time before the Americans laid heavy hands on her, then she would tell everything she knew to save her pretty skin.

Schlegel was drinking coffee when a man came into the suite. "Well?"

"I have talked to Maurice aboard the fishing boat on the scrambled circuit. The submarine is still looking."

"What does Kerr say?"

"He cannot understand why they haven't found it. He says he did the trajectory calculations himself. The satellite is there. *America* should have seen it."

Jake and Flap met on the very bow of the ship. Their wives sat in lounge chairs in the sun nearby. The two men faced into the wind, away from the ship, when they talked. Jake had a backpack hanging from a strap over one shoulder.

"Carmellini has found Zelda," Jake reported. "She's in the coronary unit in sick bay."

"Okay."

"Schlegel is in the owner's suite. Tommy didn't get in there but says one of the stewards confirms that. The stewards are carrying in food, and the doors are guarded."

"Have they found the satellite?"

"I don't know, sir."

"Do we have someone watching that loading sponson?"

"Not yet. That minisub can't rendezvous until this ship slows down, probably at one of our anchorages."

"I bow to the nautical expertise of the navy."

"Right. One of the marines is always in the stateroom where we piled the weapons and ammo. We'll be in a heap of hurt if a maid finds those weapons or someone steals them."

"Very well," Flap Le Beau said. He put his hands on the rail and swept his eyes around the horizon.

"Wanta play shuffleboard?"

Flap eyed Jake with amusement. "It's been a lot of years since we were on a ship together."

"*Columbia*. We were younger then."

Flap nodded once, remembering. "Too many years." He slapped his leg, then sat in a lounge chair beside his wife and closed his eyes.

"It isn't on this seamount," Kolnikov said. Heydrich was standing beside him staring at the Revelation screens. Turchak was at his usual station, the helm. Eck and Boldt were on the sonar.

Cold fury played across Heydrich's features. "You're sure?"

"We've covered every inch. True, there were some fissures we couldn't see into, but you've sat there looking at this thing, just as we have. What do you think?"

"I think someone has lied to us. And I think I know who."

"That won't do us much good," Kolnikov pointed out. "Unless you know where the satellite might be."

"Let me use the underwater telephone. We'll rendezvous with *Sea Wind*. Tonight if possible. Can you do that?"

Kolnikov worked at the plotting board for a moment. "If she holds her planned course and speed, we should be able to rendezvous in six hours, about oh two hundred. Have them drop their speed to two knots at that time." He gave the course and speed he wanted to Turchak, who turned the boat to the new course and advanced the power lever for more turns. Eck handed the underwater telephone to Heydrich.

At dinner the service was superlative, almost too good. Jake Grafton swept his eyes around the room. Several people looked away, almost as if they had been watching him.

For dinner I'll have the roast with a side order of paranoia, please.

He stirred the food around on his plate. The truth was that he was too nervous to eat.

"Are you okay?" Callie asked under her breath.

"Not hungry."

"Are you seasick?"

He gave her a withering look, then thought better of it. "No, dear."

"I never saw such food," Callie said with wonder in her voice. "I had no idea anyone on Earth ate like this four times a day. After two weeks of this I'll need a new wardrobe to cover my new width."

"This is nothing," the woman sitting on the other side of her declared. "We were on a cruise last year—an Italian ship and chef." She kissed her fingertips.

"I'm going to walk around on deck," Jake whispered and scooted back his chair. "Meet you in the room after a while."

The backpack was by his feet; he snagged it and took it along. As he was going toward the door, he recognized a man sitting in the far corner. Jake gaped. Yes, it was Janos Ilin.

Sitting talking to someone whose face Jake couldn't see.

He walked toward the dessert table, groaning with two dozen kinds of sweets. Jake snagged a chocolate chip cookie and took another look. He remembered the man all right. Peter Kerr.

Cookie in hand, Jake walked for the door. Out of the corner of his eye he watched Ilin, who never looked at him.

In the control room of USS *America,* the hull of *Sea Wind* projected down into the sea on the port side. Vladimir Kolnikov gestured toward it. "There she is. We've matched speeds and courses. She's about a hundred meters or so to port. That sponson is on her starboard side. Do you want someone to come along, help with the minisub?"

"No," said Heydrich, who probably refused help when he was born.

"I'll walk back there with you," Kolnikov said.

On the way aft, he said, "There will be a lot of dynamic pressure pushing you away from the liner's hull. If you have difficulty getting alongside, the ship's officer will probably order the engines stopped."

"Okay."

"Take your time, think through every task. The bottom is a long way down." They were well away from the seamount, in water a mile and a half deep.

"I have no intention of going there," Heydrich snapped.

"Good. I repeat, take your time, think through every task."

Heydrich climbed the ladder into the lock and dropped the hatch with a bang.

Kolnikov rotated a padded, spring-loaded seat down from the bulkhead and sat. He smoked a cigarette as he listened to the sounds of the minisub powering up. When he finally heard the hydraulic locks release he continued to sit, examining his shoes and thinking of Russia in the summer and this and that.

He was remembering scenes from his boyhood a lot lately. That was probably not a good sign. Paris... he should be thinking of Paris. Of that woman who sold hand-painted postcards by the Seine and smiled at him. They never spoke, but she always smiled.

He should have stayed in Paris. He knew that now. Life is like that—you always learn the important lessons too late.

The change in the feel of the ship woke Jake Grafton. He had been dozing, unable to really sleep, but when the ship's speed dropped off he came fully awake. He checked the luminous hands of his watch—almost two o'clock in the morning.

He got out of bed, pulled on slacks and a shirt, sat down to put on socks and shoes.

"What's wrong?" Callie asked from the bed.

"Ship's stopping." He didn't want to say too much because there might be bugs. "I'm going up on deck." He put on the shoulder holster, then a windbreaker.

"Be careful," she said.

He bent and kissed her. Then he grabbed the backpack and stepped through the door onto the promenade deck. He pulled the door shut, making sure it latched.

Here on the deck the wind was from the stern quarter, a good indication that the ship was making little way. He walked to the railing and looked down. Very little disturbed water. It was the absence of vibration that had awakened him. After all his years at sea, when the engines stopped throbbing the eyes popped open.

He unzipped the backpack, reached in, and found the satellite telephone. He turned it on as he walked through a passageway to the starboard side of the ship. He looked down toward the cargo sponson area. The swells reflected lights.

He moved forward a few feet to a courtesy light that was rigged on a railing post and held the phone so that he could see the keyboard. As he did so he felt something prod him in the back. "Out for a stroll around the deck?"

He froze.

"Ah, you are a wise man. We are alone on this deck and that is indeed a pistol, *mon ami*. There is no one to see you die. Raise your hands as high as they will go."

He did so. As his left arm reached full extension he let go of the backpack, which fell toward the dark ocean.

The pistol jabbed him. "Ah, you came very close. I almost squeezed this trigger to send you to your appointment with St. Peter. Hold very still. Not a single little twitch or I will put a bullet through your liver."

A hand moved over him, found the pistol, and removed it from its holster and flipped it over the side. "We will let your gun sleep with your backpack. You don't need either. *N'est-ce pas?* Any more?"

The man took the telephone from his right hand and prodded him. "Walk forward, very slowly. And lower your hands."

Jake did so and glanced over his shoulder. The man held a man-sized automatic in his right hand and looked like he knew how to use it.

"Understand you that I will shoot you down if you do not do exactly what I say?"

"I understand."

"*Très bien,*" he said. "We go. Monsieur Schlegel awaits you for to have a little chat."

Willi Schlegel was there when the slimy blackness of the minisub broke the dark water and moved slowly toward the sponson. Two sailors with lines leaped for it, then made fast the lines around recessed cleats. Other men arranged bumpers and pulled it alongside.

In a moment the hatch opened and Heydrich appeared. When he was standing beside Schlegel, he said, "It wasn't there. She lied. Where is she?"

The passengers were all asleep except for a few insomniacs. The little entourage passed only one old man in the trek to sick bay.

Heydrich zeroed in on Zelda, who was lying awake on the bed, walked over and slapped her. Then he bent down, put his face inches from hers. "It wasn't there."

"What wasn't?"

"Don't play dumb. I have come to learn the truth."

She reached to scratch him, and he grabbed her wrists. He turned to the man standing at the door. "I want her restrained. Plastic ties holding her hands together, then cuff her to the bed. We will find out how much pain she can stand."

He looked around, saw the external cardiac paddles. Reached for them. "Aah. I have always wondered. If the current will start a heart that has stopped, will it stop a healthy heart? We will do a scientific experiment."

"Is this necessary?" Willi Schlegel asked as the guard tightened a plastic tie on her wrists.

"I think so, yes," Heydrich responded. "She will tell us where she put the SuperAegis satellite or I shall butcher her right here on this table. First we will play with the electricity, then we will do the scalpels. In the morning the medical people can clean up the mess and feed what's left to the sharks."

He turned to Zelda. The guard had her cuffed to the bed rail. "We have made an enormous investment in time and money. What is your decision?"

"You'll kill me anyway."

"Ahh . . . and they said you were smart. You missed the point, Ms.

Hudson. The issue is not whether you live or die; the question is how much pain you wish to endure. What is your answer?"

She looked from face to face. They were grim, merciless men. Whatever they did out here on this ocean would never be proved. Who was going to tell on them and make it stick?

She retched. She managed to puke over the rail onto the floor.

When the spasm had stopped, she said, "Cape Barbas. Ten miles offshore, on the shelf."

Heydrich's hand shot out. The slap made her whole face go numb, almost knocked her out. "You've been listening to talk about the storm coming off Africa, haven't you? The satellite had better not be under that storm, for your sake. Try again."

Zelda retched again. She was trying to control her stomach when she felt something hot hit her leg. She jerked, then looked. Heydrich had jabbed a scalpel into the meat of her calf. The handle was all that was visible.

Schlegel walked out of the room and the other men followed, leaving her alone with Heydrich.

He smiled at her and reached for the cardiac paddles. "You know about little boys who torture animals? You know that they are sick, that they should be taken to a psychologist? You have heard all about that, yes? I was one of those boys. No one took me to a doctor. I did it because I enjoyed it. I still do."

"Well, well," Willi Schlegel said. He put his hands on his hips and stood looking at the Americans. There were ten of them, all with plastic ties on their wrists, sitting on the floor. Jake, Flap, Callie, all of them.

"We were watching the passenger list very carefully, waiting to see if the Americans sent someone to spy on us. Then boom, ten of you, at the very last minute. Troubling, that. It meant the United States government was suspicious."

He squatted in front of Flap Le Beau. "A four-star general. Commandant of the Marine Corps. Member of the Joint Chiefs. I would have never suspected that they would send such a high-ranking person." Schlegel shook his head. "I am sorry you came, General. Truly sorry."

He straightened and addressed himself to one of his entourage.

"Take them to the cargo sponson. Heydrich will be along after a while. He can take them with him."

"He will have to make two trips," the aide pointed out. "The little submarine will not hold them all."

"Two trips it is. I want all of them to go."

As they walked along the passageway, Flap whispered to Jake, "I think the bastard intends to kill us all."

"Dead men may tell tales, but they don't take the witness stand."

"Did you call the troops?"

"No, they got the telephone before—"

"Quiet!" one of Schlegel's men hissed. He slapped Jake in the face with his pistol. The admiral fell to the deck.

Flap helped him up. "You go in the first boat with Sonny. I'll take care of this crowd."

Jake got his feet under him and followed along.

There were three men with silenced submachine guns. They herded the ten of them onto the sponson. Flap worked himself to the back of the crowd, Jake with him.

They turned and faced the guards. "I've got a knife up my left sleeve," Flap said, his lips barely moving. "Get it and cut the wrist tie."

Jake got it with two fingers, pulled it out, almost dropped it. He managed to cut the plastic tie without looking down or cutting Flap.

"Keep the knife," Flap said. "Put it up your sleeve. I've got another." Of course he did. Flap Le Beau always carried two knives, the slicer up his sleeve and a throwing knife in a sheath hanging down his back.

Jake spoke loud enough for the Americans to hear him. "Men on the first boat, women on the second. Except Callie. You come with me."

They stood there for five minutes facing the three with guns before Schlegel and Heydrich came out on the sponson. Heydrich was half carrying Zelda Hudson, who was bleeding from the neck, legs, and arms.

"It was on an adjacent seamount," Heydrich explained to Schlegel. "I don't think she intended to deal honorably with you. I'll take them all aboard tonight, then meet you tomorrow night at the Azores anchorage."

"Very good," Schlegel said, bobbing his head.

Heydrich dragged Hudson along the sponson and passed her to

a sailor, who stuffed her down the hatch. Heydrich went next. Jake waited until they motioned, then followed along. The other men filed out behind him. Schlegel himself told Callie, Corina Le Beau, Rita, Lizzy, and the others to wait for the next boat. No one made an issue of the fact that Flap was at the end of the line.

The space inside the minisub was tight. Without portholes, even ones that were opaque, the feeling with six people aboard was claustrophobic. The smell was a mixture of dampness and light lubricating oil. And fear. Everyone was perspiring freely, even Jake. Sweat ran into his eyes, making them sting, but he tried to ignore it.

When his passengers were arranged and seated, Heydrich said something to the sailors, then closed the hatch. Jake thought about knifing him right then, but a dead Heydrich wouldn't get him into *America*. If there was some kind of code . . . and, of course, he didn't know how to run the minisub. Perhaps Sonny Killbuck did, but Jake had never asked. After a while Sonny was going to have to give it a try.

Sonny sat silently, looking at this and that, betraying no emotion. He met Jake's gaze for a second or two, then looked away. Toad Tarkingon seemed ready for anything. Tommy Carmellini was trying to look deadpan and succeeding.

Heydrich had a gun, a silenced automatic. He displayed it, pointed it at Zelda Hudson, who was right beside him. And he raised his voice. "If anyone moves, toward me, at me, in any direction whatsoever, I shall shoot this woman in the head. Do you understand? If *anything* happens, if anyone wants to be a hero, she dies first. Then I will see how many of you I can kill."

Zelda was in obvious pain. She was seated yet bent over at the waist, in an upright fetal position. Semiconscious, oblivious to her surroundings, she chewed on her lower lip with her eyes tightly closed. She moaned softly from time to time, but she didn't open her eyes or try to change positions.

Heydrich flashed the minisub's lights, then turned the helm, which controlled the minisub's motion in pitch and roll, much like an aircraft yoke. The rudder pedal was beneath his feet. He watched the closed-circuit monitors intently, finally engaged the prop. In a few moments the towering side of the liner disappeared from view. Heydrich began flooding the ballast tanks. The valves were audible as they opened, the water gurgled as it poured into the tanks, and the minisub swam slowly down into the dark, black, watery abyss.

With the women on the sponson, Flap Le Beau's options were limited. There were the three men with silenced submachine guns, Schlegel and two sailors, line handlers.

The sailors stayed out of the way, just in case one of the armed men decided to shoot somebody. They looked like they were from the Far East, perhaps Malaysia or Indonesia. They refused to look at the prisoners, Flap noted. If they were ever called as witnesses they would say they knew nothing. A job is a job is a job, if you have a family to feed and no skills to speak of.

Flap didn't blame them. He just hoped they stayed out of the way.

He waited patiently. Years before, when he had been a jarhead in the jungle mud, he learned patience. Let the enemy come to you in his own time.

Two of the gunmen lit cigarettes. They smoked in silence.

Then the break he had been waiting for came. Schlegel wanted to talk.

"Sorry it worked out this way, General. Obviously it would have been better for everyone if you had stayed home."

"You can't get away with this, Schlegel. The United States government knows we're here, knows you're involved. The Americans will apply excruciating pressure to the French government, which will drop you like a hot potato."

"A potato?" Schlegel asked, obviously unfamiliar with that idiom.
"Thermonuclear."

"I think not." Schlegel smiled. The man was enjoying himself hugely. Flap took a step closer. He was holding his wrists together, keeping them in against his body so that no one could see that the plastic tie was missing. It was, in fact, in his pocket.

That was the moment that Callie Grafton picked to faint. She went limp, sagged, hit the deck like a side of beef, and lay sprawled out.

Schlegel glanced at his gunmen, decided they were sufficiently fearsome to discourage heroics, and stepped over to check on Callie.

She kicked him in the balls.

As Schlegel bent over in pain, Rita Moravia delivered a right cross to the jaw that snapped his head sideways. The impact propelled him back and he lost his balance. He teetered on the edge of the sponson, his arms waving wildly. Then he fell in.

One of the three gunmen found that he had the hilt of a knife protruding from his solar plexus. He released his hold on his weapon as he sank to his knees. He tried to draw it out with both hands, but the effort was too much. He toppled slowly forward.

The gunman nearest Flap never saw him coming. He had been watching Schlegel's balancing act, so when he saw Flap coming at him out of the corner of his eye, he was flat-footed, not quite ready. The cigarette in his fingers didn't help. By the time he got his weapon turned and his hand on the trigger, Flap ripped it from his grasp and elbowed him once in the larynx, crushing it.

People holding loaded guns on other people are rarely alert, convinced that people will be paralyzed at the mere sight of a muzzle pointed in their direction. It usually works; few things in life are more horrifying.

The third gunman, also a smoker, paid for his inattention. By the time he got his weapon into action, Flap was shooting at him. His bullets went high. Flap's didn't.

The third gunman took a burst right in the chest. By the time he hit the bulkhead and slid to the deck, he was dead.

Bobbing in the water, Willi Schlegel saw the third gunman go down. And he saw the grim visage of Flap Le Beau turn in his direction and point his weapon.

"No," he screamed.

Flap fired a short burst. When the spray cleared, only the top of Schlegel's head was visible, rising and falling with the motion of the black seawater.

The general turned, ensured that the sailors didn't want any part of what he had in his hands, then motioned to the women marines. "Get these guns. Quickly now." They collected the submachine guns, spare magazines, and three pistols. Flap took the time to reload his weapon. He stuck a pistol in his waistband.

As he herded his wife and Callie off the sponson, he said to Lizzy, "You stay here. If the minisub surfaces and that dude sticks his head out of the hatch, shoot him."

"Yes, sir."

The minisub made some noise as it swam down into the blackness, but not much. Jake Grafton thought he heard the hum of the electric motor that turned the prop, or perhaps it was the fan that circulated air inside the sub. The loudest noise, he decided, was the whisper of water moving past the hull, and even that was muted.

Less than a minute after he left the surface ship, Heydrich turned on the minisub's exterior lights. They penetrated the dark water for a short distance and created the illusion that visibility was better than it was. Consequently, when the hull of *America* appeared, an intensely black presence that the lights refused to illuminate, the appearance surprised the watchers. *America* had been in the field of view for several seconds before the watchers realized what they were seeing.

Heydrich approached from the port side, made the turn behind the island to match his course and speed to the monstrous black streamlined shape, and used the searchlights to find the attachment point over the airlock.

Down the minisub came, closer and closer, the movement finally almost stopping as the two craft drifted ever so slowly together. They touched with a metallic clang. Heydrich shot the hydraulic locks, then stopped his prop and centered his controls. He threw a few more switches—Jake didn't know what they were but surmised at least one of them would connect the minisub to the mother's electrical system—then turned to his passengers.

With the pistol in his hand, he set Killbuck to opening the hatch in the minisub's belly. When the hatch opened into the airlock, he gestured with the pistol.

Killbuck went first, then the men in the minisub handed Zelda down. In places her clothes were becoming sodden with blood. She groaned when they handled her, still in obvious pain.

She hadn't shown any signs of recognizing Tommy Carmellini. When he lifted her he whispered, "Hang tough, Sarah."

She opened her eyes then. Whether she recognized him he didn't know. But she was conscious.

"What the hell is this?" Vladimir Kolnikov demanded of Heydrich. "Who are these people?"

"Americans. Looking for their submarine. And by God, they've found it!" He nudged Zelda with his foot. "This one, you know her. Zelda put the satellite in the water."

Kolnikov bent down, checked her pulse, looked at one of her bleeding wounds. "What in hell have you done to her?"

"The bitch put the satellite on a seamount twenty miles west of the one we searched. She was going to hold up Schlegel for more money. He thought she might be trying a double cross, so he grabbed her in Newark and flew her here."

Heydrich bent down and hissed at Zelda. "It had better be there. For your sake."

He turned to two of his divers, who were cradling Uzis. "Into the mess hall with these people. Leave the doors open and watch them. Check the ties on their wrists. If anyone tries anything, kill them all." He looked again at Zelda and smiled. "Except this one. I want her alive, just in case."

He waited until the divers had led the Americans away before he said to Kolnikov, "There are some more of them. Women. I am going back for them."

"What are you going to do with these people?"

"Don't play the fool. We'll leave them in the sub when we abandon it."

"And the satellite?"

"It may be there, or it may not. The bitch begged me to believe her."

He climbed back up the ladder, through the airlock into the waiting minisub.

Flap led the way up the ladders inside the cruise ship. He said to his wife, "You, Rita, and Callie go to the dining area. I want you to sit in the middle of the room, and if anyone approaches you with a weapon or demands that you go with him, scream. Make a hell of a scene." They left him on the main deck.

With the two women marines behind him, he continued up the ladders toward the bridge.

The sign on the door to the bridge proclaimed, "Crew Only." The door was locked. Flap shot out the lock and walked on through.

One of the ship's officers was at the top of the ladder when Flap reached the bridge. He saw the submachine gun hanging from a strap and took a step backward.

"The captain. Lead me to him."

The captain was wearing a nice uniform with four gold rings around each sleeve and had a trimmed gray beard. He was about sixty, Flap guessed.

"Good morning, sir," Flap said. "I am General Le Beau, United States Marine Corps."

"Captain Henri Janvier."

"Why is the ship stopped?"

"The owner has ordered it so." The captain gestured at a man wearing a sports coat standing nearby. "Monsieur Crozet, his representative."

"The owner, Willi Schlegel, was in the cargo sponson when a minisubmarine from USS *America,* a hijacked American warship, rendezvoused with this ship a few minutes ago. I assume that fact is news to you, Captain. I certainly hope so, because a conspiracy to steal a ship is considered piracy by most nations. Some of them still execute people for piracy, I believe."

"*America?* The stolen American submarine?" Janvier looked stunned.

"Yes. I suggest you get your ship under way, proceed on your schedule, and allow me to use your radio."

"But Monsieur Schlegel . . ."

"Is now deceased."

"I talked to him just an hour ago," the captain objected. "He seemed in excellent health."

"It was quite sudden," Flap told him, "An unforeseen tragedy. Alas, we are all mortal clay."

The captain didn't know what to think or do. He looked at Crozet, who was holding a pistol pointed at Flap.

"Lay down the weapons," Crozet ordered, his voice firm.

The ship's officers raised their hands. They were worried men and their faces showed it. The women marines looked at the general, waiting for orders.

Flap Le Beau removed the Uzi carrying strap from over his shoulder and, bending down, placed the weapon on the deck. He pulled the pistol from his belt and put it beside the submachine gun. He did all this in slow motion, then nodded at the women, who did likewise.

Crozet motioned for Flap to back up. Holding the pistol in his right hand, he stepped forward, crouched, reached for the guns. When he glanced down, Flap lashed out with his right foot. He caught Crozet under the chin and snapped his head back.

The first kick didn't break his neck, but the second one did.

Crozet's body came to rest wedged under a pedestal that held a radar repeater.

In the silence that followed, Flap bent down, snagged the sub-machine gun.

"I will tell you one more time, Captain. If you wish to avoid prosecution as an accomplice in piracy, get this ship under way now and proceed to your scheduled port of call. *S'il vous plaît*."

Janvier erupted in a torrent of French. The ship's officers sprang into motion. One of them seized the telegraph and rang up all ahead two-thirds.

In the midst of this activity, Flap retrieved the pistol on the deck and tucked it into his trousers. In seconds he felt the vibration as the ship's screws bit into the sea.

Keeping his eyes on the ship's officers, he bent down and felt Crozet's neck for a pulse. None. Another unexpected, unforeseen tragedy.

Heydrich was making his approach in the minisub to the cargo spon-son when *Sea Wind* began moving. The surge of water being pushed away from the hull was more than the minisub could handle. It bobbed away, the nose slewing away from the ship, quite out of control.

When Heydrich had the minisub under control he watched *Sea Wind* steam away.

He knew what it meant. Something unexpected had happened. He didn't know what the event might be, but the unexpected was always a possibility. He had decided long ago to continue with his mission. Find and recover the satellite. Everything hinged on that.

He turned the minisub back toward *America,* which was still lying just under the surface.

Kolnikov and Georgi Turchak also watched *Sea Wind* get under way. The churning of her screws just a hundred yards or so away looked like a fire on the Revelation displays, brilliant light bubbling and churning in unexpected ways. The usual control room crew was present, as well as several of the divers, who were mesmerized by the huge color displays.

"Uh-oh," Turchak said under his breath, just loud enough for Kolnikov to hear.

"Eck, what else is in the area?" Kolnikov said over the whispers that had infected the watchers.

"Nothing in the water. Perhaps an aircraft, but there is too much noise just now. When *Sea Wind* is farther away I will be able to hear better."

The minisub was visible on the display that showed the view in the aft port quarter. It was turning, coming back.

"He's going to kill those people he brought aboard," Turchak whispered. "I don't know why he didn't shoot them when he got them here."

"He doesn't want to spook the crew," Kolnikov answered.

"The bastard has been sitting in the back of the control room for weeks watching everything." Turchak caught Kolnikov's eye. "We both know he wanted to learn how to run the boat. He doesn't need us anymore."

Kolnikov pretended he hadn't heard.

There was a first aid kit marked with a red cross on the mess hall bulkhead, so Jake Grafton got to his feet and reached for it. One of the gunmen in the door said, "No. Sit!"

Jake froze. He looked at the man, who looked wound banjo-string tight. "This woman is bleeding. We'll put bandages on."

The man shook his head vigorously, gestured with the muzzle of his weapon.

"Were you hatched from an egg?" Jake asked and looked at the other man. "Did you have a mother, a sister, a girlfriend? Are you thugs or divers?"

The second man said something to the first in French, then said to Jake in English, "Put on bandages."

Jake removed the first aid kit from its brackets, sat beside Zelda, and opened it. Tommy Carmellini was holding her head in his lap. They were half under the table in the little space, so they were hard to see from the doorways, where the guards stood.

Jake started on the wound that was bleeding the worst. He used tape to close the cut, then slapped a bandage over the wound and taped it in place.

"Who did this?" he whispered.

"Heydrich."

When he got to the wound in her neck—Heydrich had sliced alongside her jugular vein—Jake whispered, "He thinks he knows where the satellite is. Did you tell him?"

Her eyes focused on him. He saw her eyebrows move.

"I'm Grafton. Rear Admiral Grafton."

The tie around his wrists impeded his efforts. The man who had put it on pulled it too tight, so his fingers were swelling. He turned her head so that he could see the neck wound better. There was disinfectant in the kit; he squirted some on the wound, then taped it shut.

"They didn't kill Zip Vance," he said. "He's in the hospital."

It was then, with her head turned so that the guards at the doors could not see her face, that she said, "It isn't where he thinks."

"Where then?"

He could barely hear her answer. "I told him and he didn't believe me. Cape Barbas. Ten miles out."

"Does Peter Kerr know where it is?"

"I don't think so."

"You there!" the first guard said loudly. "Stop talking!"

They heard the metallic clang as the minisub lowered itself onto the hull, then the solid thunks of the hydraulic locks going home. Both guards looked behind them, along the passageways. They hadn't been aboard long enough to become familiar with the sounds.

Jake used that moment to whisper to Carmellini, "Up my sleeve."

Tommy reached and in one smooth motion had the knife in his hand, hidden by his arm. He waited, and soon Jake moved his hands out of sight of the guards.

Carmellini sliced the tie that bound the admiral's wrists, then passed him the knife.

Another minute passed, then another. They heard someone coming along the passageway. Sure enough, both guards craned to see who it was. Grafton sliced the tie from Carmellini's wrists and passed him the knife.

Heydrich appeared in the doorway.

"Where are the others?" Jake asked.

"I ask the questions," Heydrich said, unwilling to give the prisoners any leverage. He nodded toward Zelda Hudson. "Is she still alive?"

"No thanks to you. I thought we ought to keep her breathing, just in case. Wouldn't want you and your pals to face a murder charge, would we?"

The guards both looked queasy. It was evident that they hadn't known murder was on the agenda when they volunteered.

"Keep them quiet and seated," Heydrich said to his colleagues and climbed the ladder toward the control room.

After a half minute or so, Jake asked conversationally, "What's the sentence in France these days for slicing up a woman? Do they still do the guillotine thing?"

"Not anymore," Toad said. "The French are pretty civilized. They did away with capital punishment, even though they eat slimy stuff."

"Quiet!" snarled the first guard. He took a half step into the room, threatened Toad and Jake with the weapon he held.

Carmellini jerked an ankle out from under him. As he did, Toad grabbed for the weapon.

They would all have been dead if the second guard had leveled his Uzi and pulled the trigger, but he didn't. He ran forward toward the crew's berthing.

"The gun," Jake said and grabbed for it. "Use the E-grenades. What's the fuse delay?"

"Three minutes."

While Toad was cutting the others loose, Carmellini removed two E-grenades from his socks, pulled the pins, and twisted the caps half a turn, starting the timers. He handed one of the things to Jake and kept one for himself.

With the Uzi at the ready, Jake Grafton started for the ladder to the control room. That's when he heard the thock of the hydraulic locks releasing the minisub.

He looked. The top of the ladder well seemed to be behind the plotting table. Jake eased his head up, crawled half out, and looked down the aisleway in front of the sonar consoles. He saw several pairs of feet.

"What is going on?" There was panic in that voice.

"Someone stole the minisub." Heydrich's voice. "See it on the sonar? We'll make a turn and run over the bastards."

Jake felt the floor tilt as Heydrich cranked the rudder and helm over. Without being told, Jake knew it was Heydrich at the controls.

He weighed the E-grenade in his hand. A minute so far?

He scrambled on up the ladder, staying low, behind the plotting table. He turned, mouthed a request to Carmellini: "More grenades."

Tommy passed up three. All had the pins removed.

Jake aimed the Uzi at the port-side sonar consoles, triggered a burst. The reports were deafening, followed by the sounds of glass showering over everything. Grafton threw an E-grenade the length of the room, then another and another.

The admiral could hear someone sobbing—it was Eck—as he pulled another E-grenade from his sock and armed it, then flipped it down the starboard aisle.

He was peering around the starboard side of the plotting table when someone grabbed him around the neck. He could feel a hand on his neck, squeezing like a vise, while another hand and arm forced his head around. From above.

Heydrich had come over the consoles and plotting table. He was on the table now, reaching down, trying to twist Jake's head from his shoulders with his right hand and arm while he choked him with his left.

Somehow Jake dropped the Uzi. Forgot he had it as the pain became unbearable.

As suddenly as it began, the pressure was released.

Jake looked up. Toad Tarkington had come up the ladderway and slashed Heydrich across the face. Cut him to the bone. Cut out an eye. Blood sprayed everywhere.

Heydrich rolled off the table screaming. He was on the floor, trying to get his pistol out of its holster in the cramped space, when the first E-grenade went off with a metallic boom and an unpleasant jolt of energy.

The lights went out. The darkness was absolutely total.

A pistol flashed. Heydrich fired a shot! He stopped screaming, struggling instead to get air in and out.

More grenades went off. Jake scrambled into the port aisle as Heydrich triggered more shots. A bullet hit something and ricocheted madly, a series of whacks.

The bastard thinks he's blind, Jake thought. He's shooting at everything.

He waited.

And was rewarded with more jolts of energy as the rest of the electromagnetic grenades exploded.

He heard Heydrich running forward, bouncing off things.

372 ★ STEPHEN COONTS

372 ★ STEPHEN COONTS

Jake stood and triggered an Uzi burst. In the hammering strobe of the muzzle flashes, he saw Heydrich disappear through the forward door to the control room. And missed him.

"Don't shoot. For God's sake, don't shoot!" That was Eck.

Boldt was somewhere forward, sobbing.

Jake slipped up the port aisle. Two men were on the floor—he could hear them. The darkness was total. Not a single form or shape could he discern.

The silence was deafening. Even the screws had stopped. *America* was a tomb.

"Okay, Sonny. Get up here and save our sorry asses."

He went forward, feeling his way.

"Don't shoot us!"

"If you people have matches," Jake said conversationally, trying to calm them down, "now would be an excellent time to strike one. Your flashlights are probably fried. Any light at all would be a help."

He heard someone fumbling. After about a half minute someone struck a match.

Sonny Killbuck walked forward down the starboard aisle.

"The reactor? Has it shut down?"

"Oh, yes," Sonny said. "The rods are held out by electrical power. In the event of a total electrical failure, springs pull the rods in, SCRAMing the reactor." He spoke to the man on the floor near him, who was Eck. "Give me those matches."

He struck one. The depth gauge showed sixty feet.

"Okay," Sonny said, trying to calm himself down. "Okay. We're dead in the water at sixty feet. What do you want to do, sir?"

"I want you to get this pigboat to the surface so we can get everyone off."

"The nearest hatch is in the next deck up, right above this compartment. I suggest we get everyone up there. When I do an emergency blow, we'll go up pretty quick. Maybe thirty seconds. Call it forty. Open the hatch and get everyone out."

"Okay," Jake said.

He turned to Toad and Carmellini and started to speak when the match burned out. The darkness was so thick it was hard to breathe. If they weren't careful, someone could start shooting. "You heard him. Toad, you and Carmellini get Zelda up to the hatch. There should be life vests by the hatch. After the blow, open it up and go out. Sonny and I will be right behind. And these two here. Then anyone else who wants out can swim for it with us."

"Okay, boss," Toad said. He and Carmellini went down the ladder and brought Zelda up. They kept climbing.

When the three of them had life vests on, Toad shouted.

"You two, go on up." Eck and Boldt scurried up the ladder.

"Anyone else?" Sonny asked.

They might be armed. Jake went to the tunnel and shouted aft, "Abandon ship." How far aft they could hear him, he didn't know.

"Do it, Sonny."

Killbuck struck another match. He was at a panel on the left. He began squeezing handles and lifting levers. Nothing electrical here— these handles pulled cables that opened valves which released compressed air into the ballast tanks, forcing the water out.

In that huge silence he heard the hissing as the valves opened. One by one, on both sides of the boat.

"Let's go," Sonny said as he came rushing toward Jake. "I couldn't get one of the valves open. She's going to be out of trim."

"What does that mean?"

"I don't know if she'll get to the surface. Or if she'll float. The shooting in the control room may have damaged something."

Trying to get life jackets on people, the hatch open, all in absolute Stygian darkness, was an exercise in terror. They handled it different ways. Tommy Carmellini was cool and deliberate; Toad kept muttering, "Come on, people"; one of the Germans was sobbing; and Zelda Hudson said nothing, tried to help but was too badly wounded. "I'm sorry," she said under her breath at one point. Grafton heard it, though no one else did.

He knew the submarine was on the surface when it rolled drunkenly as the first of the swells slammed into the sail.

Killbuck cranked madly on the hatch dogs. After a lifetime the thing opened . . . and they got their first whiff of salt spray and sea wind. And their first gleam of light. The early light of dawn was turning the sky pink—a gleam enlivened the compartment where they were.

374 ★ STEPHEN COONTS

"Out, out, out," Jake Grafton roared, unable to contain himself. He hated the darkness, he was scared, and there were still people trapped aboard.

Carmellini scampered up the ladder, then turned and jerked Zelda Hudson up and out.

A swell broke over the hatch. Cold seawater cascaded in.

Carmellini was no longer topside.

"Up you go, Toad. You and Killbuck. Out!"

Those two and the Germans from the control room were out when the next wave turned the open hatch into a drain pipe. A river of cold seawater poured in while Jake waited.

Another man was climbing the ladder, keening, desperate. He went by Jake without seeing him, ignored the life vests, and was almost washed off the ladder by the next wave.

Jake grabbed his arm. "Is there anyone back aft?"

"Oh, God! Heydrich is back there killing people. He is shooting everyone he can find."

"Out! Up the ladder and into the water. Swim away from the boat."

The man went.

Should he go aft, look for people still alive?

The deck was tilting. Staying in the boat was suicide. Jake Grafton started up the ladder, but he had waited too long. The open hatch went under and became a waterfall.

He was washed to the deck. For several seconds he waited for the deluge to stop, then he realized it wasn't going to.

The water in the compartment was going down the ladder well. Jake let go and was swept that way.

He got a grip on something, then lost it and was washed down the ladder well, fell with tons of water pushing on his shoulders and arms.

The total darkness, the cold water, the list of the boat. Raw terror grabbed him as he tried to think.

Automatically he held on to the ladder, unwilling to give up on the open hatch he knew was waiting above. He could wait in an air pocket, and when the inflow slowed, climb up and out! Yes, that was it! His one chance!

How long he clung to the ladder as water poured onto his head he didn't know. It was only when the realization sank in that the volume of water was increasing that reason prevailed.

He pushed away, tried to think, felt his way aft in the pure wet blackness, grabbing this and that as the cold water swirled about him and the air pressure pushed at his eardrums and the deck tilted.

Oh yes, my God yes! The bow is going down. She's lost buoyancy. She's going under!

The airlock aft, where the minisub docked.

The Russians and Germans hadn't closed the watertight hatches, so the boat was flooding throughout its length. Through some kink of fate, some twist in the cosmic fabric, the bow dropped, so the water ran forward, forcing the bow down even more but not drowning him.

He dimly remembered the compartments, remembered the virtual simulator, remembered the engineering drawings he had studied weeks ago in his office in Crystal City.

He fought his way up the tilting deck. The boat was perhaps twenty degrees nose-down. The weight would be carrying her down, down into the infinite depths. The steadily increasing air pressure reminded him that was so.

Then he saw a light. Dim. A battle lantern. Battery-operated. Not fried by the E-grenades. It was at the bottom of the ladder up to the airlock.

He took it from its bracket, scrambled up the tilted ladder toward the lock.

Blood. In the light he saw a vision of blood, flecked with the gleam of white bone.

Heydrich!

"Aaieee!" Heydrich screamed and swung a damage-control ax.

There wasn't room to swing it properly, and Heydrich was almost blind. He swung at what he saw, which was the gleam of light from the lantern.

The gun, Jake thought. Where?

He had lost it somewhere.

Heydrich drew the ax back and swung again.

Jake ducked down the hatch to avoid the bite of the blade, which struck the combing, then grabbed for the handle before Heydrich could raise it again.

Heydrich was screaming now, keening steadily. His strength was unbelievable. He raised the ax with Jake grimly holding on to the handle . . . and dragged Grafton up into the compartment. The lantern went onto the deck.

They struggled. Jake felt the ax bite him, but he was beyond caring. This maniac stood between him and life!

Grafton went nuts. He kicked, gouged, bit, hammered at the insane diver, all the while fighting for the ax.

Then he realized he had it in his hands. He reversed it, drew it back at his waist, and swung with all his strength. He buried the blade in Heydrich's stomach. The man doubled over, collapsed on the deck.

Jake grabbed the lantern, climbed into the lock, and closed the hatch.

Instructions! In his condition he found that the printed words on the bulkhead were indecipherable. He stopped, took three deep breaths, tried to calm himself.

"You're going to make it, Jake Grafton," he reassured himself. "This is your chance. God gave you one more."

A hood. He didn't have an escape hood.

Well, he would have to go without it.

There was a tool to open the water valve, which was a safety handle. He used both hands. The water began coming slowly, then faster and faster as he opened the valve. He opened it all the way. As the water flooded in he looked at the hatch above him, examined it with the lantern light.

The water was cold. Cold as death.

He fought the urge to attack the upper hatch.

No. Wait. Not yet. He could hear a voice talking to him. Not yet, Jake Grafton.

The battle lantern stayed lit even though covered by water. The rising water was rapidly compressing the air that Grafton was breathing. There was a hood, a shelter of clear, thick Plexiglas, and he stood so his head was in it as the water poured in, filling the space.

He concentrated on breathing as he watched the rising water. Thank God for the battle lantern!

How deep was the boat?

If it was too deep, he would never make the surface. . . .

The water filled the last of the space. Standing with his head in the hood, he could still breathe. He felt a great calm.

The wheel that rotated the dogs was stiff. Whoever had left in the minisub had really cranked this thing down.

He let the air fill his lungs, then turned the wheel with all the strength that was in him.

The handle rotated and the hatch flew open.

Jake took his last breath, ducked down under the edge of the Plexiglas hood, then climbed and kicked his way up through the open hatch. Into absolute darkness.

Far above he could see light, the dawn lighting the surface of the ocean.

He exhaled steadily. If he didn't, the submariners had told him, his lungs would burst as he rose.

Up, up, up, exhaling as slowly as he could, sure he would run out of air before he reached the surface.

He heard a great roaring in his ears, fought the fear, fought his way up toward that light on the surface of the sea, fought his way up toward life.

Jake Grafton shot out of the water, his head and shoulders rising above the swells. He gasped for air as he fell back with a splash.

Amazingly, he still had the lantern.

The sky in the east was a bluish yellow. In minutes the sun would rise.

He turned, looking, and saw two hydrofoils. Roaring, snorting, exhaust plumes cutting the air.

He waved the battle lantern, pointed it at the nearest one.

And it came toward him. As it approached he saw the flag over the bridge streaming in the breeze, the Stars and Stripes.

CHAPTER TWENTY-TWO

Written on the hulls of the hydrofoils in large black letters was "U.S. Navy." Jake Grafton had never been so glad to see anything in his life. One of the boats settled into the water upwind of him. As the marines on deck lowered a rope ladder over the side, a man wearing a wet suit leaped into the ocean to help him.

Climbing the rope ladder took all the strength he had. Jake clambered over the rail, puking seawater. Toad Tarkington was the first person he saw—the Toadman was grinning as if his face would split. He grabbed Jake and collapsed with him in a heap on the deck as Jake continued to retch.

Lying in the open sea, the hydrofoil wallowed and pitched in the swells. After what Jake had been through, the corkscrewing deck and salty sea breeze felt absolutely terrific. He wanted to hug Toad, but as his stomach did somersaults the best he could manage was a death grip on his leg.

"Don't ever scare me like that again, boss. I don't know if my heart can take it. When I realized you hadn't made it out, the big Uh-Oh got loose and started chewing on my ass."

Toad wrapped him in a blanket while Jake vomited the last of the seawater.

When he could finally sit up, Jake saw that Tommy Carmellini and Sonny Killbuck had Zelda stretched out on the deck. They had stripped her to her panties and were slapping fresh bandages on every wound. The marines in helmets and combat gear hunkered nearby pretended to look the other way.

By the time Jake could stand, the hydrofoil crew had her in the only bunk. The corpsman wrapped her in blankets and plugged in an IV.

"How's she doing?" Jake asked Carmellini when he came back on deck.

"I dunno," the CIA officer said. "She's lost a lot of blood. In shock, I guess." He examined the place on Jake's arm where Heydrich's ax had taken off a small hunk of hide, smeared it with antiseptic, and put a bandage on. When he was finished with that he slapped Jake Grafton on the back.

"Risking your life to save those pirates wasn't the smartest thing I've ever seen done, but I'd like to shake your hand."

"I wasn't trying to save anyone but little ol' me," Jake protested. "I was trying desperately to get myself through that hatch. I felt like a salmon swimming up a fire hose."

"Right! Just what I expected you to say." Carmellini pumped Jake's hand, gave him a hug, then looked a little embarrassed. "I'm just glad I know you."

When he got his legs under him, Jake went to the hydrofoil's wheelhouse, a tiny bridge, and talked to the captain, a master chief petty officer. "Your foil is sure a pretty sight."

"We were waiting for that beacon, Admiral. When the P-3 picked it up, we mounted up and headed out. I'm telling you, I was the most surprised man on Earth when that submarine surfaced and people started bailing out."

"The beacon was in a backpack," Jake explained. "Saltwater activated. I tossed it over the side of *Sea Wind* but wasn't sure enough water would get to it to activate it."

"Worked great," the master chief assured him. "We've been on the radio to *Sea Wind*. Apparently there was an altercation aboard after you left, and something happened to Schlegel. General Le Beau is on the bridge now with the captain, who says he just follows orders."

"Callie Grafton? My wife? Is she okay?"

"Fine, sir, according to General Le Beau. He said everything is under control aboard *Sea Wind*. He ordered us back to Rota."

"You're sure you were talking to General Le Beau?"

The master chief had close-cropped gray hair and a tanned, lined face. "Yes, sir," he said. "The general is pretty salty."

"So something happened to Schlegel, eh?" Jake had thought that something probably would. Flap Le Beau was crawling through the jungle slitting throats while Willi Schlegel was playing with dueling swords in college. Welcome to the major leagues, fella.

Soon he was on the radio to Flap. *Sea Wind* was not in sight.

"Tell Callie I'm all right," he said.

"Things are under control here," the general boomed. "Schlegel is technically missing, deceased I think. Captain Janvier has decided to proceed to the Madeiras. We've been talking to the authorities on the radio. A delegation of officials will meet us there."

When Jake's turn to talk came, he said, "I suggest you find a reason to have Peter Kerr arrested and sent back to the States. He's aboard someplace. Maybe under a false name and passport."

"The missing NASA guy? I can do that. Oh, I talked to Callie, Rita, and Corina a few minutes ago, told them you guys had been pulled out of the drink."

"Where is she now?" Jake asked, meaning Callie.

"Uh, they went to breakfast. Callie hoped you'd meet her in Las Palmas for the rest of the cruise. She said since the cruise is paid for . . ."

That was when Jake realized the crisis was really over. Callie didn't want to go back to candles and canned food in a powerless flat in Rosslyn. And he didn't blame her. In his mind's eye he saw her as she must have looked when she broke the news to Flap Le Beau, and laughed aloud. Then he couldn't stop. Callie was what he had to go home to. Schlegel and Jouany—they weren't rich. Oh, they had money, but they weren't *rich*! He was! He laughed so hard he had to sit.

When he finally calmed down a sailor brought him a cup of coffee and a sandwich that had been brought aboard the hydrofoil that morning. He had to hold on to the coffee with both hands, the boat was rolling so badly. He managed to get a sip, wolfed down the sandwich, and felt better.

The master chief wanted to talk. "I don't want to leave this area until I'm sure there are no more survivors." He told Jake how many people the hydrofoil crews had pulled from the water, even passed him a list of names. Only three of the pirates had been rescued. Kolnikov and Turchak weren't on the list.

"How deep is the water?"

"The depth is marked on the chart, sir, as seventy-nine hundred feet."

Just then two F/A-18s flew slowly overhead. They were about a thousand feet in the air, loafing along.

When the sound of their engines faded, Jake Grafton said, "The sub's reactor was dead and her main hatch was open, so she was taking water. As she goes down, any compartment not open to the sea will be crushed—the bulkheads will collapse. If there are any more survivors, they are on the surface now."

"I thought we should search for another hour or so, just to be sure."

"Fine," Jake Grafton said. "Satisfy yourself. But talk to your corpsman. Let's not let our injured woman bleed to death while we hunt for nonexistent survivors."

"I'll talk to the corpsman," the master chief promised. His voice had an edge. Obviously he had already thought of that.

Jake went below, to the small office/mess deck/galley, the topside compartment under the wheelhouse. The dozen marines who were aboard had to stay out on the deck. Out of the wind and reasonably warm, Jake settled into a corner, pulled the blanket tightly around him, and went to sleep as the boat rocked on the swells.

He awoke when the master chief powered up the hydrofoil. The deck and bulkheads—everything—vibrated as the two huge gas turbine engines lit off and came up to speed. And the motion of the vessel changed. The rocking and pitching steadied, with longer and longer periods as the small ship accelerated. Jake went out on deck where the marines were hunkered down against the increasing wind. Soon the vessel had her hull out of the water and was rock steady.

With the blanket still pulled around him, Jake went up the ladder to the wheelhouse. The hydrofoils were in formation, skimming the sea, headed toward Rota.

"How fast are we going?"

"Working up to fifty-two knots, sir. Be back at base in three hours."

Zelda Hudson was in the one sick bay berth hooked up to an IV, awake, pale, and hurting. The corpsman was there. After a last look at Zelda, he withdrew from the tiny compartment to give Jake a little privacy. "I'll be right outside, Admiral." Someone had passed the word about Jake's rank.

With the door closed, the sound level was tolerable. Jake asked Zelda, "How are you doing?"

"That bastard cut me to pieces, and he enjoyed every moment of it."

"There are people like that out there."

"Ten more minutes and he would have got to my face." A tremor went through her.

Jake reached for her hand, which was ice-cold. "I'm Grafton."

"I remember."

"We're going to be in Rota in three hours. The docs at the base hospital will stitch you up. They'll probably do a whole-blood IV with major antibiotics. When they say it's okay, we'll fly you to the States. The FBI will be waiting. Heck, they'll probably be waiting on the dock in Rota."

She nodded. He released her hand and backed away a step.

"I can't promise you anything, Ms. Hudson. I have no authority to make deals. You're going to need a good lawyer. Maybe your lawyer can cut a deal, maybe he can't. My guess is you're going to do a serious stretch in a federal pen. Be that as it may, I'd hate to see Antoine Jouany dance all the way to the bank with his billions, laughing like hell."

"What do you want to know?"

"I want to know enough so that the feds can seize his assets in the United States. If he doesn't like that, he'll have to file suit in federal court to get them back. Odds are he won't."

She fixed her eyes on his face and began talking.

When he got back to the United States from Spain, Tommy Carmellini went to Langley to see his boss, Pulzelli. When he arrived, Pulzelli was packing the items in his office in cardboard boxes.

"Ah, the prodigal son returns," Pulzelli said. "It's about time. I've been wondering where you were."

"It's a long story, sir, and I—"

Pulzelli waved him into silence. "I've been reading of your exploits. Admiral Grafton sends messages, you know."

"Oh." Carmellini sank into a chair and watched Pulzelli empty a drawer item by item into a box.

"Are you opening a new office in Kandahar, or taking that movie role in Hollywood?"

"I'm moving into Herman Watring's office. Alas, he's left us."

Carmellini gaped. "Dead?" he asked hopefully.

"No," said Pulzelli, who disappeared behind his desk as he cleaned out a bottom drawer. "He was arrested. It seems that one of the computer criminals is talking to the FBI. Vance, I think. Spilling his guts, as the saying goes. According to him, Watring and our man in London, McSweeney, helped set Zelda Hudson up with Antoine Jouany. The FBI arrested them both."

"Oh, man, I would have loved to have been here to see them take him away!" Carmellini exclaimed. "Did they slap the cuffs on him?"

Pulzelli lifted his head above the top of the desk and made eye contact with Carmellini. "Try to control yourself. Please. For my sake. I have been promoted to department head, and you are now in charge of this division. You'll want to move into this office, of course, as soon as I remove my things."

So Tommy Carmellini didn't quit the CIA. He thought about it for two minutes, but he liked Pulzelli, and with Watring gone, things were looking up. Oh, and a raise went with his promotion. After all, he reflected, the jewelry stores and museums would always be there if he ever got bored.

When the telephone technicians had the system in his new office up and running again, he sat staring at it. He should call someone, but who?

Lizzy, he decided. Before he did he looked in the sports section of the newspaper. After four telephone calls, he tracked her down at the marine base at Quantico.

"Lizzy, Tommy Carmellini. Just checking in."

She was cool. She hadn't forgiven him for not making a pass at her.

"I was calling to see if you would like to go to the wrestling match this weekend in Richmond. Saturday night."

"What is this? Are you jerking me around?"

"Actually, I'm trying to get a date to the wrestling match this weekend. I thought of you."

"I suppose I could go," she said tentatively.

"Do you think your boyfriend would mind, the one who snaps bones?"

"There's no boyfriend. I just told you that so you wouldn't think I was trolling."

"I understand perfectly. A woman must think of her reputation. Saturday afternoon, may I pick you up at Quantico about three?"

She was quickly warming up. "That would be good." She gave him the building number, then added, "You'll *love* wrestling! It's a new art form, a distillation of the true essence of life. This will open your eyes."

"I'm sure it will."

"And to think that you asked me to go with you to your very first performance! How romantic!"

"Isn't it?" Tommy Carmellini agreed.

Jake did make it to Las Palmas. For a day. Flap and Corina Le Beau left the ship there and flew back to the States. At Jake's insistence, Callie continued to cruise while Jake and Janos Ilin flew back to Rota and sailed aboard a chartered deep-sea salvage vessel.

A week later the vessel pulled up the third stage of the SuperAegis launch vehicle, right where Zelda Hudson said it would be, ten miles off Cape Barbas.

Three days after that, back at the dock in Rota, Jake Grafton and Janos Ilin watched as the third stage was craned aboard a U.S. Navy frigate and secured to the deck for the trip back to the United States.

"So, what are your plans?" Jake asked Ilin. The two were standing on the frigate's bridge drinking coffee and watching the sailors install tie-down chains on the third stage.

"Is that a subtle way of asking if I am going back to Washington to enjoy your hospitality in Crystal City?"

"Yeah. Sort of, I guess."

"You know that the U.S. government won't let me back into the country, or if they do, will throw me out in short order. I watched the satellite broadcasts of CNN while we were at sea. The government has announced that Hudson and Vance are both cooperating. They seized Jouany's assets the day *America* went down. Apparently that created quite a stir."

"So what do you think Hudson and Vance are saying?"

Ilin laughed. "Aah, friend Grafton. Amigo. I like your style. I really do."

He took his time getting a cigarette going. With the sea breeze coming in off the Atlantic, he had a hard time getting the lighter to work. When the weed was burning satisfactorily, Ilin bestowed another amused look on the American naval officer. "I think Zelda Hudson is telling the FBI that she stole a lot of secrets and sold them to the highest bidder. Occasionally that was me. She was a first-class, high-tech entrepreneur."

"She was more than that," Jake said. "She played the system like a violin."

Ilin smoked in silence.

"Where is Kolnikov?" Jake asked. "He swiped the minisub off *America*'s back and sailed away before we popped the E-grenades and destroyed the computers."

"Did he? Perhaps he is at the bottom of the sea with Heydrich."

"Sleeping with the fishes? I think not," Jake said. "Kolnikov struck me as a smart, smooth operator. Where is he now?"

"Do you want him?"

"Stealing a submarine and firing missiles at American cities were acts of war. And there was *La Jolla*."

"He was not SVR. You know that? He was not working for any branch of the Russian government. I swear to you, no official in the Russian government had any idea Kolnikov or anyone else would steal an American submarine."

"They tell you these things, do they?" Jake snapped. "So you can take blanket oaths?"

Ilin didn't turn a hair. He smoked in silence.

Finally Jake asked, "Zelda Hudson didn't tell you it was going to happen before it did?"

"No," said Janos Ilin.

Perhaps it didn't matter, Jake reflected. He doubted that the politicians would want to push the issue with the Europeans or the Russian government. The airlines were flying again, telephone and electrical services were being restored in Washington and New York, bills were pending in Congress to fund the necessary repairs, life in America was rapidly returning to normal. Even the stock and currency markets were rebounding. Precipitating another major international crisis over a disaster that was past didn't seem like something that would strike the Beltway politicians as a good idea.

The politicians were also smart enough to know that if the FBI talked to Kolnikov, it was possible he would say things they didn't want to hear. As the wise man once said, "If you think you might not like the answer, don't ask the question." Still . . .

"I want to know where he is," Jake told Ilin. "Just in case someone wants to hear it from his lips. Or wants a pound of flesh."

Ilin flipped his cigarette butt away from the ship. The brisk breeze caught it and carried it into the scummy harbor water. He turned up his collar and buried his hands in his coat pockets. "The situation is as I have told you." He looked Grafton square in the eyes. "If you want to talk to Vladimir Kolnikov, try Paris. If I were looking for him I would look there."

Ilin held out his hand, and Jake shook it. Then he went down the ladders to the main deck, walked over to the third stage and patted it, then headed for the gangway. As he crossed it he waved to Jake Grafton on the bridge. And Grafton waved back.

On Jake Grafton's first day back at the office a federal marshal delivered a joint congressional committee subpoena. The date and time were set for the next day, which required that he waive the usual waiting period. Jake called the committee staff and told them he would be there.

Jouany had friends in Congress and the financial community. Rich, powerful friends who were making a lot of noise over the seizure of his American assets. In a way the situation was unfortunate for Jouany—the closed markets and New York power problems meant that his trades during the crisis couldn't be settled as they usually were. In the two weeks Jake had been gone the power grid and telephone systems had been returned to normal function and the financial markets were once again in full operation . . . but almost five billion dollars had been in the Jouany bank accounts or clearinghouse channels when the feds latched on to everything.

Jake went to see Flap in the Pentagon. The commandant had also been subpoenaed and, like Jake, had waived the time requirement. Tomorrow morning at ten.

After Jake had told the general about the recovery of the satellite and his conversation with Janos Ilin, Flap had some choice words for the senators and congresspeople who insisted that the flag officers' investments in the Jouany firms be investigated fully. "It's blackmail," Flap fumed. "Hardball. They know nobody over here played the currency futures or took a bribe. And they're throwing all the mud they can get their hands on. For their buddy Jouany, who's a slimy son of a bitch."

"Oh, no," Jake pointed out. "He's a *rich,* slimy son of a bitch."

Flap gave the admiral The Look.

Grafton grinned. He hadn't been stewing in Washington for ten days, as Flap had, reading the papers every morning. "What was that fine old phrase, 'twisting slowly in the wind'?"

"That's it. Defamation by innuendo is the name of this game."

"Sir, may I use your telephone?"

Flap frowned and nodded a curt yes. Jake called a lawyer who had a beach house two blocks from his. After he identified himself, he asked the question, "Can a subpoenaed witness before Congress be sued for libel or slander?"

"You mean for something he said while testifying under oath?"

"That's right."

"No. The testimony is privileged. The witness can be prosecuted for perjury, though, if the testimony is false. You know anybody going to the Hill to bare his soul?"

"Me. Tomorrow morning at ten. And General Le Beau. Watch us on television. We're going to be famous. Not rich, just famous."

"The proper word to describe that condition is infamous."

Jake chuckled and asked the lawyer to dinner the following Saturday night, then thanked him and rang off.

Flap was up to speed. He grinned wolfishly at Grafton. "You should have been a marine," he said.

"If you don't mind, sir, I'd like to go first tomorrow. I'll read a statement, telling what I know about Zelda Hudson and Antoine Jouany and EuroSpace. The only way to shut these people up is to throw the truth in their faces."

"The prosecutors won't like it."

"Not my problem," Jake said and laced his fingers behind his head. He was alive and home, and he felt pretty damned good.

Jake wore his dress blue uniform the next morning. Callie was home from Europe, so she came and sat in the gallery. Carmellini sat with her and Corina Le Beau, while Toad sat at the long wooden witness table beside Jake and Flap so it wouldn't look as if they hadn't a friend in the world.

Finally the television lights came on and the chairman made a few remarks. "I understand the commandant has suggested that you go first, Admiral. Do you wish to make a statement?"

"Yes, sir." Jake began reading from his handwritten notes: "This is a story of superpower politics, cutting-edge technology, and greed. . . ."

About the Author

One of today's best action-adventure writers, Stephen Coonts is the author of ten published novels. His writing, he says, is the culmination of a lifelong love affair with books.

Mr. Coonts enlisted in the Naval Reserve during his sophomore year at West Virginia University "to avoid the draft," and because the Navy promised to send him to flight school. The Navy kept its promise, ordering him to flight training at NAS Pensacola, Florida, upon his graduation in 1968. He received his Navy wings in August 1969. After completion of fleet replacement training in the A-6 Intruder aircraft, he reported to Attack Squadron 196 at NAS Whidbey Island, Washington. He made two combat cruises as a member of this squadron aboard USS *Enterprise* during the final years of the Vietnam War. After the war he served as a flight instructor on A-6 aircraft for two years, then did a tour as an assistant catapult and arresting gear officer aboard USS *Nimitz*. He left active duty in 1977 and moved to Colorado.

After short stints as a taxi driver and police officer, Mr. Coonts entered the University of Colorado School of Law in the fall of 1977. He received his law degree in December 1979. He was practicing law as a staff attorney for a large independent oil company when his first novel, *Flight of the Intruder,* the classic novel of naval aviation in the jet era, was published in 1986.

Since his first flight as a student naval aviator, Mr. Coonts has been flying whenever finances permit. His nonfiction flying adventure, *The Cannibal Queen*, first published in 1992, has been hailed by critics as a general aviation classic. "That," he says, "is the book I hope they remember me for fifty years from now. Over half the fan mail I receive is inspired by that book. After reading it, many people decide they know me pretty well, so they write me a long letter telling me of their life's adventure. Receiving letters like that is the coolest part of being a writer."

In addition to flying, Mr. Coonts collects and shoots rifles. "Av gas and gunpowder are my substances of choice. They'll be illegal someday, so I'm burning all I can right now."

He maintains a Web site at www.coonts.com. He and his wife, Deborah Buell Coonts, live in Las Vegas with their son, Tyler.